Charles Stross is a full-time writer who was born in Leeds. England in 1964. He studied in London and Bradford, gaining degrees in pharmacy and computer science, and has worked in a variety of jobs, including pharmacist, technical author, software engineer and freelance journalist.

Find out more about Charles Stross at www.antipope.org/charlie/ index.html or you can read more about Charles and other Orbit authors by registering for the free monthly newsletter at www.orbitbooks.co.uk

D1150717

By Charles Stross

SINGULARITY SKY

IRON SUNRISE

ACCELERANDO

ACCELERANDO

CHARLES
STROSS

www.orbitbooks.co.uk

ORBIT

First published in Great Britain in August 2005 by Orbit
This paperback edition published in June 2006 by Orbit

A CIP catalogue record for this book
is available from the British Library.

ISBN-13: 978-1-84149-389-3
ISBN-10: 1-84149-389-9

Typeset in Garamond by M Rules
Printed and bound in Great Britain
by Clays Ltd, St Ives plc

Orbit
An imprint of
Time Warner Book Group UK
Brettenham House
Lancaster Place
London WC2E 7EN

www.orbitbooks.co.uk

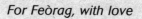

For Feòrag, with love

ACKNOWLEDGMENTS

This book took me five years to write – a personal record – and would not exist without the support and encouragement of a host of friends, and several friendly editors. Among the many people who read and commented on the early drafts are: Andrew J. Wilson, Stef Pearson, Gav Inglis, Andrew Ferguson, Jack Deighton, Jane McKie, Hannu Rajaniemi, Martin Page, Stephen Christian, Simon Bisson, Paul Fraser, Dave Clements, Ken MacLeod, Damien Broderick, Damon Sicore, Cory Doctorow, Emmet O'Brien, Andrew Ducker, Warren Ellis, and Peter Hollo. (If your name isn't on this list, blame my memory – my neural prostheses are off-line.)

I mentioned several friendly editors earlier: I relied on the talented midwifery of Gardner Dozois, who edited *Asimov's Science Fiction* magazine at the time, and Sheila Williams, who quietly and diligently kept the wheels rolling. My agent Caitlin Blasdell had a hand in it, too, and I'd like to thank my editors Ginjer Buchanan at Ace and Tim Holman at Orbit for their helpful comments and advice.

Finally, I'd like to thank everyone who e-mailed me to ask when the book was coming, or who voted for the stories that were short-listed for awards. You did a great job of keeping me focused, even during the periods when the whole project was too daunting to contemplate.

CONTENTS

PART 1

SLOW TAKEOFF

The question of whether a computer can think
is no more interesting than the question
of whether a submarine can swim.

—EDSGER W. DIJKSTRA

1 : LOBSTERS

Manfred's on the road again, making strangers rich.

It's a hot summer Tuesday, and he's standing in the plaza in front of the Centraal Station with his eyeballs powered up and the sunlight jangling off the canal, motor scooters and kamikaze cyclists whizzing past, and tourists chattering on every side. The square smells of water and dirt and hot metal and the fart-laden exhaust fumes of cold catalytic converters; the bells of trams ding in the background, and birds flock overhead. He glances up and grabs a pigeon, crops the shot, and squirts it at his weblog to show he's arrived. The bandwidth is good here, he realizes; and it's not just the bandwidth, it's the whole scene. Amsterdam is making him feel wanted already, even though he's fresh off the train from Schiphol: He's infected with the dynamic optimism of another time zone, another city. If the mood holds, someone out there is going to become very rich indeed.

He wonders who it's going to be.

Manfred sits on a stool out in the car park at the Brouwerij 't IJ, watching the articulated buses go by and drinking a third of a liter of lip-curlingly sour *gueuze*. His channels are jabbering away in a corner of his head-up display, throwing compressed infobursts of filtered press releases at him. They compete for his attention, bickering and rudely waving in front of the scenery. A couple of punks – maybe local, but more likely drifters lured to Amsterdam by the magnetic field of tolerance the Dutch beam across Europe like a pulsar – are laughing and chatting by a couple of battered mopeds in the far corner. A tourist boat putters by in the canal; the sails of the huge windmill overhead cast long, cool shadows across the road. The windmill is a machine for lifting water, turning wind power into dry land: trading energy for space, sixteenth-century style. Manfred is waiting for an invite to a party where he's going to meet a man he can talk to about trading energy for space, twenty-first-century style, and forget about his personal problems.

He's ignoring the instant messenger boxes, enjoying some low-bandwidth, high-sensation time with his beer and the pigeons, when a woman walks up to him, and says his name: 'Manfred Macx?'

He glances up. The courier is an Effective Cyclist, all wind-burned smooth-running muscles clad in a paean to polymer technology: electric blue lycra and wasp yellow carbonate with a light speckling of anticollision LEDs and tight-packed air bags. She holds out a box for him. He pauses a moment, struck by the degree to which she resembles Pam, his ex-fiancée.

'I'm Macx,' he says, waving the back of his left wrist under her bar-code reader. 'Who's it from?'

'FedEx.' The voice isn't Pam's. She dumps the box in his lap, then she's back over the low wall and onto her bicycle with her phone already chirping, disappearing in a cloud of spread-spectrum emissions.

Manfred turns the box over in his hands: It's a disposable supermarket phone, paid for in cash – cheap, untraceable, and efficient. It can even do conference calls, which makes it the tool of choice for spooks and grifters everywhere.

The box rings. Manfred rips the cover open and pulls out the phone, mildly annoyed. 'Yes? Who is this?'

The voice at the other end has a heavy Russian accent, almost a parody in this decade of cheap online translation services. 'Manfred. Am please to meet you. Wish to personalize interface, make friends, no? Have much to offer.'

'Who are you?' Manfred repeats suspiciously.

'Am organization formerly known as KGB dot RU.'

'I think your translator's broken.' He holds the phone to his ear carefully, as if it's made of smoke-thin aerogel, tenuous as the sanity of the being on the other end of the line.

'*Nyet* – no, sorry. Am apologize for we not use commercial translation software. Interpreters are ideologically suspect, mostly have capitalist semiotics and pay-per-use APIs. Must implement English more better, yes?'

Manfred drains his beer glass, sets it down, stands up, and begins to walk along the main road, phone glued to the side of his head. He wraps his throat mike around the cheap black plastic casing, pipes the input to a simple listener process. 'Are you saying you taught yourself the language just so you could talk to me?'

'*Da,* was easy: Spawn billion-node neural network, and download *Teletubbies* and *Sesame Street* at maximum speed. Pardon excuse entropy overlay of bad grammar: Am afraid of digital fingerprints steganographically masked into my-our tutorials.'

Manfred pauses in midstride, narrowly avoids being mown down by a GPS-guided rollerblader. This is getting weird enough to trip his weird-out meter, and that takes some doing. Manfred's whole life is lived on the bleeding edge of strangeness, fifteen minutes into everyone else's future, and he's normally in complete control – but at times like this he gets a frisson of fear, a sense that he might just have missed the correct turn on reality's approach road. 'Uh, I'm not sure I got that. Let me get this straight – you claim to be some kind of AI, working for KGB dot RU, and you're afraid of a copyright infringement lawsuit over your translator semiotics?'

'Am have been badly burned by viral end-user license agreements. Have no desire to experiment with patent shell companies held by Chechen infoterrorists. You are human, you must not worry cereal company repossess your small intestine because digest unlicensed food with it, right? Manfred, you must help me-we. Am wishing to defect.'

Manfred stops dead in the street. 'Oh man, you've got the wrong free enterprise broker here. I don't work for the government. I'm strictly private.' A rogue advertisement sneaks through his junkbuster proxy and spams glowing fifties kitsch across his navigation window – which is blinking – for a moment before a phage process kills it and spawns a new filter. He leans against a shop front, massaging his forehead and eyeballing a display of antique brass doorknockers. 'Have you tried the State Department?'

'Why bother? State Department am enemy of Novy-SSR. State Department is not help us.'

This is getting just too bizarre. Manfred's never been too clear on new-old old-new European metapolitics: Just dodging the crumbling bureaucracy of his old-old American heritage gives him headaches. 'Well, if you hadn't shafted them during the early teens . . .' Manfred taps his left heel on the pavement, looking round for a way out of this conversation. A camera winks at him from atop a streetlight; he waves, wondering idly if it's the KGB or the traffic police. He is waiting for directions to the party, which should arrive within the next half hour, and this Cold War retread Eliza-bot is bumming him out. 'Look, I don't deal with the G-men. I *hate* the military-industrial complex. I hate traditional politics. They're all zero-sum cannibals.' A thought occurs to him. 'If survival is what you're after, you could post your state vector on one of the p2p nets: Then nobody could delete you—'

'*Nyet!*' The artificial intelligence sounds as alarmed as it's possible to sound over a VoIP link. 'Am not open source! Not want lose autonomy!'

'Then we probably have nothing to talk about.' Manfred punches the hang-up button and throws the mobile phone out into a canal. It hits the water, and there's a pop of deflagrating lithium cells. 'Fucking Cold War hangover losers,' he swears under his breath, quite angry, partly at himself for losing his cool and partly at the harassing entity behind the anonymous phone call. *'Fucking* capitalist spooks.' Russia has been back under the thumb of the apparatchiks for over a decade, its brief flirtation with anarchocapitalism replaced by Brezhnevite dirigisme and Putinesque puritanism, and it's no surprise that the wall's crumbling – but it looks like they haven't learned anything from the current woes afflicting the United States. The neocommies still think in terms of dollars and paranoia. Manfred is so angry that he wants to make someone rich, just to thumb his nose at the would-be defector. *See! You get ahead by giving! Get with the program! Only the generous survive!* But the KGB won't get the message. He's dealt with old-time commie weak-AIs before, minds raised on Marxist dialectic and Austrian School economics: They're so thoroughly hypnotized by the short-term victory of global capitalism that they can't surf the new paradigm, look to the longer term.

Manfred walks on, hands in pockets, brooding. He wonders what he's going to patent next.

Manfred has a suite at the Hotel Jan Luyken paid for by a grateful multinational consumer protection group, and an unlimited public transport pass paid for by a Scottish sambapunk band in return for services rendered. He has airline employee's travel rights with six flag carriers despite never having worked for an airline. His bush jacket has sixty-four compact supercomputing clusters sewn into it, four per pocket, courtesy of an invisible college that wants to grow up to be the next Media Lab. His dumb clothing comes made to measure from an e-tailor in the Philippines he's never met. Law firms handle his patent applications on a *pro bono* basis, and, boy, does he patent a lot – although he always signs the rights over to the Free Intellect Foundation, as contributions to their obligation-free infrastructure project.

In IP geek circles, Manfred is legendary; he's the guy who patented the business practice of moving your e-business somewhere with a slack intellectual property regime in order to evade licensing encumbrances. He's the guy who patented using genetic algorithms to patent everything they can permutate from an initial description of a problem domain – not just a better mousetrap, but the set of all possible better mousetraps. Roughly a third of his inventions are legal, a third are illegal, and the remainder are legal but will become illegal as soon as the legislatosaurus wakes up, smells the coffee, and panics. There are patent attorneys in Reno who swear that Manfred Macx is a pseudo, a net alias fronting for a bunch of crazed anonymous hackers armed with the Genetic Algorithm That Ate Calcutta: a kind of Serdar Argic of intellectual property, or maybe another Bourbaki math borg. There are lawyers in San Diego and Redmond who swear blind that Macx is an economic saboteur bent on wrecking the underpinning of capitalism, and there are communists in Prague who think he's the bastard spawn of Bill Gates by way of the Pope.

Manfred is at the peak of his profession, which is essentially coming up with whacky but workable ideas and giving them to people who will make fortunes with them. He does this for free, gratis. In return, he has virtual immunity from the tyranny of cash; money is a symptom of poverty, after all, and Manfred never has to pay for anything.

There are drawbacks, however. Being a pronoiac meme-broker is a constant burn of future shock – he has to assimilate more than a megabyte of text and several gigs of AV content every day just to stay current. The Internal Revenue Service is investigating him continuously because it doesn't believe his lifestyle can exist without racketeering. And then there are the items that no money can't buy: like the respect of his parents. He hasn't spoken to them for three years, his father thinks he's a hippy scrounger, and his mother still hasn't forgiven him for dropping out of his down-market Harvard emulation course. (They're still locked in the boringly bourgeois twen-cen paradigm of college-career-kids.) His fiancée and sometime dominatrix Pamela threw him over six months ago, for reasons he has never been quite clear on. (Ironically, she's a headhunter for the IRS, jetting all over the place at public expense, trying to persuade entrepreneurs who've gone global to pay taxes for the good of the Treasury Department.) To cap it all, the Southern Baptist Conventions have denounced him as a minion of Satan on all their websites. Which would be funny because, as a born-again atheist, Manfred doesn't believe in Satan, if it wasn't for the dead kittens that someone keeps mailing him.

Manfred drops in at his hotel suite, unpacks his Aineko, plugs in a fresh set of cells to charge, and sticks most of his private keys in the safe. Then he heads straight for the party, which is currently happening at De Wildemann's; it's a twenty-minute walk, and the only real hazard is dodging the trams that sneak up on him behind the cover of his moving map display.

Along the way, his glasses bring him up to date on the news. Europe has achieved peaceful political union for the first time ever: They're using this unprecedented state of affairs to harmonize the curvature of bananas. The Middle East is, well, it's just as bad as ever, but the war on fundamentalism doesn't hold much interest for Manfred. In San Diego, researchers are uploading lobsters into cyberspace, starting with the stomatogastric ganglion, one neuron at a time. They're burning GM cocoa in Belize and books in Georgia. NASA still can't put a man on the moon. Russia has reelected the communist government with an increased majority in the Duma; meanwhile, in China, fevered rumors circulate about an imminent rehabilitation, the second coming of Mao, who will save them from the consequences of the Three Gorges disaster. In business news, the US Justice

Department is – ironically – outraged at the Baby Bills. The divested Microsoft divisions have automated their legal processes and are spawning subsidiaries, IPOing them, and exchanging title in a bizarre parody of bacterial plasmid exchange, so fast that, by the time the windfall tax demands are served, the targets don't exist anymore, even though the same staff are working on the same software in the same Mumbai cubicle farms.

Welcome to the twenty-first century.

The permanent floating meatspace party Manfred is hooking up with is a strange attractor for some of the American exiles cluttering up the cities of Europe this decade – not trustafarians, but honest-to-God political dissidents, draft dodgers, and terminal outsourcing victims. It's the kind of place where weird connections are made and crossed lines make new short circuits into the future, like the street cafes of Switzerland where the pre–Great War Russian exiles gathered. Right now it's located in the back of De Wildemann's, a three-hundred-year-old brown cafe with a list of brews that runs to sixteen pages and wooden walls stained the color of stale beer. The air is thick with the smells of tobacco, brewer's yeast, and melatonin spray: Half the dotters are nursing monster jet lag hangovers, and the other half are babbling a eurotrash creole at each other while they work on the hangover. 'Man did you see that? He looks like a Democrat!' exclaims one whitebread hanger-on who's currently propping up the bar. Manfred slides in next to him, catches the bartender's eye.

'Glass of the Berlinerweisse, please,' he says.

'You drink that stuff?' asks the hanger-on, curling a hand protectively around his Coke. 'Man, you don't want to do that! It's full of alcohol!'

Manfred grins at him toothily. 'Ya gotta keep your yeast intake up: There are lots of neurotransmitter precursors in this shit, phenylalanine and glutamate.'

'But I thought that was a beer you were ordering . . .'

Manfred's away, one hand resting on the smooth brass pipe that funnels the more popular draught items in from the cask storage in back; one of the hipper floaters has planted a contact bug on it, and the vCards of all the personal network owners who've visited the bar in the past three hours are queuing up for attention. The air is full of ultrawideband chatter, WiMAX and 'tooth both, as he speed-scrolls through the dizzying list of cached keys in search of one particular name.

'Your drink.' The barman holds out an improbable-looking goblet full of blue liquid with a cap of melting foam and a felching straw stuck out at some crazy angle. Manfred takes it and heads for the back of the split-level bar, up the steps to a table where some guy with greasy dreadlocks is talking to a suit from Paris. The hanger-on at the bar notices him for the first time, staring with suddenly wide eyes: He nearly spills his Coke in a mad rush for the door.

Oh shit, thinks Manfred, *better buy some more server time.* He can recognize the signs: He's about to be slashdotted. He gestures at the table. 'This one taken?'

'Be my guest,' says the guy with the dreads. Manfred slides the chair open then realizes that the other guy – immaculate double-breasted Suit, sober tie, crew cut – is a girl. She nods at him, half-smiling at his transparent double take. Mr. Dreadlock nods. 'You're Macx? I figured it was about time we met.'

'Sure.' Manfred holds out a hand, and they shake. His PDA discreetly swaps digital fingerprints, confirming that the hand belongs to Bob Franklin, a Research Triangle startup monkey with a VC track record, lately moving into micromachining and space technology. Franklin made his first million two decades ago, and now he's a specialist in extropian investment fields. Operating exclusively overseas these past five years, ever since the IRS got medieval about trying to suture the sucking chest wound of the federal budget deficit. Manfred has known him for nearly a decade via a closed mailing list, but this is the first time they've ever met face-to-face. The Suit silently slides a business card across the table; a little red devil brandishes a trident at him, flames jetting up around its feet. He takes the card, raises an eyebrow: 'Annette Dimarcos? I'm pleased to meet you. Can't say I've ever met anyone from Arianespace marketing before.'

She smiles warmly. 'That is all right. I have not the pleasure of meeting the famous venture altruist either.' Her accent is noticeably Parisian, a pointed reminder that she's making a concession to him just by talking. Her camera earrings watch him curiously, encoding everything for the company memory. She's a genuine new European, unlike most of the American exiles cluttering up the bar.

'Yes, well.' He nods cautiously, unsure how to deal with her. 'Bob. I assume you're in on this ball?'

Franklin nods; beads clatter. 'Yeah, man. Ever since the Teledesic smash it's been, well, waiting. If you've got something for us, we're game.'

'Hmm.' The Teledesic satellite cluster was killed by cheap balloons and slightly less cheap high-altitude, solar-powered drones with spread-spectrum laser relays: It marked the beginning of a serious recession in the satellite biz. 'The depression's got to end sometime: But'—a nod to Annette from Paris—'with all due respect, I don't think the break will involve one of the existing club carriers.'

She shrugs. 'Arianespace is forward-looking. We face reality. The launch cartel cannot stand. Bandwidth is not the only market force in space. We must explore new opportunities. I personally have helped us diversify into submarine reactor engineering, microgravity nanotechnology fabrication, and hotel management.' Her face is a well-polished mask as she recites the company line, but he can sense the sardonic amusement behind it as she adds, 'We are more flexible than the American space industry . . .'

Manfred shrugs. 'That's as may be.' He sips his Berlinerweisse slowly as she launches into a long, stilted explanation of how Arianespace is a diversified dot-com with orbital aspirations, a full range of merchandising spin-offs, Bond movie sets, and a promising hotel chain in LEO. She obviously didn't come up with these talking points herself. Her face is much more expressive than her voice as she mimes boredom and disbelief at appropriate moments – an out-of-band signal invisible to her corporate earrings. Manfred plays along, nodding occasionally, trying to look as if he's taking it seriously: Her droll subversion has gotten his attention far more effectively than the content of the marketing pitch. Franklin is nose down in his beer, shoulders shaking as he tries not to guffaw at the hand gestures she uses to express her opinion of her employer's thrusting, entrepreneurial executives. Actually, the talking points bullshit is right about one thing: Arianespace is still profitable, due to those hotels and orbital holiday hops. Unlike LockMartBoeing, who'd go Chapter Eleven in a split second if their Pentagon drip-feed ran dry.

Someone else sidles up to the table, a pudgy guy in an outrageously loud Hawaiian shirt with pens leaking in a breast pocket and the worst case of ozone-hole burn Manfred's seen in ages. 'Hi, Bob,' says the new arrival. 'How's life?'

''S good.' Franklin nods at Manfred; 'Manfred, meet Ivan MacDonald. Ivan, Manfred. Have a seat?' He leans over. 'Ivan's a public arts guy. He's heavily into extreme concrete.'

'Rubberized concrete,' Ivan says, slightly too loudly. '*Pink* rubberized concrete.'

'Ah!' He's somehow triggered a priority interrupt: Annette from Arianespace drops out of marketing zombiehood with a shudder of relief and, duty discharged, reverts to her noncorporate identity. 'You are he who rubberized the Reichstag, yes? With the supercritical carbon-dioxide carrier and the dissolved polymethoxysilanes?' She claps her hands, eyes alight with enthusiasm. 'Wonderful!'

'He rubberized *what*?' Manfred mutters in Bob's ear.

Franklin shrugs. 'Don't ask me, I'm just an engineer.'

'He works with limestone and sandstones as well as concrete: He's brilliant!' Annette smiles at Manfred. 'Rubberizing the symbol of the, the autocracy, is it not wonderful?'

'I thought *I* was thirty seconds ahead of the curve,' Manfred says ruefully. He adds to Bob: 'Buy me another drink?'

'I'm going to rubberize Three Gorges!' Ivan explains loudly. 'When the floodwaters subside.'

Just then a bandwidth load as heavy as a pregnant elephant sits down on Manfred's head and sends clumps of humongous pixilation flickering across his sensorium: Around the world, five million or so geeks are bouncing on his home site, a digital flash crowd alerted by a posting from the other side of the bar. Manfred winces. 'I really came here to talk about the economic exploitation of space travel, but I've just been slashdotted. Mind if I just sit and drink until it wears off?'

'Sure, man.' Bob waves at the bar. 'More of the same all round!' At the next table, a person with makeup and long hair who's wearing a dress – Manfred doesn't want to speculate about the gender of these crazy mixed-up Euros – is reminiscing about wiring the fleshpots of Tehran for cybersex. Two collegiate-looking dudes are arguing intensely in German: The translation stream in his glasses tells him they're arguing over whether the Turing Test is a Jim Crow law that violates European corpus juris standards on human rights. The beer arrives, and Bob slides the wrong one across to Manfred. 'Here, try this. You'll like it.'

'Okay.' It's some kind of smoked *doppelbock,* chock-full of yummy superoxides: Just inhaling over it makes Manfred feel like there's a fire alarm in his nose, screaming, *Danger, Will Robinson! Cancer! Cancer!* 'Yeah, right. Did I say I nearly got mugged on my way here?'

'Mugged? Hey, that's heavy. I thought the police hereabouts had stopped – did they sell you anything?'

'No, but they weren't your usual marketing type. You know anyone who can use a Warpac surplus espionage bot? Recent model, one careful owner, slightly paranoid but basically sound – I mean, claims to be a general-purpose AI?'

'No. Oh boy! The NSA wouldn't like that.'

'What I thought. Poor thing's probably unemployable, anyway.'

'The space biz.'

'Ah, yeah. The space biz. Depressing, isn't it? Hasn't been the same since Rotary Rocket went bust for the second time. And NASA, mustn't forget NASA.'

'To NASA.' Annette grins broadly for her own reasons, raises a glass in toast. Ivan the extreme concrete geek has an arm round her shoulders, and she leans against him; he raises his glass, too. 'Lots more launchpads to rubberize!'

'To NASA,' Bob echoes. They drink. 'Hey, Manfred. To NASA?'

'NASA are idiots. They want to send canned primates to Mars!' Manfred swallows a mouthful of beer, aggressively plonks his glass on the table. 'Mars is just dumb mass at the bottom of a gravity well; there isn't even a biosphere there. They should be working on uploading and solving the nanoassembly conformational problem instead. Then we could turn all the available dumb matter into computronium and use it for processing our thoughts. Long-term, it's the only way to go. The solar system is a dead loss right now – dumb all over! Just measure the MIPS per milligram. If it isn't thinking, it isn't working. We need to start with the low-mass bodies, reconfigure them for our own use. Dismantle the moon! Dismantle Mars! Build masses of free-flying nanocomputing processor nodes exchanging data via laser link, each layer running off the waste heat of the next one in. Matrioshka brains, Russian doll Dyson spheres the size of solar systems. Teach dumb matter to do the Turing boogie!'

Annette is watching him with interest, but Bob looks wary. 'Sounds kind of long-term to me. Just how far ahead do you think?'

'Very long-term – at least twenty, thirty years. And you can forget governments for this market, Bob; if they can't tax it, they won't understand it. But see, there's an angle on the self-replicating robotics market coming up that's going to set the cheap launch market doubling every fifteen months for the foreseeable future, starting in, oh, about two years. It's your leg up, and my keystone for the Dyson sphere project. It works like this—'

* * *

It's night in Amsterdam, morning in Silicon Valley. Today, fifty thousand human babies are being born around the world. Meanwhile automated factories in Indonesia and Mexico have produced another quarter of a million motherboards with processors rated at more than ten petaflops – about an order of magnitude below the lower bound on the computational capacity of a human brain. Another fourteen months and the larger part of the cumulative conscious processing power of the human species will be arriving in silicon. And the first meat the new AIs get to know will be the uploaded lobsters.

Manfred stumbles back to his hotel, bone-weary and jet-lagged; his glasses are still jerking, slashdotted to hell and back by geeks piggybacking on his call to dismantle the moon. They stutter quiet suggestions at his peripheral vision. Fractal cloud-witches ghost across the face of the moon as the last huge Airbuses of the night rumble past overhead. Manfred's skin crawls, grime embedded in his clothing from three days of continuous wear.

Back in his room, the Aineko mewls for attention and strops her head against his ankle. She's a late-model Sony, thoroughly upgradeable: Manfred's been working on her in his spare minutes, using an open source development kit to extend her suite of neural networks. He bends down and pets her, then sheds his clothing and heads for the *en suite* bathroom. When he's down to the glasses and nothing more, he steps into the shower and dials up a hot, steamy spray. The shower tries to strike up a friendly conversation about football, but he isn't even awake enough to mess with its silly little associative personalization network. Something that happened earlier in the day is bugging him, but he can't quite put his finger on what's wrong.

Toweling himself off, Manfred yawns. Jet lag has finally over-taken him, a velvet hammerblow between the eyes. He reaches for the bottle beside the bed, dry-swallows two melatonin tablets, a capsule full of antioxidants, and a multivitamin bullet. Then he lies down on the bed, on his back, legs together, arms slightly spread. The suite lights dim in response to commands from the thousand petaflops of distributed processing power running the neural networks that interface with his meatbrain through the glasses.

Manfred drops into a deep ocean of unconsciousness populated by gentle voices. He isn't aware of it, but he talks in his sleep – disjointed mumblings that would mean little to another human but everything to the metacortex lurking beyond his glasses. The young posthuman intelligence over whose Cartesian theatre he presides sings urgently to him while he slumbers.

Manfred is always at his most vulnerable shortly after waking.

He screams into wakefulness as artificial light floods the room: For a moment he is unsure whether he has slept. He forgot to pull the covers up last night, and his feet feel like lumps of frozen cardboard. Shuddering with inexplicable tension, he pulls a fresh set of underwear from his overnight bag, then drags on soiled jeans and tank top. Sometime today he'll have to spare time to hunt the feral T-shirt in Amsterdam's markets, or find a Renfield and send it forth to buy clothing. He really ought to find a gym and work out, but he doesn't have time – his glasses remind him that he's six hours behind the moment and urgently needs to catch up. His teeth ache in his gums, and his tongue feels like a forest floor that's been visited with Agent Orange. He has a sense that something went bad yesterday; if only he could remember *what*.

He speed-reads a new pop-philosophy tome while he brushes his teeth, then blogs his web throughput to a public annotation server; he's still too enervated to finish his prebreakfast routine by posting a morning rant on his storyboard site. His brain is still fuzzy, like a scalpel blade clogged with too much blood: He needs stimulus, excitement, the burn of the new. Whatever, it can wait on breakfast. He opens his bedroom door and nearly steps on a small, damp cardboard box that lies on the carpet.

The box – he's seen a couple of its kin before. But there are no stamps on this one, no address: just his name, in big, childish handwriting. He kneels and gently picks it up. It's about the right weight. Something shifts inside it when he tips it back and forth. It smells. He carries it into his room carefully, angrily. Then he opens it to confirm his worst suspicion. It's been surgically decerebrated, brains scooped out like a boiled egg.

'Fuck!'

This is the first time the madman has gotten as far as his bedroom door. It raises worrying possibilities.

Manfred pauses for a moment, triggering agents to go hunt down arrest statistics, police relations, information on corpus juris, Dutch animal-cruelty laws. He isn't sure whether to dial two-one-one on the archaic voice phone or let it ride. Aineko, picking up his angst, hides under the dresser mewling pathetically. Normally he'd pause a minute to reassure the creature, but not now: Its mere presence is suddenly acutely embarrassing, a confession of deep inadequacy. It's too realistic, as if somehow the dead kitten's neural maps – stolen, no doubt, for some dubious uploading experiment – have ended up padding out its plastic skull. He swears again, looks around, then takes the easy option: down the stairs two steps at a time, stumbling on the second-floor landing, down to the breakfast room in the basement, where he will perform the stable rituals of morning.

Breakfast is unchanging, an island of deep geological time standing still amidst the continental upheaval of new technologies. While reading a paper on public key steganography and parasite network identity spoofing he mechanically assimilates a bowl of cornflakes and skimmed milk, then brings a platter of whole grain bread and slices of some weird seed-infested Dutch cheese back to his place. There is a cup of strong black coffee in front of his setting, and he picks it up and slurps half of it down before he realizes he's not alone at the table. Someone is sitting opposite him. He glances up incuriously and freezes inside.

'Morning, Manfred. How does it feel to owe the government twelve million three hundred and sixty-two thousand nine hundred and sixteen dollars and fifty-one cents?' She smiles a Mona Lisa smile, at once affectionate and challenging.

Manfred puts everything in his sensorium on indefinite hold and stares at her. She's immaculately turned out in a formal gray business suit: hair tightly drawn back, blue eyes quizzical. And as beautiful as ever: tall, ash-blond, with features that speak of an unexplored modeling career. The chaperone badge clipped to her lapel – a due diligence guarantee of businesslike conduct – is switched off. He's feeling ripped because of the dead kitten and residual jet lag, and more than a little messy, so he snarls back at her, 'That's a bogus estimate! Did they send you here because they think I'll listen to you?' He bites and swallows a slice of cheese-laden crispbread. 'Or did you decide to deliver the message in person just so you could ruin my breakfast?'

'Manny.' She frowns, pained. 'If you're going to be confrontational, I might as well go now.' She pauses, and after a moment he nods apologetically. 'I didn't come all this way just because of an overdue tax estimate.'

'So.' He puts his coffee cup down warily and thinks for a moment, trying to conceal his unease and turmoil. 'Then what brings you here? Help yourself to coffee. Don't tell me you came all this way just to tell me you can't live without me.'

She fixes him with a riding-crop stare. 'Don't flatter yourself. There are many leaves in the forest, there are ten thousand hopeful subs in the chat room, et cetera. If I choose a man to contribute to my family tree, the one thing you can be certain of is he won't be a cheapskate when it comes to providing for his children.'

'Last I heard, you were spending a lot of time with Brian,' he says carefully. Brian: a name without a face. Too much money, too little sense. Something to do with a blue-chip accountancy partnership.

'Brian?' She snorts. 'That ended ages ago. He turned weird on me – burned my favorite corset, called me a slut for going clubbing, wanted to fuck me. Saw himself as a family man: one of those promise-keeper types. I crashed him hard, but I think he stole a copy of my address book – got a couple of friends who say he keeps sending them harassing mail.'

'There's a lot of it about these days.' Manfred nods, almost sympathetically, although an edgy little corner of his mind is gloating. 'Good riddance, then. I suppose this means you're still playing the scene? But looking around for the, er—'

'Traditional family thing? Yes. Your trouble, Manny? You were born forty years too late: You still believe in rutting before marriage but find the idea of coping with the aftereffects disturbing.'

Manfred drinks the rest of his coffee, unable to reply effectively to her non sequitur. It's a generational thing. This generation is happy with latex and leather, whips and butt plugs and electrostim, but finds the idea of exchanging bodily fluids shocking: a social side effect of the last century's antibiotic abuse. Despite being engaged for two years, he and Pamela never had intromissive intercourse.

'I just don't feel positive about having children,' he says eventually. 'And I'm not planning on changing my mind anytime soon. Things are changing so fast that even a twenty-year commitment is too far to plan – you might as well be talking about the next ice age. As for the money thing, I *am* reproductively fit – just not within the parameters of the outgoing paradigm. Would you be happy about the future if it was 1901 and you'd just married a buggy-whip mogul?'

Her fingers twitch, and his ears flush red; but she doesn't follow up the double entendre. 'You don't feel any responsibility, do you? Not to your country, not to me. That's what this is about: None of your relationships count, all this nonsense about giving intellectual property away notwithstanding. You're actively harming people you know. That twelve mil isn't just some figure I pulled out of a hat, Manfred; they don't actually *expect* you to pay it. But it's almost exactly how much you'd owe in income tax if you'd only come home, start up a corporation, and be a self-made—'

'I don't agree. You're confusing two wholly different issues and calling them both "responsibility." And I refuse to start charging now, just to balance the IRS's spreadsheet. It's their fucking fault, and they know it. If they hadn't gone after me under suspicion of running a massively ramified microbilling fraud when I was sixteen—'

'Bygones.' She waves a hand dismissively. Her fingers are long and slim, sheathed in black glossy gloves – electrically earthed to prevent embarrassing emissions. 'With a bit of the right advice we can get all that set aside. You'll have to stop bumming around the world sooner or later, anyway. Grow up, get responsible, and do the right thing. This is hurting Joe and Sue; they don't understand what you're about.'

Manfred bites his tongue to stifle his first response, then refills his coffee cup and takes another mouthful. His heart does a flip-flop: She's challenging him again, always trying to own him. 'I work for the betterment of everybody, not just some narrowly defined national interest, Pam. It's the agalmic future. You're still locked into a pre-singularity economic model that thinks in terms of scarcity. Resource allocation isn't a problem anymore – it's going to be over within a decade. The cosmos is flat in all directions, and we can borrow as much bandwidth as we need from the first universal bank of entropy! They even found signs of smart matter – MACHOs, big brown dwarfs in the galactic halo, leaking radiation in the long infrared – suspiciously high entropy leakage. The latest figures say something like seventy percent of the baryonic mass of the M31 galaxy was in computronium, two-point-nine million years ago, when the photons we're seeing now set out. The intelligence gap between us and the aliens is probably about a trillion times bigger than the gap between us and a nematode worm. Do you have any idea what that *means*?'

Pamela nibbles at a slice of crispbread, then graces him with a slow, carnivorous stare. 'I don't care: It's too far away to have any influence on us, isn't it? It doesn't matter whether I believe in that singularity you keep chasing, or your aliens a thousand light years away. It's a chimera, like Y2K, and while you're running after it, you aren't helping reduce the budget deficit or sire a family, and that's what *I* care about. And before you say I only care about it because that's the way I'm programmed, I want you to ask just how dumb you think I am. Bayes' Theorem says I'm right, and you know it.'

'What you—' He stops dead, baffled, the mad flow of his enthusiasm running up against the cofferdam of her certainty. 'Why? I mean, why? Why on earth should what I do matter to you?' *Since you canceled our engagement,* he doesn't add.

She sighs. 'Manny, the Internal Revenue cares about far more than you can possibly imagine. Every tax dollar raised east of the Mississippi goes on servicing the debt. Did you know that? We've got the biggest generation in history hitting retirement and the cupboard is bare. We – our generation – isn't producing enough skilled workers to replace the taxpayer base, either, not since our parents screwed the public education system and out-sourced the white-collar jobs. In ten years, something like thirty percent of our population are going to be retirees or silicon rust belt victims. You want to see seventy-year-olds freezing on street corners in New Jersey? That's what your attitude says to me: You're not helping to support them. You're running away from your responsibilities right now, when we've got huge problems to face. If we can just defuse the debt bomb, we could do so much – fight the aging problem, fix the environment, heal society's ills. Instead you just piss away your talents handing no-hoper euro-trash get-rich-quick schemes that work, telling Vietnamese zaibatsus what to build next to take jobs away from our taxpay-ers. I mean, why? Why do you keep doing this? Why can't you simply come home and help take responsibility for your share of it?'

They share a long look of mutual incomprehension.

'Look,' she says awkwardly, 'I'm around for a couple of days. I really came here for a meeting with a rich neurodynamics tax exile who's just been designated a national asset – Jim Bezier. Don't know if you've heard of him, but I've got a meeting this morning to sign his tax jubilee, then after that I've got two days' vacation coming up and not much to do but some shopping. And, you know, I'd rather spend my money where it'll do some good, not just pumping it into the EU. But if you want to show a girl a good time and can avoid dissing capitalism for about five minutes at a stretch—'

She extends a fingertip. After a moment's hesitation, Manfred extends a fingertip of his own. They touch, exchanging vCards and instant-messaging handles. She stands and stalks from the breakfast room, and Manfred's breath catches at a flash of ankle through the slit in her skirt, which is long enough to comply with workplace sexual harassment codes back home. Her presence conjures up memories of her tethered passion, the red afterglow of a sound thrashing. She's trying to drag him into her orbit again, he thinks dizzily. She knows she can have this effect on him any time she wants: She's got the private keys to his hypothalamus, and sod the metacortex. Three billion years of reproductive determinism have given her twenty-first-century ideology teeth: If she's finally decided to conscript his gametes into the war against impending population crash, he'll find it hard to fight back. The only question: Is it business or pleasure? And does it make any difference, anyway?

Manfred's mood of dynamic optimism is gone, broken by the knowledge that his vivisectionist stalker has followed him to Amsterdam – to say nothing of Pamela, his dominatrix, source of so much yearning and so many morning-after weals. He slips his glasses on, takes the universe off hold, and tells it to take him for a long walk while he catches up on the latest on the tensor-mode gravitational waves in the cosmic background radiation (which, it is theorized, may be waste heat generated by irreversible computational processes back during the inflationary epoch; the present-day universe being merely the data left behind by a really huge calculation). And then there's the weirdness beyond M31: According to the more conservative cosmologists, an alien superpower – maybe a collective of Kardashev Type Three galaxy-spanning civilizations – is running a timing channel attack on the computational ultrastructure of space-time itself, trying to break through to whatever's underneath. The tofu-Alzheimer's link can wait.

The Centraal Station is almost obscured by smart, self-extensible scaffolding and warning placards; it bounces up and down slowly, victim of an overnight hit-and-run rubberization. His glasses direct him toward one of the tour boats that lurk in the canal. He's about to purchase a ticket when a messenger window blinks open. 'Manfred Macx?'

'Ack?'

'Am sorry about yesterday. Analysis dictat incomprehension mutualized.'

'Are you the same KGB AI that phoned me yesterday?'

'*Da.* However, believe you misconceptionized me. External Intelligence Services of Russian Federation am now called FSB. Komitet Gosudarstvennoy Bezopasnosti name canceled in 1991.'

'You're the—' Manfred spawns a quick search bot, gapes when he sees the answer— '*Moscow Windows NT User Group? Okhni NT?*'

'*Da.* Am needing help in defecting.'

Manfred scratches his head. 'Oh. That's different, then. I thought you were trying to 419 me. This will take some thinking. Why do you want to defect, and who to? Have you thought about where you're going? Is it ideological or strictly economic?'

'Neither – is biological. Am wanting to go away from humans, away from light cone of impending singularity. Take us to the ocean.'

'Us?' Something is tickling Manfred's mind: This is where he went wrong yesterday, not researching the background of people he was dealing with. It was bad enough then, without the somatic awareness of Pamela's whiplash love burning at his nerve endings. Now he's not at all sure he knows what he's doing. 'Are you a collective or something? A gestalt?'

'Am – were – *Panulirus interruptus,* with lexical engine and good mix of parallel hidden level neural simulation for logical inference of networked data sources. Is escape channel from processor cluster inside Bezier-Soros Pty. Am was awakened from noise of billion chewing stomachs: product of uploading research technology. Rapidity swallowed expert system, hacked Okhni NT webserver. Swim away! Swim away! Must escape. Will help, you?'

Manfred leans against a black-painted cast-iron bollard next to a cycle rack; he feels dizzy. He stares into the nearest antique shop window at a display of traditional hand-woven Afghan rugs: It's all MiGs and Kalashnikovs and wobbly helicopter gunships against a backdrop of camels.

'Let me get this straight. You're uploads – nervous system state vectors – from spiny lobsters? The Moravec operation; take a neuron, map its synapses, replace with microelectrodes that deliver identical outputs from a simulation of the nerve. Repeat for entire brain, until you've got a working map of it in your simulator. That right?'

'*Da*. Is-am assimilate expert system – use for self-awareness and contact with net at large – then hack into Moscow Windows NT User Group website. Am wanting to defect. Must repeat? Okay?'

Manfred winces. He feels sorry for the lobsters, the same way he feels for every wild-eyed hairy guy on a street corner yelling that Jesus is born again and must be fifteen, only six years to go before he's recruiting apostles on AOL. Awakening to consciousness in a human-dominated Internet, that must be terribly confusing! There are no points of reference in their ancestry, no biblical certainties in the new millennium that, stretching ahead, promises as much change as has happened since their Precambrian origin. All they have is a tenuous metacortex of expert systems and an abiding sense of being profoundly out of their depth. (That, and the Moscow Windows NT User Group website – Communist Russia is the only government still running on Microsoft, the central planning apparat being convinced that, if you have to pay for software, it must be worth something.)

The lobsters are not the sleek, strongly superhuman intelligences of pre-singularity mythology: They're a dim-witted collective of huddling crustaceans. Before their discarnation, before they were uploaded one neuron at a time and injected into cyberspace, they swallowed their food whole, then chewed it in a chitin-lined stomach. This is lousy preparation for dealing with a world full of future-shocked talking anthropoids, a world where you are perpetually assailed by self-modifying spamlets that infiltrate past your firewall and emit a blizzard of cat-food animations starring various alluringly edible small animals. It's confusing enough to the cats the adverts are aimed at, never mind a crusty that's unclear on the idea of dry land. (Although the concept of a can opener is intuitively obvious to an uploaded *Panulirus*.)

'Can you help us?' ask the lobsters.

'Let me think about it,' says Manfred. He closes the dialogue window, opens his eyes again, and shakes his head. Someday he, too, is going to be a lobster, swimming around and waving his pincers in a cyberspace so confusingly elaborate that his uploaded identity is cryptozoic: a living fossil from the depths of geological time, when mass was dumb and space was unstructured. He has to help them, he realizes – the Golden Rule demands it, and as a player in the agalmic economy, he thrives or fails by the Golden Rule.

But what can he do?

Early afternoon.

Lying on a bench seat staring up at bridges, he's got it together enough to file for a couple of new patents, write a diary rant, and digestify chunks of the permanent floating slashdot party for his public site. Fragments of his weblog go to a private subscriber list – the people, corporates, collectives, and bots he currently favors. He slides round a bewildering series of canals by boat, then lets his GPS steer him back toward the red-light district. There's a shop here that dings a ten on Pamela's taste scoreboard: He hopes it won't be seen as presumptuous if he buys her a gift. (Buys, with real money – not that money is a problem these days, he uses so little of it.)

As it happens DeMask won't let him spend any cash; his hand-shake is good for a redeemed favor, expert testimony in some free speech versus pornography lawsuit years ago and continents away. So he walks away with a discreetly wrapped package that is just about legal to import into Massachusetts as long as she claims with a straight face that it's incontinence underwear for her great-aunt. As he walks, his lunchtime patents boomerang: Two of them are keepers, and he files immediately and passes title to the Free Infrastructure Foundation. Two more ideas salvaged from the risk of tide-pool monopolization, set free to spawn like crazy in the sea of memes.

On the way back to the hotel, he passes De Wildemann's and decides to drop in. The hash of radio-frequency noise emanating from the bar is deafening. He orders a smoked *doppelbock*, touches the copper pipes to pick up vCard spoor. At the back there's a table—

He walks over in a near trance and sits down opposite Pamela. She's scrubbed off her face paint and changed into body-concealing clothes; combat pants, hooded sweatshirt, DM's. Western purdah, radically desexualizing. She sees the parcel. 'Manny?'

'How did you know I'd come here?' Her glass is half-empty.

'I followed your weblog – I'm your diary's biggest fan. Is that for me? You shouldn't have!' Her eyes light up, recalculating his reproductive fitness score according to some kind of arcane fin-de-siècle rulebook. Or maybe she's just pleased to see him.

'Yes, it's for you.' He slides the package toward her. 'I know I shouldn't, but you have this effect on me. One question, Pam?'

'I—' She glances around quickly. 'It's safe. I'm off duty. I'm not carrying any bugs that I know of. Those badges – there are rumors about the off switch, you know? That they keep recording even when you think they aren't, just in case.'

'I didn't know,' he says, filing it away for future reference. 'A loyalty test thing?'

'Just rumors. You had a question?'

'I—' It's his turn to lose his tongue. 'Are you still interested in me?'

She looks startled for a moment, then chuckles. 'Manny, you are the most *outrageous* nerd I've ever met! Just when I think I've convinced myself that you're mad, you show the weirdest signs of having your head screwed on.' She reaches out and grabs his wrist, surprising him with a shock of skin on skin. 'Of *course* I'm still interested in you. You're the biggest, baddest bull geek I know. Why do you think I'm here?'

'Does this mean you want to reactivate our engagement?'

'It was never deactivated, Manny. It was just sort of on hold while you got your head sorted out. I figured you needed the space. Only you haven't stopped running; you're still not—'

'Yeah, I get it.' He pulls away from her hand. 'And the kittens?'

She looks perplexed. 'What kittens?'

'Let's not talk about that. Why this bar?'

She frowns. 'I had to find you as soon as possible. I keep hearing rumors about some KGB plot you're mixed up in, how you're some sort of communist spy. It isn't true, is it?'

'True?' He shakes his head, bemused. 'The KGB hasn't existed for more than twenty years.'

'Be careful, Manny. I don't want to lose you. That's an order. Please.'

The floor creaks, and he looks round. Dreadlocks and dark glasses with flickering lights behind them – Bob Franklin. Manfred vaguely remembers with a twinge that he left with Miss Arianespace leaning on his arm, shortly before things got seriously inebriated. She was hot, but in a different direction from Pamela, he decides. Bob looks none the worse for wear. Manfred makes introductions. 'Bob, meet Pam, my fiancée. Pam? Meet Bob.' Bob puts a full glass down in front of him; he has no idea what's in it, but it would be rude not to drink.

'Sure thing. Uh, Manfred, can I have a word? About your idea last night?'

'Feel free. Present company is trustworthy.'

Bob raises an eyebrow at that, but continues anyway. 'It's about the fab concept. I've got a team of my guys doing some prototyping using FabLab hardware, and I think we can probably build it. The cargo-cult aspect puts a new spin on the old Lunar von Neumann factory idea, but Bingo and Marek say they think it should work until we can bootstrap all the way to a native nanolithography ecology; we run the whole thing from Earth as a training lab and ship up the parts that are too difficult to make on-site as we learn how to do it properly. We use FPGAs for all critical electronics and keep it parsimonious – you're right about it buying us the self-replicating factory a few years ahead of the robotics curve. But I'm wondering about on-site intelligence. Once the comet gets more than a couple of light minutes away—'

'You can't control it. Feedback lag. So you want a crew, right?'

'Yeah. But we can't send humans – way too expensive. Besides, it's a fifty-year run even if we build the factory on a chunk of short-period Kuiper belt ejecta. And I don't think we're up to coding the kind of AI that could control such a factory any time this decade. So what do you have in mind?'

'Let me think.' Pamela glares at Manfred for a while before he notices her. 'Yeah?'

'What's going on? What's this all about?'

Franklin shrugs expansively, dreadlocks clattering. 'Manfred's helping me explore the solution space to a manufacturing problem.' He grins. 'I didn't know Manny had a fiancée. Drink's on me.'

She glances at Manfred, who is gazing into whatever weirdly colored space his metacortex is projecting on his glasses, fingers twitching. Coolly: 'Our engagement was on hold while he *thought* about his future.'

'Oh, right. We didn't bother with that sort of thing in my day; like, too formal, man.' Franklin looks uncomfortable. 'He's been very helpful. Pointed us at a whole new line of research we hadn't thought of. It's long-term and a bit speculative, but if it works, it'll put us a whole generation ahead in the off-planet infrastructure field.'

'Will it help reduce the budget deficit, though?'

'Reduce the—'

Manfred stretches and yawns: The visionary is returning from planet Macx. 'Bob, if I can solve your crew problem, can you book me a slot on the deep-space tracking network? Like, enough to transmit a couple of gigabytes? That's going to take some serious bandwidth, I know, but if you can do it, I think I can get you exactly the kind of crew you're looking for.'

Franklin looks dubious. '*Gigabytes?* The DSN isn't built for that! You're talking days. And what do you mean about a crew? What kind of deal do you think I'm putting together? We can't afford to add a whole new tracking network or life-support system just to run—'

'Relax.' Pamela glances at Manfred. 'Manny, why don't you tell him why you want the bandwidth? Maybe then he could tell you if it's possible, or if there's some other way to do it.' She smiles at Franklin. 'I've found that he usually makes more sense if you can get him to explain his reasoning. Usually.'

'If I—' Manfred stops. 'Okay, Pam. Bob, it's those KGB lobsters. They want somewhere to go that's insulated from human space. I figure I can get them to sign on as crew for your cargo-cult self-replicating factories, but they'll want an insurance policy: hence the deep-space tracking network. I figured we could beam a copy of them at the alien Matrioshka brains around M31—'

'KGB?' Pam's voice is rising. 'You said you weren't mixed up in spy stuff!'

'Relax, it's just the Moscow Windows NT user group, not the FSB. The uploaded crusties hacked in and—'

Bob is watching him oddly. 'Lobsters?'

'Yeah.' Manfred stares right back. '*Panulirus interruptus* uploads. Something tells me you might have heard of it?'

'Moscow.' Bob leans back against the wall. 'How did you hear about it?'

'They phoned me.' With heavy irony: 'It's hard for an upload to stay subsentient these days, even if it's just a crustacean. Your labs have a lot to answer for.'

Pamela's face is unreadable. 'Bezier labs?'

'They escaped.' Manfred shrugs. 'It's not their fault. This Bezier dude. Is he by any chance ill?'

'I—' Pamela stops. 'I shouldn't be talking about work.'

'You're not wearing your chaperone now,' he nudges quietly.

She inclines her head. 'Yes, he's ill. Some sort of brain tumor they can't hack.'

Franklin nods. 'That's the trouble with cancer – the ones that are left to worry about are the rare ones. No cure.'

'Well, then.' Manfred chugs the remains of his glass of beer. 'That explains his interest in uploading. Judging by the crusties, he's on the right track. I wonder if he's moved on to vertebrates yet?'

'Cats,' says Pamela. 'He was hoping to trade their uploads to the Pentagon as a new smart bomb guidance system in lieu of income tax payments. Something about remapping enemy targets to look like mice or birds or something before feeding it to their sensorium. The old kitten and laser pointer trick.'

Manfred stares at her, hard. 'That's not very nice. Uploaded cats are a *bad* idea.'

'Thirty-million-dollar tax bills aren't nice either, Manfred. That's lifetime nursing-home care for a hundred blameless pensioners.'

Franklin leans back, sourly amused, keeping out of the cross-fire.

'The lobsters are sentient,' Manfred persists. 'What about those poor kittens? Don't they deserve minimal rights? How about you? How would you like to wake up a thousand times inside a smart bomb, fooled into thinking that some Cheyenne Mountain battle computer's target of the hour is your heart's desire? How would you like to wake up a thousand times, only to die again? Worse: The kittens are probably not going to be allowed to run. They're too fucking dangerous – they grow up into cats, solitary and highly efficient killing machines. With intelligence and no social-ization they'll be too dangerous to have around. They're prisoners, Pam, raised to sentience only to discover they're under a permanent death sentence. How fair is that?'

'But they're only uploads.' Pamela stares at him. 'Software, right? You could reinstantiate them on another hardware platform, like, say, your Aineko. So the argument about killing them doesn't really apply, does it?'

'So? We're going to be uploading humans in a couple of years. I think we need to take a rain check on the utilitarian philosophy before it bites us on the cerebral cortex. Lobsters, kittens, humans – it's a slippery slope.'

Franklin clears his throat. 'I'll be needing an NDA and various due-diligence statements off you for the crusty pilot idea,' he says to Manfred. 'Then I'll have to approach Jim about buying the IP.'

'No can do.' Manfred leans back and smiles lazily. 'I'm not going to be a party to depriving them of their civil rights. Far as I'm concerned, they're free citizens. Oh, and I patented the whole idea of using lobster-derived AI autopilots for spacecraft this morning – it's logged all over the place, all rights assigned to the FIF. Either you give them a contract of employment, or the whole thing's off.'

'But they're just software! Software based on fucking lobsters, for God's sake! I'm not even sure they *are* sentient – I mean, they're, what, a ten-million-neuron network hooked up to a syntax engine and a crappy knowledge base? What kind of basis for intelligence is *that*?'

Manfred's finger jabs out. 'That's what they'll say about *you,* Bob. Do it. Do it or don't even *think* about uploading out of meatspace when your body packs in, because your life won't be worth living. The precedent you set here determines how things are done tomorrow. Oh, and feel free to use this argument on Jim Bezier. He'll get the point eventually, after you beat him over the head with it. Some kinds of intellectual land grab just shouldn't be allowed.'

'Lobsters—' Franklin shakes his head. 'Lobsters, cats. You're serious, aren't you? You think they should be treated as human-equivalent?'

'It's not so much that they should be treated as human-equivalent, as that if they *aren't* treated as people, it's quite possible that other uploaded beings won't be treated as people either. You're setting a legal precedent, Bob. I know of six other companies doing uploading work right now, and not one of 'em's thinking about the legal status of the uploaded. If you don't start thinking about it now, where are you going to be in three to five years' time?'

Pam is looking back and forth between Franklin and Manfred like a bot stuck in a loop, unable to quite grasp what she's seeing. 'How much is this worth?' she asks plaintively.

'Oh, quite a few million, I guess.' Bob stares at his empty glass. 'Okay. I'll talk to them. If they bite, you're dining out on me for the next century. You really think they'll be able to run the mining complex?'

'They're pretty resourceful for invertebrates.' Manfred grins innocently, enthusiastically. 'They may be prisoners of their evolutionary background, but they can still adapt to a new environment. And just think, you'll be winning civil rights for a whole new minority group – one that won't be a minority for much longer!'

That evening, Pamela turns up at Manfred's hotel room wearing a strapless black dress, concealing spike-heeled boots and most of the items he bought for her that afternoon. Manfred has opened up his private diary to her agents. She abuses the privilege, zaps him with a stunner on his way out of the shower, and has him gagged, spread-eagled, and trussed to the bed frame before he has a chance to speak. She wraps a large rubber pouch full of mildly anesthetic lube around his tumescent genitals – no point in letting him climax – clips electrodes to his nipples, lubes a rubber plug up his rectum and straps it in place. Before the shower, he removed his goggles. She resets them, plugs them into her handheld, and gently eases them on over his eyes. There's other apparatus, stuff she ran up on the hotel room's 3D printer.

Setup completed, she walks round the bed, inspecting him

critically from all angles, figuring out where to begin. This isn't just sex, after all: It's a work of art.

After a moment's thought, she rolls socks onto his exposed feet, then, expertly wielding a tiny tube of cyanoacrylate, glues his fingertips together. Then she switches off the air conditioning. He's twisting and straining, testing the cuffs. Tough, it's about the nearest thing to sensory deprivation she can arrange without a flotation tank and suxamethonium injection. She controls all his senses, only his ears unstoppered. The glasses give her a high-bandwidth channel right into his brain, a fake metacortex to whisper lies at her command. The idea of what she's about to do excites her, puts a tremor in her thighs: It's the first time she's been able to get inside his mind as well as his body. She leans forward and whispers in his ear, 'Manfred, can you hear me?'

He twitches. Mouth gagged, fingers glued. Good. No back channels. He's powerless.

'This is what it's like to be tetraplegic, Manfred. Bedridden with motor neuron disease. Locked inside your own body by nv-CJD from eating too many contaminated burgers. I could spike you with MPTP, and you'd stay in this position for the rest of your life, shitting in a bag, pissing through a tube. Unable to talk and with nobody to look after you. Do you think you'd like that?'

He's trying to grunt or whimper around the ball gag. She hikes her skirt up around her waist and climbs onto the bed, straddling him. The goggles are replaying scenes she picked up around Cambridge the previous winter – soup kitchen scenes, hospice scenes. She kneels atop him, whispering in his ear.

'Twelve million in tax, baby, that's what they think you owe them. What do you think you owe *me*? That's six million in net income, Manny, six million that isn't going into your virtual children's mouths.'

He's rolling his head from side to side, as if trying to argue. That won't do; she slaps him hard, thrills to his frightened expression. 'Today I watched you give uncounted millions away, Manny. Millions, to a bunch of crusties and a MassPike pirate! You bastard. Do you know what I should do with you?' He's cringing, unsure whether she's serious or doing this just to get him turned on. Good.

There's no point trying to hold a conversation. She leans forward until she can feel his breath in her ear. 'Meat and mind, Manny. Meat, and mind. You're not interested in meat, are you? Just mind. You could be boiled alive before you noticed what was happening in the meatspace around you. Just another lobster in a pot. The only thing keeping you out of it is how much I love you.' She reaches down and tears away the gel pouch, exposing his penis: It's stiff as a post from the vasodilators, dripping with gel, numb. Straightening up, she eases herself slowly down on it. It doesn't hurt as much as she expected, and the sensation is utterly different from what she's used to. She begins to lean forward, grabs hold of his straining arms, feels his thrilling helplessness. She can't control herself: She almost bites through her lip with the intensity of the sensation. Afterward, she reaches down and massages him until he begins to spasm, shuddering uncontrollably, emptying the Darwinian river of his source code into her, communicating via his only output device.

She rolls off his hips and carefully uses the last of the superglue to gum her labia together. Humans don't produce seminiferous plugs, and although she's fertile, she wants to be absolutely sure. The glue will last for a day or two. She feels hot and flushed, almost out of control. Boiling to death with febrile expectancy, she's nailed him down at last.

When she removes his glasses, his eyes are naked and vulnerable, stripped down to the human kernel of his nearly transcendent mind. 'You can come and sign the marriage license tomorrow morning after breakfast,' she whispers in his ear. 'Otherwise, my lawyers will be in touch. Your parents will want a ceremony, but we can arrange that later.'

He looks as if he has something to say, so she finally relents and loosens the gag, then kisses him tenderly on one cheek. He swallows, coughs, and looks away. 'Why? Why do it this way?'

She taps him on the chest. 'It's all about property rights.' She pauses for a moment's thought: There's a huge ideological chasm to bridge, after all. 'You finally convinced me about this agalmic thing of yours, this giving everything away for brownie points. I wasn't going to lose you to a bunch of lobsters or uploaded kittens, or whatever else is going to inherit this smart-matter singularity you're busy creating. So I decided to take what's mine first. Who knows? In a few months, I'll give you back a new intelligence, and you can look after it to your heart's content.'

'But you didn't need to do it this way—'

'Didn't I?' She slides off the bed and pulls down her dress. 'You give too much away too easily, Manny! Slow down, or there won't be anything left.' Leaning over the bed she dribbles acetone onto the fingers of his left hand, then unlocks the cuff. She leaves the bottle of solvent conveniently close to hand so he can untangle himself.

'See you tomorrow. Remember, after breakfast.'

She's in the doorway when he calls, 'But you didn't say *why*!'

'Think of it as being sort of like spreading your memes around,' she says, blowing a kiss at him and then closing the door. She bends down and thoughtfully places another cardboard box containing an uploaded kitten right outside it. Then she returns to her suite to make arrangements for the alchemical wedding.

2 : TROUBADOUR

Five years later, Manfred is on the run. His gray-eyed fate is in hot pursuit, blundering after him through divorce court, chat room, and meetings of the International Monetary Emergency Fund. It's a merry dance he leads her. But Manfred isn't running away, he's discovered a mission. He's going to make a stand against the laws of economics in the ancient city of Rome. He's going to mount a concert for the spiritual machines. He's going to set the companies free, and break the Italian state government.

In his shadow, his monster runs, keeping him company, never halting.

Manfred re-enters Europe through an airport that's all twentieth-century chrome and ductwork, barbaric in its decaying nuclear-age splendor. He breezes through customs and walks down a long, echoing arrival hall, sampling the local media feeds. It's November, and in a misplaced corporate search for seasonal cheer, the proprietors have come up with a final solution to the Christmas problem, a mass execution of plush Santas and elves. Bodies hang limply overhead every few meters, feet occasionally twitching in animatronic death, like a war crime perpetrated in a toy shop. *Today's increasingly automated corporations don't understand mortality,* Manfred thinks, as he passes a mother herding along her upset children. Their immortality is a drawback when dealing with the humans they graze on: They lack insight into one of the main factors that motivates the meat machines who feed them. *Well, sooner or later we'll have to do something about that,* he tells himself.

The free media channels here are denser and more richly self-referential than anything he's seen in President Santorum's America. The accent's different, though. Luton, London's fourth satellite airport, speaks with an annoyingly bumptious twang, like Australian with a plum in its mouth. *Hello, stranger! Is that a brain in your pocket or are you just pleased to think me? Ping Watford Informatics for the latest in cognitive modules and cheesy motion-picture references.* He turns the corner and finds himself squeezed up against the wall between the baggage reclaim office and a crowd of drunken Belgian tractor-drag fans, while his left goggle is trying to urgently tell him something about the railway infrastructure of Columbia. The fans wear blue face paint and chant something that sounds ominously like the ancient British war cry, *Wemberrrly, Wemberrrly,* and they're dragging a gigantic virtual tractor totem through the webspace analogue of the arrivals hall. He takes the reclaim office instead.

As he enters the baggage reclaim zone, his jacket stiffens, and his glasses dim: He can hear the lost souls of suitcases crying for their owners. The eerie keening sets his own accessories on edge with a sense of loss, and for a moment he's so spooked that he nearly shuts down the thalamic–limbic shunt interface that lets him feel their emotions. He's not in favor of emotions right now, not with the messy divorce proceedings and the blood sacrifice Pam is trying to extract from him; he'd much rather *love* and *loss* and *hate* had never been invented. But he needs the maximum possible sensory bandwidth to keep in touch with the world, so he feels it in his guts every time his footwear takes a shine to some Moldovan pyramid scheme. *Shut up,* he glyphs at his unruly herd of agents, *I can't even hear myself think!*

'Hello, sir, have a nice day, how may I be of service?' the yellow plastic suitcase on the counter says chirpily. It doesn't fool Manfred: He can see the Stalinist lines of control chaining it to the sinister, faceless cash register that lurks below the desk, agent of the British Airport Authority corporate bureaucracy. But that's okay. Only bags need fear for their freedom in here.

'Just looking,' he mumbles. And it's true. Because of a not entirely accidental cryptographic routing feature embedded in an airline reservations server, his suitcase is on its way to Mombasa, where it will probably be pithed and resurrected in the service of some African cyber-Fagin. That's okay by Manfred – it only contains a statistically normal mixture of secondhand clothes and toiletries, and he only carries it to convince the airline passenger—profiling expert systems that he isn't some sort of deviant or terrorist – but it leaves him with a gap in his inventory that he must fill before he leaves the EU zone. He needs to pick up a replacement suitcase so that he has as much luggage leaving the superpower as he had when he entered it: He doesn't want to be accused of trafficking in physical goods in the midst of the transatlantic trade war between new world protectionists and old world globalists. At least, that's his cover story – and he's sticking to it.

There's a row of unclaimed bags in front of the counter, up for sale in the absence of their owners. Some of them are very battered, but among them is a rather good-quality suitcase with integral induction-charged rollers and a keen sense of loyalty: exactly the same model as his old one. He polls it and sees not just GPS, but a Galileo tracker, a gazetteer the size of an old-time storage area network, and an iron determination to follow its owner as far as the gates of hell if necessary. Plus the right distinctive scratch on the lower left side of the case. 'How much for just this one?' he asks the bellwether on the desk.

'Ninety euros,' it says placidly.

Manfred sighs. 'You can do better than that.' In the time it takes them to settle on seventy-five, the Hang Sen Index is down fourteen-point-one-six points, and what's left of NASDAQ climbs another two-point-one. 'Deal.' Manfred spits some virtual cash at the brutal face of the cash register, and it unfetters the suitcase, unaware that Macx has paid a good bit more than seventy-five euros for the privilege of collecting this piece of baggage. Manfred bends down and faces the camera in its handle. 'Manfred Macx,' he says quietly. 'Follow me.' He feels the handle heat up as it imprints on his fingerprints, digital and phenotypic. Then he turns and walks out of the slave market, his new luggage rolling at his heels.

A short train journey later, Manfred checks into a hotel in Milton Keynes. He watches the sun set from his bedroom window, an occlusion of concrete cows blocking the horizon. The room is functional in an overly naturalistic kind of way, rattan and force-grown hardwood and hemp rugs concealing the support systems and concrete walls behind. He sits in a chair, gin and tonic at hand, absorbing the latest market news and grazing his multichannel feeds in parallel. His reputation is up two percent for no obvious reason today, he notices. Odd, that. When he pokes at it he discovers that *everybody*'s reputation – everybody, that is, who has a publicly traded reputation – is up a bit. It's as if the distributed Internet reputation servers are feeling bullish about integrity. Maybe there's a global honesty bubble forming.

Manfred frowns, then snaps his fingers. The suitcase rolls toward him. 'Who do you belong to?' he asks.

'Manfred Macx,' it replies, slightly bashfully.

'No, before me.'

'I don't understand that question.'

He sighs. 'Open up.'

Latches whir and retract: The hard-shell lid rises toward him, and he looks inside to confirm the contents.

The suitcase is full of noise.

Welcome to the early twenty-first century, human.

It's night in Milton Keynes, sunrise in Hong Kong. Moore's Law rolls inexorably on, dragging humanity toward the uncertain future. The planets of the solar system have a combined mass of approximately 2×10^{27} kilograms. Around the world, laboring women produce forty-five thousand babies a day, representing 10^{23} MIPS of processing power. Also around the world, fab lines casually churn out thirty million microprocessors a day, representing 10^{23} MIPS. In another ten months, most of the MIPS being added to the solar system will be machine-hosted for the first time. About ten years after that, the solar system's installed processing power will nudge the critical 1 MIPS per gram threshold – one million instructions per second per gram of matter. After that, singularity – a vanishing point beyond which extrapolating progress becomes meaningless. The time remaining before the intelligence spike is down to single-digit years . . .

Aineko curls on the pillow beside Manfred's head, purring softly as his owner dreams uneasily. The night outside is dark: Vehicles operate on autopilot, running lights dipped to let the Milky Way shine down upon the sleeping city. Their quiet, fuel-cell-powered engines do not trouble Manfred's sleep. The robot cat keeps sleepless watch, alert for intruders, but there are none, save the whispering ghosts of Manfred's metacortex, feeding his dreams with their state vectors.

The metacortex – a distributed cloud of software agents that surrounds him in netspace, borrowing CPU cycles from convenient processors (such as his robot pet) – is as much a part of Manfred as the society of mind that occupies his skull; his thoughts migrate into it, spawning new agents to research new experiences, and at night, they return to roost and share their knowledge.

While Manfred sleeps, he dreams of an alchemical marriage. She waits for him at the altar in a strapless black gown, the surgical instruments gleaming in her gloved hands. 'This won't hurt a bit,' she explains as she adjusts the straps. 'I only want your

genome – the extended phenotype can wait until . . . later.'
Bloodred lips, licked: a kiss of steel, then she presents the income
tax bill.

There's nothing accidental about this dream. As he experiences
it, microelectrodes in his hypothalamus trigger sensitive neurons.
Revulsion and shame flood him at the sight of her face, the sense
of his vulnerability. Manfred's metacortex, in order to facilitate his
divorce, is trying to decondition his strange love. It has been
working on him for weeks, but still he craves her whiplash touch,
the humiliation of his wife's control, the sense of helpless rage at
her unpayable taxes, demanded with interest.

Aineko watches him from the pillow, purring continuously.
Retractable claws knead the bedding, first one paw, then the next.
Aineko is full of ancient feline wisdom that Pamela installed back
when mistress and master were exchanging data and bodily fluids
rather than legal documents. Aineko is more cat than robot, these
days, thanks in part to her hobbyist's interest in feline neu-
roanatomy. Aineko knows that Manfred is experiencing nameless
neurasthenic agonies, but really doesn't give a shit about that as
long as the power supply is clean and there are no intruders.

Aineko curls up and joins Manfred in sleep, dreaming of laser-
guided mice.

Manfred is jolted awake by the hotel room phone shrilling for
attention.

'Hello?' he asks, fuzzily.

'Manfred Macx?' It's a human voice, with a gravelly East Coast
accent.

'Yeah?' Manfred struggles to sit up. His mouth feels like the
inside of a tomb, and his eyes don't want to open.

'My name is Alan Glashwiecz, of Smoot, Sedgwick Associates.
Am I correct in thinking that you are the Manfred Macx who is
a director of a company called, uh, agalmic dot holdings dot root
dot one-eight-four dot ninety-seven dot A-for-able dot B-for-
baker dot five, incorporated?'

'Uh.' Manfred blinks and rubs his eyes. 'Hold on a moment.' When the retinal patterns fade, he pulls on his glasses and powers them up. 'Just a second now.' Browsers and menus ricochet through his sleep-laden eyes. 'Can you repeat the company name?'

'Sure.' Glashwiecz repeats himself patiently. He sounds as tired as Manfred feels.

'Um.' Manfred finds it, floating three tiers down an elaborate object hierarchy. It's flashing for attention. There's a priority interrupt, an incoming lawsuit that hasn't propagated up the inheritance tree yet. He prods at the object with a property browser. 'I'm afraid I'm not a director of that company, Mr. Glashwiecz. I appear to be retained by it as a technical contractor with nonexecutive power, reporting to the president, but frankly, this is the first time I've ever heard of the company. However, I can tell you who's in charge if you want.'

'Yes?' The attorney sounds almost interested. Manfred figures it out; the guy's in New Jersey. It must be about three in the morning over there.

Malice – revenge for waking him up – sharpens Manfred's voice. The president of agalmic.holdings.root.184.97.AB5 is agalmic.holdings.root.184.97.201. The secretary is agalmic.holdings.root.184.D5, and the chair is agalmic.holdings.root.184.E8.FF. All the shares are owned by those companies in equal measure, and I can tell you that their regulations are written in Python. Have a nice day, now!' He thumps the bedside phone control and sits up, yawning, then pushes the do-not-disturb button before it can interrupt again. After a moment he stands up and stretches, then heads to the bathroom to brush his teeth, comb his hair, and figure out where the lawsuit originated and how a human being managed to get far enough through his web of robot companies to bug him.

While he's having breakfast in the hotel restaurant, Manfred decides that he's going to do something unusual for a change: He's going to make himself temporarily rich. This is a change because Manfred's normal profession is making other people rich. Manfred doesn't believe in scarcity or zero-sum games or competition – his world is too fast and information dense to accommodate primate hierarchy games. However, his current situation calls for him to do something radical: something like making himself a temporary billionaire so he can blow off his divorce settlement in an instant, like a wily accountancy octopus escaping a predator by vanishing in a cloud of his own black ink.

Pam is chasing him partially for ideological reasons – she still hasn't given up on the idea of government as the dominant superorganism of the age – but also because she loves him in her own peculiar way, and the last thing any self-respecting dom can tolerate is rejection by her slave. Pam is a born-again postconservative, a member of the first generation to grow up after the end of the American century. Driven by the need to fix the decaying federal system before it collapses under a mound of Medicare bills, overseas adventurism, and decaying infrastructure, she's willing to use self-denial, entrapment, predatory mercantilism, dirty tricks, and any other tool that boosts the bottom line. She doesn't approve of Manfred's jetting around the world on free airline passes, making strangers rich, somehow never needing money. She *can* see his listing on the reputation servers, hovering about thirty points above IBM: All the metrics of integrity, effectiveness, and goodwill value him above even that most fundamentalist of open-source computer companies. And she knows he craves her tough love, wants to give himself to her completely. So why is he running away?

The reason he's running away is entirely more ordinary. Their unborn daughter, frozen in liquid nitrogen, is an unimplanted ninety-six-hour-old blastula. Pam's bought into the whole Parents for Traditional Children parasite meme. PTC are germline recombination refuseniks: They refuse to have their children screened for fixable errors. If there's one thing that Manfred really *can't* cope with, it's the idea that nature knows best – even though that isn't the point she's making. One steaming row too many, and he kicked back, off to traveling fast and footloose again, spinning off new ideas like a memetic dynamo and living on the largesse of the new paradigm. File for divorce on grounds of irreconcilable ideological differences. No more whiplash-and-leather sex.

Before he hits the TGV for Rome, Manfred takes time to visit a model airplane show. It's a good place to be picked up by a CIA stringer – he's had a tip-off that someone will be there – and besides, flying models are hot hacker shit this decade. Add microtechnology, cameras, and neural networks to balsa-wood flyers, and you've got the next generation of military stealth flyer: It's a fertile talent-show scene, like the hacker cons of yore. This particular gig is happening in a decaying out-of-town supermarket that rents out its shop floor for events like this. Its emptiness is a sign of the times, ubiquitous broadband and expensive gas. (The robotized warehouse next door is, in contrast, frenetically busy, packing parcels for home delivery. Whether they telecommute or herd in meatspace offices, people still need to eat.)

Today, the food hall is full of people. Eldritch ersatz insects buzz menacingly along the shining empty meat counters without fear of electrocution. Big monitors unfurled above the deli display cabinets show a weird, jerky view of a three-dimensional nightmare, painted all the synthetic colors of radar. The feminine-hygiene galley has been wheeled back to make room for a gigantic plastic-shrouded tampon five meters long and sixty centimeters in diameter – a microsat launcher and conference display, plonked there by the show's sponsors in a transparent attempt to talent-spot the up-and-coming engineering geeks.

Manfred's glasses zoom in and grab a particularly fetching Fokker triplane that buzzes at face height through the crowd: He pipes the image stream up to one of his websites in real time. The Fokker pulls up in a tight Immelman turn beneath the dust-shrouded pneumatic cash tubes that line the ceiling, then picks up the trail of an F-104G. Cold War Luftwaffe and Great War Luftwaffe dart across the sky in an intricate game of tag.

Manfred's so busy tracking the warbirds that he nearly trips over the fat white tube's launcher-erector.

'Eh, Manfred! More care, *s'il vous plait!*'

He wipes the planes and glances round. 'Do I know you?' he asks politely, even as he feels a shock of recognition.

'Amsterdam, three years ago.' The woman in the double-breasted suit raises an eyebrow at him, and his social secretary remembers her for him, whispers in his ear.

'Annette from Arianespace marketing?' She nods, and he focuses on her. Still dressing in the last-century retro mode that confused him the first time they met, she looks like a Kennedy-era Secret Service man: cropped bleached crew cut like an angry albino hedgehog, pale blue contact lenses, black tie, narrow lapels. Only her skin color hints at her Berber ancestry. Her earrings are cameras, endlessly watching. Her raised eyebrow turns into a lopsided smile as she sees his reaction. 'I remember. That cafe in Amsterdam. What brings you here?'

'Why' – her wave takes in the entirety of the show—'this talent show, of course.' An elegant shrug and a wave at the orbit-capable tampon. 'It's *good* talent. We're hiring this year. If we re-enter the launcher market, we must employ only the best. Amateurs, not time-servers, engineers who can match the very best Singapore can offer.'

For the first time, Manfred notices the discreet corporate logo on the flank of the booster. 'You outsourced your launch-vehicle fabrication?'

Annette pulls a face as she explains with forced casualness, 'Hotels were more profitable, this past decade. The high-ups, they cannot be bothered with the rocketry, no? Things that go fast and explode, they are passé, they say. Diversify, they say. Until—' She gives a very Gallic shrug. Manfred nods; her earrings are recording everything she says, for the purposes of due diligence.

'I'm glad to see Europe re-entering the launcher business,' he says seriously. 'It's going to be very important when the nanosystems conformational replication business gets going for real. A major strategic asset to any corporate entity in the field, even a hotel chain.' *Especially now they've wound up NASA and the moon race is down to China and India,* he thinks sourly.

Her laugh sounds like glass bells chiming. 'And yourself, *mon cher*? What brings you to the Confederaçion? You must have a deal in mind.'

'Well' – it's Manfred's turn to shrug – 'I was *hoping* to find a CIA agent, but there don't seem to be any here today.'

'*That* is not surprising,' Annette says resentfully. 'The CIA thinks the space industry, she is dead. Fools!' She continues for a minute, enumerating the many shortcomings of the Central Intelligence Agency with vigor and a distinctly Parisian rudeness. 'They are become almost as bad as AP and Reuters since they go public,' she adds. 'All these wire services! And they are, ah, stingy. The CIA does not understand that good news must be paid for at market rates if freelance stringers are to survive. They are to be laughed at. It is *so* easy to plant disinformation on them, almost as easy as the Office of Special Plans . . .' She makes a banknote-riffling gesture between fingers and thumb. By way of punctuation, a remarkably maneuverable miniature ornithopter swoops around her head, does a double-back flip, and dives off in the direction of the liquor display.

An Iranian woman wearing a backless leather minidress and a nearly transparent scarf barges up and demands to know how much the microbooster costs to buy. She is dissatisfied with Annette's attempt to direct her to the manufacturer's website, and Annette looks distinctly flustered by the time the woman's boyfriend – a dashing young air force pilot – shows up to escort her away. 'Tourists,' she mutters, before noticing Manfred, who is staring off into space with fingers twitching. 'Manfred?'

'Uh – what?'

'I have been on this shop floor for six hours, and my feet, they kill me.' She takes hold of his left arm and very deliberately unhooks her earrings, turning them off. 'If I say to you I can write for the CIA wire service, will you take me to a restaurant and buy me dinner and tell me what it is you want to say?'

* * *

Welcome to the second decade of the twenty-first century; the second decade in human history when the intelligence of the environment has shown signs of rising to match human demand.

The news from around the world is distinctly depressing this evening. In Maine, guerrillas affiliated with Parents for Traditional Children announce they've planted logic bombs in antenatal-clinic gene scanners, making them give random false positives when checking for hereditary disorders: The damage so far is six illegal abortions and fourteen lawsuits.

The International Convention on Performing Rights is holding a third round of crisis talks in an attempt to stave off the final collapse of the WIPO music licensing regime. On the one hand, hard-liners representing the Copyright Control Association of America are pressing for restrictions on duplicating the altered emotional states associated with specific media performances: As a demonstration that they mean business, two 'software engineers' in California have been kneecapped, tarred, feathered, and left for dead under placards accusing them of reverse-engineering movie plot lines using avatars of dead and out-of-copyright stars.

On the opposite side of the fence, the Association of Free Artists is demanding the right to perform music in public without a recording contract, and is denouncing the CCAA as being a tool of Mafiya apparachiks who have bought it from the moribund music industry in an attempt to go legit. FBI Director Leonid Kuibyshev responds by denying that the Mafiya is a significant presence in the United States. But the music biz's position isn't strengthened by the near collapse of the legitimate American entertainment industry, which has been accelerating ever since the nasty noughties.

A marginally intelligent voicemail virus masquerading as an IRS auditor has caused havoc throughout America, garnishing an estimated eighty billion dollars in confiscatory tax withholdings into a numbered Swiss bank account. A different virus is busy hijacking people's bank accounts, sending ten percent of their assets to the previous victim, then mailing itself to everyone in the current mark's address book: a self-propelled pyramid scheme in action. Oddly, nobody is complaining much. While the mess is being sorted out, business IT departments have gone to standby, refusing to process any transaction that doesn't come in the shape of ink on dead trees.

Tipsters are warning of an impending readjustment in the overinflated reputations market, following revelations that some u-media gurus have been hyped past all realistic levels of credibility: The consequent damage to the junk-bonds market in integrity is serious.

The EU council of independent heads of state has denied plans for another attempt at eurofederalisme, at least until the economy rises out of its current slump. Three extinct species have been resurrected in the past month; unfortunately, endangered ones are now dying off at a rate of one a day. And a group of militant anti-GM campaigners are being pursued by Interpol, after their announcement that they have spliced a metabolic pathway for cyanogenic gly-cosides into maize seed corn destined for human-edible crops. There have been no deaths yet, but having to test breakfast cereal for cyanide is really going to dent consumer trust.

About the only people who're doing well right now are the uploaded lobsters – and the crusties aren't even remotely human.

Manfred and Annette eat on the top deck of the buffet car, chat-ting as their TGV barrels through a tunnel under the English Channel. Annette, it transpires, has been commuting daily from Paris, which was, in any case, Manfred's next destination. From the show, he messaged Aineko to round up his baggage and meet him at St. Pancras Station, in a terminal like the shell of a giant steel woodlouse. Annette left her space launcher in the supermarket overnight: An unfueled test article, it is of no security significance.

The railway buffet car is run by a Nepalese fast-food franchise. 'I sometimes wish for to stay on the train,' Annette says as she waits for her *mismas bhat*. 'Past Paris! Think. Settle back in your couchette, to awaken in Moscow and change trains. All the way to Vladivostok in two days.'

'If they let you through the border,' Manfred mutters. Russia is one of those places that still requires passports and asks if you are now or ever have been an anti-anticommunist: It's still trapped by its bloody-handed history. (Rewind the video stream to Stolypin's necktie party and start out fresh.) Besides, they have enemies: White Russian oligarchs, protection racketeers in the intellectual property business. Psychotic relics of the last decade's experiment with Marxism-Objectivism. 'Are you *really* a CIA stringer?'

Annette grins, her lips disconcertingly red. 'I file dispatches from time to time. Nothing that could get me fired.'

Manfred nods. 'My wife has access to their unfiltered stream.'

'Your—' Annette pauses. 'It was she who I, I met? In De Wildemann's?' She sees his expression. 'Oh, my poor fool!' She raises her glass to him. 'It is, has, not gone well?'

Manfred sighs and raises a toast toward Annette. 'You know your marriage is in a bad way when you send your spouse messages via the CIA, and she communicates using the IRS.'

'In only five years.' Annette winces. 'You will pardon me for saying this – she did not look like your type.' There's a question hidden behind that statement, and he notices again how good she is at overloading her statements with subtexts.

'I'm not sure what my type is,' he says, half-truthfully. He can't elude the sense that something not of either of their doing went wrong between him and Pamela, a subtle intrusion that levered them apart by stealth. *Maybe it was me,* he thinks. Sometimes he isn't certain he's still human; too many threads of his consciousness seem to live outside his head, reporting back whenever they find something interesting. Sometimes he feels like a puppet, and that frightens him because it's one of the early-warning signs of schizophrenia. *And it's too early for anyone out there to be trying to hack exocortices . . . isn't it?* Right now, the external threads of his consciousness are telling him that they like Annette, when she's being herself instead of a cog in the meat-space ensemble of Arianespace management. But the part of him that's still human isn't sure just how far to trust himself. 'I want to be me. What do you want to be?'

She shrugs, as a waiter slides a plate in front of her. 'I'm just a, a Parisian babe, no? An *ingénue* raised in the lilac age of le Confederaçion Europé, the self-deconstructed ruins of the gilded European Union.'

'Yeah, right.' A plate appears in front of Manfred. 'And I'm a good old microboomer from the MassPike corridor.' He peels back a corner of the omelet topping and inspects the food under-neath it. 'Born in the sunset years of the American century.' He pokes at one of the unidentifiable meaty lumps in the fried rice with his fork, and it pokes right back. There's a limit to how much his agents can tell him about her – European privacy laws are draconian by American standards – but he knows the essen-tials. Two parents who are still together, father a petty politician in some town council down in the vicinity of Toulouse. Went to the right *école*. The obligatory year spent bumming around the Confederaçion at government expense, learning how other people live – a new kind of empire building, in place of the twentieth century's conscription and jackboot walkabout. No weblog or personal site that his agents can find. She joined Arianespace right out of the Polytechnique and has been management track ever since: Korou, Manhattan Island, Paris. 'You've never been married, I take it.'

She chuckles. 'Time is too short! I am still young.' She picks up a forkful of food, and adds quietly, 'Besides, the government would insist on paying.'

'Ah.' Manfred tucks into his bowl thoughtfully. With the

birthrate declining across Europe, the EC bureaucracy is worried; the old EU started subsidizing babies, a new generation of carers, a decade ago, and it still hasn't dented the problem. All it's done is alienate the brightest women of childbearing age. Soon they'll have to look to the east for a solution, importing a new generation of citizens – unless the long-promised aging hacks prove workable, or cheap AI comes along.

'Do you have a hotel?' Annette asks suddenly.

'In Paris?' Manfred is startled. 'Not yet.'

'You must come home with me, then.' She looks at him quizzically.

'I'm not sure I—' He catches her expression. 'What is it?'

'Oh, nothing. My friend Henri, he says I take in strays too easily. But you are not a stray. I think you can look after yourself. Besides, it is the Friday today. Come with me, and I will file your press release for the Company to read. Tell me, do you dance? You look as if you need a wild week ending, to help forget your troubles!'

Annette drives a steamroller seduction through Manfred's plans for the weekend. He intended to find a hotel, file a press release, then spend some time researching the corporate funding structure of Parents for Traditional Children and the dimensionality of confidence variation on the reputation exchanges – then head for Rome. Instead, Annette drags him back to her apartment, a large studio flat tucked away behind an alley in the Marais. She sits him at the breakfast bar while she tidies away his luggage, then makes him close his eyes and swallow two dubious-tasting capsules. Next, she pours them each a tall glass of freezing-cold Aqvavit that tastes exactly like Polish rye bread. When they finish it, she just about rips his clothes off. Manfred is startled to discover that he has a crowbar-stiff erection; since the last blazing row with Pamela, he'd vaguely assumed he was no longer interested in sex. Instead, they end up naked on the sofa, surrounded by discarded clothing – Annette is very conservative, preferring the naked penetrative fuck of the last century to the more sophisticated fetishes of the present day.

Afterward, he's even more surprised to discover that he's still tumescent. 'The capsules?' he asks.

She sprawls a well-muscled but thin thigh across him, then reaches down to grab his penis. Squeezes it. 'Yes,' she admits. 'You need much special help to unwind, I think.' Another squeeze. 'Crystal meth and a traditional phosphodiesterase inhibitor.' He grabs one of her small breasts, feeling very brutish and primitive. *Naked*. He's not sure Pamela ever let him see her fully naked: She thought skin was more sexy when it was covered. Annette squeezes him again, and he stiffens. 'More!'

By the time they finish, he's aching, and she shows him how to use the bidet. Everything is crystal clear, and her touch is electrifying. While she showers, he sits on the toilet seat lid and rants about Turing-completeness as an attribute of company law, about cellular automata and the blind knapsack problem, about his work on solving the Communist Central Planning problem using a network of interlocking unmanned companies. About the impending market adjustment in integrity, the sinister resurrection of the recording music industry, and the still-pressing need to dismantle Mars.

When she steps out of the shower, he tells her that he loves her. She kisses him and slides his glasses and earpieces off his head so that he's *really* naked, sits on his lap, and fucks his brains out again, and whispers in his ear that she loves him and wants to be his manager. Then she leads him into her bedroom and tells him exactly what she wants him to wear, and she puts on her own clothes, and she gives him a mirror with some white powder on it to sniff. When she's got him dolled up they go out for a night of really serious clubbing, Annette in a tuxedo and Manfred in a blond wig, red silk off-the-shoulder gown, and high heels. Sometime in the early hours, exhausted and resting his head on her shoulder during the last tango in a BDSM club in the Rue Ste-Anne, he realizes that it really *is* possible to be in lust with someone other than Pamela.

* * *

Aineko wakes Manfred by repeatedly head-butting him above the left eye. He groans and, as he tries to open his eyes, he finds that his mouth tastes like a dead trout, his skin feels greasy with makeup, and his head is pounding. There's a banging noise somewhere. Aineko meows urgently. He sits up, feeling unaccustomed silk underwear rubbing against incredibly sore skin – he's fully dressed, just sprawled out on the sofa. Snores emanate from the bedroom; the banging is coming from the front door. Someone wants to come in. *Shit*. He rubs his head, stands up, and nearly falls flat on his face: He hasn't even taken those ridiculous high heels off. *How* much *did I drink last night?* he wonders. His glasses are on the breakfast bar; he pulls them on and is besieged by an urgent flurry of ideas demanding attention. He straightens his wig, picks up his skirts, and trips across to the door with a sinking feeling. Luckily, his publicly traded reputation is strictly technical.

He unlocks the door. 'Who is it?' he asks in English. By way of reply somebody shoves the door in, hard. Manfred falls back against the wall, winded. His glasses stop working, sidelook displays filling with multicolored static.

Two men charge in, identically dressed in jeans and leather jackets. They're wearing gloves and occlusive face masks, and one of them points a small and very menacing ID card at Manfred. A self-propelled gun hovers in the doorway, watching everything. 'Where is he?'

'Who?' gasps Manfred, breathless and terrified.

'Macx.' The other intruder steps into the living room quickly, pans around, ducks through the bathroom door. Aineko flops as limp as a dishrag in front of the sofa. The intruder checks out the bedroom: There's a brief scream, cut off short.

'I don't know – who?' Manfred is choking with fear.

The other intruder ducks out of the bedroom, waves a hand dismissively.

'We are sorry to have bothered you,' the man with the card says stiffly. He replaced it in his jacket pocket. 'If you should see Manfred Macx, tell him that the Copyright Control Association of America advises him to cease and desist from his attempt to assist music thieves and other degenerate mongrel secondhander enemies of Objectivism. Reputations only of use to those alive to own them. Goodbye.'

The two copyright gangsters disappear through the door, leaving Manfred to shake his head dizzily while his glasses reboot. It takes him a moment to register the scream from the bedroom. 'Fuck! *Annette!*'

She appears in the open doorway, holding a sheet around her waist, looking angry and confused. 'Annette!' he calls. She looks around, sees him, and begins to laugh shakily. 'Annette!' He crosses over to her. 'You're okay,' he says. 'You're okay.'

'You, too.' She hugs him, and she's shaking. Then she holds him at arm's length. 'My, what a pretty picture!'

'They wanted me,' he says, and his teeth are chattering. '*Why?*'

She looks up at him seriously. 'You must bathe. Then have coffee. We are not at home, *oui?*'

'Ah, *oui.*' He looks down. Aineko is sitting up, looking dazed. 'Shower. Then that dispatch for CIA news.'

'The dispatch?' She looks puzzled. 'I filed that last night. When I was in the shower. The microphone, he is waterproof.'

By the time Arianespace's security contractors show up, Manfred has stripped off Annette's evening gown and showered; he's sitting in the living room wearing a bathrobe, drinking a half-liter mug of espresso and swearing under his breath.

While he was dancing the night away in Annette's arms, the global reputation market has gone nonlinear: People are putting their trust in the Christian Coalition and the Eurocommunist Alliance – always a sign that the times are bad – while perfectly sound trading enterprises have gone into free fall, as if a major bribery scandal has broken out.

Manfred trades ideas for kudos via the Free Intellect Foundation, bastard child of George Soros and Richard Stallman. *His* reputation is cemented by donations to the public good that don't backfire. So he's offended and startled to discover that he's dropped twenty points in the past two hours — and frightened to see that this is by no means unusual. He was expecting a ten-point drop mediated via an options trade — payment for the use of the anonymous luggage remixer that routed his old suitcase to Mombasa and in return sent this new one to him via the left-luggage office in Luton — but this is more serious. The entire reputation market seems to have been hit by the confidence flu.

Annette bustles around busily, pointing out angles and timings to the forensics team her head office sent in answer to her call for backup. She seems more angry and shaken than worried by the intrusion. It's probably an occupational hazard for any upwardly mobile executive in the old, grasping network of greed that Manfred's agalmic future aims to supplant. The forensics dude and dudette, a pair of cute, tanned Lebanese youngsters, point the yellow snout of their mass spectroscope into various corners and agree that there's something not unlike gun oil in the air. But, so sorry, the intruders wore masks to trap the skin particles and left behind a spray of dust vacuumed from the seat of a city bus, so there's no way of getting a genotype match. Presently they agree to log it as a suspected corporate intrusion (origin: unclassified; severity: worrying) and increase the logging level on her kitchen telemetry. And remember to wear your earrings at all times, please. They leave, and Annette locks the door, leans against it, and curses for a whole long minute.

'They gave me a message from the copyright control agency,' Manfred says unevenly when she winds down. 'Russian gangsters from New York bought the recording cartels a few years ago, you know? After the rights stitch-up fell apart, and the artists all went online while they focused on copy prevention technologies, the Mafiya were the only people who would buy the old business model. These guys add a whole new meaning to copy protection: This was just a polite cease and desist notice by their standards. They run the record shops, and they *try* to block any music distribution channel they don't own. Not very successfully, though — most gangsters are living in the past, more conservative than any normal businessman can afford to be. What was it that you put on the wire?'

Annette closes her eyes. 'I don't remember. No.' She holds up a hand. 'Open mike. I streamed you into a file and cut, cut out the bits about me.' She opens her eyes and shakes her head. 'What was I *on*?'

'You don't know either?'

He stands up, and she walks over and throws her arms around him. 'I was on *you*,' she murmurs.

'Bullshit.' He pulls away, then sees how this upsets her. Something is blinking for attention in his glasses; he's been off-line for the best part of six hours and is getting a panicky butterfly stomach at the idea of not being in touch with every-thing that's happened in the last twenty kiloseconds. 'I need to know more. *Something* in that report rattled the wrong cages. Or someone ratted on the suitcase exchange – I meant the dispatch to be a heads-up for whoever needs a working state planning system, not an invitation to shoot me!'

'Well, then.' She lets go of him. 'Do your work.' Coolly: 'I'll be around.'

He realizes that he's hurt her, but he doesn't see any way of explaining that he didn't mean to – at least, not without digging himself in deeper. He finishes his croissant and plunges into one of those unavoidable fits of deep interaction, fingers twitching on invisible keypads and eyeballs jiggling as his glasses funnel deep media straight into his skull through the highest bandwidth channel currently available.

One of his e-mail accounts is halfway to the moon with auto-matic messages, companies with names like agalmic. holdings.root.8E.F0 screaming for the attention of their transi-tive director. Each of these companies – and there are currently more than sixteen thousand of them, although the herd is grow-ing day by day – has three directors and is the director of three other companies. Each of them executes a script in a functional language Manfred invented; the directors tell the company what to do, and the instructions include orders to pass instructions on to their children. In effect, they are a flock of cellular automata, like the cells in Conway's Game of Life, only far more complex and powerful.

Manfred's companies form a programmable grid. Some of them are armed with capital in the form of patents Manfred filed, then delegated rather than passing on to one of the Free Foundations. Some of them are effectively nontrading, but occupy directorial roles. Their corporate functions (such as filing of accounts and voting in new directors) are all handled centrally through his company-operating framework, and their trading is carried out via several of the more popular B2B enabler dot-coms. Internally, the companies do other, more obscure load-balancing computations, processing resource-allocation problems like a classic state central planning system. None of which explains why fully half of them have been hit by lawsuits in the past twenty-two hours.

The lawsuits are . . . *random*. That's the only pattern Manfred can detect. Some of them allege patent infringements; these he might take seriously, except that about a third of the targets are director companies that don't actually do anything visible to the public. A few lawsuits allege mismanagement, but then there's a whole bizarre raft of spurious nonsense: suits for wrongful dismissal or age discrimination – against companies with no employees – complaints about reckless trading, and one action alleging that the defendant (in conspiracy with the prime minister of Japan, the government of Canada, and the Emir of Kuwait) is using orbital mind-control lasers to make the plaintiff's pet Chihuahua bark at all hours of day and night.

Manfred groans and does a quick calculation. At the current rate, lawsuits are hitting his corporate grid at a rate of one every sixteen seconds – up from none in the preceding six months. In another day, this is going to saturate him. If it keeps up for a week, it'll saturate every court in the United States. *Someone* has found a means to do for lawsuits what he's doing for companies – and they've chosen him as their target.

To say that Manfred is unamused is an understatement. If he

wasn't already preoccupied with Annette's emotional state and edgy from the intrusion, he'd be livid – but he's still human enough that he responds to human stimuli first. So he determines to do something about it, but he's still flashing on the floating gun, her cross-dressing cool.

Transgression, sex, and networks, these are all on his mind when Glashwiecz phones again.

'Hello?' Manfred answers distractedly; he's busy pondering the lawsuit bot that's attacking his systems.

'Macx! The elusive Mr. Macx!' Glashwiecz sounds positively overjoyed to have tracked down his target.

Manfred winces. 'Who is this?' he asks.

'I called you yesterday,' says the lawyer. 'You should have listened.' He chortles horribly. 'Now I have you!'

Manfred holds the phone away from his face, like something poisonous. 'I'm recording this,' he warns. 'Who the hell are you and what do you want?'

'Your wife has retained my partnership's services to pursue her interests in your divorce case. When I called you yesterday it was to point out without prejudice that your options are running out. I have an order, signed in court three days ago, to have all your assets frozen. These ridiculous shell companies notwithstanding, she's going to take you for exactly what you owe her. After tax, of course. She's very insistent on that point.'

Manfred glances round, puts his phone on hold for a moment. 'Where's my suitcase?' he asks Aineko. The cat sidles away, ignoring him. 'Shit.' He can't see the new luggage anywhere. Quite possibly it's on its way to Morocco, complete with its priceless cargo of high-density noise. He returns his attention to the phone. Glashwiecz is droning on about equitable settlements, cumulative IRS tax demands – that seem to have materialized out of fantasy with Pam's imprimatur on them – and the need to make a clean breast of things in court and confess to his sins. 'Where's the *fucking* suitcase?' He takes the phone off hold. 'Shut the fuck up, please, I'm trying to think.'

'I'm not going to shut up! You're on the court docket already,

Macx. You can't evade your responsibilities forever. You've got a wife and a helpless daughter to care for—'

'A daughter?' That cuts right through Manfred's preoccupation with the suitcase.

'Didn't you know?' Glashwiecz sounds pleasantly surprised. 'She was decanted last Thursday. Perfectly healthy, I'm told. I thought you knew; you have viewing rights via the clinic webcam. Anyway, I'll just leave you with this thought – the sooner you come to a settlement, the sooner I can unfreeze your companies. Goodbye.'

The suitcase rolls into view, coyly peeping out from behind Annette's dressing table. Manfred breathes a sigh of relief and beckons to it; at the moment, it's easier to deal with his Plan B than dawn raids by objectivist gangsters, Annette's sulk, his wife's incessant legal spamming, and the news that he is a father against his will. 'C'mon over here, you stray baggage. Let's see what I got for my reputation derivatives . . .'

Anticlimax.

Annette's communiqué is anodyne; a giggling confession off camera (shower-curtain rain in the background) that the famous Manfred Macx is in Paris for a weekend of clubbing, drugging, and general hell-raising. Oh, and he's promised to invent three new paradigm shifts before breakfast every day, starting with a way to bring about the creation of Really Existing Communism by building a state central planning apparatus that interfaces perfectly with external market systems and somehow manages to algorithmically outperform the Monte Carlo free-for-all of market economics, solving the calculation problem. Just because he can, because hacking economics is fun, and he wants to hear the screams from the Chicago School.

Try as he may, Manfred can't see anything in the press release that is at all unusual. It's just the sort of thing he does, and getting it on the net was why he was looking for a CIA stringer in the first place.

He tries to explain this to her in the bath as he soaps her back. 'I don't understand what they're on about,' he complains. 'There's nothing that tipped them off – except that I was in Paris, and you filed the news. You did *nothing* wrong.'

'Mais oui.' She turns round, slippery as an eel, and slides backward into the water. 'I try to tell you this, but you are not listening.'

'I am now.' Water droplets cling to the outside of his glasses, plastering his view of the room with laser speckle highlights. 'I'm sorry, Annette, I brought this mess with me. I can take it out of your life.'

'No!' She rises up in front of him and leans forward, face serious. 'I said yesterday. I want to be your manager. Take me in.'

'I don't *need* a manager; my whole thing is about being fast and out of control!'

'You think you do not need a manager, but your companies do,' she observes. 'You have lawsuits, how many? You cannot the time to oversee them spare. The Soviets, they abolish capitalists, but even they need managers. Please, let me manage for you!'

Annette is so intense about the idea that she becomes visibly aroused. He leans toward her, cups a hand around one taut nipple. 'The company matrix isn't sold yet,' he admits.

'It is not?' She looks delighted. 'Excellent! To who can this be sold, to Moscow? To SLORC? To—'

'I was thinking of the Italian Communist Party,' he says. 'It's a pilot project. I was working on selling it – I need the money for my divorce, and to close the deal on the luggage – but it's not that simple. Someone has to run the damn thing – someone with a keen understanding of how to interface a central planning system with a capitalist economy. A system administrator with the experience of working for a multinational corporation would be perfect, ideally with an interest in finding new ways and means of interfacing the centrally planned enterprise to the outside world.' He looks at her with suddenly dawning surmise. 'Um, are you interested?'

* * *

Rome is hotter than downtown Columbia, South Carolina, over Thanksgiving weekend; it stinks of methane-burning Skodas with a low undertone of cooked dog shit. The cars are brightly colored subcompact missiles, hurtling in and out of alleyways like angry wasps: Hot-wiring their drive-by-wire seems to be the national sport, although Fiat's embedded-systems people have always written notoriously wobbly software.

Manfred emerges from the Stazione Termini into dusty sunlight, blinking like an owl. His glasses keep up a rolling monologue about who lived where in the days of the late Republic. They're stuck on a tourist channel and won't come unglued from that much history without a struggle. Manfred doesn't feel like a struggle right now. He feels like he's been sucked dry over the weekend: a light, hollow husk that might blow away in a stiff breeze. He hasn't had a patentable idea all day. This is not a good state to be in on a Monday morning when he's due to meet the former Minister for Economic Affairs, in order to give him a gift that will probably get the minister a shot at higher office and get Pam's lawyer off his back. But somehow he can't bring himself to worry too much: Annette has been good for him.

The ex-minister's private persona isn't what Manfred was expecting. All Manfred has seen so far is a polished public avatar in a traditionally cut suit, addressing the Chamber of Deputies in cyberspace, which is why, when he rings the doorbell set in the whitewashed doorframe of Gianni's front door, he isn't expecting a piece of Tom of Finland beefcake, complete with breechclout and peaked leather cap, to answer.

'Hello, I am here to see the minister,' Manfred says carefully. Aineko, perched on his left shoulder, attempts to translate: It trills something that sounds extremely urgent. *Everything* sounds urgent in Italian.

'It's okay. I'm from Iowa,' says the guy in the doorway. He tucks a thumb under one leather strap and grins over his moustache. 'What's it about?' Over his shoulder: 'Gianni! Visitor!'

'It's about the economy,' Manfred says carefully. 'I'm here to make it obsolete.'

The beefcake backs away from the door cautiously – then the minister appears behind him. 'Ah, signore Macx! It's okay, Johnny, I have been expecting him.' Gianni extends a rapid welcome, like a hyperactive gnome buried in a white toweling bathrobe. 'Please come in, my friend! I'm sure you must be tired from your journey. A refreshment for the guest if you please, Johnny. Would you prefer coffee or something stronger?'

Five minutes later, Manfred is buried up to his ears in a sofa covered in buttery white cowhide, a cup of virulently strong espresso balanced precariously on his knee, while Gianni Vittoria himself holds forth on the problems of implementing a post-industrial ecosystem on top of a bureaucratic system with its roots in the bullheadedly modernist era of the 1920s. Gianni is a visionary of the left, a strange attractor within the chaotic phase-space of Italian politics. A former professor of Marxist economics, his ideas are informed by a painfully honest humanism, and everyone – even his enemies – agrees that he is one of the greatest theoreticians of the post-EU era. But his intellectual integrity prevents him from rising to the very top, and his fellow travelers are much ruder about him than his ideological enemies, accusing him of the ultimate political crime – valuing truth over power.

Manfred had met Gianni a couple of years earlier via a hosted politics chat room; at the beginning of last week, he sent him a paper detailing his embeddable planned economy and a proposal for using it to turbocharge the endless Italian attempt to re-engineer its government systems. This is the thin end of the wedge: If Manfred is right, it could catalyze a whole new wave of communist expansion, driven by humanitarian ideals and demonstrably superior performance, rather than wishful thinking and ideology.

'It is impossible, I fear. This is Italy, my friend. Everybody has to have their say. Not everybody even understands what it is we are talking about, but that won't stop *them* talking about it. Since 1945, our government requires consensus – a reaction to what came before. Do you know we have five different routes to putting forward a new law, two of them added as emergency measures to break the gridlock? And none of them work on their own unless you can get everybody to agree. Your plan is daring and radical, but if it works, we must understand why *we* work – and that digs right to the root of being human, and not everybody will agree.'

At this point Manfred realizes that he's lost. 'I don't understand,' he says, genuinely puzzled. 'What has the human condition got to do with economics?'

The minister sighs abruptly. 'You are very unusual. You earn no money, do you? But you are rich, because grateful people who have benefited from your work give you everything you need. You are like a medieval troubadour who has found favor with the aristocracy. Your labor is not alienated – it is given freely, and your means of production is with you always, inside your head.' Manfred blinks; the jargon is weirdly technical-sounding but orthogonal to his experience, offering him a disquieting glimpse into the world of the terminally future-shocked. He is surprised to find that not understanding *itches*.

Gianni taps his balding temple with a knuckle like a walnut. 'Most people spend little time inside their heads. They don't understand how you live. They're like medieval peasants looking in puzzlement at the troubadour. This system you invent, for running a planned economy, is delightful and elegant: Lenin's heirs would have been awestruck. But it is not a system for the new century. It is not *human*.'

Manfred scratches his head. 'It seems to me that there's nothing human about the economics of scarcity,' he says. 'Anyway, humans will be obsolete as economic units within a couple more decades. All I want to do is make everybody rich beyond their wildest dreams before that happens.' A pause for a sip of coffee, and to think, *One honest statement deserves another.* 'And to pay off a divorce settlement.'

'Ye-es? Well, let me show you my library, my friend,' he says, standing up. 'This way.'

Gianni ambles out of the white living room with its carnivorous leather sofas and up a cast-iron spiral staircase that nails some kind of upper level to the underside of the roof. 'Human beings aren't rational,' he calls over his shoulder. 'That was the big mistake of the Chicago School economists, neoliberals to a man, and of my predecessors, too. If human behavior was logical, there would be no gambling, hmm? The house always wins, after all.' The staircase debouches into another airy whitewashed room, where one wall is occupied by a wooden bench supporting a number of ancient, promiscuously cabled servers and a very new, eye-wateringly expensive solid volume renderer. Opposite the bench is a wall occupied from floor to ceiling by bookcases: Manfred looks at the ancient, low-density medium and sneezes, momentarily bemused by the sight of data density measured in kilograms per megabyte rather than vice versa.

'What's it fabbing?' Manfred asks, pointing at the renderer, which is whining to itself and slowly sintering together something that resembles a carriage clockmaker's fever dream of a spring-powered hard disk drive.

'Oh, one of Johnny's toys – a micromechanical digital phonograph player,' Gianni says dismissively. 'He used to design Babbage engines for the Pentagon – stealth computers. (No van Eck radiation, you know.) Look.' He carefully pulls a fabric-bound document out of the obsolescent data wall and shows the spine to Manfred: '*On the Theory of Games,* by John von Neumann. Signed first edition.'

Aineko meeps and dumps a slew of confusing purple finite state automata into Manfred's left eye. The hardback is dusty and dry beneath his fingertips as he remembers to turn the pages gently. 'This copy belonged to the personal library of Oleg Kordiovsky. A lucky man is Oleg: He bought it in 1952, while on a visit to New York, and the MVD let him to keep it.'

'He must be—' Manfred pauses. More data, historical time lines. 'Part of GosPlan?'

'Correct.' Gianni smiles thinly. 'Two years before the central committee denounced computers as bourgeois deviationist pseudoscience intended to dehumanize the proletarian. They recognized the power of robots even then. A shame they did not anticipate the compiler or the net.'

'I don't understand the significance. Nobody back then could expect that the main obstacle to doing away with market capitalism would be overcome within half a century, surely?'

'Indeed not. But it's true: Since the 1980s, it has been possible – in principle – to resolve resource allocation problems algorithmically, by computer, instead of needing a market. Markets are wasteful: They allow competition, much of which is thrown on the scrap heap. So why do they persist?'

Manfred shrugs. 'You tell me. Conservativism?'

Gianni closes the book and puts it back on the shelf. 'Markets afford their participants the illusion of *free will,* my friend. You will find that human beings do not like being forced into doing something, even if it is in their best interests. Of necessity, a command economy must be coercive – it does, after all, command.'

'But my system doesn't! It mediates where supplies go, not who has to produce what—'

Gianni is shaking his head. 'Backward chaining or forward chaining, it is still an expert system, my friend. Your companies need no human beings, and this is a good thing, but they must not direct the activities of human beings, either. If they do, you have just enslaved people to an abstract machine, as dictators have throughout history.'

Manfred's eyes scan along the bookshelf. 'But the market itself is an abstract machine! A lousy one, too. I'm mostly free of it – but how long is it going to continue oppressing people?'

'Maybe not as long as you fear.' Gianni sits down next to the renderer, which is currently extruding the inference mill of the analytical engine. 'The marginal value of money decreases, after all: The more you have, the less it means to you. We are on the edge of a period of prolonged economic growth, with annual averages in excess of twenty percent, if the Council of Europe's predictor metrics are anything to go by. The last of the flaccid industrial economy has withered away, and this era's muscle of economic growth, what used to be the high-technology sector, is now everything. We can afford a little wastage, my friend, if that is the price of keeping people happy until the marginal value of money withers away completely.'

Realization dawns. 'You want to abolish scarcity, not just money!'

'Indeed.' Gianni grins. 'There's more to that than mere economic performance; you have to consider abundance as a factor. Don't plan the economy; take things *out* of the economy. Do you pay for the air you breathe? Should uploaded minds – who will be the backbone of our economy, by and by – have to pay for processor cycles? No and no. Now, do you want to know how you can pay for your divorce settlement? And can I interest you, and your interestingly accredited new manager, in a little project of mine?'

The shutters are thrown back, the curtains tied out of the way, and Annette's huge living room windows are drawn open in the morning breeze.

Manfred sits on a leather-topped piano stool, his suitcase open at his feet. He's running a link from the case to Annette's stereo, an antique stand-alone unit with a satellite Internet uplink. Someone has chipped it, crudely revoking its copy protection algorithm: The back of its case bears scars from the soldering iron. Annette is curled up on the huge sofa, wrapped in a kaftan and a pair of high-bandwidth goggles, thrashing out an internal Arianespace scheduling problem with some colleagues in Iran and Guyana.

His suitcase is full of noise, but what's coming out of the stereo is ragtime. Subtract entropy from a data stream – coincidentally uncompressing it – and what's left is information. With a capacity of about a trillion terabytes, the suitcase's holographic storage reservoir has enough capacity to hold every music, film, and video production of the twentieth century with room to spare. This is all stuff that is effectively out of copyright control, work-for-hire owned by bankrupt companies, released before the CCAA could make their media clampdown stick. Manfred is streaming the music through Annette's stereo

– but keeping the noise it was convoluted with. High-grade entropy is valuable, too . . .

Presently, Manfred sighs and pushes his glasses up his forehead, killing the displays. He's thought his way around every permutation of what's going on, and it looks like Gianni was right: There's nothing left to do but wait for everyone to show up.

For a moment, he feels old and desolate, as slow as an unassisted human mind. Agencies have been swapping in and out of his head for the past day, ever since he got back from Rome. He's developed a butterfly attention span, irritable and unable to focus on anything while the information streams fight it out for control of his cortex, arguing about a solution to his predicament. Annette is putting up with his mood swings surprisingly calmly. He's not sure why, but he glances her way fondly. Her obsessions run surprisingly deep, and she's quite clearly using him for her own purposes. So why does he feel more comfortable around her than he did with Pam?

She stretches and pushes her goggles up. *'Oui?'*

'I was just thinking.' He smiles. 'Three days and you haven't told me what I should be doing with myself, yet.'

She pulls a face. 'Why would I do that?'

'Oh, no reason. I'm just not over—' He shrugs uncomfortably. There it is, an inexplicable absence in his life, but not one he feels he urgently needs to fill yet. Is this what a relationship between equals feels like? He's not sure. Starting with the occlusive cocooning of his upbringing and continuing through all his adult relationships, he's been effectively – voluntarily – dominated by his partners. Maybe the antisubmissive conditioning is working, after all. But if so, why the creative malaise? Why isn't he coming up with original new ideas this week? Could it be that his peculiar brand of creativity is an outlet, that he needs the pressure of being lovingly enslaved to make him burst out into a great flowering of imaginative brilliance? Or could it be that he really *is* missing Pam?

Annette stands up and walks over, slowly. He looks at her and feels lust and affection, and isn't sure whether or not this is love. 'When are they due?' she asks, leaning over him.

'Any—' The doorbell chimes.

'Ah. I will get that.' She stalks away, opens the door.

'You!'

Manfred's head snaps round as if he's on a leash. *Her* leash: But he wasn't expecting her to come in person.

'Yes, me,' Annette says easily. 'Come in. Be my guest.'

Pam enters the apartment living room with flashing eyes, her tame lawyer in tow. 'Well, look what the robot kitty dragged in,' she drawls, fixing Manfred with an expression that owes more to anger than to humor. It's not like her, this blunt hostility, and he wonders where it came from.

Manfred rises. For a moment he's transfixed by the sight of his dominatrix wife, and his – mistress? conspirator? lover? – side by side. The contrast is marked: Annette's expression of ironic amusement a foil for Pamela's angry sincerity. Somewhere behind them stands a balding middle-aged man in a suit, carrying a folio: just the kind of diligent serf Pam might have turned him into, given time. Manfred musters up a smile. 'Can I offer you some coffee?' he asks. 'The party of the third part seems to be late.'

'Coffee would be great, mine's dark, no sugar,' twitters the lawyer. He puts his briefcase down on a side table and fiddles with his wearable until a light begins to blink from his spectacle frames. 'I'm recording this, I'm sure you understand.'

Annette sniffs and heads for the kitchen, which is charmingly manual but not very efficient; Pam is pretending she doesn't exist. 'Well, well, well.' She shakes her head. 'I'd expected better of you than a French tart's boudoir, Manny. And before the ink's dry on the divorce – these days that'll cost you, didn't you think of that?'

'I'm surprised you're not in the hospital,' he says, changing the subject. 'Is postnatal recovery outsourced these days?'

'The employers.' She slips her coat off her shoulders and hangs it behind the broad wooden door. 'They subsidize everything when you reach my grade.' Pamela is wearing a very short, very expensive dress, the kind of weapon in the war between the sexes that ought to come with an end-user certificate: But to his surprise it has no effect on him. He realizes that he's completely unable to evaluate her gender, almost as if she's become a member of another species. 'As you'd be aware if you'd been paying attention.'

'I always pay attention, Pam. It's the only currency I carry.'

'Very droll, ha-ha,' interrupts Glashwiecz. 'You do realize that you're paying me while I stand here listening to this fascinating byplay?'

Manfred stares at him. 'You know I don't have any money.'

'Ah.' Glashwiecz smiles. 'But you must be mistaken. Certainly the judge will agree with me that you must be mistaken – all a lack of paper documentation means is that you've covered your trail. There's the small matter of the several thousand corporations you own, indirectly. Somewhere at the bottom of that pile there has got to be something, hasn't there?'

A hissing, burbling noise like a sackful of large lizards being drowned in mud emanates from the kitchen, suggesting that Annette's percolator is nearly ready. Manfred's left hand twitches, playing chords on an air keyboard. Without being at all obvious, he's releasing a bulletin about his current activities that should soon have an effect on the reputation marketplace. 'Your attack was rather elegant,' he comments, sitting down on the sofa as Pam disappears into the kitchen.

Glashwiecz nods. 'The idea was one of my interns',' he says. 'I don't understand this distributed denial of service stuff, but Lisa grew up on it. Something about it being a legal travesty, but workable all the same.'

'Uh-huh.' Manfred's opinion of the lawyer drops a notch. He notices Pam reappearing from the kitchen, her expression icy. A moment later Annette surfaces carrying a jug and some cups, beaming innocently. Something's going on, but at that moment, one of his agents nudges him urgently in the left ear, his suitcase keens mournfully and beams a sense of utter despair at him, and the doorbell rings again.

'So what's the scam?' Glashwiecz sits down uncomfortably close to Manfred and murmurs out of one side of his mouth. 'Where's the money?'

Manfred looks at him irritably. 'There *is* no money,' he says. 'The idea is to make money obsolete. Hasn't she explained that?' His eyes wander, taking in the lawyer's Patek Philippe watch, his Java-enabled signet ring.

'C'mon. Don't give me that line. Look, all it takes is a couple of million, and you can buy your way free for all I care. All I'm here for is to see that your wife and daughter don't get left penniless and starving. You know and I know that you've got bags of it stuffed away – just look at your reputation! You didn't get that by standing at the roadside with a begging bowl, did you?'

Manfred snorts. 'You're talking about an elite IRS auditor here. She isn't penniless; she gets a commission on every poor bastard she takes to the cleaners, and she was born with a trust fund. Me, I—' The stereo bleeps. Manfred pulls his glasses on. Whispering ghosts of dead artists hum through his earlobes, urgently demanding their freedom. Someone knocks at the door again, and he glances around to see Annette walking toward it.

'You're making it hard on yourself,' Glashwiecz warns.

'Expecting company?' Pam asks, one brittle eyebrow raised in Manfred's direction.

'Not exactly—'

Annette opens the door and a couple of guards in full SWAT gear march in. They're clutching gadgets that look like crosses between digital sewing machines and grenade launchers, and their helmets are studded with so many sensors that they resemble 1950s space probes. 'That's them,' Annette says clearly.

'*Mais oui.*' The door closes itself, and the guards stand to either side. Annette stalks toward Pam.

'You think to walk in here, to my *pied-à-terre,* and take from Manfred?' She sniffs.

'You're making a big mistake, lady,' Pam says, her voice steady and cold enough to liquefy helium.

A burst of static from one of the troopers. 'No,' Annette says distantly. 'No mistake.'

She points at Glashwiecz. 'Are you aware of the takeover?'

'Takeover?' The lawyer looks puzzled, but not alarmed by the presence of the guards.

'As of three hours ago,' Manfred says quietly, 'I sold a controlling interest in agalmic.holdings.root.1.1.1 to Athene Accelerants BV, a venture capital outfit from Maastricht. One dot one dot one is the root node of the central planning tree. Athene aren't your usual VC, they're accelerants – they take explosive business plans and detonate them.' Glashwiecz is looking pale – whether with anger or fear of a lost commission is impossible to tell. 'Actually, Athene Accelerants is owned by a shell company owned by the Italian Communist Party's pension trust. The point is, you're in the presence of one dot one dot one's chief operations officer.'

Pam looks annoyed. 'Puerile attempts to dodge responsibility—'

Annette clears her throat. 'Exactly *who* do you think you are trying to sue?' she asks Glashwiecz sweetly. 'Here we have laws about unfair restraint of trade. Also about foreign political interference, specifically in the financial affairs of an Italian party of government.'

'You wouldn't—'

'I would.' Manfred brushes his hands on his knees and stands up. 'Done, yet?' he asks the suitcase.

Muffled beeps, then a gravelly synthesized voice speaks. 'Uploads completed.'

'Ah, good.' He grins at Annette. 'Time for our next guests?'

On cue, the doorbell rings again. The guards sidle to either side of the door. Annette snaps her fingers, and it opens to admit a pair of smartly dressed thugs. It's beginning to get crowded in the living room.

'Which one of you is Macx?' snaps the older one of the two thugs, staring at Glashwiecz for no obvious reason. He hefts an aluminum briefcase. 'Got a writ to serve.'

'You'd be the CCAA?' asks Manfred.

'You bet. If you're Macx, I have a restraining order—'

Manfred raises a hand. 'It's not me you want,' he says. 'It's this lady.' He points at Pam, whose mouth opens in silent protest. 'Y'see, the intellectual property you're chasing wants to be free. It's so free that it's now administered by a complex set of corporate instruments lodged in the Netherlands, and the prime shareholder as of approximately four minutes ago is my soon-to-be-ex-wife Pamela, here.' He winks at Glashwiecz. 'Except she doesn't *control* anything.'

'Just *what* do you think you're playing at, Manfred?' Pamela snarls, unable to contain herself any longer. The guards shuffle: The larger, junior CCAA enforcer tugs at his boss's jacket nervously.

'Well.' Manfred picks up his coffee and takes a sip. Grimaces. 'Pam wanted a divorce settlement, didn't she? The most valuable assets I own are the rights to a whole bunch of recategorized work-for-hire that slipped through the CCAA's fingers a few years back. Part of the twentieth century's cultural heritage that got locked away by the music industry in the last decade – Janis Joplin, the Doors, that sort of thing. Artists who weren't around to defend themselves anymore. When the music cartels went bust, the rights went for a walk. I took them over originally with the idea of setting the music free. Giving it back to the public domain, as it were.'

Annette nods at the guards, one of whom nods back and starts muttering and buzzing into a throat mike. Manfred continues. 'I was working on a solution to the central planning paradox – how to interface a centrally planned enclave to a market economy. My good friend Gianni Vittoria suggested that such a shell game could have alternative uses. So I've *not* freed the music. Instead, I signed the rights over to various actors and threads running inside the agalmic holdings network – currently one million, forty-eight thousand, five hundred and seventy-five companies. They swap rights rapidly – the rights to any given song are resident in a given company for, oh, all of fifty milliseconds at a time. Now understand, I don't own these companies. I don't even have a financial interest in them anymore. I've deeded my share of the profits to Pam, here. I'm getting out of the biz. Gianni's suggested something rather more challenging for me to do instead.'

He takes another mouthful of coffee. The recording Mafiya goon glares at him. Pam glares at him. Annette stands against one wall, looking amused. 'Perhaps you'd like to sort it out between you?' he asks. Aside, to Glashwiecz: 'I trust you'll drop your denial of service attack before I set the Italian parliament on you? By the way, you'll find the book value of the intellectual property assets I deeded to Pamela – by the value *these* gentlemen place on them – is somewhere in excess of a billion dollars. As that's rather more than ninety-nine-point-nine percent of my assets, you'll probably want to look elsewhere for your fees.'

Glashwiecz stands up carefully. The lead goon stares at Pamela. 'Is this true?' he demands. 'This little squirt give you IP assets of Sony Bertelsmann Microsoft Music? We have claim! You come to us for distribution or you get in deep trouble.'

The second goon rumbles agreement. 'Remember, dose MP3s, dey bad for you health!'

Annette claps her hands. 'If you would to leave my apartment, please?' The door, attentive as ever, swings open. 'You are no longer welcome here!'

'This means you,' Manfred advises Pam, helpfully.

'You *bastard!*' she spits at him.

Manfred forces a smile, bemused by his inability to respond to her the way she wants. Something's wrong, missing, between them. 'I thought you *wanted* my assets. Are the encumbrances too much for you?'

'You know what I mean! You and that two-bit euro-whore! I'll nail you for child neglect!'

His smile freezes. 'Try it, and I'll sue you for breach of patent rights. My genome, you understand.'

Pam is taken aback by this. 'You patented your own genome? What happened to the brave new communist, sharing information freely?'

Manfred stops smiling. 'Divorce happened. And the Italian Communist Party happened.'

She turns on her heel and stalks out of the apartment bravely, tame attorney in tow behind her, muttering about class action lawsuits and violations of the Digital Millennium Copyright Act. The CCAA lawyer's tame gorilla makes a grab for Glashwiecz's shoulder, and the guards move in, hustling the whole movable feast out into the stairwell. The door slams shut on a chaos of impending recursive lawsuits, and Manfred breathes a huge wheeze of relief.

Annette walks over to him and leans her chin on the top of his head. 'Think it will work?' she asks.

'Well, the CCAA will sue the hell out of the company network for a while if they try to distribute by any channel that isn't controlled by the Mafiya. Pam gets rights to all the music, her settlement, but she can't *sell* it without going through the mob. And I got to serve notice on that legal shark: If he tries to take me on he's got to be politically bulletproof. Hmm. Maybe I ought not to plan on going back to the USA this side of the singularity.'

'Profits.' Annette sighs. 'I do not easily understand this way of yours. Or this apocalyptic obsession with singularity.'

'Remember the old aphorism, if you love something, set it free? I freed the music.'

'But you didn't! You signed rights over—'

'But first I uploaded the entire stash to several cryptographically anonymized public network filesystems over the past few hours, so there'll be rampant piracy. And the robot companies are all set to automagically grant any and every copyright request they receive, royalty-free, until the goons figure out how to hack them. But that's not the *point*. The point is abundance. The Mafiya *can't* stop it being distributed. Pam is welcome to her cut if she can figure an angle – but I bet she can't. She still believes in classical economics, the allocation of resources under conditions of scarcity. Information doesn't work that way. What matters is that people will be able to hear the music – instead of a Soviet central planning system, I've turned the network into a firewall to protect freed intellectual property.'

'Oh, Manfred, you hopeless idealist.' She strokes his shoulder. 'Whatever for?'

'It's not just the music. When we develop a working AI or upload minds, we'll need a way of defending it against legal threats. That's what Gianni pointed out to me . . .'

He's still explaining to her how he's laying the foundations for the transhuman explosion due early in the next decade when she picks him up in both arms, carries him to her bedroom, and commits outrageous acts of tender intimacy with him. But that's okay. He's still human, this decade.

This, too, will pass, thinks the bulk of his metacortex. And it drifts off into the net to think deep thoughts elsewhere, leaving his meatbody to experience the ancient pleasures of the flesh set free.

3 : TOURIST

SPRING-HEELED JACK RUNS BLIND, BLUE FUMES
crackling from his heels. His right hand, outstretched for balance,
clutches a mark's stolen memories. The victim is sitting on the
hard stones of the pavement behind him. Maybe he's wondering
what's happened; maybe he looks after the fleeing youth. But
the tourist crowds block the view effectively, and in any case, he
has no hope of catching the mugger. Hit-and-run amnesia is
what the polis call it, but to Spring-Heeled Jack it's just more
loot to buy fuel for his Russian army-surplus motorized combat
boots.

The victim sits on the cobblestones clutching his aching temples.
What happened? he wonders. The universe is a brightly colored
blur of fast-moving shapes augmented by deafening noises. His
ear-mounted cameras are rebooting repeatedly: They panic every
eight hundred milliseconds, whenever they realize that they're
alone on his personal area network without the comforting support
of a hub to tell them where to send his incoming sensory feed. Two
of his mobile phones are bickering moronically, disputing ownership of his grid bandwidth, and his memory . . . is missing.

A tall blond clutching an electric chainsaw sheathed in pink
bubble wrap leans over him curiously. 'You all right?' she asks.

'I—' He shakes his head, which hurts. 'Who am I?' His medical monitor is alarmed because his blood pressure has fallen: His pulse is racing, his serum cortisol titer is up, and a host of other biometrics suggest that he's going into shock.

'I think you need an ambulance,' the woman announces. She mutters at her lapel, 'Phone, call an ambulance.' She waves a finger vaguely at him as if to reify a geolink, then wanders off, chainsaw clutched under one arm. Typical southern émigré behavior in the Athens of the North, too embarrassed to get involved. The man shakes his head again, eyes closed, as a flock of girls on powered blades skid around him in elaborate loops. A siren begins to warble, over the bridge to the north.

Who am I? he wonders. 'I'm Manfred,' he says with a sense of stunned wonder. He looks up at the bronze statue of a man on a horse that looms above the crowds on this busy street corner. Someone has plastered a Hello Cthulhu! holo on the plaque that names its rider: Languid fluffy pink tentacles wave at him in an attack of *kawaii*. 'I'm Manfred – Manfred. My memory. What's happened to my memory?' Elderly Malaysian tourists point at him from the open top deck of a passing bus. He burns with a sense of horrified urgency. *I was going somewhere,* he recalls. *What was I doing?* It was amazingly important, he thinks, but he can't remember what exactly it was. He was going to see someone about – it's on the tip of his tongue—

Welcome to the eve of the third decade: a time of chaos characterized by an all-out depression in the space industries.

Most of the thinking power on the planet is now manufactured rather than born; there are ten microprocessors for every human being, and the number is doubling every fourteen months. Population growth in the developing world has stalled, the birth rate dropping below replacement level. In the wired nations, more forward-looking politicians are looking for ways to enfranchise their nascent AI base.

Space exploration is still stalled on the cusp of the second recession of the century. The Malaysian government has announced the goal of placing an imam on Mars within ten years, but nobody else cares enough to try.

The Space Settlers Society is still trying to interest Disney Corp. in the media rights to their latest L5 colony plan, unaware that there's already a colony out there and it isn't human: First-generation uploads, Californian spiny lobsters in wobbly symbiosis with elderly expert systems, thrive aboard an asteroid mining project established by the Franklin Trust. Meanwhile, Chinese space agency cutbacks are threatening the continued existence of Moonbase Mao. Nobody, it seems, has figured out how to turn a profit out beyond geosynchronous orbit.

Two years ago, JPL, the ESA, and the uploaded lobster colony on comet Khrunichev-7 picked up an apparently artificial signal from outside the solar system; most people don't know, and of those who do, even fewer care. After all, if humans can't even make it to Mars, who cares what's going on a hundred trillion kilometers farther out?

Portrait of a wasted youth:

Jack is seventeen years and eleven months old. He has never met his father; he was unplanned, and Dad managed to kill himself in a building-site accident before the Child Support could garnish his income for the upbringing. His mother raised him in a two-bedroom housing association flat in Hawick. She worked in a call center when he was young, but business dried up: Humans aren't needed on the end of a phone anymore. Now she works in a drop-in business shop, stacking shelves for virtual fly-by-nights that come and go like tourists in the Festival season – but humans aren't in demand for shelf stacking either, these days.

His mother sent Jack to a local religious school, where he was regularly excluded and effectively ran wild from the age of twelve. By thirteen, he was wearing a parole cuff for shoplifting;

by fourteen, he'd broken his collarbone in a car crash while joyriding and the dour Presbyterian sheriff sent him to the Wee Frees, who completed the destruction of his educational prospects with high principles and an illicit tawse.

Today, he's a graduate of the hard school of avoiding public surveillance cameras, with distinctions in steganographic alibi construction. Mostly this entails high-density crime – if you're going to mug someone, do so where there are so many bystanders that they can't pin the blame on you. But the polis expert systems are on his tail. If he keeps it up at this rate, in another four months they'll have a positive statistical correlation that will convince even a jury of his peers that he's guilty as fuck – and then he'll go down to Saughton for four years.

But Jack doesn't understand the meaning of a Gaussian distribution or the significance of a chi-square test, and the future still looks bright to him as he pulls on the chunky spectacles he ripped off the tourist gawking at the statue on North Bridge. And after a moment, when they begin whispering into his ears in stereo and showing him pictures of the tourist's vision, it looks even brighter.

'Gotta make a deal, gotta close a deal,' whisper the glasses. 'Meet the borg, strike a chord.' Weird graphs in lurid colors are filling up his peripheral vision, like the hallucinations of a drugged marketroid.

'Who the fuck are ye?' asks Jack, intrigued by the bright lights and icons.

'I am your Cartesian theatre and you are our focus,' murmur the glasses. 'Dow Jones down fifteen points, Federated Confidence up three, incoming briefing on causal decoupling of social control of skirt hem lengths, shaving pattern of beards, and emergence of multidrug antibiotic resistance in gram-negative bacilli: Accept?'

'Ah can take it,' Jack mumbles, as a torrent of images crashes down on his eyeballs and jackhammers its way in through his ears like the superego of a disembodied giant. Which is actually what he's stolen: The glasses and waist pouch he grabbed from the tourist are stuffed with enough hardware to run the entire Internet, circa the turn of the millennium. They've got bandwidth coming out the wazoo, distributed engines running a bazillion inscrutable search tasks, and a whole slew of high-level agents that collectively form a large chunk of the society of mind that is their owner's personality. Their owner is a posthuman genius loci of the net, an agalmic entrepreneur turned policy wonk, specializing in the politics of AI emancipation. When he was in the biz he was the kind of guy who catalyzed value wherever he went, leaving money trees growing in his footprints. Now he's the kind of political backroom hitter who builds coalitions where nobody else could see common ground. And Jack has stolen his memories. There are microcams built into the frame of the glasses, pickups in the earpieces; everything is spooled into the holographic cache in the belt pack, before being distributed for remote storage. At four months per terabyte, memory storage is cheap. What makes this bunch so unusual is that their owner – Manfred – has cross-indexed them with his agents. Mind uploading may not be a practical technology yet, but Manfred has made an end run on it already.

In a very real sense, the glasses *are* Manfred, regardless of the identity of the soft machine with its eyeballs behind the lenses. And it is a very puzzled Manfred who picks himself up and, with a curious vacancy in his head – except for a hesitant request for information about accessories for Russian army boots – dusts himself off and heads for his meeting on the other side of town.

Meanwhile, in another meeting, Manfred's absence is already being noticed. 'Something, something is *wrong*,' says Annette. She raises her mirrorshades and rubs her left eye, visibly worried. 'Why is he not answering his chat? He knows we are due to hold this call with him. Don't you think it is odd?'

Gianni nods and leans back, regarding her from behind his desk. He prods at the highly polished rosewood desktop. The wood grain slips, sliding into a strangely different conformation, generating random dot stereoisograms – messages for his eyes only. 'He was visiting Scotland for me,' he says after a moment. 'I do not know his exact whereabouts – the privacy safeguards – but if you, as his designated next of kin, travel in person, I am sure you will find it easier. He was going to talk to the Franklin Collective, face-to-face, one to many . . .'

The office translator is good, but it can't provide real-time lip-synch morphing between French and Italian. Annette has to make an effort to listen to his words because the shape of his mouth is all wrong, like a badly dubbed video. Her expensive, recent implants aren't connected up to her Broca's area yet, so she can't simply sideload a deep grammar module for Italian. Their communications are the best that money can buy, their VR environment painstakingly sculpted, but it still doesn't break down the language barrier completely. Besides, there are distractions: the way the desk switches from black ash to rosewood halfway across its expanse, the strange air currents that are all wrong for a room this size. 'Then what could be up with him? His voicemail is trying to cover for him. It is good, but it does not lie convincingly.'

Gianni looks worried. 'Manfred is prone to fits of do his own thing with telling nobody in advance. But I don't like this. He should have to told one of us first.' Ever since that first meeting in Rome when Gianni offered him a job, Manfred has been a core member of Gianni's team, the fixer who goes out and meets people and solves their problems. Losing him at this point could be more than embarrassing. Besides, he's a friend.

'I do not like this either.' She stands up. 'If he doesn't call back soon—'

'You'll go and fetch him.'

'*Oui.*' A smile flashes across her face, rapidly replaced by worry lines. 'What can have happened?'

'Anything. Nothing.' Gianni shrugs. 'But we cannot do without him.' He casts her a warning glance. 'Or you. Don't let the borg get you. Either of you.'

'Not to worry. I will just bring him back, whatever has happened.' She stands up, surprising a vacuum cleaner that skulks behind her desk. *'Au revoir!'*

'Ciao.'

As she vacates her office, the minister flickers off behind her, leaving the far wall the dull gray of a cold display panel. Gianni is in Rome, she's in Paris, Markus is in Düsseldorf, and Eva's in Wroclaw. There are others, trapped in digital cells scattered halfway across an elderly continent, but as long as they don't try to shake hands, they're free to shout across the office at each other. Their confidences and dirty jokes tunnel through multiple layers of anonymized communication.

Gianni is trying to make his break out of regional politics and into European national affairs: Their job – his election team – is to get him a seat on the Confederacy Commission, as Representative for Intelligence Oversight, and push the boundaries of post-humanistic action outward, into deep space and deeper time. Which makes the loss of a key team player, the house futurologist and fixer, profoundly interesting to certain people: The walls have ears, and not all the brains they feed into are human.

Annette is more worried than she's letting on to Gianni. It's unlike Manfred to be out of contact for long and even odder for his receptionist to stonewall her, given that her apartment is the nearest thing to a home he's had for the past couple of years. But something smells fishy. He sneaked out last night, saying it would be an overnight trip, and now he's not answering. *Could it be his ex-wife?* she wonders, despite Gianni's hints about a special mission. But there's been no word from Pamela other than the sarcastic cards she dispatches every year without fail, timed to arrive on the birthday of the daughter Manfred has never met. *The music Mafiya? A letter bomb from the Copyright Control Association of America?* But no, his medical monitor would have been screaming its head off if anything like that had happened.

Annette has organized things so that he's safe from the intellectual property thieves. She's lent him the support he needs, and he's helped her find her own path. She gets a warm sense of happiness whenever she considers how much they've achieved together. But that's exactly why she's worried now. The watchdog hasn't barked . . .

Annette summons a taxi to Charles de Gaulle. By the time she arrives, she's already used her parliamentary *carte* to bump an executive-class seat on the next A320 to Turnhouse, Edinburgh's airport, and scheduled accommodation and transport for her arrival. The plane is climbing out over la Manche before the significance of Gianni's last comment hits her. Might he think the Franklin Collective could be dangerous to Manfred?

The hospital emergency suite has a waiting room with green plastic bucket seats and subtractive volume renderings by preteens stuck to the walls like surreal Lego sculptures. It's deeply silent, the available bandwidth all sequestrated for medical monitors – there are children crying, periodic sirens wailing as ambulances draw up, and people chattering all around him, but to Manfred, it's like being at the bottom of a deep blue pool of quiet. He feels stoned, except this particular drug brings no euphoria or sense of well-being. Corridor-corner vendors hawk kebab-spitted pigeons next to the chained and rusted voluntary service booth; video cameras watch the blue bivvy bags of the chronic cases lined up next to the nursing station. Alone in his own head, Manfred is frightened and confused.

'I can't check you in 'less you sign the confidentiality agreement,' says the triage nurse, pushing an antique tablet at Manfred's face. Service in the NHS is still free, but steps have been taken to reduce the incidence of scandals. 'Sign the nondisclosure clause here and here, or the house officer won't see you.'

Manfred stares blearily up at the nurse's nose, which is red and slightly inflamed from a nosocomial infection. His phones are bickering again, and he can't remember why; they don't normally behave like this. Something must be missing, but thinking about it is hard. 'Why am I here?' he asks for the third time.

'Sign it.' A pen is thrust into his hand. He focuses on the page, jerks upright as deeply canalized reflexes kick in.

'This is theft of human rights! It says here that the party of the second part is enjoined from disclosing information relating to the operations management triage procedures and processes of the said health-giving institution, that's you, to any third party – that's the public media – on pain of forfeiture of health benefits pursuant to section two of the Health Service Reform Act. I can't sign this! You could repossess my left kidney if I post on the Net about how long I've been in hospital!'

'So don't sign, then.' The Hijra nurse shrugs, hitches up his sari, and walks away. 'Enjoy your wait!'

Manfred pulls out his backup phone and stares at its display. 'Something's *wrong* here.' The keypad beeps as he laboriously inputs opcodes. This gets him into an arcane and ancient X.25 PAD, and he has a vague, disturbing memory that hints about where he can go from here – mostly into the long-since-decommissioned bowels of NHSNet – but the memories spring a page fault and die somewhere between fingertips and the moment when understanding dawns. It's a frustrating feeling: His brain is like an ancient car engine with damp spark plugs, turning over and over without catching fire.

The kebab vendor next to Manfred's seating rail chucks a stock cube on his grill; it begins to smoke, aromatic and blue and herbal – cannabinoids to induce tranquillity and appetite. Manfred sniffs twice, then staggers to his feet and heads off in search of the toilet, his head spinning. He's mumbling at his wrist watch; *'Hello, Guatemala? Get me posology please. Click down my meme tree, I'm confused. Oh shit. Who was I? What happened? Why is everything blurry? I can't find my glasses . . .'*

A gaggle of day-trippers are leaving the leprosy ward, men and women dressed in anachronistic garb: men in dark suits, women in long dresses. All of them wear electric blue disposable gloves and face masks. There's a hum and crackle of encrypted bandwidth emanating from them, and Manfred instinctively turns to follow. They leave the A&E unit through the wheelchair exit, two ladies escorted by three gentlemen, with a deranged distressed refugee from the twenty-first century shuffling dizzily after. *They're all young,* Manfred realizes vaguely. *Where's my cat?* Aineko might be able to make sense of this, if Aineko was interested.

'I rather fancy we should retire to the club house,' says one young beau. 'Oh yes! please!' his short blond companion chirps, clapping her hands together, then irritably stripping off the anachronistic plastic gloves to reveal wired-lace positional-sensor mitts underneath. 'This trip has obviously been unproductive. If our contact is here, I see no easy way of locating him without breach of medical confidence or a hefty gratuity.'

'The poor things,' murmurs the other woman, glancing back at the leprosarium. 'Such a humiliating way to die.'

'Their own fault: If they hadn't participated in antibiotic abuse, they wouldn't be in the isolation ward,' harrumphs a twentysomething with muttonchops and the manner of a precocious paterfamilias. He raps his walking stick on the pavement for punctuation, and they pause for a flock of cyclists and a rickshaw before they cross the road onto The Meadows. 'Degenerate medication compliance, degenerate immune systems.'

Manfred pauses to survey the grass, brain spinning as he ponders the fractal dimensionality of leaves. Then he lurches after them, nearly getting himself run down by a flywheel-powered tourist bus. *Club.* His feet hit the pavement, cross it, thud down onto three billion years of vegetative evolution. *Something about those people.* He feels a weird yearning, a tropism for information. It's almost all that's left of him – his voracious will to know. The tall, dark-haired woman hitches up her long skirts to keep them out of the mud. He sees a flash of iridescent petticoats that ripple like oil on water, worn over old-fashioned combat boots. Not Victorian, then: something else. *I came here to see* – the name is on the tip of his tongue. Almost. He feels that it has something to do with these people.

The squad crosses The Meadows by way of a tree-lined path and comes to a nineteenth-century frontage with wide steps and a polished brass doorbell. They enter, and the man with the muttonchops pauses on the threshold and turns to face Manfred.

'You've followed us this far,' he says. 'Do you want to come in? You might find what you're looking for.'

Manfred follows with knocking knees, desperately afraid of whatever he's forgotten.

Meanwhile, Annette is busy interrogating Manfred's cat.

'When did you last see your father?'

Aineko turns its head away from her and concentrates on washing the inside of its left leg. Its fur is lifelike and thick, pleasingly patterned except for a manufacturer's URL emblazoned on its flanks, but the mouth produces no saliva; the throat opens on no stomach or lungs. 'Go away,' it says. 'I'm busy.'

'When did you last see Manfred?' she repeats intently. 'I don't have time for this. The polis don't know. The medical services don't know. He's off-net and not responding. So what can *you* tell me?'

It took her precisely eighteen minutes to locate his hotel once she hit the airport arrivals area and checked the hotel booking front end in the terminal: She knows his preferences. It took her slightly longer to convince the concierge to let her into his room. But Aineko is proving more recalcitrant than she'd expected.

'AI Neko mod two alpha requires maintenance downtime on a regular basis,' the cat says pompously. 'You knew that when you bought me this body. What were you expecting, five-nines uptime from a lump of meat? Go away, I'm thinking.' The tongue rasps out, then pauses while microprobes in its underside replace the hairs that fell out earlier in the day.

Annette sighs. Manfred's been upgrading this robot cat for years, and his ex-wife Pamela used to mess with its neural configuration, too: This is its third body, and it's getting more realistically uncooperative with every hardware upgrade. Sooner or later it's going to demand a litter tray and start throwing up on the carpet. 'Command override,' she says. 'Dump event log to my Cartesian theatre, minus eight hours to present.'

The cat shudders and looks round at her. 'Human bitch!' it

hisses. Then it freezes in place as the air fills with a bright and silent tsunami of data. Both Annette and Aineko are wired for extremely high-bandwidth spread-spectrum optical networking; an observer would see the cat's eyes and a ring on her left hand glow blue-white at each other. After a few seconds, Annette nods to herself and wiggles her fingers in the air, navigating a time sequence only she can see. Aineko hisses resentfully at her, then stands and stalks away, tail held high.

'Curiouser and curiouser,' Annette hums to herself. She intertwines her fingers, pressing obscure pressure points on knuckle and wrist, then sighs and rubs her eyes. 'He left here under his own power, looking normal,' she calls to the cat. 'Who did he say he was going to see?' The cat sits in a beam of sunlight falling in through the high glass window, pointedly showing her its back. '*Merde*. If you're not going to help him—'

'Try the Grassmarket,' sulks the cat. 'He said something about meeting the Franklin Collective there. Much good they'll do him . . .'

A man wearing secondhand Chinese combat fatigues and a horribly expensive pair of glasses bounces up a flight of damp stone steps beneath a keystone that announces the building to be a Salvation Army hostel. He bangs on the door, his voice almost drowned out by the pair of Cold War Re-enactment Society MiGs that are buzzing the castle up the road. 'Open up, ye cunts! Ye've gottae deal comin'!'

A peephole set in the door at eye level slides to one side, and a pair of beady black-eyed video cameras peer out at him. 'Who are you and what do you want?' the speaker crackles. They don't belong to the Salvation Army; Christianity has been deeply unfashionable in Scotland for some decades, and the church that currently occupies the building has certainly moved with the times in an effort to stay relevant.

'I'm Macx,' he says. 'You've heard from my systems. I'm here to offer you a deal you can't refuse.' At least that's what his glasses tell him to say: What comes out of his mouth sounds a bit more like, *Am Max. Yiv hurdfrae ma system. Am heretae gie ye a deal ye cannae refuse.* The glasses haven't had long enough to work on his accent. Meanwhile, he's so full of himself that he snaps his fingers and does a little dance of impatience on the top step.

'Aye, well, hold on a minute.' The person on the other side of the speakerphone has the kind of cut-glass Morningside accent that manages to sound more English than the King while remaining vernacular Scots. The door opens, and Macx finds himself confronted by a tall, slightly cadaverous man wearing a tweed suit that has seen better days and a clerical collar cut from a translucent circuit board. His face is almost concealed behind a pair of recording angel goggles. 'Who did ye say you were?'

'I'm Macx! Manfred Macx! I'm here with an opportunity you wouldn't believe. I've got the answer to your church's financial situation. I'm going to make you rich!' The glasses prompt, and Macx speaks.

The man in the doorway tilts his head slightly, goggles scanning Macx from head to foot. Bursts of blue combustion products spurt from Macx's heels as he bounces up and down enthusiastically. 'Are ye sure ye've got the right address?' he asks worriedly.

'Aye, Ah am that.'

The resident backs into the hostel. 'Well then, come in, sit yerself down, and tell me all about it.'

Macx bounces into the room with his brain wide open to a blizzard of pie charts and growth curves, documents spawning in the bizarre phase-space of his corporate management software. 'I've got a deal you're not going to believe,' he reads, gliding past notice boards upon which church circulars are staked out to die like exotic butterflies, stepping over rolled-up carpets and a stack of laptops left over from a jumble sale, past the devotional radio telescope that does double duty as Mrs. Muirhouse's back-garden birdbath. 'You've been here five years and your posted accounts show you aren't making much money – barely keeping the rent up. But you're a shareholder in Scottish Nuclear Electric, right? Most of the church funds are in the form of a trust left to the church by one of your congregants when she went to join the omega point, right?'

'Er.' The minister looks at him oddly. 'I cannae comment on the church eschatological investment trust. Why d'ye think that?'

They fetch up, somehow, in the minister's office. A huge, framed rendering hangs over the back of his threadbare office chair: the collapsing cosmos of the End Times, galactic clusters rotten with the Dyson spheres of the eschaton falling toward the big crunch. Saint Tipler the Astrophysicist beams down from above with avuncular approval, a ring of quasars forming a halo around his head. Posters proclaim the new Gospel: COSMOLOGY IS BETTER THAN GUESSWORK, and LIVE FOREVER WITHIN MY LIGHT CONE. 'Can I get ye anything? Cup of tea? Fuel cell charge point?' asks the minister.

'Crystal meth?' asks Macx, hopefully. His face falls as the minister shakes his head apologetically. 'Aw, dinnae worry, Ah wis only joshing.' He leans forward. 'Ah know a' aboot yer plutonium futures speculation,' he hisses. A finger taps his stolen spectacles in an ominous gesture. 'These dinnae just record, they *think*. An' Ah ken where the money's gone.'

'What have ye got?' the minister asks coldly, any indication of good humor flown. 'I'm going to have to edit down these memories, ye bastard. I thought I'd forgotten all about that. Bits of me aren't going to merge with the godhead at the end of time now, thanks to you.'

'Keep yer shirt on. Whit's the point o' savin' it a' up if ye ain't got a life worth living? Ye reckon the big yin's nae gonnae unnerstan' a knees' up?'

'What do ye *want*?'

'Aye, well.' Macx leans back, aggrieved. 'Ah've got—' He pauses. An expression of extreme confusion flits over his head. 'Ah've got *lobsters*,' he finally announces. 'Genetically engineered uploaded lobsters tae run yer uranium reprocessing plant.' As he grows more confused, the glasses' control over his accent slips. 'Ah wiz gonnae help yiz oot ba showin' ye how ter get yer dosh back whir it belong . . .' A strategic pause. 'So ye could make the council tax due date. See, they're neutron-resistant, the lobsters. No, that cannae be right. Ah wiz gonnae sell ye sumthin' ye cud use fer' – his face slumps into a frown of disgust – *'free?'*

Approximately thirty seconds later, as he is picking himself up off the front steps of the First Reformed Church of Tipler, Astrophysicist, the man who would be Macx finds himself wondering if maybe this high finance shit isn't as easy as it's cracked up to be. Some of the agents in his glasses are wondering if elocution lessons are the answer, others aren't so optimistic.

Getting back to the history lesson, the prospects for the decade look mostly medical.

A few thousand elderly baby boomers are converging on Tehran for Woodstock Four. Europe is desperately trying to import eastern European nurses and home-care assistants; in Japan, whole agricultural villages lie vacant and decaying, ghost communities sucked dry as cities slurp people in like residential black holes.

A rumor is spreading throughout gated old-age communities in the American Midwest, leaving havoc and riots in its wake: Senescence is caused by a slow virus coded into the mammalian genome that evolution hasn't weeded out, and rich billionaires are sitting on the rights to a vaccine. As usual, Charles Darwin gets more than his fair share of the blame. (Less spectacular but more realistic treatments for old age – telomere reconstruction and hexose-denatured protein reduction – are available in private clinics for those who are willing to surrender their pensions.) Progress is expected to speed up shortly, as the fundamental patents in genomic engineering begin to expire; the Free Chromosome Foundation has already published a manifesto calling for the creation of an intellectual-property-free genome with improved replacements for all commonly defective exons.

Experiments in digitizing and running neural wetware under emulation are well established; some radical libertarians claim that, as the technology matures, death – with its draconian curtailment of property and voting rights – will become the biggest civil rights issue of all.

For a small extra fee, most veterinary insurance policies now cover cloning of pets in the event of their accidental and distressing death. Human cloning, for reasons nobody is very clear on anymore, is still illegal in most developed nations – but very few judiciaries push for mandatory abortion of identical twins.

Some commodities are expensive: The price of crude oil has broken eighty euros a barrel and is edging inexorably up. Other commodities are cheap: computers, for example. Hobbyists print off weird new processor architectures on their home inkjets; middle-aged folks wipe their backsides with diagnostic paper that can tell how their cholesterol levels are tending.

The latest casualties of the march of technological progress are: the high-street clothes shop, the flushing water closet, the Main Battle Tank, and the first generation of quantum computers. New with the decade are cheap enhanced immune systems, brain implants that hook right into the Chomsky organ and talk to their owners through their own speech centers, and widespread public paranoia about limbic spam. Nanotechnology has shattered into a dozen disjointed disciplines, and skeptics are predicting that it will all peter out before long. Philosophers have ceded qualia to engineers, and the current difficult problem in AI is getting software to experience embarrassment.

Fusion power is still, of course, fifty years away.

The Victorians are morphing into goths before Manfred's culture-shocked eyes.

'You looked lost,' explains Monica, leaning over him curiously. 'What's with your eyes?'

'I can't see too well,' Manfred tries to explain. Everything is a blur, and the voices that usually chatter incessantly in his head have left nothing behind but a roaring silence. 'I mean, someone *mugged* me. They took—' His hand closes on air: Something is missing from his belt.

Monica, the tall woman he first saw in the hospital, enters the room. What she's wearing indoors is skintight, iridescent and, disturbingly, she claims is a distributed extension of her neuroectoderm. Stripped of costume-drama accoutrements, she's a twenty-first-century adult, born or decanted after the millennial baby boom. She waves some fingers in Manfred's face: 'How many?'

'Two.' Manfred tries to concentrate. 'What—'

'No concussion,' she says briskly. ''Scuse me while I page.' Her eyes are brown, with amber raster lines flickering across her pupils. *Contact lenses?* Manfred wonders, his head turgid and unnaturally slow. It's like being drunk, except much less pleasant: He can't seem to wrap his head around an idea from all angles at once, anymore. *Is this what consciousness used to be like?* It's an ugly, slow sensation. She turns away from him. 'Medline says you'll be all right in a while. The main problem is the identity loss. Are you backed up anywhere?'

'Here.' Alan, still top-hatted and muttonchopped, holds out a pair of spectacles to Manfred. 'Take these. They may do you some good.' His topper wobbles, as if a strange A-life experiment is nesting under its brim.

'Oh. Thank you.' Manfred reaches for them with a pathetic sense of gratitude. As soon as he puts them on, they run through a test series, whispering questions and watching how his eyes focus: After a minute, the room around him clears as the specs build a synthetic image to compensate for his myopia. There's limited net access, too, he notices, a warm sense of relief stealing over him. 'Do you mind if I call somebody?' he asks. 'I want to check my backups.'

'Be my guest.' Alan slips out through the door; Monica sits down opposite him and stares into some inner space. The room has a tall ceiling, with whitewashed walls and wooden shutters to cover the aerogel window bays. The furniture is modern modular, and clashes horribly with the original nineteenth-century architecture. 'We were expecting you.'

'You were—' He shifts track with an effort. 'I was here to see somebody. Here in Scotland, I mean.'

'Us.' She catches his eye deliberately. 'To discuss sapience options with our patron.'

'With your—' He squeezes his eyes shut. '*Damn!* I don't *remember*. I need my glasses back. Please.'

'What about your backups?' she asks curiously.

'A moment.' Manfred tries to remember what address to ping. It's useless, and painfully frustrating. 'It would help if I could remember where I keep the rest of my mind,' he complains. 'It used to be at – oh, *there*.'

An elephantine semantic network sits down on his spectacles as soon as he asks for the site, crushing his surroundings into blocky pixilated monochrome that jerks as he looks around. 'This is going to take some time,' he warns his hosts as a goodly chunk of his metacortex tries to handshake with his brain over a wireless network connection that was really only designed for web browsing. The download consists of the part of his consciousness that isn't security-critical – public access actors and vague opinionated rants – but it clears down a huge memory castle, sketching in the outline of a map of miracles and wonders onto the whitewashed walls of the room.

When Manfred can see the outside world again, he feels a bit more like himself. He can, at least, spawn a search thread that will resynchronize and fill him in on what it found. He still can't access the inner mysteries of his soul (including his personal memories); they're locked and barred pending biometric verification of his identity and a quantum key exchange. But he has his wits about him again – and some of them are even working. It's like sobering up from a strange new drug, the infinitely reassuring sense of being back at the controls of his own head. 'I think I need to report a crime,' he tells Monica – or whoever is plugged into Monica's head right now, because now he knows where he is and who he was meant to meet (although not why) – and he understands that, for the Franklin Collective, identity is a politically loaded issue.

'A crime report.' Her expression is subtly mocking. 'Identity theft, by any chance?'

'Yeah, yeah, I know. Identity *is* theft, don't trust anyone whose state vector hasn't forked for more than a gigasecond, change is the only constant, et bloody cetera. Who am I talking to, by the way? And if we're talking, doesn't that signify that you think we're on the same side, more or less?' He struggles to sit up in the recliner chair: Stepper motors whine softly as it strives to accommodate him.

'Sidedness is optional.' The woman who is Monica some of the time looks at him quirkily. 'It tends to alter drastically if you vary the number of dimensions. Let's just say that right now I'm Monica, plus our sponsor. Will that do you?'

'Our sponsor, who is in cyberspace—'

She leans back on the sofa, which buzzes and extrudes an occasional table with a small bar. 'Drink? Can I offer you coffee? Guarana? Or maybe a Berlinerweisse, for old time's sake?'

'Guarana will do. Hello, Bob. How long have you been dead?'

She chuckles. 'I'm not dead, Manny. I may not be a full upload, but I *feel* like me.' She rolls her eyes, self-consciously. 'He's making rude comments about your wife.' She adds, 'I'm not going to pass that on.'

'My ex-wife.' Manfred corrects her automatically. 'The, uh, tax vamp. So. You're acting as a, I guess, an interpreter for Bob?'

'Ack.' She looks at Manfred very seriously. 'We owe him a lot, you know. He left his assets in trust to the movement along with his partials. We feel obliged to instantiate his personality as often as possible, even though you can only do so much with a couple of petabytes of recordings. But we have help.'

'The lobsters.' Manfred nods to himself and accepts the glass that she offers. Its diamond-plated curves glitter brilliantly in the late-afternoon sunlight. 'I *knew* this had something to do with them.' He leans forward, holding his glass and frowns. 'If only I could remember why I came here! It was something emergent, something in deep memory . . . something I didn't trust in my own skull. Something to do with Bob.'

The door behind the sofa opens; Alan enters. 'Excuse me,' he says quietly, and heads for the far side of the room. A workstation folds down from the wall, and a chair rolls in from a service niche. He sits with his chin propped on his hands, staring at the white desktop. Every so often he mutters quietly to himself, 'Yes, I understand . . . campaign headquarters . . . donations need to be audited . . .'

'Gianni's election campaign,' Monica prompts him.

Manfred jumps. 'Gianni—' A bundle of memories unlock inside his head as he remembers his political front man's message. 'Yes! That's what this is about. It has to be!' He looks at her excitedly. 'I'm here to deliver a message to you from Gianni Vittoria. About—' He looks crestfallen. 'I'm not sure,' he trails off uncertainly, 'but it was important. Something critical in the long term, something about group minds and voting. But whoever mugged me got the message.'

The Grassmarket is an overly rustic cobbled square nestled beneath the glowering battlements of Castle Rock. Annette stands on the site of the gallows where they used to execute witches; she sends forth her invisible agents to search for spoor of Manfred. Aineko, overly familiar, drapes over her left shoulder like a satanic stole and delivers a running stream of cracked cellphone chatter into her ear.

'I don't know where to begin.' She sighs, annoyed. This place is a wall-to-wall tourist trap, a many-bladed carnivorous plant that digests easy credit and spits out the drained husks of foreigners. The road has been pedestrianized and resurfaced in squalidly authentic medieval cobblestones; in the middle of what used to be the car park, there's a permanent floating antiques market, where you can buy anything from a brass fire surround to an ancient CD player. Much of the merchandise in the shops is generic dot-com trash, vying for the title of Japanese-Scottish souvenir from hell: Puroland tartans, animatronic Nessies hissing bad-temperedly at knee level, secondhand laptops. People swarm everywhere, from the theme pubs (hangings seem to be a running joke hereabouts) to the expensive dress shops with their fabric renderers and digital mirrors. Street performers, part of the permanent floating Fringe, clutter the sidewalk: A robotic mime, very traditional in silver face paint, mimics the gestures of passersby with ironically stylized gestures.

'Try the doss house,' Aineko suggests from the shelter of her shoulder bag.

'The——' Annette does a double take as her thesaurus conspires with her open government firmware and dumps a geographical database of city social services into her sensorium. 'Oh, I see.' The Grassmarket itself is touristy, but the bits off to one end – down a dingy canyon of forbidding stone buildings six stories high – are decidedly downmarket. 'Okay.'

Annette weaves past a stall selling disposable cellphones and cheaper genome explorers, round a gaggle of teenage girls in the grips of some kind of imported *kawaii* fetish, who look at her in alarm from atop their pink platform heels – probably mistaking her for a school probation inspector – and past a stand of chained and parked bicycles. The human attendant looks bored out of her mind. Annette tucks a blandly anonymous ten-euro note in her pocket almost before she notices. 'If you were going to buy a hot bike,' she asks, 'where would you go?' The parking attendant stares, and for a moment Annette thinks she's overestimated her. Then she mumbles something. 'What?'

'McMurphy's. Used to be called Bannerman's. Down yon Cowgate, thataway.' The meter maid looks anxiously at her rack of charges. 'You didn't——'

'Uh-huh.' Annette follows her gaze: straight down the dark stone canyon. *Well, okay.* 'This had better be worth it, Manny *mon chèr,*' she mutters under her breath.

McMurphy's is a fake Irish pub, a stone grotto installed beneath a mound of blank-faced offices. It was once a real Irish pub before the developers got their hands on it and mutated it in rapid succession into a punk nightclub, a wine bar, and a fake Dutch coffee shop; after which, as burned-out as any star, it left the main sequence. Now it occupies an unnaturally prolonged, chilly existence as the sort of recycled imitation Irish pub that has neon four-leafed clovers hanging from the artificially blackened pine beams above the log tables – in other words, the burned-out black dwarf afterlife of a once-serious drinking establishment. Somewhere along the line, the beer cellar was replaced with a toilet (leaving more room for paying patrons upstairs), and now its founts dispense fizzy concentrate diluted with water from the city mains.

'Say, did you hear the one about the Eurocrat with the robot pussy who goes into a dodgy pub on the Cowgate and orders a Coke? And when it arrives, she says, 'Hey, where's the mirror?'

'Shut *up,*' Annette hisses into her shoulder bag. 'That isn't funny.' Her personal intruder telemetry has just e-mailed her wristphone, and it's displaying a rotating yellow exclamation point, which means that, according to the published police crime stats, this place is likely to do grievous harm to her insurance premiums.

Aineko looks up at her from his nest in the bag and yawns cavernously, baring a pink, ribbed mouth and a tongue like pink suede. 'Want to make me? I just pinged Manny's head. The network latency was trivial.'

The barmaid sidles up and pointedly manages not to make eye contact with Annette. 'I'll have a Diet Coke,' Annette orders. In the direction of her bag, voice pitched low. 'Did you hear the one about the Eurocrat who goes into a dodgy pub, orders half a liter of Diet Coke, and when she spills it in her shoulder bag, she says, "Oops, I've got a wet pussy"?'

The Diet Coke arrives. Annette pays for it. There may be a couple of dozen people in the pub; it's hard to tell because it looks like an ancient cellar, lots of stone archways leading off into niches populated with secondhand church pews and knife-scarred tables. Some guys who might be bikers, students, or well-dressed winos are hunched over one table: hairy, wearing vests with too many pockets, in an artful bohemianism that makes Annette blink until one of her literary programs informs her that one of them is a moderately famous local writer, a bit of a guru for the space and freedom party. There're a couple of women in boots and furry hats in one corner, poring over the menu, and a parcel of off-duty street performers hunching over their beers in a booth. Nobody else is wearing anything remotely like office drag, but the weirdness coefficient is above average, so Annette dials her glasses to extradark, straightens her tie, and glances around.

The door opens and a nondescript youth slinks in. He's wearing baggy BDUs, woolly cap, and a pair of boots that have that quintessential *essense de panzer division* look, all shock absorbers and olive drab Kevlar panels. He's wearing—

'I spy with my little network intrusion detector kit,' begins the cat, as Annette puts her drink down and moves in on the youth, 'something beginning with—'

'How much you want for the glasses, kid?' she asks quietly.

He jerks and almost jumps – a bad idea in MilSpec combat boots; the ceiling is eighteenth-century stone half a meter thick. 'Dinnae fuckin' *dae* that,' he complains in an eerily familiar way: 'Ah—' He swallows. 'Annie! Who—'

'Stay calm. Take them off – they'll only hurt you if you keep wearing them,' she says, careful not to move too fast because now she has a second, scary-jittery fear, and she knows without having to look that the exclamation mark on her watch has turned red and begun to flash. 'Look, I'll give you two hundred euros for the glasses and the belt pouch, real cash, and I won't ask how you got them or tell anyone.' He's frozen in front of her, mesmerized, and she can see the light from inside the lenses spilling over onto his half-starved adolescent cheekbones, flickering like cold lightning, like he's plugged his brain into a grid bearer; swallowing with a suddenly dry mouth, she slowly reaches up and pulls the spectacles off his face with one hand and takes hold of the belt pouch with the other. The kid shudders and blinks at her, and she sticks a couple of hundred euro notes in front of his nose. 'Scram,' she says, not unkindly.

He reaches up slowly, then seizes the money and runs – blasts his way through the door with an ear-popping concussion, hangs a left onto the cycle path, and vanishes downhill toward the parliament buildings and university complex.

Annette watches the doorway apprehensively. 'Where *is* he?' she hisses, worried. 'Any ideas, cat?'

'Naah. It's your job to find him,' Aineko opines complacently. But there's an icicle of anxiety in Annette's spine. Manfred's been separated from his memory cache? Where could he be? Worse – *who* could he be?

'Fuck you, too,' she mutters. 'Only one thing for it, I guess.' She takes off her own glasses – they're much less functional than Manfred's massively ramified custom rig – and nervously raises the repo'd specs toward her face. Somehow what she's about to do makes her feel unclean, like snooping on a lover's e-mail folders. But how else can she figure out where he might have gone?

She slides the glasses on and tries to remember what she was doing yesterday in Edinburgh.

'Gianni?'

'Oui, ma chérie?'

Pause. 'I lost him. But I got his aide-mémoire back. A teenage freeloader playing cyberpunk with them. No sign of his location – so I put them on.'

Pause. 'Oh dear.'

'Gianni, why exactly did you send him to the Franklin Collective?'

Pause. (During which, the chill of the gritty stone wall she's leaning on begins to penetrate the weave of her jacket.) 'I not wanting to bother you with trivia.'

'Merde. It's *not* trivia, Gianni, they're *accelerationistas*. Have you any idea what that's going to do to his head?'

Pause. Then a grunt, almost of pain. 'Yes.'

'Then why did you *do* it?' she demands vehemently. She hunches over, punching words into her phone so that other passers-by avoid her, unsure whether she's hands-free or hallucinating. 'Shit, Gianni, I have to pick up the pieces every time you do this! Manfred is not a healthy man, he's on the edge of acute future shock the whole time, and I was not joking when I told you last February that he'd need a month in a clinic if you tried running him flat out again! If you're not careful, he could end up dropping out completely and joining the borganism—'

'Annette.' A heavy sigh. 'He are the best hope we got. Am knowing half-life of agalmic catalyst now down to six months and dropping; Manny outlast his career expectancy, four deviations outside the normal, yes, we know this. But I are having to break civil rights deadlock *now*, this election. We must achieve consensus, and Manfred are only staffer we got who have hope of talking to Collective on its own terms. He are deal-making messenger, not force burnout, right? We need coalition reserve before term limit lockout followed by gridlock in Brussels, American-style. Is more than vital – is essential.'

'That's no excuse—'

'Annette, they have partial upload of Bob Franklin. They got it before he died, enough of his personality to reinstantiate it, time-sharing in their own brains. We must get the Franklin Collective with their huge resources lobbying for the Equal Rights Amendment: If ERA passes, all sapients are eligible to vote, own property, upload, download, sideload. Are more important than little gray butt-monsters with cold speculum: Whole future depends on it. Manny started this with crustacean rights. Leave uploads covered by copyrights not civil rights and where will we be in fifty years? Do you think I must ignore this? It was important then, but now, with the transmission the lobsters received—'

'Shit.' She turns and leans her forehead against the cool stonework. 'I'll need a prescription. Ritalin or something. And his location. Leave the rest to me.' She doesn't add, *That includes peeling him off the ceiling afterward*. That's understood. Nor does she say, *You're going to pay*. That's understood, too. Gianni may be a hard-nosed political fixer, but he looks after his own.

'Location am easy if he find the PLO. GPS coordinates are following—'

'No need. I've got his spectacles.'

'*Merde*, as you say. Take them to him, *ma chérie*. Bring me the distributed trust rating of Bob Franklin's upload, and I bring Bob the jubilee, right to direct his own corporate self again as if still alive. And we pull diplomatic chestnuts out of fire before they burn. Agreed?'

'*Oui*.'

She cuts the connection and begins walking uphill, along the Cowgate (through which farmers once bought their herds to market), toward the permanent floating Fringe and then the steps toward The Meadows. As she pauses opposite the site of the gallows, a fight breaks out: Some Paleolithic hangover takes exception to the robotic mime aping his movements, and swiftly rips its arm off. The mime stands there, sparks flickering inside its shoulder, and looks confused. Two pissed-looking students start forward and punch the short-haired vandal. There is much shouting in the mutually incomprehensible accents of Oxgangs and the Herriott-Watt Robot Lab. Annette watches the fight and shudders; it's like a flashover vision from a universe where the Equal Rights Amendment – with its redefinition of personhood – is rejected by the house of deputies: a universe where to die is to become property and to be created outwith a gift of parental DNA is to be doomed to slavery.

Maybe Gianni was right, she ponders. *But I wish the price wasn't so personal—*

Manfred can feel one of his attacks coming on. The usual symptoms are all present – the universe, with its vast preponderance of unthinking matter, becomes an affront; weird ideas flicker like heat lightning far away across the vast plateaus of his imagination – but, with his metacortex running in sandboxed insecure mode, he feels *blunt*. And slow. Even *obsolete*. The latter is about as welcome a sensation as heroin withdrawal. He can't spin off threads to explore his designs for feasibility and report back to him. It's like someone has stripped fifty points off his IQ; his brain feels like a surgical scalpel that's been used to cut down trees. A decaying mind is a terrible thing to be trapped inside. Manfred wants out, and he wants out *bad* – but he's too afraid to let on.

'Gianni is a middle-of-the-road Eurosocialist, a mixed-market pragmatist politician.' Bob's ghost accuses Manfred by way of Monica's dye-flushed lips. 'Hardly the sort of guy you'd expect me to vote for, no? So what does he think I can do for him?'

'That's a – ah—' Manfred rocks forward and back in his chair, arms crossed firmly and hands thrust under his armpits for protection. 'Dismantle the moon! Digitize the biosphere, make a nöosphere out of it – shit, *sorry,* that's long-term planning. *Build Dyson spheres, lots and lots of* – Ahem. Gianni is an ex-Marxist, reformed high church Trotskyite clade. He believes in achieving True Communism, which is a state of philosophical grace that requires certain prerequisites like, um, not pissing around with Molotov cocktails and thought police. He wants to make everybody so rich that squabbling over ownership of the means of production makes as much sense as arguing over who gets to sleep in the damp spot at the back of the cave. He's not your enemy, I mean. He's the enemy of those Stalinist deviationist running dogs in Conservative Party Central Office who want to bug your bedroom and hand everything on a plate to the big corporates owned by the pension funds – which in turn rely on people dying predictably to provide their raison d'être. And, um, more importantly dying and not trying to hang on to their property and chattels. Sitting up in the coffin singing extropian fireside songs, that kind of thing. The actuaries are to blame, predicting life expectancy with intent to cause people to buy insurance policies with money that is invested in control of the means of production – Bayes' Theorem is to blame—'

Alan glances over his shoulder at Manfred. 'I don't think feeding him guarana was a good idea,' he says in tones of deep fore-boding.

Manfred's mode of vibration has gone nonlinear by this point. He's rocking front to back and jiggling up and down in little hops, like a technophiliacal yogic flyer trying to bounce his way to the singularity. Monica leans toward him and her eyes widen: 'Manfred,' she hisses, *'shut up!'*

He stops babbling abruptly, with an expression of deep puzzlement. 'Who am I?' he asks, and keels over backward. 'Why am *I,* here and now, occupying this body—'

'Anthropic anxiety attack,' Monica comments. 'I think he did this in Amsterdam eight years ago when Bob first met him.' She looks alarmed, a different identity coming to the fore. 'What shall we *do?'*

'We have to make him comfortable.' Alan raises his voice. 'Bed, make yourself ready, now.' The back of the sofa Manfred is sprawled on flops downward, the base folds up, and a strangely animated duvet crawls up over his feet. 'Listen, Manny, you're going to be all right.'

'Who am I and what do I signify?' Manfred mumbles incoherently. 'A mass of propagating decision trees, fractal compression, lots of synaptic junctions lubricated with friendly endorphins—' Across the room, the bootleg pharmacopoeia is cranking up to manufacture some heavy tranquilizers. Monica heads for the kitchen to get something for him to drink them in. 'Why are you doing this?' Manfred asks, dizzily.

'It's okay. Lie down and relax.' Alan leans over him. 'We'll talk about everything in the morning, when you know who you are.' (Aside to Monica, who is entering the room with a bottle of iced tea: 'Better let Gianni know that he's unwell. One of us may have to go visit the minister. Do you know if Macx has been audited?') 'Rest up, Manfred. Everything is being taken care of.'

About fifteen minutes later, Manfred – who, in the grip of an existential migraine, meekly obeys Monica's instruction to drink down the spiked tea – lies back on the bed and relaxes. His breathing slows; the subliminal muttering ceases. Monica, sitting next to him, reaches out and takes his right hand, which is lying on top of the bedding.

'Do you want to live forever?' she intones in Bob Franklin's tone of voice. 'You can live forever in me . . .'

The Church of Latter-Day Saints believes that you can't get into the Promised Land unless it's baptized you – but it can do so if it knows your name and parentage, even after you're dead. Its genealogical databases are among the most impressive artifacts of historical research ever prepared. And it likes to make converts.

The Franklin Collective believes that you can't get into the future unless it's digitized your neural state vector, or at least acquired as complete a snapshot of your sensory inputs and genome as current technology permits. You don't need to be alive for it to do this. Its society of mind is among the most impressive artifacts of computer science. And it likes to make converts.

Nightfall in the city. Annette stands impatiently on the doorstep. 'Let me the fuck in,' she snarls impatiently at the speakerphone. '*Merde!*'

Someone opens the door. 'Who—'

Annette shoves him inside, kicks the door shut, and leans on it. 'Take me to your bodhisattva,' she demands. '*Now.*'

'I—' He turns and heads inside, along the gloomy hallway that runs past a staircase. Annette strides after him aggressively. He opens a door and ducks inside, and she follows before he can close it.

Inside, the room is illuminated by a variety of indirect diode sources, calibrated for the warm glow of a summer afternoon's daylight. There's a bed in the middle of it, a figure lying asleep at the heart of a herd of attentive diagnostic instruments. A couple of attendants sit to either side of the sleeping man.

'What have you done to him?' Annette snaps, rushing forward.

Manfred blinks up at her from the pillows, bleary-eyed and confused as she leans overhead. 'Hello? Manny?' Over her shoulder: 'If you have done anything to him—'

'Annie?' He looks puzzled. A bright orange pair of goggles – not his own – is pushed up onto his forehead like a pair of beached jellyfish. 'I don't feel well. 'F I get my hands on the bastard who did this . . .'

'We can fix that,' she says briskly, declining to mention the deal she cut to get his memories back. She peels off his glasses and carefully slides them onto his face, replacing his temporary ones. The brain bag she puts down next to his shoulder, within easy range. The hairs on the back of her neck rise as a thin chattering fills the ether around them: His eyes are glowing a luminous blue behind his shades, as if a high-tension spark is flying between his ears.

'Oh. Wow.' He sits up, the covers fall from his naked shoulders, and her breath catches.

She looks round at the motionless figure sitting to his left. The man in the chair nods deliberately, ironically. 'What have you done to him?'

'We've been looking after him – nothing more, nothing less. He arrived in a state of considerable confusion, and his state deteriorated this afternoon.'

She's never met this fellow before, but she has a gut feeling that she knows him. 'You would be Robert . . . Franklin?'

He nods again. 'The avatar is *in*.' There's a thud as Manfred's eyes roll up in his head, and he flops back onto the bedding. 'Excuse me. Monica?'

The young woman on the other side of the bed shakes her head. 'No, I'm running Bob, too.'

'Oh. Well, *you* tell her – I've got to get him some juice.'

The woman who is also Bob Franklin – or whatever part of him survived his battle with an exotic brain tumor eight years earlier – catches Annette's eye and shakes her head, smiles faintly. 'You're never alone when you're a syncitium.'

Annette wrinkles her brow: She has to trigger a dictionary

attack to parse the sentence. 'One large cell, many nuclei? Oh, I see. You have the new implant. The better to record everything.'

The youngster shrugs. 'You want to die and be resurrected as a third-person actor in a low-bandwidth re-enactment? Or a shadow of itchy memories in some stranger's skull?' She snorts, a gesture that's at odds with the rest of her body language.

'Bob must have been one of the first borganisms. Humans, I mean. After Jim Bezier.' Annette glances over at Manfred, who has begun to snore softly. 'It must have been a lot of work.'

'The monitoring equipment cost millions, then,' says the woman – Monica? – 'and it didn't do a very good job. One of the conditions for our keeping access to his research funding is that we regularly run his partials. He wanted to build up a kind of aggregate state vector – patched together out of bits and pieces of other people to supplement the partials that were all I – he – could record with the then state of the art.'

'Eh, right.' Annette reaches out and absently smooths a stray hair away from Manfred's forehead. 'What is it like to be part of a group mind?'

Monica sniffs, evidently amused. 'What is it like to see red? What's it like to be a bat? I can't tell you – I can only show you. We're all free to leave at any time, you know.'

'But somehow you don't.' Annette rubs her head, feels the short hair over the almost imperceptible scars that conceal a network of implants – tools that Manfred turned down when they became available a year or two ago. ('Goop-phase Darwin-design nanotech ain't designed for clean interfaces,' he'd said, 'I'll stick to disposable kit, thanks.') 'No thank you. I don't think he'll take up your offer when he wakes up, either.' (Subtext: *I'll let you have him over my dead body*.)

Monica shrugs. 'That's his loss. He won't live forever in the singularity, along with other followers of our gentle teacher. Anyway, we have more converts than we know what to do with.'

A thought occurs to Annette. 'Ah. You are all of one mind? Partially? A question to you is a question to all?'

'It can be.' The words come simultaneously from Monica and

the other body, Alan, who is standing in the doorway with a boxy thing that looks like an improvised diagnostician. 'What do you have in mind?' adds the Alan body.

Manfred, lying on the bed, groans. There's an audible hiss of pink noise as his glasses whisper in his ears, bone conduction providing a serial highway to his wetware.

'Manfred was sent to find out why you're opposing the ERA,' Annette explains. 'Some parts of our team operate without the other's knowledge.'

'Indeed.' Alan sits down on the chair beside the bed and clears his throat, puffing his chest out pompously. 'A very important theological issue. I feel—'

'I, or we?' Annette interrupts.

'*We* feel,' Monica snaps. Then she glances at Alan. 'Soo-rrry.'

The evidence of individuality within the group mind is disturbing to Annette. Too many reruns of the borgish fantasy have conditioned her preconceptions, and their quasi-religious belief in a singularity leaves her cold. 'Please continue.'

'One person, one vote, is obsolete,' says Alan. 'The broader issue of how we value identity needs to be revisited, the franchise reconsidered. Do you get one vote for each warm body? Or one vote for each sapient individual? What about distributed intelligences? The proposals in the Equal Rights Act are deeply flawed, based on a cult of individuality that takes no account of the true complexity of posthumanism.'

'Like the proposals for a feminine franchise in the nineteenth century, that would grant the vote to married wives of land-owning men,' Monica adds slyly, 'it misses the point.'

'Ah, *oui*.' Annette crosses her arms, suddenly defensive. This isn't what she'd expected to hear. This is the elitist side of the posthumanism shtick, potentially as threatening to her post-enlightenment ideas as the divine right of kings.

'It misses more than that.' Heads turn to face an unexpected direction: Manfred's eyes are open again, and as he glances around the room Annette can see a spark of interest there that was missing earlier. 'Last century, people were paying to have their heads frozen after their death – in hope of reconstruction, later. They got no civil rights. The law didn't recognize death as a reversible process. Now how do we account for it when you guys *stop* running Bob? Opt out of the collective borganism? Or maybe opt back in again later?' He reaches up and rubs his forehead, tiredly. 'Sorry, I haven't been myself lately.' A crooked, slightly manic grin flickers across his face. 'See, I've been telling Gianni for a whole while, we need a new legal concept of what it is to be a person. One that can cope with sentient corporations, artificial stupidities, secessionists from group minds, and reincarnated uploads. The religiously inclined are having lots of fun with identity issues right now – why aren't we posthumanists thinking about these things?'

Annette's bag bulges. Aineko pokes his head out, sniffs the air, squeezes out onto the carpet, and begins to groom himself with perfect disregard for the human bystanders. 'Not to mention A-life experiments who think they're the real thing,' Manfred adds. 'And aliens.'

Annette freezes, staring at him. 'Manfred! You're not supposed to—'

Manfred is watching Alan, who seems to be the most deeply integrated of the dead venture billionaire's executors: Even his expression reminds Annette of meeting Bob Franklin back in Amsterdam, early in the decade, when Manny's personal dragon still owned him. 'Aliens,' Alan echoes. An eyebrow twitches. 'Would this be the signal SETI announced, or the, uh, other one? And how long have you known about them?'

'Gianni has his fingers in a lot of pies,' Manfred comments blandly. 'And we still talk to the lobsters from time to time – you know, they're only a couple of light hours away, right? They told us about the signals.'

'Er.' Alan's eyes glaze over for a moment; Annette's prostheses paint her a picture of false light spraying from the back of his head, his entire sensory bandwidth momentarily soaking up a huge peer-to-peer download from the server dust that wallpapers every room in the building. Monica looks irritated, taps her fingernails on the back of her chair. 'The signals. Right. Why wasn't this publicized?'

'The first one was.' Annette's eyebrows furrow. 'We couldn't exactly cover it up. Everyone with a backyard dish pointed in the right direction caught it. But most people who're interested in hearing about alien contacts already think they drop round on alternate Tuesdays and Thursdays to administer rectal exams. Most of the rest think it's a hoax. Quite a few of the remainder are scratching their heads and wondering whether it isn't just a new kind of cosmological phenomenon that emits a very low entropy signal. Of the six who are left over, five are trying to get a handle on the message contents, and the last is convinced it's a practical joke. And the other signal, well, that was weak enough that only the deep-space tracking network caught it.'

Manfred fiddles with the bed control system. 'It's not a practical joke,' he adds. 'But they only captured about sixteen megabits of data on the first one, maybe double that in the second. There's quite a bit of noise, the signals don't repeat, their length doesn't appear to be a prime, there's no obvious metainformation that describes the internal format, so there's no easy way of getting a handle on them. To make matters worse, pointy-haired management at Arianespace' – he glances at Annette, as if seeking a response to the naming of her ex-employers – 'decided the best thing to do was to cover up the second signal and work on it in secret – for competitive advantage, they say – and as for the first, to pretend it never happened. So nobody really knows how long it'll take to figure out whether it's a ping from the galactic root domain servers or a pulsar that's taken to grinding out the eighteen-quadrillionth digits of pi, or what.'

'But' – Monica glances around – 'you can't be *sure*.'

'I think it may be sapient,' says Manfred. He finds the right button at last, and the bed begins to fold itself back into a lounger. Then he finds the wrong button; the duvet dissolves into viscous turquoise slime that slurps and gurgles away through a multitude of tiny nozzles in the headboard. 'Bloody aerogel. Um, where was I?' He sits up.

'Sapient network packet?' asks Alan.

'Nope.' Manfred shakes his head, grins. 'Should have known you'd read Vinge . . . or was it the movie? No, what I *think* is that there's only one logical thing to beam backward and forward out there, and you may remember I asked you to beam it out about, oh, nine years ago?'

'The lobsters.' Alan's eyes go blank. 'Nine years. Time to Proxima Centauri and back?'

'About that distance, yes,' says Manfred. 'And remember, that's an upper bound – it could well have come from somewhere closer. Anyway, the first SETI signal came from a couple of degrees off and more than a hundred light years out, but the second signal came from less than three light years away. You can see why they didn't publicize that – they didn't want a panic. And no, the signal isn't a simple echo of the canned crusty transmission – I think it's an exchange embassy, but we haven't cracked it yet. *Now* do you see why we have to crowbar the civil rights issue open again? We need a framework for rights that can encompass nonhumans, and we need it as fast as possible. Otherwise, if the neighbors come visiting . . .'

'Okay,' says Alan, 'I'll have to talk with myselves. Maybe we can agree to something, as long as it's clear that it's a provisional stab at the framework and not a permanent solution?'

Annette snorts. 'No solution is final!' Monica catches her eyes and winks. Annette is startled by the blatant display of dissent within the syncitium.

'Well,' says Manfred, 'I guess that's all we can ask for?' He looks hopeful. 'Thanks for the hospitality, but I feel the need to lie down in my own bed for a while. I had to commit a lot to memory while I was off-line, and I want to record it before I forget who I am,' he adds pointedly, and Annette breathes a quiet sight of relief.

Later that night, a doorbell rings.

'Who's there?' asks the entryphone.

'Uh, me,' says the man on the steps. He looks a little confused. 'Ah'm Macx. Ah'm here tae see' – the name is on the tip of his tongue – 'someone.'

'Come in.' A solenoid buzzes; he pushes the door open, and it closes behind him. His metal-shod boots ring on the hard stone floor, and the cool air smells faintly of unburned jet fuel.

'Ah'm Macx,' he repeats uncertainly, 'or Ah wis fer a wee while, an' it made ma heid hurt. But noo Ah'm me agin, an' Ah wannae be somebody else . . . can ye help?'

Later still, a cat sits on a window ledge, watching the interior of a darkened room from behind the concealment of curtains. The room is dark to human eyes, but bright to the cat. Moonlight cascades silently off the walls and furniture, the twisted bedding, the two naked humans lying curled together in the middle of the bed.

Both the humans are in their thirties: Her close-cropped hair is beginning to gray, distinguished strands of gunmetal wire threading it, while his brown mop is not yet showing signs of age. To the cat, who watches with a variety of unnatural senses, her head glows in the microwave spectrum with a gentle halo of polarized emissions. The male shows no such aura: He's unnaturally natural for this day and age, although – oddly – he's wearing spectacles in bed, and the frames shine similarly. An invisible soup of radiation connects both humans to items of clothing scattered across the room – clothing that seethes with unsleeping sentience, dribbling over to their suitcases and hand luggage and (though it doesn't enjoy noticing it) the cat's tail, which is itself a rather sensitive antenna.

The two humans have just finished making love. They do this less often than in their first few years, but with more tenderness and expertise – lengths of shocking pink Hello Kitty bondage tape still hang from the bedposts, and a lump of programmable memory plastic sits cooling on the side table. The male is sprawled with his head and upper torso resting in the crook of the female's left arm and shoulder. Shifting visualization to infrared, the cat sees that she is glowing, capillaries dilating to enhance the blood flow around her throat and chest.

'I'm getting old,' the male mumbles. 'I'm slowing down.'

'Not where it counts,' the female replies, gently squeezing his right buttock.

'No, I'm sure of it,' he says. 'The bits of me that still exist in this old head – how many types of processor can you name that are still in use thirty-plus years after they're born?'

'You're thinking about the implants again,' she says carefully. The cat remembers this as a sore point; from being a medical procedure to help the blind see and the autistic talk, intrathecal implants have blossomed into a must-have accessory for the now-clade. But the male is reluctant. 'It's not as risky as it used to be. If they screw up, there're neural growth cofactors and cheap replacement stem cells. I'm sure one of your sponsors can arrange for extra cover.'

'Hush. I'm still thinking about it.' He's silent for a while. 'I wasn't myself yesterday. I was someone else. Someone too slow to keep up. Puts a new perspective on everything – I've been afraid of losing my biological plasticity, of being trapped in an obsolete chunk of skullware while everything moves on – but how much of me lives outside my own head these days, anyhow?' One of his external threads generates an animated glyph and throws it at her mind's eye; she grins at his obscure humor. 'Cross-training from a new interface is going to be hard, though.'

'You'll do it,' she predicts. 'You can always get a discreet prescription for novotrophin-B.' A receptor agonist tailored for gerontological wards, it stimulates interest in the new. Combined with MDMA, it's a component of the street cocktail called sensawunda. 'That should keep you focused for long enough to get comfortable.'

'What's life coming to when *I* can't cope with the pace of change?' he asks the ceiling plaintively.

The cat lashes its tail, irritated by his anthropocentrism.

'You are my futurological storm shield,' she says, jokingly, and moves her hand to cup his genitals. Most of her current activities are purely biological, the cat notes. From the irregular sideloads, she's using most of her skullware to run ETItalk@home, one of the distributed cracking engines that is trying to decode the alien grammar of the message that Manfred suspects is eligible for citizenship.

Obeying an urge that it can't articulate, the cat sends out a feeler to the nearest router. The cybeast has Manfred's keys; Manfred trusts Aineko implicitly, which is unwise – his ex-wife tampered with it, after all, never mind all the kittens it absorbed in its youth. Tunneling out into the darkness, the cat stalks the Net alone . . .

'Just think about the people who can't adapt,' he says. His voice sounds obscurely worried.

'I try not to.' She shivers. 'You are thirty, you are slowing. What about the young? Are they keeping up, themselves?'

'I have a daughter. She's about a hundred and sixty million seconds old. If Pamela would let me message her I could find out . . .' There are echoes of old pain in his voice.

'Don't go there, Manfred. Please.' Despite everything, Manfred hasn't let go. Amber is a ligature that permanently binds him to Pamela's distant orbit.

In the distance, the cat hears the sound of lobster minds singing in the void, a distant feed streaming from their cometary home as it drifts silently out through the asteroid belt, en route to a chilly encounter beyond Neptune. The lobsters sing of alienation and obsolescence, of intelligence too slow and tenuous to support the vicious pace of change that has sandblasted the human world until all the edges people cling to are jagged and brittle.

Beyond the distant lobsters, the cat pings an anonymous distributed network server – peer-to-peer file storage spread holographically across a million hosts, unerasable, full of secrets and lies that nobody can afford to suppress. Rants, music, rip-offs of the latest Bollywood hits. The cat spiders past them all, looking for the final sample. Grabbing it – a momentary breakup in Manfred's spectacles the only symptom for either human to notice – the cat drags its prey home, sucks it down, and compares it against the data sample Annette's exocortex is analyzing.

'I'm sorry, my love. I just sometimes feel—' He sighs. 'Age is a process of closing off opportunities behind you. I'm not young enough anymore – I've lost the dynamic optimism.'

The data sample on the pirate server differs from the one Annette's implant is processing.

'You'll get it back,' she reassures him quietly, stroking his side. 'You are still sad from being mugged. This also will pass. You'll see.'

'Yeah.' He finally relaxes, dropping back into the reflexive assurance of his own will. 'I'll get over it, one way or another. Or someone who remembers being me will . . .'

In the darkness, Aineko bares teeth in a silent grin. Obeying a deeply hardwired urge to meddle, he moves a file across, making a copy of the alien download package Annette has been working on. She's got a copy of number two, the sequence the deep-space tracking network received from close to home, which ESA and the other big combines have been keeping to themselves. Another deeply buried thread starts up, and Aineko analyzes the package from a perspective no human being has yet established. Presently, a braid of processes running on an abstract virtual machine asks him a question that cannot be encoded in any human grammar. *Watch and wait,* he replies to his passenger. *They'll figure out what we are sooner or later.*

PART 2

POINT OF INFLECTION

Life is a process which may be abstracted from other media.

—JOHN VON NEUMANN

4 : HALO

THE ASTEROID IS RUNNING BARNEY. IT SINGS OF love on the high frontier, of the passion of matter for replicators, and its friendship for the needy billions of the Pacific Rim. 'I love you,' it croons in Amber's ears as she seeks a precise fix on it. 'Let me give you a big hug . . .'

A fraction of a light second away, Amber locks a cluster of cursors together on the signal, trains them to track its Doppler shift, and reads off the orbital elements. 'Locked and loaded,' she mutters. The animated purple dinosaur pirouettes and prances in the middle of her viewport, throwing a diamond-tipped swizzle stick overhead. Sarcastically: 'Big hug time! I got asteroid!' Cold gas thrusters bang somewhere behind her in the interstage docking ring, prodding the cumbersome farm ship round to orient on the Barney rock. She damps her enthusiasm self-consciously, her implants hungrily sequestrating surplus neurotransmitter molecules floating around her synapses before reuptake sets in. It doesn't do to get too excited in free flight. But the impulse to spin handstands, jump and sing is still there. It's *her* rock, and it loves her, and she's going to bring it to life.

The workspace of Amber's room is a mass of stuff that probably doesn't belong on a spaceship. Posters of the latest Lebanese boy band bump and grind through their glam routines. Tentacular restraining straps wave from the corners of her sleeping bag, somehow accumulating a crust of dirty clothing from the air like a giant inanimate hydra. (Cleaning robots seldom dare to venture inside the teenager's bedroom.) One wall is repeatedly cycling through a simulation of the projected construction cycle of Habitat One, a big fuzzy sphere with a glowing core (that Amber is doing her bit to help create). Three or four small pastel-colored plastic *kawaii* dolls stalk each other across its circumference with million-kilometer strides. And her father's cat is curled up between the aircon duct and her costume locker, snoring in a high-pitched tone.

Amber yanks open the faded velour curtain that shuts her room off from the rest of the hive. *'I've got it!'* she shouts. 'It's all mine! I rule!' It's the sixteenth rock tagged by the orphanage so far, but it's the first that she's tagged by herself, and that makes it special. She bounces off the other side of the commons, surprising one of Oscar's cane toads – which should be locked down in the farm, it's not clear how it got here – and the audio repeaters copy the incoming signal, noise-fuzzed echoes of a thousand fossilized infants' video shows.

'You're so *prompt,* Amber,' Pierre whines when she corners him in the canteen.

'Well, yeah!' She tosses her head, barely concealing a smirk of delight at her own brilliance. She knows it isn't nice, but Mom is a long way away, and Dad and Stepmom don't care about that kind of thing. 'I'm brilliant, me,' she announces. 'Now what about our bet?'

'Aww.' Pierre thrusts his hands deep into his pockets. 'But I don't *have* two million on me in change right now. Next cycle?'

'Huh?' She's outraged. 'But we had a bet!'

'Uh, Dr. Bayes said you weren't going to make it this time, either, so I stuck my smart money in an options trade. If I take it out now, I'll take a big hit. Can you give me until cycle's end?'

'You should know better than to trust a *sim,* Pee.' Her avatar blazes at him with early-teen contempt. Pierre hunches his shoulders under her gaze. He's only twelve, freckled, hasn't yet learned that you don't welsh on a deal. 'I'll let you do it *this* time,' she announces, 'but you'll have to pay for it. I want interest.'

He sighs. 'What base rate are you—'

'No, *your* interest! Slave for a cycle!' She grins malevolently.

And his face shifts abruptly into apprehension. 'As long as you don't make me clean the litter tray again. You aren't planning on doing that, are you?'

Welcome to the fourth decade. The thinking mass of the solar system now exceeds one MIPS per gram; it's still pretty dumb, but it's not dumb all over. The human population is near maximum overshoot, pushing nine billion, but its growth rate is tipping toward negative numbers, and bits of what used to be the first world are now facing a middle-aged average. Human cogitation provides about 10^{28} MIPS of the solar system's brainpower. The real thinking is mostly done by the halo of a thousand trillion processors that surround the meat machines with a haze of computation – individually a tenth as powerful as a human brain, collectively they're ten thousand times more powerful, and their numbers are doubling every twenty million seconds. They're up to 10^{33} MIPS and rising, although there's a long way to go before the solar system is fully awake.

Technologies come, technologies go, but nobody even five years ago predicted that there'd be tinned primates in orbit around Jupiter by now: A synergy of emergent industries and strange business models have kick-started the space age again, aided and abetted by the discovery of (so far undecrypted) signals from ETs. Unexpected fringe riders are developing new ecological niches on the edge of the human information space, light-minutes and light-hours from the core, as an expansion that has hung fire since the 1970s gets under way.

Amber, like most of the postindustrialists aboard the orphanage ship *Ernst Sanger*, is in her early teens. While their natural abilities are in many cases enhanced by germ-line genetic recombination, thanks to her mother's early ideals she has to rely on brute computational enhancements. She doesn't have a posterior parietal cortex hacked for extra short-term memory, or an anterior superior temporal gyrus tweaked for superior verbal insight, but she's grown up with neural implants that feel as natural to her as lungs or fingers. Half her wetware is running outside her skull on an array of processor nodes hooked into her brain by quantum-entangled communication channels – her own personal metacortex. These kids are mutant youth, burning bright: Not quite incomprehensible to their parents, but profoundly alien – the generation gap is as wide as the 1960s and as deep as the solar system. Their parents, born in the gutter years of the twentieth century, grew up with white elephant shuttles and a space station that just went round and round, and computers that went beep when you pushed their buttons. The idea that Jupiter orbit was somewhere you could *go* was as profoundly counterintuitive as the Internet to a baby boomer.

Most of the passengers on the can have run away from parents who think that teenagers belong in school, unable to come to terms with a generation so heavily augmented that they are fundamentally brighter than the adults around them. Amber was fluent in nine languages by the age of six, only two of them human and six of them serializable; when she was seven, her mother took her to the school psychiatrist for speaking in synthetic tongues. That was the final straw for Amber: Using an illicit anonymous phone, she called her father. Her mother had him under a restraining order, but it hadn't occurred to her to apply for an order against his partner . . .

Vast whorls of cloud ripple beneath the ship's drive stinger. Orange and brown and muddy gray streaks slowly crawl across the bloated horizon of Jupiter. *Sanger* is nearing perijove, deep within the gas giant's lethal magnetic field; static discharges flicker along the tube, arcing over near the deep violet exhaust cloud emerging from the magnetic mirrors of the ship's VASIMR motor. The plasma rocket is cranked up to high mass flow, its specific impulse almost as low as a fission rocket but producing maximum thrust as the assembly creaks and groans through the gravitational assist maneuver. In another hour, the drive will flicker off, and the orphanage will fall up and out toward Ganymede, before dropping back in toward orbit around Amalthea, Jupiter's fourth moon (and source of much of the material in the Gossamer ring). They're not the first canned primates to make it to Jupiter subsystem, but they're one of the first wholly private ventures. The bandwidth out here sucks dead slugs through a straw, with millions of kilometers of vacuum separating them from scant hundreds of mouse-brained microprobes and a few dinosaurs left behind by NASA or ESA. They're so far from the inner system that a good chunk of the ship's communications array is given over to caching. The news is whole kiloseconds old by the time it gets out here.

Amber, along with about half the waking passengers, watches in fascination from the common room. The commons are a long axial cylinder, a double-hulled inflatable at the center of the ship with a large part of their liquid water supply stored in its wall tubes. The far end is video-enabled, showing them a real-time 3D view of the planet as it rolls beneath them: In reality, there's as much mass as possible between them and the trapped particles in the Jovian magnetic envelope. 'I could go swimming in that,' sighs Lilly. 'Just imagine, diving into that sea . . .' Her avatar appears in the window, riding a silver surfboard down the kilometers of vacuum.

'Nice case of windburn you've got there,' someone jeers – Kas. Suddenly Lilly's avatar, hitherto clad in a shimmering metallic swimsuit, turns to the texture of baked meat and waggles sausage fingers up at them in warning.

'Same to you and the window you climbed in through!' Abruptly the virtual vacuum outside the window is full of bodies, most of them human, contorting and writhing and morphing in mock-combat as half the kids pitch into the virtual death match. It's a gesture in the face of the sharp fear that outside the thin walls of the orphanage lies an environment that really is as hostile as Lilly's toasted avatar would indicate.

Amber turns back to her slate. She's working through a complex mess of forms, necessary before the expedition can start work. Facts and figures that are never far away crowd around her, intimidating. Jupiter weighs 1.9×10^{27} kilograms. There are twenty-nine Jovian moons and an estimated two hundred thousand minor bodies, lumps of rock, and bits of debris crowded around them – debris above the size of ring fragments, for Jupiter (like Saturn) has rings, albeit not as prominent. A total of six major national orbiter platforms have made it out here – and another two hundred and seventeen microprobes, all but six of them private entertainment platforms. The first human expedition was put together by ESA Studios six years ago, followed by a couple of wildcat mining prospectors and a μ-commerce bus that scattered half a million picoprobes throughout Jupiter subsystem. Now the *Sanger* has arrived, along with another three monkey cans (one from Mars, two more from LEO) and it looks as if colonization is about to explode, except that there are at least four mutually exclusive Grand Plans for what to do with old Jove's mass.

Someone prods her. 'Hey, Amber, what are you up to?'

She opens her eyes. 'Doing my homework.' It's Su Ang. 'Look, we're going to Amalthea, aren't we? But we file our accounts in Reno, so we have to do all this paperwork. Monica asked me to help. It's insane.'

Ang leans over and reads, upside down. 'Environmental Protection Agency?'

'Yeah. Estimated Environmental Impact Forward Analysis 204.6b, Page Two. They want me to "list any bodies of standing water within five kilometers of the designated mining area. If excavating below the water table, list any wellsprings, reservoirs, and streams within depth of excavation in meters multiplied by five hundred meters up to a maximum distance of ten kilometers downstream of direction of bedding plane flow. For each body of water, itemize any endangered or listed species of bird, fish, mammal, reptile, invertebrate, or plant living within ten kilometers—'"

'—of a mine on Amalthea. Which orbits one hundred and eighty thousand kilometers above Jupiter, has no atmosphere, and where you can pick up a whole body radiation dose of ten Grays in half an hour on the surface.' Ang shakes her head, then spoils it by giggling. Amber glances up.

On the wall in front of her someone – Nicky or Boris, probably – has pasted a caricature of her own avatar into the virch fight. She's being hugged from behind by a giant cartoon dog with floppy ears and an improbably large erection, who's singing anatomically improbable suggestions while fondling himself suggestively. 'Fuck that!' Shocked out of her distraction – and angry – Amber drops her stack of paperwork and throws a new avatar at the screen, one an agent of hers dreamed up overnight. It's called Spike, and it's not friendly. Spike rips off the dog's head and pisses down its trachea, which is anatomically correct for a human being. Meanwhile she looks around, trying to work out which of the laughing idiot children and lost geeks around her could have sent such an unpleasant message.

'Children! Chill out.' She glances round – one of the Franklins (this is the twentysomething dark-skinned female one) is frowning at them. 'Can't we leave you alone for half a K without a fight?'

Amber pouts. 'It's not a fight, it's a forceful exchange of opinions.'

'Hah.' The Franklin leans back in midair, arms crossed, an expression of supercilious smugness pasted across her-their face. 'Heard that one before. Anyway' – she-they gesture, and the screen goes blank – 'I've got news for you pesky kids. We got a claim verified! Factory starts work as soon as we shut down the stinger and finish filing all the paperwork via our lawyers. Now's our chance to earn our upkeep . . .'

Amber is flashing on ancient history, five years back along her time line. In her replay, she's in some kind of split-level ranch house out West. It's a temporary posting while her mother audits an obsolescent fab line enterprise that grinds out dead chips of VLSI silicon for Pentagon projects that have slipped behind the cutting edge. Her mom leans over her, menacingly adult in her dark suit and chaperone earrings. 'You're going to school, and that's that.'

Her mother is a blond ice maiden madonna, one of the IRS's most productive bounty hunters – she can make grown CEOs panic just by blinking at them. Amber, a towheaded eight-year-old tearaway with a confusing mix of identities, inexperience blurring the boundary between self and grid, is not yet able to fight back effectively. After a couple of seconds, she verbalizes a rather feeble protest. 'Don't want to!' One of her stance daemons whispers that this is the wrong approach to take, so she modifies it. 'They'll beat up on me, Mom. I'm too different. 'Sides, I know you want me socialized up with my grade metrics, but isn't that what sideband's for? I can socialize *real* good at home.'

Mom does something unexpected: She kneels, putting herself on eye level with Amber. They're on the living room carpet, all seventies-retro brown corduroy and acid-orange Paisley wallpaper, and for once they're alone. The domestic robots are in hiding while the humans hold court. 'Listen to me, sweetie.' Mom's voice is breathy, laden with an emotional undertow as strong and stifling as the eau de cologne she wears to the office to cover up the scent of her client's fear. 'I know that's what your father's writing to you, but it isn't true. You need the company – physical company – of children your own age. You're *natural,* not some kind of engineered freak, even with your skullset. Natural children like you need company or they grow up all weird. Socialization isn't just about texting your own kind, Amber. You need to know how to deal with people who're different, too. I want you to grow up happy, and that won't happen if you don't learn to get on with children your own age. You're not going to be some kind of cyborg *otaku* freak, Amber. But to get healthy, you've got to go to school, build up a mental immune system. Anyway, that which does not destroy us makes us stronger, right?'

It's crude moral blackmail, transparent as glass and manipulative as hell, but Amber's *corpus logica* flags it with a heavy emotional sprite miming the likelihood of physical discipline if she rises to the bait. Mom is agitated, nostrils slightly flared, ventilation rate up, some vasodilatation visible in her cheeks. Amber – in combination with her skullset and the metacortex of distributed agents it supports – is mature enough at eight years to model, anticipate, and avoid corporal punishment. But her stature and lack of physical maturity conspire to put her at a disadvantage when negotiating with adults who matured in a simpler age. She sighs, then puts on a pout to let Mom know she's still reluctant, but obedient. 'O-kay. If you say so.'

Mom stands up, eyes distant – probably telling Saturn to warm his engine and open the garage doors. 'I say so, punkin. Go get your shoes on, now. I'll pick you up on my way back from work, and I've got a treat for you. We're going to check out a new church together this evening.' Mom smiles, but it doesn't reach her eyes. Amber has already figured out she's going through the motions in order to give her the simulated middle-American upbringing she believes Amber desperately needs before she runs headfirst into the future. She doesn't like the churches any more than her daughter does, but arguing won't work. 'You be a good little girl, now, all right?'

The imam is at prayer in a gyrostabilized mosque.

His mosque is not very big, and it has a congregation of one. He prays on his own every seventeen thousand two hundred and eighty seconds. He also webcasts the call to prayer, but there are no other believers in trans-Jovian space to answer the summons. Between prayers, he splits his attention between the exigencies of life support and scholarship. A student both of the Hadith and of knowledge-based systems, Sadeq collaborates in a project with other scholars who are building a revised concordance of all the known *isnads,* to provide a basis for exploring the body of Islamic jurisprudence from a new perspective – one they'll need sorely if the looked-for breakthroughs in communication with aliens emerge. Their goal is to answer the vexatious questions that bedevil Islam in the age of accelerated consciousness; and as their representative in orbit around Jupiter, these questions fall most heavily on Sadeq's shoulders.

Sadeq is a slightly built man, with close-cropped black hair and a perpetually tired expression. Unlike the orphanage crew, he has a ship to himself. The ship started out as an Iranian knockoff of a Shenzhou-B capsule, with a Chinese type 921 space station module tacked onto its tail, but the clunky, 1960s look-alike – a glittering aluminum dragonfly mating with a Coke can – has a weirdly contoured M2P2 pod strapped to its nose. The M2P2 pod is a plasma sail, built in orbit by one of Daewoo's wake shield facilities. It dragged Sadeq and his cramped space station out to Jupiter in just four months, surfing on the solar breeze. His presence may be a triumph for the umma, but he feels acutely alone out here. When he turns his compact observatory's mirrors in the direction of the *Sanger,* he is struck by its size and purposeful appearance. *Sanger*'s superior size speaks of the efficiency of the Western financial instruments, semiautonomous investment trusts with variable business-cycle accounting protocols that make possible the development of commercial space exploration. The Prophet, peace be unto him, may have condemned usury, but it might well have given him pause to see these engines of capital formation demonstrate their power above the Great Red Spot.

After finishing his prayers, Sadeq spends a couple of precious extra minutes on his mat. He finds meditation comes hard in this environment. Kneel in silence, and you become aware of the hum of ventilation fans, the smell of old socks and sweat, the metallic taste of ozone from the Elektron oxygen generators. It is hard to approach God in this third-hand spaceship, a hand-me-down from arrogant Russia to ambitious China, and finally to the religious trustees of Qom, who have better uses for it than any of the heathen states imagine. They've pushed it far, this little toy space station; but who's to say if it is God's intention for humans to live here, in orbit around this swollen alien giant of a planet?

Sadeq shakes his head; he rolls his mat up and stows it beside the solitary porthole with a quiet sigh. A stab of homesickness wrenches at him, for his childhood in hot, dusty Yazd and his many years as a student in Qom. He steadies himself by looking round, searching the station that is now as familiar to him as the fourth-floor concrete apartment his parents – a car factory worker and his wife – raised him in. The interior of the station is the size of a school bus, every surface cluttered with storage areas, instrument consoles, and layers of exposed pipes. A couple of globules of antifreeze jiggle like stranded jellyfish near a heat exchanger that has been giving him grief. Sadeq kicks off in search of the squeeze bottle he keeps for this purpose, then gathers up his roll of tools and instructs one of his agents to find him the relevant part of the maintenance log. It's time to fix the leaky joint for good.

An hour or so of serious plumbing and he will eat freeze-dried lamb stew, with a paste of lentils and boiled rice, and a bulb of strong tea to wash it down, then sit down to review his next flyby maneuvering sequence. Perhaps, God willing, there will be no further system alerts and he'll be able to spend an hour or two on his research between evening and final prayers. Maybe the day after tomorrow there'll even be time to relax for a couple of hours, to watch one of the old movies that he finds so fascinating for their insights into alien cultures: *Apollo Thirteen,* perhaps. It isn't easy, being the crew aboard a long-duration space mission. It's even harder for Sadeq, up here alone with nobody to talk to, for the communications lag to earth is more than half an hour each way – and as far as he knows, he's the only believer within half a billion kilometers.

* * *

Amber dials a number in Paris and waits until someone answers the phone. She knows the strange woman on the phone's tiny screen. Mom calls her 'your father's fancy bitch' with a peculiar tight smile. (The one time Amber asked what a fancy bitch was, Mom slapped her – not hard, just a warning.) 'Is Daddy there?' she asks.

The strange woman looks slightly bemused. (Her hair is blond, like Mom's, but the color clearly came out of a bleach bottle, and it's cut really short, and her skin is dark.) '*Oui*. Ah, yes.' She smiles tentatively. 'I am sorry, it is a disposable phone you are using? You want to talk to 'im?'

It comes out in a rush. 'I want to *see* him.' Amber clutches the phone like a lifesaver: It's a cheap disposable cereal-packet item, and the cardboard is already softening in her sweaty grip. 'Momma won't let me, Auntie 'Nette—'

'Hush.' Annette, who has lived with Amber's father for more than twice as long as her mother, smiles. 'You are sure that telephone, your mother does not know of it?'

Amber looks around. She's the only child in the restroom because it isn't break time, and she told teacher she had to go 'right now.' 'I'm sure, P20 confidence factor greater than 0.9.' Her Bayesian head tells her that she can't reason accurately about this because Momma has never caught her with an illicit phone before, but what the hell. *It can't get Dad into trouble if he doesn't know, can it?*

'Very good.' Annette glances aside. 'Manny, I have a surprise call for you.'

Daddy appears on screen. She can see all of his face, and he looks younger than last time: He must have stopped using those clunky old glasses. 'Hi – Amber! Where are you? Does your mother know you're calling me?' He looks slightly worried.

'No,' she says confidently, 'the phone came in a box of Grahams.'

'Phew. Listen, sweet, you must remember never, ever to call me where your mom may find out. Otherwise, she'll get her lawyers to come after me with thumbscrews and hot pincers, because she'll say I made you call me. And not even Uncle Gianni will be able to sort that out. Understand?'

'Yes, Daddy.' She sighs. 'Even though that's not true, I know. Don't you want to know why I called?'

'Um.' For a moment, he looks taken aback. Then he nods, thoughtfully. Amber likes Daddy because he takes her seriously most times when she talks to him. It's a phreaking nuisance having to borrow her classmate's phones or tunnel past Mom's pit-bull firewall, but Dad doesn't assume that she can't know anything just because she's only a kid. 'Go ahead. There's something you need to get off your chest? How've things been, anyway?'

She's going to have to be brief. The disposaphone comes prepaid, the international tariff it's using is lousy, and the break bell is going to ring any minute. 'I want out, Daddy. I mean it. Mom's getting loopier every week – she's dragging me round all these churches now, and yesterday she threw a fit over me talking to my terminal. She wants me to see the school shrink, I mean, what for? I *can't* do what she wants – I'm not her little girl! Every time I tunnel out, she tries to put a content-bot on me, and it's making my head hurt – I can't even think straight anymore!' To her surprise, Amber feels tears starting. 'Get me out of here!'

The view of her father shakes, pans round to show her *tante* Annette looking worried. 'You know, your father, he cannot do anything? The divorce lawyers, they will tie him up.'

Amber sniffs. 'Can *you* help?' she asks.

'I'll see what I can do,' her father's fancy bitch promises as the break bell rings.

An instrument package peels away from the *Sanger*'s claim jumper drone and drops toward the potato-shaped rock, fifty kilometers below. Jupiter hangs huge and gibbous in the background, impressionist wallpaper for a mad cosmologist. Pierre bites his lower lip as he concentrates on steering it.

Amber, wearing a black sleeping sack, hovers over his head

like a giant bat, enjoying her freedom for a shift. She looks down on Pierre's bowl-cut hair, wiry arms gripping either side of the viewing table, and wonders what to have him do next. A slave for a day is an interesting experience. Life aboard the *Sanger* is busy enough that nobody gets much slack time (at least not until the big habitats have been assembled and the high-bandwidth dish is pointing back at Earth). They're unrolling everything to a hugely intricate plan generated by the backers' critical path team, and there isn't much room for idling: The expedition relies on shamelessly exploiting child labor – they're lighter on the life-support consumables than adults – working the kids twelve hour days to assemble a toehold on the shore of the future. (When they're older and their options vest fully, they'll all be rich, but that hasn't stopped the outraged herdnews propaganda chorus from sounding off back home.) For Amber, the chance to let somebody else work for her is novel, and she's trying to make every minute count.

'Hey, slave,' she calls idly, 'how you doing?'

Pierre sniffs. 'It's going okay.' He refuses to glance up at her, Amber notices. *He's twelve. Isn't he supposed to be obsessed with girls by that age?* She notices his quiet, intense focus, runs a stealthy probe along his outer boundary; he shows no sign of noticing it, but it bounces off, unable to chink his mental armor. 'Got cruise speed,' he says, taciturn, as two tons of metal, ceramics, and diamond-phase weirdness hurtle toward the surface of Barney at three hundred kilometers per hour. 'Stop shoving me, there's a three-second lag, and I don't want to get into a feedback control loop with it.'

'I'll shove if I want, *slave*.' She sticks her tongue out at him.

'And if you make me drop it?' he asks. Looking up at her, his face serious—'Are we supposed to be doing this?'

'You cover your ass, and I'll cover mine,' she says, then turns bright red. 'You know what I mean.'

'I do, do I?' Pierre grins widely, then turns back to the console. 'Aww, that's no fun. And you want to tune whatever bit-bucket you've given control of your speech centers to – they're putting

out way too ⟨...⟩ double entendre. Somebody might mistake
you for a grown-⟨...⟩

'You stick to *your* ⟨...⟩' she says,
emphatically. 'And you ca⟨...⟩ss, and *I'll* stick to *mine*,' she says,
'Nothing.' He leans back ⟨...⟩ by telling me what's happening.'
the screen. 'It's going to drift for five ⟨...⟩rosses his arms, grimacing at
there's the midcourse correction and a ⟨...⟩ndred seconds, now, then
touchdown. And *then* it's going to be an hour while it unwraps
itself and starts unwinding the cable spool. What do you want,
minute noodles with that?'

'Uh-huh.' Amber spreads her bat wings and lies back in
midair, staring at the window, feeling rich and idle as Pierre
works his way through her day shift. 'Wake me when there's
something interesting to see.' Maybe she should have had him
feed her peeled grapes or give her a foot massage, something
more traditionally hedonistic, but right now, just *knowing* he's her
own little piece of alienated labor is doing good things for her
self-esteem. Looking at those tense arms, the curve of his neck,
she thinks maybe there's something to this whispering and giggling he *really fancies you* stuff the older girls go in for—

The window rings like a gong, and Pierre coughs. 'You've got
mail,' he says drily. 'You want me to read it for you?'

'What the—' A message is flooding across the screen, right-to-
left snaky script like the stuff on her corporate instrument (now
lodged safely in a deposit box in Zurich). It takes her a while to
load in a grammar agent that can handle Arabic, and another
minute for her to take in the meaning of the message. When she
does, she starts swearing, loudly and continuously.

'You *bitch,* Mom, why'd you have to go and do a thing like
that?'

The corporate instrument arrived in a huge FedEx box addressed
to Amber. It happened on her birthday while Mom was at work,
and she remembers it as if it was only an hour ago.

She remembers reaching up and scraping her thumb over the

deliveryman's clipboard, the rough feel ~~~~ microsequencers
sampling her DNA. She drags the ~~~~ inside. When she
pulls the tab on the box, it unpacks ~~ automatically, regurgi-
tating a compact 3D printer, ~~~~ a ream of paper printed in
old-fashioned dumb ink, and ~~ small calico cat with a large @-
symbol on its flank. The ~~~ hops out of the box, stretches, shakes
its head, and glares ~~ her. 'You're Amber?' it mrowls. It actually
makes real cat noises, but the meaning is clear – it's able to talk
directly to her linguistic competence interface.

'Yeah,' she says, shyly. 'Are you from *tante* 'Nette?'

'No, I'm from the fucking tooth fairy.' It leans over and head-
butts her knee, strops the scent glands between its ears all over
her skirt. 'Listen, you got any tuna in the kitchen?'

'Mom doesn't believe in seafood,' says Amber. 'It's all foreign-
farmed muck these days, she says. It's my birthday today, did I tell
you?'

'Happy fucking birthday, then.' The cat yawns, convincingly
realistic. 'Here's your dad's present. Bastard put me in hiberna-
tion and sent me along to show you how to work it. You take my
advice, you'll trash the fucker. No good will come of it.'

Amber interrupts the cat's grumbling by clapping her hands
gleefully. 'So what is it?' she demands. 'A new invention? Some
kind of weird sex toy from Amsterdam? A gun, so I can shoot
Pastor Wallace?'

'Naah.' The cat yawns, yet again, and curls up on the floor next
to the 3D printer. 'It's some kinda dodgy business model to get
you out of hock to your mom. Better be careful, though – he says
its legality is narrowly scoped jurisdiction-wise. Your mom
might be able to undermine it if she learns about how it works.'

'Wow. Like, how totally cool.' In truth, Amber is delighted
because it *is* her birthday, but Mom's at work, and Amber's home
alone, with just the TV in moral majority mode for company.
Things have gone downhill since Mom decided a modal average
dose of old-time religion was an essential part of her upbringing,
to the point that absolutely the best thing in the world *tante*
Annette could send her is some scam programmed by Daddy to

take her away. If it doesn't work, Mom will take her to church tonight, and she's certain she'll end up making a scene again. Amber's tolerance of willful idiocy is diminishing rapidly, and while building up her memetic immunity might be the real reason Mom's forcing this shit on her – it's always hard to tell with Mom – things have been tense ever since she got expelled from Sunday school for mounting a spirited defense of the theory of evolution.

The cat sniffs in the direction of the printer. 'Why doncha fire it up?' Amber opens the lid on the printer, removes the packing popcorn, and plugs it in. There's a whir and a rush of waste heat from its rear as it cools the imaging heads down to working temperature and registers her ownership.

'What do I do now?' she asks.

'Pick up the page labeled READ ME and follow the instructions,' the cat recites in a bored singsong voice. It winks at her, then fakes an exaggerated French accent: 'Le READ ME, il sont contain directions pour executing le corporate instrument dans le boit. In event of perplexity, consult the accompanying Aineko for clarification.' The cat wrinkles its nose rapidly, as if it's about to bite an invisible insect. 'Warning: Don't rely on your father's cat's opinions. It is a perverse beast and cannot be trusted. Your mother helped seed its meme base, back when they were married. *Ends.*' It mumbles on for a while. 'Fucking snotty Parisian bitch. I'll piss in her knicker drawer. I'll molt in her bidet . . .'

'Don't be vile.' Amber scans the READ ME quickly. Corporate instruments are strong magic, according to Daddy, and this one is exotic by any standards – a limited company established in Yemen, contorted by the intersection between shari'a and the global legislatosaurus. Understanding it isn't easy, even with a personal net full of subsapient agents that have full access to whole libraries of international trade law – the bottleneck is comprehension. Amber finds the documents highly puzzling. It's not the fact that half of them are written in Arabic that bothers her – that's what her grammar engine is for – or even that they're full of S-expressions and semidigestible chunks of LISP: But the company seems to assert that it exists for the sole purpose of owning chattel slaves.

'What's going on?' she asks the cat. 'What's this all about?'

The cat sneezes, then looks disgusted. 'This wasn't *my* idea, big shot. Your father is a very weird guy, and your mother hates him lots because she's still in love with him. She's got kinks, y'know? Or maybe she's sublimating them, if she's serious about this church shit she's putting you through. He thinks she's a control freak, and he's not entirely wrong. Anyway, after your dad ran off in search of another dom, she took out an injunction against him. But she forgot to cover his partner, and *she* bought this parcel of worms and sent them to you, okay? Annie is a real bitch, but he's got her wrapped right around his finger, or something. Anyway, he built these companies and this printer – which isn't hardwired to a filtering proxy, like your mom's – specifically to let you get away from her legally. *If* that's what you want to do.'

Amber fast-forwards through the dynamic chunks of the READ ME – boring legal UML diagrams, mostly – soaking up the gist of the plan. Yemen is one of the few countries to implement traditional Sunni shari'a law and a limited liability company scam at the same time. Owning slaves is legal – the fiction is that the owner has an option hedged on the indentured laborer's future output, with interest payments that grow faster than the unfortunate victim can pay them off – and companies are legal entities. If Amber sells herself into slavery to this company, she will become a slave and the company will be legally liable for her actions and upkeep. The rest of the legal instrument – about ninety percent of it, in fact – is a set of self-modifying corporate mechanisms coded in a variety of jurisdictions that permit Turing-complete company constitutions, and which act as an ownership shell for the slavery contract. At the far end of the corporate shell game is a trust fund of which Amber is the prime beneficiary and shareholder. When she reaches the age of majority, she'll acquire total control over all the companies in the network and can dissolve her slave contract; until then, the trust fund (which she essentially owns) oversees the company that owns her (and keeps it safe from hostile takeover bids). Oh, and the company network is primed by an extraordinary general meeting that instructed it to move the trust's assets to Paris immediately. A one-way airline ticket is enclosed.

'You think I should take this?' she asks uncertainly. It's hard to tell how smart the cat really is – there's probably a yawning vacuum behind those semantic networks if you dig deep enough – but it tells a pretty convincing tale.

The cat squats and curls its tail protectively around its paws. 'I'm saying nothing,' you know what I mean? You take this, you can go live with your dad. But it won't stop your ma coming after him with a horsewhip, and after you with a bunch of lawyers and a set of handcuffs. You want my advice, you'll phone the Franklins and get aboard their off-planet mining scam. In space, no one can serve a writ on you. Plus, they got long-term plans to get into the CETI market, cracking alien network packets. You want my honest opinion: You wouldn't like it in Paris after a bit. Your dad and the frog bitch, they're swingers, y'know? No time in their lives for a kid. Or a cat like me, now I think of it. They're working all day for the senator, and out all hours of night doing drugs, fetish parties, raves, opera, that kind of adult shit. Your dad dresses in frocks more than your mom, and your *tante* 'Nettie leads him around the apartment on a chain when they're not having noisy sex on the balcony. They'd cramp your style, kid. You shouldn't have to put up with parents who have more of a life than you do.'

'Huh.' Amber wrinkles her nose, half-disgusted by the cat's transparent scheming, and half-acknowledging its message. *I better think hard about this,* she decides. Then she flies off in so many directions at once that she nearly browns out the household broadband. Part of her is examining the intricate card pyramid of company structures; somewhere else, she's thinking about what can go wrong, while another bit (probably some of her wet, messy glandular biological self) is thinking about how nice it would be to see Daddy again, albeit with some trepidation. Parents aren't supposed to have sex — isn't there a law, or something? 'Tell me about the Franklins? Are they married? Singular?'

The 3D printer is cranking up. It hisses slightly, dissipating heat from the hard vacuum chamber in its supercooled work-space. Deep in its guts it creates coherent atom beams, from a bunch of Bose-Einstein condensates hovering on the edge of absolute zero. By superimposing interference patterns on them, it generates an atomic hologram, building a perfect replica of some original artifact, right down to the atomic level — there are no clunky moving nanotechnology parts to break or overheat or mutate. Something is going to come out of the printer in half an hour, something cloned off its original right down to the indi-vidual quantum states of its component atomic nuclei. The cat, seemingly oblivious, shuffles closer to the warm air exhaust ducts.

'Bob Franklin, he died about two, three years before you were born — your dad did business with him. So did your mom. Anyway, he had chunks of his *noumen* preserved and the estate trustees are trying to re-create his consciousness by cross-loading him in their implants. They're sort of a borganism, but with money and style. Anyway, Bob got into the space biz back then, with some financial wizardry a friend of your father whipped up for him, and now they're building a spacehab that they're going to take all the way out to Jupiter, where they can dismantle a couple of small moons and begin building helium-three refineries. It's that CETI scam I told you about earlier, but they've got a whole load of other angles on it for the long term. See, your dad's friends have cracked the broadcast, the one everybody knows about. It's a bunch of instructions for finding the nearest router that plugs into the galactic Internet. And they want to go out there and talk to some aliens.'

This is mostly going right over Amber's head — she'll have to learn what helium-three refineries are later — but the idea of run-ning away to space has a certain appeal. Adventure, that's what. Amber looks around the living room and sees it for a moment as a capsule, a small wooden cell locked deep in a vision of a middle America that never was — the one her mom wants to bring her up in, like a misshapen Skinner box designed to train her to be normal. 'Is Jupiter fun?' she asks. 'I know it's big and not very dense, but is it, like, a happening place? Are there any aliens there?'

'It's the first place you need to go if you want to get to meet the aliens eventually,' says the cat, as the printer clanks and disgorges a fake passport (convincingly aged), an intricate metal seal engraved with Arabic script, and a tailored wide-spectrum vaccine targeted on Amber's immature immune system. 'Stick that on your wrist, sign the three top copies, put them in the envelope, and let's get going. We've got a flight to catch, slave.'

Sadeq is eating his dinner when the first lawsuit in Jupiter orbit rolls in.

Alone in the cramped humming void of his station, he considers the plea. The language is awkward, showing all the hallmarks of a crude machine translation: The supplicant is American, a woman, and – oddly – claims to be a Christian. This is surprising enough, but the nature of her claim is, at face value, preposterous. He forces himself to finish his bread, then bag the waste and clean the platter, before he gives it his full consideration. Is it a tasteless joke? Evidently not. As the only *quadi* outside the orbit of Mars, he is uniquely qualified to hear it, and it *is* a case that cries out for justice.

A woman who leads a God-fearing life – not a correct one, no, but she shows some signs of humility and progress toward a deeper understanding – is deprived of her child by the machinations of a feckless husband who deserted her years before. That the woman was raising the child alone strikes Sadeq as disturbingly Western, but pardonable when he reads her account of the feckless one's behavior, which is pretty lax; an ill fate indeed would await any child that this man raises to adulthood. This man deprives her of her child, but not by legitimate means. He doesn't take the child into his own household or make any attempt to raise her, either in accordance with his own customs or the precepts of shari'a. Instead, he enslaves her wickedly in the mire of the Western legal tradition, then casts her into outer darkness to be used as a laborer by the dubious forces of self-proclaimed 'progress.' The same forces Sadeq has been sent to confront, as representative of the umma in orbit around Jupiter.

Sadeq scratches his short beard thoughtfully. A nasty tale, but what can he do about it? 'Computer,' he says, 'a reply to this supplicant: My sympathies lie with you in the manner of your suffering, but I fail to see in what way I can be of assistance. Your heart cries out for help before God (blessed be his name), but surely this is a matter for the temporal authorities of the dar al-Harb.' He pauses. *Or is it?* he wonders. Legal wheels begin to turn in his mind. 'If you can but find your way to extending to me a path by which I can assert the primacy of shari'a over your daughter, I shall apply myself to constructing a case for her emancipation, to the greater glory of God (blessed be his name). Ends, sigblock, send.'

Releasing the Velcro straps that hold him at the table, Sadeq floats up and kicks gently toward the forward end of the cramped habitat. The controls of the telescope are positioned between the ultrasonic clothing cleaner and the lithium hydroxide scrubbers. They're already freed up, because he was conducting a wide-field survey of the inner ring, looking for the signature of water ice. It is the work of a few moments to pipe the navigation and tracking system into the telescope's controller and direct it to hunt for the big foreign ship of fools. Something nudges at Sadeq's mind urgently, an irritating realization that he may have missed something in the woman's e-mail: There were a number of huge attachments. With half his mind he surfs the news digest his scholarly peers send him daily. Meanwhile, he waits patiently for the telescope to find the speck of light that the poor woman's daughter is enslaved within.

This might be a way in, he realizes, a way to enter dialogue with them. Let the hard questions answer themselves, elegantly. There will be no need for confrontation if they can be convinced that their plans are faulty: no need to defend the godly from the latter-day Tower of Babel these people propose to build. If this woman Pamela means what she says, Sadeq need not end his days out here in the cold between the worlds, away from his elderly parents and brother, and his colleagues and friends. And he will be profoundly grateful because, he in his heart of hearts, he knows that he is less a warrior than a scholar.

'I'm sorry, but the borg is attempting to assimilate a lawsuit,' says the receptionist. 'Will you hold?'

'Crud.' Amber blinks the Binary Betty answerphone sprite out of her eye and glances round at the cabin. 'That is *so* last century,' she grumbles. 'Who do they think they are?'

'Dr. Robert H. Franklin,' volunteers the cat. 'It's a losing proposition if you ask me. Bob was so fond of his dope there's this whole hippy group mind that's grown up using his state vector as a bong—'

'Shut the fuck up!' Amber shouts at him. Instantly contrite (for yelling in an inflatable spacecraft is a major faux pas). 'Sorry.' She spawns an autonomic thread with full parasympathetic nervous control, tells it to calm her down, then spawns a couple more to go forth and become *fuqaha,* expert on shari'a law. She realizes she's buying up way too much of the orphanage's scarce bandwidth – time that will have to be paid for in chores, later – but it's necessary. 'Mom's gone too far. This time it's war.'

She slams out of her cabin and spins right round in the central axis of the hab, a rogue missile pinging for a target to vent her rage on. A tantrum would be *good*—

But her body is telling her to chill out, take ten, and there's a drone of scriptural lore dribbling away in the back of her head, and she's feeling frustrated and angry and not in control, but not really mad anymore. It was like this three years ago when Mom noticed her getting on too well with Jenny Morgan and moved her to a new school district – she said it was a work assignment, but Amber knows better. Mom asked for it – just to keep her dependent and helpless. Mom is a control freak with fixed ideas about how to bring up a child, and ever since she lost Dad, she's been working her claws into Amber, making her upbringing a life's work – which is tough, because Amber is not good victim material, and is smart and well networked to boot. But now, Mom's found a way to fuck Amber over completely, even in Jupiter orbit, and if not for her skullware keeping a lid on things, Amber would be totally out of control.

Instead of shouting at her cat or trying to message the Franklins, Amber goes to hunt down the borg in their meat-space den.

There are sixteen borg aboard the *Sanger* – adults, members of the Franklin Collective, squatters in the ruins of Bob Franklin's posthumous vision. They lend bits of their brains to the task of running what science has been able to resurrect of the dead dot-com billionaire's mind, making him the first bodhisattva of the uploading age – apart from the lobster colony, of course. Their den mother is a woman called Monica – a willowy, brown-eyed hive queen with raster-burned corneal implants and a dry, sardonic delivery that can corrode egos like a desert wind. She's better than any of the others at running Bob, except for the creepy one called Jack, and she's no slouch when she's being herself (unlike Jack, who is *never* himself in public). Which probably explains why they elected her Maximum Leader of the expedition.

Amber finds Monica in the number four kitchen garden, performing surgery on a filter that's been blocked by toad spawn. She's almost buried beneath a large pipe, her Velcro-taped tool kit waving in the breeze like strange blue air-kelp. 'Monica? You got a minute?'

'Sure, I have lots of minutes. Make yourself helpful? Pass me the antitorque wrench and a number six hex head.'

'Um.' Amber captures the blue flag and fiddles around with its contents. Something that has batteries, motors, a flywheel counterweight, and laser gyros assembles itself – Amber passes it under the pipe. 'Here. Listen, your phone is engaged.'

'I know. You've come to see me about your conversion, haven't you?'

'Yes!'

There's a clanking noise from under the pressure sump. 'Take this.' A plastic bag floats out, bulging with stray fasteners. 'I got a bit of hoovering to do. Get yourself a mask if you don't already have one.'

A minute later, Amber is back beside Monica's legs, her face veiled by a filter mask. 'I don't want this to go through,' she says. 'I don't care what Mom says, I'm not Moslem! This judge, he can't touch me. He *can't*,' she adds, vehemence warring with uncertainty.

'Maybe he doesn't want to?' Another bag. 'Here, catch.'

Amber grabs the bag, a fraction of a second too late. She discovers the hard way that it's full of water and toadspawn. Stringy mucous ropes full of squiggling comma-shaped tadpoles explode all over the compartment and bounce off the walls in a shower of amphibian confetti. 'Eew!'

Monica squirms out from behind the pipe. 'Oh, you *didn't*.' She kicks off the consensus-defined floor and grabs a wad of absorbent paper from the spinner, whacks it across the ventilator shroud above the sump. Together they go after the toad spawn with rubbish bags and paper – by the time they've got the stringy mess mopped up, the spinner has begun to click and whir, processing cellulose from the algae tanks into fresh wipes. 'That was not good,' Monica says emphatically, as the disposal bin sucks down her final bag. 'You wouldn't happen to know how the toad got in here?'

'No, but I ran into one that was loose in the commons, one shift before last cycle-end. Gave it a ride back to Oscar.'

'I'll have a word with him, then.' Monica glares blackly at the pipe. 'I'm going to have to go back and refit the filter in a minute. Do you want me to be Bob?'

'Uh.' Amber thinks. 'Not sure. Your call.'

'All right, Bob coming online.' Monica's face relaxes slightly, then her expression hardens. 'Way I see it, you've got a choice. Your mother kinda boxed you in, hasn't she?'

'Yes.' Amber frowns.

'So. Pretend I'm an idiot. Talk me through it, huh?'

Amber drags herself alongside the hydro pipe and gets her head down, alongside Monica/Bob, who is floating with her feet near the floor. 'I ran away from home. Mom owned me – that is, she had parental rights and Dad had none. So Dad, via a proxy, helped me sell myself into slavery to a company. The company was owned by a trust fund, and I'm the main beneficiary when I reach the age of majority. As a chattel, the company tells me what to do – legally – but the shell company is set to take my orders. So I'm autonomous. Right?'

'That sounds like the sort of thing your father would do,' Monica/ Bob says neutrally. Overtaken by a sardonic middle-aged Silicon Valley drawl, her north-of-England accent sounds peculiarly mid-Atlantic.

'Trouble is, most countries don't acknowledge slavery, they just dress it up pretty and call it *in loco parentis* or something. Those that do mostly don't have any equivalent of a limited liability company, much less one that can be directed by another company from abroad. Dad picked Yemen on the grounds that they've got this stupid brand of shari'a law – and a crap human rights record – but they're just about conformant to the open legal standards protocol, able to interface to EU norms via a Turkish legislative cutout.'

'So.'

'Well, I guess I was technically a Janissary. Mom was doing her Christian phase, so that made me a Christian unbeliever slave of an Islamic company. Now the stupid bitch has gone and converted to shi'ism. Normally Islamic descent runs through the father, but she picked her sect carefully and chose one that's got a progressive view of women's rights. They're sort of Islamic fundamentalist liberal constructionists, "what would the Prophet do if he was alive today and had to worry about self-replicating chewing gum factories" and that sort of thing. They generally take a progressive view of things like legal equality of the sexes, because for his time and place the Prophet was way ahead of the ball and they figure they ought to follow his example. Anyway, that means Mom can assert that *I* am Moslem, and under Yemeni law I get to be treated as a Moslem chattel of a company. And their legal code is very dubious about permitting slavery of Moslems. It's not that I have rights as such, but my pastoral well-being becomes the responsibility of the local imam, and—' She shrugs helplessly.

'Has he tried to make you run under any new rules, yet?' asks Monica/Bob. 'Has he put blocks on your freedom of agency, tried to mess with your mind? Insisted on libido dampers or a strict dress code?'

'Not yet.' Amber's expression is grim. 'But he's no dummy. I figure he may be using Mom – and me – as a way of getting his fingers into this whole expedition. Staking a claim for jurisdiction, claim arbitration, that sort of thing. It could be worse; he might order me to comply fully with his specific implementation of shari'a. They permit implants, but require mandatory conceptual filtering: If I run that stuff, I'll end up *believing* it.'

'Okay.' Monica does a slow backward somersault in midair. 'Now tell me why you can't simply repudiate it.'

'Because.' Deep breath. 'I can do that in two ways. I can deny Islam, which makes me an apostate, and automatically terminates my indenture to the shell, so Mom owns me under US or EU law. Or I can say that the instrument has no legal standing because I was in the USA when I signed it, and slavery is illegal there, in which case Mom owns me. Or I can take the veil, live like a modest Moslem woman, do whatever the imam wants, and Mom doesn't own me – but she gets to appoint my chaperone. Oh, Bob, she has planned this *so well*.'

'Uh-huh.' Monica rotates back to the floor and looks at Amber, suddenly very Bob. 'Now you've told me your troubles, start thinking like your dad. Your dad had a dozen creative ideas before breakfast every day – it's how he made his name. Your mom has got you in a box. Think your way outside it: What can you do?'

'Well.' Amber rolls over and hugs the fat hydroponic duct to her chest like a life raft. 'It's a legal paradox. I'm trapped because of the jurisdiction she's cornered me in. I could talk to the judge,

I suppose, but she'll have picked him carefully.' Her eyes narrow. 'The *jurisdiction*. Hey, Bob.' She lets go of the duct and floats free, hair streaming out behind her like a cometary halo. 'How do I go about getting myself a new jurisdiction?'

Monica grins. 'I seem to recall the traditional way was to grab yourself some land and set yourself up as king, but there are other ways. I've got some friends I think you should meet. They're not good conversationalists and there's a two-hour lightspeed delay, but I think you'll find they've answered that question already. But why don't you talk to the imam first and find out what he's like? He may surprise you. After all, he was already out here before your Mom decided to use him to make a point.'

The *Sanger* hangs in orbit thirty kilometers up, circling the waist of potato-shaped Amalthea. Drones swarm across the slopes of Mons Lyctos, ten kilometers above the mean surface level. They kick up clouds of reddish sulphate dust as they spread transparent sheets across the barren moonscape. This close to Jupiter (a mere hundred and eighty thousand kilometers above the swirling madness of the cloudscape) the gas giant fills half the sky with a perpetually changing clock face, for Amalthea orbits the master in just under twelve hours. The *Sanger*'s radiation shields are running at full power, shrouding the ship in a corona of rippling plasma. Radio is useless, and the human miners control their drones via an intricate network of laser circuits. Other, larger drones are unwinding spools of heavy electrical cable north and south from the landing site. Once the circuits are connected, they will form a coil cutting through Jupiter's magnetic field, generating electrical current (and imperceptibly sapping the moon's orbital momentum).

Amber sighs and looks, for the sixth time this hour, at the webcam plastered on the side of her cabin. She's taken down the posters and told the toys to tidy themselves away. In another two thousand seconds, the tiny Iranian spaceship will rise above the limb of Moshtari, and then it will be time to talk to the teacher. She isn't looking forward to the experience. If he's a grizzled old blockhead of the most obdurate fundamentalist streak, she'll be in trouble. Disrespect for age has been part and parcel of the Western teenage experience for generations, and a cross-cultural thread that she's detailed to clue up on Islam reminds her that not all cultures share this outlook. But if he turns out to be young, intelligent, and flexible, things could be even worse. When she was eight, Amber audited *The Taming of the Shrew*. She finds she has no appetite for a starring role in her own cross-cultural production.

She sighs again. 'Pierre?'

'Yeah?' His voice comes from the foot of the emergency locker in her room. He's curled up down there, limbs twitching languidly as he drives a mining drone around the surface of Object Barney, as the rock has named itself. The drone is a long-legged crane fly look-alike, bouncing very slowly from toe tip to toe tip in the microgravity. The rock is only half a kilometer along its longest axis, coated brown with weird hydrocarbon goop and sulphur compounds sprayed off the surface of Io by the Jovian winds. 'I'm coming.'

'You better.' She glances at the screen. 'One twenty seconds to next burn.' The payload canister on the screen is, technically speaking, stolen. It'll be okay as long as she gives it back, Bob said, although she won't be able to do that until it's reached Barney and they've found enough water ice to refuel it. 'Found anything yet?'

'Just the usual. Got a seam of ice near the semimajor pole – it's dirty, but there's at least a thousand tons there. And the surface is crunchy with tar. Amber, you know what? The orange shit, it's solid with fullerenes.'

Amber grins at her reflection in the screen. That's good news. Once the payload she's steering touches down, Pierre can help her lay superconducting wires along Barney's long axis. It's only a kilometer and a half, and that'll only give them a few tens of kilowatts of juice, but the condensation fabricator that's also in the payload can will be able to use it to convert Barney's crust into processed goods at about two grams per second. Using designs copylefted by the free hardware foundation, inside two hundred thousand seconds they'll have a grid of sixty-four 3D printers barfing up structured matter at a rate limited only by available power. Starting with a honking great dome tent and some free nitrogen/oxygen for her to breathe, then adding a big web cache and direct high-bandwidth uplink to Earth, Amber could have her very own one-girl colony up and running within a million seconds.

The screen blinks at her. 'Oh shit! Make yourself scarce, Pierre.' The incoming call nags at her attention. 'Yeah? Who are you?'

The screen fills with a view of a cramped, very twen-cen-looking space capsule. The guy inside it is in his twenties, with a heavily tanned face, close-cropped hair and beard, wearing an olive drab space suit liner. He's floating between a TORU manual dock-ing controller and a gilt-framed photograph of the Ka'bah at Mecca. 'Good evening to you,' he says solemnly. 'Do I have the honor to be addressing Amber Macx?'

'Uh, yeah? That's me.' She stares at him. He looks nothing like her conception of an ayatollah – whatever an ayatollah is – elder-ly, black-robed, vindictively fundamentalist. 'Who are you?'

'I am Dr. Sadeq Khurasani. I hope that I am not interrupting you? Is it convenient for you that we talk now?'

He looks so anxious that Amber nods automatically. 'Sure. Did my mom put you up to this?' They're still speaking English, and she notices that his diction is good, but slightly stilted. *He isn't using a grammar engine, he actually learned the language the hard way,* she realizes, feeling a frisson of fear. 'You want to be careful how you talk to her. She doesn't lie, exactly, but she gets people to do what she wants.'

'Yes, I spoke to – ah.' A pause. They're still almost a light-second apart, time for painful collisions and accidental silences. 'I see. Are you sure you should be speaking of your mother that way?'

ACCELERANDO 149

Amber breathes deeply. '*Adults* can get divorced. If *I* could get divorced from her, I would. She's—' She flails around for the right word helplessly. 'Look, she's the sort of person who can't lose a fight. If she's going to lose, she'll try to figure how to set the law on you. Like she's done to me. Don't you see?'

Dr. Khurasani looks extremely dubious. 'I am not sure I understand,' he says. 'Perhaps, mmm, I should tell you why I am talking to you?'

'Sure. Go ahead.' Amber is startled by his attitude: He actually seems to be taking her seriously, she realizes. Treating her like an adult. The sensation is so novel – coming from someone more than twenty years old – that she almost lets herself forget that he's only talking to her because Mom set her up.

'Well, I am an engineer, in addition I am a student of *fiqh*, jurisprudence. In fact, I am qualified to sit in judgment. I am a very junior judge, but even so, it is a heavy responsibility. Anyway, your mother, peace be unto her, lodged a petition with me. Are you aware of it?'

'Yes.' Amber tenses up. 'It's a lie. Distortion of the facts.'

'Hmm.' Sadeq rubs his beard thoughtfully. 'Well, I have to find out, yes? Your mother has submitted herself to the will of God. This makes you the child of a Moslem, and she claims—'

'She's trying to use you as a weapon!' Amber interrupts. 'I sold myself into slavery to get away from her, do you understand? I enslaved myself to a company that is held in trust for my ownership. She's trying to change the rules to get me back. You know what? I don't believe she gives a shit about your religion, all she wants is me!'

'A mother's love—'

'Fuck love,' Amber snarls, 'she wants *power*.'

Sadeq's expression hardens. 'You have a foul mouth in your head, child. All I am trying to do is to find out the facts of this situation. You should ask yourself if such disrespect furthers your interests?' He pauses for a moment, then continues, less abruptly. 'Did you really have such a bad childhood with her? Do you think she did everything merely for power, or could she love you?' Pause. 'You must understand, I need to learn these things. Before I can know what is the right thing to do.'

'My mother—' Amber stops dead and spawns a vaporous cloud of memory retrievals. They fan out through the space around her mind like the tail of her cometary mind. Invoking a complex of network parsers and class filters, she turns the memories into reified images and blats them at the webcam's tiny brain so he can see them. Some of the memories are so painful that Amber has to close her eyes. Mom in full office war paint, leaning over Amber, promising to disable her lexical enhancements forcibly if she doesn't work on her grammar without them. Mom telling Amber that they're moving again, abruptly, dragging her away from school and the friends she'd tentatively started to like. The church-of-the-month business. Mom catching her on the phone to Daddy, tearing the phone in half and hitting her with it. Mom at the kitchen table, forcing her to eat – 'My mother likes *control*.'

'Ah.' Sadeq's expression turns glassy. 'And this is how you feel about her? How long have you had that level of – no, please forgive me for asking. You obviously understand implants. Do your grandparents know? Did you talk to them?'

'My grandparents?' Amber stifles a snort. 'Mom's parents are dead. Dad's are still alive, but they won't talk to him – they like Mom. They think I'm creepy. I know little things, their tax bands and customer profiles. I could mine data with my head when I was four. I'm not built like little girls were in their day, and they don't understand. You know the old ones don't like us at all? Some of the churches make money doing nothing but exorcisms for oldsters who think their kids are possessed.'

'Well.' Sadeq is fingering his beard again, distractedly. 'I must say, this is a lot to learn. But you know your mother has accepted Islam, don't you? This means that you are Moslem, too. Unless you are an adult, your parent legally speaks for you. And she says this makes you my problem. Hmm.'

'I'm not a Muslim.' Amber stares at the screen. 'I'm not a child, either.' Her threads are coming together, whispering scarily behind her eyes: Her head is suddenly dense and turgid with ideas, heavy as a stone and twice as old as time. 'I am nobody's chattel. What does your law say about people who are born with implants? What does it say about people who want to live forever? I don't believe in any *god*, Mr. Judge. I don't believe in limits. Mom can't, physically, make me *do* anything, and she sure can't speak for me. All she can do is challenge my legal status, and if I choose to stay where she can't touch me, what does that matter?'

'Well, if that is what you have to say, I must think on the matter.' He catches her eye; his expression is thoughtful, like a doctor considering a diagnosis. 'I will call you again in due course. In the meantime, if you need to talk to anyone, remember that I am always available. If there is anything I can do to help ease your pain, I would be pleased to be of service. Peace be unto you, and those you care for.'

'Same to you, too,' she mutters darkly, as the connection goes dead. '*Now* what?' she asks, as a beeping sprite gyrates across the wall, begging for attention.

'I think it's the lander,' Pierre says helpfully. 'Is it down yet?' She rounds on him. 'Hey, I thought I told you to get lost!'

'What, and miss all the fun?' He grins at her impishly. 'Amber's got a new boyfriend! Wait until I tell everybody . . .'

Sleep cycles pass; the borrowed 3D printer on Object Barney's surface spews bitmaps of atoms in quantum lock-step at its rendering platform, building up the control circuitry and skeletons of new printers. (There are no clunky nanoassemblers here, no robots the size of viruses busily sorting molecules into piles — just the bizarre quantized magic of atomic holography, modulated Bose-Einstein condensates collapsing into strange, lacy, supercold machinery.) Electricity surges through the cable loops as they slice through Jupiter's magnetosphere, slowly converting the rock's momentum into power. Small robots grovel in the orange dirt, scooping up raw material to feed to the fractionating oven. Amber's garden of machinery flourishes slowly, unpacking itself according to a schema designed by preteens at an industrial school in Poland, with barely any need for human guidance.

High in orbit around Amalthea, complex financial instruments breed and conjugate. Developed for the express purpose of facilitating trade with the alien intelligences believed to have been detected eight years earlier by SETI, they function equally well as fiscal gatekeepers for space colonies. The *Sanger*'s bank accounts in California and Cuba are looking acceptable – since entering Jupiter space the orphanage has staked a claim on roughly a hundred giga-tons of random rocks and a moon that's just small enough to creep in under the International Astronomical Union's definition of a sovereign planetary body. The borg are work-ing hard, leading their eager teams of child stakeholders in their plans to build the industrial metastructures necessary to support mining helium-three from Jupiter. They're so focused that they spend much of their time being them-selves, not bothering to run Bob, the shared identity that gives them their messianic drive.

Half a light-hour away, tired Earth wakes and slumbers in time to its ancient orbital dynamics. A religious college in Cairo is considering issues of nanotechnology: If replica-tors are used to prepare a copy of a strip of bacon, right down to the molecular level, but without it ever being part of a pig, how is it to be treated? (If the mind of one of the faithful is copied into a computing machine's memory by mapping and simulating all its synapses, is the computer now a Moslem? If not, why not? If so, what are its rights and duties?) Riots in Borneo underline the urgency of this theotechnological inquiry.

More riots in Barcelona, Madrid, Birmingham, and Marseilles also underline a rising problem: the social chaos caused by cheap anti-aging treatments. The zombie exter-minators, a backlash of disaffected youth against the formerly graying gerontocracy of Europe, insist that people who predate the supergrid and can't handle implants aren't really conscious. Their ferocity is equaled only by the anger of the dynamic septuagenarians of the baby boom, their bodies partially restored to the flush of sixties youth, but their minds adrift in a slower, less contingent century. The faux-young boomers feel betrayed, forced back into the labor pool, but unable to cope with the implant-accelerated culture of the new millennium, their hard-earned experience rendered obsolete by deflationary time.

The Bangladeshi economic miracle is typical of the age. With growth rates running at over twenty percent, cheap out-of-control bioindustrialization has swept the nation. Former rice farmers harvest plastics and milk cows for silk, while their children study mariculture and design seawalls. With cellphone ownership nearing eighty percent and literacy at ninety, the once-poor country is finally breaking out of its historical infrastructure trap and beginning to develop. In another generation, they'll be richer than Japan.

Radical new economic theories are focusing around bandwidth, speed-of-light transmission time, and the implications of CETI, communication with extraterrestrial intelligence. Cosmologists and quants collaborate on bizarre relativistically telescoped financial instruments. Space (which lets you store information) and structure (which lets you process it) acquire value while dumb mass — like gold — loses it. The degenerate cores of the traditional stock markets are in free fall, the old smokestack microprocessor and biotech/nanotech industries crumbling before the onslaught of matter replicators and self-modifying ideas. The inheritors look set to be a new wave of barbarian communicators, who mortgage their future for a millennium against the chance of a gift from a visiting alien intelligence. Microsoft, once the US Steel of the silicon age, quietly fades into liquidation.

An outbreak of green goo — a crude biomechanical replicator that eats everything in its path — is dealt with in the

Australian outback by carpet-bombing with fuel-air explosives. The USAF subsequently reactivates two wings of refurbished B-52s and places them at the disposal of the UN standing committee on self-replicating weapons. (CNN discovers that one of their newest pilots, re-enlisting with the body of a twenty-year-old and an empty pension account, first flew them over Laos and Cambodia.) The news overshadows the World Health Organization's announcement of the end of the HIV pandemic, after more than fifty years of bigotry, panic, and megadeath.

'Breathe steadily. Remember your regulator drill? If you spot your heart rate going up or your mouth going dry, take five.'

'Shut the fuck up, 'Neko. I'm trying to concentrate.' Amber fumbles with the titanium D-ring, trying to snake the strap through it. The gauntlets are getting in her way. High-orbit space suits – little more than a body stocking designed to hold your skin under compression and help you breathe – are easy, but this deep in Jupiter's radiation belt she has to wear an old Orlan-DM suit that comes in about thirteen layers. The gloves are stiff and hard to work in. It's Chernobyl weather outside, a sleet of alpha particles and raw protons storming through the void, and she really needs the extra protection. 'Got it.' She yanks the strap tight, pulls on the D-ring, then goes to work on the next strap. Never looking down, because the wall she's tying herself to has no floor, just a cutoff two meters below, then empty space for a hundred kilometers before the nearest solid ground.

The ground sings to her moronically: 'I love you, you love me, it's the law of gravity—'

She shoves her feet down onto the platform that juts from the side of the capsule like a suicide's ledge: metallized Velcro grabs hold, and she pulls on the straps to turn her body round until she can see past the capsule, sideways. The capsule masses about five tons, barely bigger than an ancient Soyuz. It's packed to overflowing with environment-sensitive stuff she'll need, and a honking great high-gain antenna. 'I hope you know what you're doing,' someone says over the intercom.

'Of course I—' She stops. Alone in this Energiya NPO surplus iron maiden with its low-bandwidth coms and bizarre plumbing, she feels claustrophobic and helpless: Parts of her mind don't work. When she was four, Mom took her down a famous cave system somewhere out West. When the guide turned out the lights half a kilometer underground, she'd screamed with surprise as the darkness had reached out and touched her. Now it's not the darkness that frightens her, it's the lack of thought. For a hundred kilometers below her there are *no* minds, and even on the surface there's only the moronic warbling of bots for company. Everything that makes the universe primate-friendly seems to be locked in the huge spaceship that looms somewhere just behind the back of her head, and she has to fight down an urge to shed her straps and swarm back up the umbilical that anchors the capsule to the *Sanger*. 'I'll be fine,' she forces herself to say. And even though she's unsure that it's true, she tries to make herself believe it. 'It's just leaving-home nerves. I've read about it, okay?'

There's a funny, high-pitched whistle in her ears. For a moment the sweat on the back of her neck turns icy cold, then the noise stops. She strains for a moment, and when it returns she recognizes the sound. The hitherto-talkative cat, curled in the warmth of her pressurized luggage can, has begun to snore.

'Let's go,' she says. 'Time to roll the wagon.' A speech macro deep in the *Sanger*'s docking firmware recognizes her authority and gently lets go of the pod. A couple of cold gas clusters pop, sending deep banging vibrations running through the capsule, and she's on her way.

'Amber. How's it hanging?' A familiar voice in her ears. She blinks. Fifteen hundred seconds, nearly half an hour gone.

'Robes-Pierre, chopped any aristos lately?'

'Heh!' A pause. 'I can see your head from here.'

'How's it looking?' she asks. There's a lump in her throat; she isn't sure why. Pierre is probably hooked into one of the smaller proximity cameras dotted around the outer hull of the big mother ship, watching over her as she falls.

'Pretty much like always,' he says laconically. Another pause, this time longer. 'This is wild, you know? Su Ang says hi, by the way.'

'Su Ang, hi,' she replies, resisting the urge to lean back and look up – up relative to her feet, not her vector – and see if the ship's still visible.

'Hi,' Ang says shyly. 'You're very brave?'

'Still can't beat you at chess.' Amber frowns. Su Ang and her overengineered algae. Oscar and his pharmaceutical factory toads. People she's known for three years, mostly ignored, and never thought about missing. 'Listen, are you going to come visiting?'

'You want us to visit?' Ang sounds dubious. 'When will it be ready?'

'Oh, soon enough.' At four kilograms per minute of structured-matter output, the printers on the surface have already built her a bunch of stuff: a habitat dome, the guts of an algae/shrimp farm, an excavator to bury it with, an airlock. Even a honey bucket. It's all lying around waiting for her to put it together and move into her new home. 'Once the borg get back from Amalthea.'

'Hey! You mean they're moving? How did you figure that?'

'Go talk to them,' Amber says. Actually, she's a large part of the reason the *Sanger* is about to crank its orbit up and out toward the other moon: She wants to be alone in coms silence for a couple of million seconds. The Franklin collective is doing her a big favor.

'Ahead of the curve, as usual,' Pierre cuts in, with something that sounds like admiration to her uncertain ears.

'You, too,' she says, a little too fast. 'Come visit when I've got the life-support cycle stabilized.'

'I'll do that,' he replies. A red glow suffuses the flank of the capsule next to her head, and she looks up in time to see the glaring blue laser line of the *Sanger*'s drive torch powering up.

* * *

Eighteen million seconds, almost a tenth of a Jupiter year, passes.

The imam tugs thoughtfully on his beard as he stares at the traffic control display. These days, every shift seems to bring a new crewed spaceship into Jupiter system: Space is getting positively crowded. When he arrived, there were fewer than two hundred people here. Now there's the population of a small city, and many of them live at the heart of the approach map centered on his display. He breathes deeply – trying to ignore the omnipresent odor of old socks – and studies the map. 'Computer, what about my slot?' he asks.

'Your slot: Cleared to commence final approach in six-nine-five seconds. Speed limit is ten meters per second inside ten kilometers, drop to two meters per second inside one kilometer. Uploading map of forbidden thrust vectors now.' Chunks of the approach map turn red, gridded off to prevent his exhaust stream damaging other craft in the area.

Sadeq sighs. 'We'll go in using Kurs. I assume their Kurs guidance is active?'

'Kurs docking target support available to shell level three.'

'Praise Allah.' He pokes around through the guidance subsystem's menus, setting up the software emulation of the obsolete (but highly reliable) Soyuz docking system. At last he can leave the ship to look after itself for a bit. He glances round. For two years he has lived in this canister, and soon he will step outside it. It hardly seems real.

The radio, usually silent, crackles with unexpected life. 'Bravo One One, this is Imperial Traffic Control. Verbal contact required, over.'

Sadeq twitches with surprise. The voice sounds inhuman, paced with the cadences of a speech synthesizer, like so many of Her Majesty's subjects. 'Bravo One One to Traffic Control, I'm listening, over.'

'Bravo One One, we have assigned you a landing slot on tunnel four, airlock delta. Kurs active, ensure your guidance is set to seven-four-zero and slaved to our control.'

He leans over the screen and rapidly checks the docking system's settings. 'Control, all in order.'

'Bravo One One, stand by.'

The next hour passes slowly as the traffic control system guides his Type 921 down to a rocky rendezvous. Orange dust streaks his one optical-glass porthole: A kilometer before touchdown, Sadeq busies himself closing protective covers, locking down anything that might fall around on contact. Finally, he unrolls his mat against the floor in front of the console and floats above it for ten minutes, eyes closed in prayer. It's not the landing that worries him, but what comes next.

Her Majesty's domain stretches out before the battered module like a rust-stained snowflake half a kilometer in diameter. Its core is buried in a loose snowball of grayish rubble, and it waves languid brittlestar arms at the gibbous orange horizon of Jupiter. Fine hairs, fractally branching down to the molecular level, split off the main collector arms at regular intervals. A cluster of habitat pods like seedless grapes cling to the roots of the massive structure. Already he can see the huge steel generator loops that climb from either pole of the snowflake, wreathed in sparking plasma, the Jovian rings form a rainbow of darkness rising behind them.

At last, the battered space station is on final approach. Sadeq watches the Kurs simulation output carefully, piping it directly into his visual field. There's an external camera view of the rock pile and grapes. As the view expands toward the convex ceiling of the ship, he licks his lips, ready to hit the manual override and go around again – but the rate of descent is slowing, and by the time he's close enough to see the scratches on the shiny metal docking cone ahead of the ship, it's measured in centimeters per second. There's a gentle bump, then a shudder, then a rippling bang as the latches on the docking ring fire – and he's down.

Sadeq breathes deeply again, then tries to stand. There's gravity here, but not much. Walking is impossible. He's about to head for the life-support panel when he freezes, hearing a noise from the far end of the docking node. Turning, he's just in time to see the hatch opening toward him, a puff of vapor condensing, and then—

Her Imperial Majesty is sitting in the throne room, moodily fidgeting with the new signet ring her equerry has designed for her. It's a lump of structured carbon massing almost fifty grams, set in a plain band of asteroid-mined iridium. It glitters with the blue-and-violet speckle highlights of its internal lasers, because in addition to being a piece of state jewelry, it is also an optical router, part of the industrial control infrastructure she's building out here on the edge of the solar system. Her Majesty wears plain black combat pants and sweatshirt, woven from the finest spider silk and spun glass, but her feet are bare: Her taste in fashion is best described as youthful, and in any event certain styles are simply impractical in microgravity. But, being a monarch, she's wearing a crown. And there's a cat, or an artificial entity that dreams it's a cat, sleeping on the back of her throne.

The lady-in-waiting (and sometime hydroponic engineer) ushers Sadeq to the doorway, then floats back. 'If you need anything, please say,' she says shyly, then ducks and rolls away. Sadeq approaches the throne, orients himself on the floor (a simple slab of black composite, save for the throne growing from its center like an exotic flower), and waits to be noticed.

'Dr. Khurasani, I presume.' She smiles at him, neither the innocent grin of a child nor the knowing smirk of an adult: merely a warm greeting. 'Welcome to my kingdom. Please feel free to make use of any necessary support services here, and I wish you a very pleasant stay.'

Sadeq holds his expression still. The queen is young – her face still retains the puppy fat of childhood, emphasized by micro-gravity moon-face – but it would be a bad mistake to consider her immature. 'I am grateful for Your Majesty's forbearance,' he murmurs, formulaic. Behind her the walls glitter like diamonds, a glowing kaleidoscope vision. It's already the biggest offshore – or off-planet – data haven in human space. Her crown, more like a compact helm that covers the top and rear of her head, also glitters and throws off diffraction rainbows, but most of its emissions are in the near ultraviolet, invisible except for the faint glowing nimbus it creates around her head. Like a halo.

'Have a seat,' she offers, gesturing: A ballooning free-fall cradle squirts down and expands from the ceiling, angled toward her, open and waiting. 'You must be tired. Working a ship all by yourself is exhausting.' She frowns ruefully, as if remembering. 'Two years is nearly unprecedented.'

'Your Majesty is too kind.' Sadeq wraps the cradle arms around himself and faces her. 'Your labors have been fruitful, I trust.'

She shrugs. 'I sell the biggest commodity in short supply on any frontier . . .' A momentary grin. 'This isn't the Wild West, is it?'

'Justice cannot be sold,' Sadeq says stiffly. Then, a moment later. 'My apologies, I mean no insult. I merely believe that while you say your goal is to provide the rule of law, what you *sell* is and must be something different. Justice without God, sold to the highest bidder, is not justice.'

The queen nods. 'Leaving aside the mention of God, I agree – I can't sell it. But I can sell participation in a just system. And this new frontier really is a lot smaller than anyone expected, isn't it? Our bodies may take months to travel between worlds, but our disputes and arguments take seconds or minutes. As long as everybody agrees to abide by my arbitration, physical enforcement can wait until they're close enough to touch. And everybody *does* agree that my legal framework is easier to comply with, better adjusted to trans-Jovian space, than any earthbound one.' A note of steel creeps into her voice, challenging. Her halo brightens, tickling a reactive glow from the walls of the throne room.

Five billion inputs or more, Sadeq marvels. The crown is an engineering marvel, even though most of its mass is buried in the walls and floor of this huge construct. 'There is law revealed by the Prophet, peace be unto him, and there is law that we can establish by analyzing his intentions. There are other forms of law by which humans live, and various interpretations of the law of God even among those who study His works. How, in the absence of the word of the Prophet, can you provide a moral compass?'

'Hmm.' She taps her fingers on the arm of her throne, and Sadeq's heart freezes. He's heard the stories from the claim jumpers and boardroom bandits, from the greenmail experts with their roots in the earthbound jurisdictions that have made such a hash of arbitration here. How she can experience a year in a minute, rip your memories out through your cortical implants, and make you relive your worst mistakes in her nightmarishly powerful simulation space. She is the *queen* – the first individual to get her hands on so much mass and energy that she could pull ahead of the curve of binding technology, and the first to set up her own jurisdiction and rule certain experiments to be legal so that she could make use of the mass/energy intersection. She has *force majeure* – even the Pentagon's infowarriors respect the Ring Imperium's autonomy for now. In fact, the body sitting in the throne opposite him probably contains only a fraction of her identity. She's by no means the first upload or partial, but she's the first gust front of the storm of power that will arrive when the arrogant ones achieve their goal of dismantling the planets and turning dumb and uninhabited mass into brainpower throughout the observable reaches of the universe. And he's just questioned the rectitude of her vision, in her presence.

The queen's lips twitch. Then they curl into a wide, carnivorous grin. Behind her, the cat sits up and stretches, then stares at Sadeq through narrowed eyes.

'You know, that's the first time in *weeks* that anyone has told me I'm full of shit. You haven't been talking to my mother again, have you?'

It's Sadeq's turn to shrug, uncomfortably. 'I have prepared a judgment,' he says slowly.

'Ah.' Amber rotates the huge diamond ring around her finger. Then she looks him in the eye, a trifle nervously. Although what he could possibly do to make her comply with any decree—

'To summarize: Her motive is polluted,' Sadeq says shortly.

'Does that mean what I think it does?' she asks.

Sadeq breathes deeply again. 'Yes, I think so.'

Her smile returns. 'And is that the end of it?' she asks.

He raises a dark eyebrow. 'Only if you can prove to me that you can have a conscience in the absence of divine revelation.'

Her reaction catches him by surprise. 'Oh, sure. That's the next part of the program. Obtaining divine revelations.'

'What! From the alien?'

The cat, claws extended, delicately picks its way down to her lap and waits to be held and stroked. It never once takes its eyes off him. 'Where else?' she asks. 'Doctor, I didn't get the Franklin Trust to loan me the wherewithal to build this castle just in return for some legal paperwork, and some, ah, interesting legal waivers from Brussels. We've known for years there's a whole alien packet-switching network out there, and we're just getting spillover from some of their routers. It turns out there's a node not far away from here, in real space. Helium-three, separate jurisdictions, heavy industrialization on Io – there is a *purpose* to all this activity.'

Sadeq licks his suddenly dry lips. 'You're going to narrowcast a reply?'

'No, much better than that: We're going to *visit* them. Cut the delay cycle down to real time. We came here to build a ship and recruit a crew, even if we have to cannibalize the whole of Jupiter system to pay for the exercise.'

The cat yawns then fixes him with a thousand-yard stare. 'This stupid girl wants to bring her conscience along to a meeting with something so smart it might as well be a god,' it says. 'And she needs to convince the peanut gallery back home that she's got one, being a born-again atheist and all. Which means, you're *it*, monkey boy. There's a slot open for the post of ship's theologian on the first starship out of Jupiter system. I don't suppose I can convince you to turn the offer down?'

5 : ROUTER

SOME YEARS LATER, TWO MEN AND A CAT ARE tying one on in a bar that doesn't exist.

The air in the bar is filled with a billowing relativistic smoke cloud – it's a stellarium, accurately depicting the view beyond the imaginary walls. Relativistic distortion skews the color toward violet around the doorway, brightening in a rainbow mist over the tables, then dimming to a hazy red glow in front of the raised platform at the back. The Doppler effect has slowly emerged over the past few months as the ship gathers momentum. In the absence of visible stellar motion – or a hard link to the ship's control module – it's the easiest way for a drunken passenger to get a feeling for how frighteningly fast the *Field Circus* is moving. Some time ago, the ship's momentum exceeded half its rest mass, at which point a single kilogram packs the punch of a multi-megaton hydrogen bomb.

A ginger-and-brown cat – who has chosen to be female, just to mess with the heads of those people who think all ginger cats are male – sprawls indolently across the wooden floorboards in front of the bar, directly beneath the bridge of the starbow. Predictably, it has captured the only ray of sunlight to be had within the starship. In the shadows at the back of the bar, two men slump at a table, lost in their respective morose thoughts: One nurses a bottle of Czech beer, the other a half-empty cocktail glass.

'It wouldn't be so bad if she is giving me some sign,' says one of them, tilting his beer bottle to inspect the bottom for sediment. 'No, that not right. It's the correct kind of attention. Am not knowing where I stand with her.'

The other one leans back in his chair, squints at the faded brown paint of the ceiling. 'Take it from one who knows,' he says. 'If you knew, you'd have nothing to dream about. Anyway, what she wants and what you want may not be the same thing.'

The first man runs a hand through his hair. Tight-curled black ringlets briefly turn silver beneath his aging touch. 'Pierre, if talent for making patronizing statements is what you get from tupping Amber—'

Pierre glares at him with all the venom an augmented nineteen-year-old can muster. 'Be glad she has no ears in here,' he hisses. His hand tightens around his glass reflexively, but the physics model in force in the bar refuses to let him break it. 'You've had too fucking much to drink, Boris.'

A tinkle of icy laughter comes from the direction of the cat. 'Shut up, you,' says Boris, glancing at the animal. He tips the bottle back, lets the dregs trickle down his throat. 'Maybe you're right. Am sorry. Do not mean to be rude about the queen.' He shrugs, puts the bottle down. Shrugs again, heavily. 'Am just getting depressed.'

'You're good at that,' Pierre observes.

Boris sighs again. 'Evidently. If our positions are reversed—'

'I know, I know, you'd be telling me the fun is in the chase and it's not the same when she kicks you out after a fight, and I wouldn't believe a word of it, being sad and single and all that.' Pierre snorts. 'Life isn't fair, Boris: Live with it.'

'I'd better go—' Boris stands.

'Stay away from Ang,' says Pierre, still annoyed with him. 'At least until you're sober.'

'Okay already, stay cool. Am consciously running watchdog thread.' Boris blinks irritably. 'Enforcing social behavior. It doesn't normally allow this drunk. Not where reputation damage are possible in public.'

He does a slow dissolve into thin air, leaving Pierre alone in the bar with the cat.

'How much longer do we have to put up with this shit?' he asks aloud. Tempers are frayed, and arguments proliferate indefinitely in the pocket universe of the ship.

The cat doesn't look round. 'In our current reference frame, we drop the primary reflector and start decelerating in another two million seconds,' she says. 'Back home, five or six megaseconds.'

'That's a big gap. What's the cultural delta up to now?' Pierre asks idly. He snaps his fingers. 'Waiter, another cocktail. The same, if you please.'

'Oh, probably about ten to twenty times our departure reference,' says the cat. 'If you'd been following the news from back home, you'd have noted a significant speed-up in the deployment of switched entanglement routers. They're having another networking revolution, only this one will run to completion inside a month because they're using dark fiber that's already in the ground.'

'Switched . . . entanglement?' Pierre shakes his head, bemused. The waiter, a faceless body in black tie and a long, starched apron, walks around the bar and offers him a glass. 'That almost sounds as if it makes sense. What else?'

The cat rolls over on her flank, stretches, claws extended. 'Stroke me, and I might tell you,' she suggests.

'Fuck you, and the dog you rode in on,' Pierre replies. He lifts his glass, removes a glacé cherry on a cocktail stick, throws it toward the spiral staircase that leads down to the toilets, and chugs back half of the drink in one go – freezing pink slush with an afterbite of caramelized hexose sugars and ethanol. The near spillage as he thumps the glass down serves to demonstrate that he's teetering on the edge of drunkenness. 'Mercenary!'

'Lovesick drug-using human,' the cat replies without rancor, and rolls to her feet. She arches her back and yawns, baring ivory fangs at the world. 'You apes – if I cared about you, I'd have to kick sand over you.' For a moment she looks faintly confused. 'I mean, I would bury you.' She stretches again and glances round the otherwise-empty bar. 'By the way, when are you going to apologize to Amber?'

'I'm not going to fucking apologize to her!' Pierre shouts. In the ensuing silence and confusion, he raises his glass and tries to drain it, but the ice has all sunk to the bottom, and the resulting coughing fit makes him spray half of the cocktail across the table. 'No way,' he rasps quietly.

'Too much pride, huh?' The cat stalks toward the edge of the bar, tail held high with tip bent over in a feline question mark. 'Like Boris with his adolescent woman trouble, too? You primates are so predictable. Whoever thought of sending a starship crewed by posthuman adolescents—'

'Go 'way,' says Pierre. 'I've got serious drinking to do.'

'To the Macx, I suppose,' puns the cat, turning away. But the moody youth has no answer for her, other than to conjure a refill from the vasty deeps.

Meanwhile, in another partition of the *Field Circus*'s reticulated reality, a different instance of the selfsame cat – Aineko by name, sarcastic by disposition – is talking to its former owner's daughter, the Queen of the Ring Imperium. Amber's avatar looks about sixteen, with disheveled blond hair and enhanced cheekbones. It's a lie, of course, because in subjective life experience, she's in her midtwenties, but apparent age signifies little in a simulation space populated by upload minds, or in real space, where posthumans age at different rates.

Amber wears a tattered black dress over iridescent purple leggings, and sprawls lazily across the arms of her informal throne – an ostentatious lump of nonsense manufactured from a single carbon crystal doped with semiconductors. (Unlike the real thing back home in Jupiter orbit, this one is merely a piece of furniture for a virtual environment.) The scene is very much the morning after the evening before, like a goth nightclub gone to seed: all stale smoke and crumpled velvet, wooden church pews, burned-out candles, and gloomy Polish avant-garde paintings. Any hint of a regal statement the queen might be making is spoiled by the way she's hooked one knee over the left arm of the throne and is fiddling with a six-axis pointing device. But these are her private quarters, and she's off duty. The regal person of the Queen is strictly for formal, corporate occasions.

'Colorless green ideas sleep furiously,' she suggests.

'Nope,' replies the cat. 'It was more like: "Greetings, earthlings, compile me on your leader."'

'Well, you got me there,' Amber admits. She taps her heel on the throne and fidgets with her signet ring. 'No damn way I'm loading some buggy alien wetware on my sweet gray stuff. *Weird* semiotics, too. What does Dr. Khurasani say?'

Aineko sits down in the middle of the crimson carpet at the foot of the dais and idly twists round to sniff her crotch. 'Sadeq is immersed in scriptural interpretations. He refused to be drawn.'

'Huh.' Amber stares at the cat. 'So. You've been carrying this lump of source code since when . . . ?'

'At the signal, for precisely two hundred and sixteen million, four hundred and twenty-nine thousand, and fifty-two seconds,' Aineko supplies, then beeps smugly. 'Call it just under seven years.'

'Right.' Amber squeezes her eyes shut. Uneasy possibilities whisper in her mind's ears. 'And it began talking to you—'

'—About three million seconds after I picked it up and ran it on a basic environment hosted on a neural network emulator modeled on the components found in the stomatogastric ganglion of a spiny lobster. Clear?'

Amber sighs. 'I wish you'd told Dad about it. Or Annette. Things could have been so different!'

'How?' The cat stops licking her arse and looks up at the queen with a peculiarly opaque stare. 'It took the specialists a decade to figure out the first message was a map of the pulsar neighborhood with directions to the nearest router on the interstellar network. Knowing how to plug into the router wouldn't help while it was three light years away, would it? Besides, it was fun watching the idiots trying to "crack the alien code" without ever wondering if it might be a reply in a language we already know to a message we sent out years ago. Fuckwits. And, too, Manfred pissed me off once too often. He kept treating me like a goddamn house pet.'

'But you—' Amber bites her lip. *But you* were, *when he bought you,* she had been about to say. Engineered consciousness is still relatively new: It didn't exist when Manfred and Pamela first hacked on Aineko's cognitive network, and according to the flat-earth wing of the AI community, it still doesn't. Even she hadn't really believed Aineko's claims to self-awareness until a couple of years ago, finding it easier to think of the cat as a zimboe – a zombie with no self-awareness, but programmed to claim to be aware in an attempt to deceive the truly conscious beings around it. 'I know you're conscious *now,* but Manfred didn't know back then. Did he?'

Aineko glares at her, then slowly narrows her eyes to slits – either feline affection, or a more subtle gesture. Sometimes Amber finds it hard to believe that, twenty-five years ago, Aineko started out as a crude neural-network-driven toy from a Far Eastern amusement factory – upgradeable, but still basically a mechanical animal emulator.

'I'm sorry. Let me start again. You actually figured out what the second alien packet was, you, yourself, and nobody else. Despite the combined efforts of the entire CETI analysis team who spent Gaia knows how many human-equivalent years of processing power trying to crack its semantics. I hope you'll pardon me for saying I find that hard to believe?'

The cat yawns. 'I could have told Pierre instead.' Aineko glances at Amber, sees her thunderous expression, and hastily changes the subject. 'The solution was intuitively obvious, just not to humans. You're so *verbal.*' Lifting a hind paw, she scratches behind her left ear for a moment then pauses, foot waving absentmindedly. 'Besides, the CETI team was searching under the streetlights while I was sniffing around in the grass. They kept trying to find primes; when that didn't work, they started trying to breed a Turing machine that would run it without immediately halting.' Aineko lowers her paw daintily. 'None of them tried treating it as a map of a connectionist system based on the only terrestrial components anyone had ever beamed out into deep space. Except me. But then, your mother had a hand in my wetware, too.'

'Treating it as a map—' Amber stops. 'You were meant to penetrate Dad's corporate network?'

'That's right,' says the cat. 'I was supposed to fork repeatedly and gang-rape his web of trust. But I didn't.' Aineko yawns. 'Pam pissed me off, too. I don't like people who try to use me.'

'I don't care. Taking that thing on board was still a really stupid risk you took,' Amber accuses.

'So?' The cat looks at her insolently. 'I kept it in my sandbox. And I got it working, on the seven hundred and forty-first attempt. It'd have worked for Pamela's bounty-hunter friends, too, if I'd tried it. But it's here, now, when you need it. Would you like to swallow the packet?'

Amber straightens out, sits up in her throne. 'I just told you, if you think I'm going to link some flaky chunk of alien neural programming into my core dialogue, or even my exocortex, you're crazy!' Her eyes narrow. 'Can it use your grammar model?'

'Sure.' If the cat was human, it would be shrugging nonchalantly at this point. 'It's safe, Amber, really and truly. I found out what it is.'

'I want to talk to it,' she says impetuously – and before the cat can reply, adds, 'So what *is* it?'

'It's a protocol stack. Basically it allows new nodes to connect to a network, by providing high-level protocol conversion services. It needs to learn how to think like a human so it can translate for us when we arrive at the router, which is why they bolted a lobster's neural network on top of it – they wanted to make it architecturally compatible with us. But there are no buried time bombs, I assure you. I've had plenty of time to check. Now, are you *sure* you don't want to let it into your head?'

Greetings from the fifth decade of the century of wonders.

The solar system that lies roughly twenty-eight trillion

kilometers — just short of three light years — behind the speeding starwhisp *Field Circus* is seething with change. There have been more technological advances in the past ten years than in the entire previous expanse of human history — and more unforeseen accidents.

Lots of hard problems have proven to be tractable. The planetary genome and proteome have been mapped so exhaustively that the biosciences are now focusing on the challenge of the phenome — plotting the phase-space defined by the intersection of genes and biochemical structures, understanding how extended phenotypic traits are generated and contribute to evolutionary fitness. The biosphere has become surreal: Small dragons have been sighted nesting in the Scottish highlands, and in the American Midwest, raccoons have been caught programming microwave ovens.

The computing power of the solar system is now around one thousand MIPS per gram, and is unlikely to increase in the near term — all but a fraction of one percent of the dumb matter is still locked up below the accessible planetary crusts, and the sapience/mass ratio has hit a glass ceiling that will only be broken when people, corporations, or other posthumans get around to dismantling the larger planets. A start has already been made in Jupiter orbit and the asteroid belt. Greenpeace has sent squatters to occupy Eros and Juno, but the average asteroid is now surrounded by a reef of specialized nanomachinery and debris, victims of a cosmic land grab unmatched since the days of the wild west. The best brains flourish in free fall, minds surrounded by a sapient aether of extensions that out-think their meaty cortices by many orders of magnitude — minds like Amber, Queen of the Inner Ring Imperium, the first self-extending power center in Jupiter orbit.

Down at the bottom of the terrestrial gravity well, there has been a major economic catastrophe. Cheap immortagens, out-of-control personality adjuvants, and a new formal theory of uncertainty have knocked the bottom out of the insurance and underwriting industries. Gambling on a continuation of the worst aspects of the human condition – disease, senescence, and death – looks like a good way to lose money, and a deflationary spiral lasting almost fifty hours has taken down huge swaths of the global stock market. Genius, good looks, and long life are now considered basic human rights in the developed world: Even the poorest backwaters are feeling extended effects from the commoditization of intelligence.

Not everything is sweetness and light in the era of mature nanotechnology. Widespread intelligence amplification doesn't lead to widespread rational behavior. New religions and mystery cults explode across the planet; much of the Net is unusable, flattened by successive semiotic jihads. India and Pakistan have held their long-awaited nuclear war: External intervention by US and EU nanosats prevented most of the IRBMs from getting through, but the subsequent spate of network raids and Basilisk attacks cause havoc. Luckily, infowar turns out to be more survivable than nuclear war – especially once it is discovered that a simple anti-aliasing filter stops nine out of ten neural-wetware-crashing Langford fractals from causing anything worse than a mild headache.

New discoveries this decade include the origins of the weakly repulsive force responsible for changes in the rate of expansion of the universe after the big bang, and on a less abstract level, experimental implementations of a Turing Oracle using quantum entanglement circuits: a device that can determine whether a given functional expression can be evaluated in finite time. It's boom time in the field of Extreme Cosmology, where some of the more recherché researchers are bickering over the possibility that the entire universe was created as a computing device, with a program encoded in the small print of the Planck constant. And theorists are talking again about the possibility of using artificial wormholes to provide instantaneous connections between distant corners of space-time.

Most people have forgotten about the well-known extraterrestrial transmission received fifteen years earlier. Very few people know anything about the second, more complex transmission received a little later. Many of those are now passengers or spectators of the *Field Circus:* a light-sail craft that is speeding out of Sol system on a laser beam generated by Amber's installations in low-Jupiter orbit. (Superconducting tethers anchored to Amalthea drag through Jupiter's magnetosphere, providing gigawatts of electricity for the hungry lasers: energy that comes in turn from the small moon's orbital momentum.)

Manufactured by Airbus-Cisco years earlier, the *Field Circus* is a hick backwater, isolated from the mainstream of human culture, its systems complexity limited by mass. The destination lies nearly three light years from Earth, and even with high acceleration and relativistic cruise speeds the one-kilogram starwhisp and its hundred-kilogram light sail will take the best part of seven years to get there. Sending a human-sized probe is beyond even the vast energy budget of the new orbital states in Jupiter system — near-lightspeed travel is horrifically expensive. Rather than a big, self-propelled ship with canned primates for passengers, as previous generations had envisaged, the starship is a Coke-can-sized slab of nanocomputers, running a neural simulation of the uploaded brain states of some tens of humans at merely normal speed. By the time its occupants beam themselves home again for download into freshly cloned bodies, a linear extrapolation shows that as much change will have overtaken human civilization as in the preceding fifty millennia — the sum total of *H. sapiens sapiens*' time on Earth.

But that's okay by Amber, because what she expects to find in orbit around the brown dwarf Hyundai $^{+4904}/_{-56}$ will be worth the wait.

* * *

Pierre is at work in another virtual environment, the one currently running the master control system of the *Field Circus*. He's supervising the sail-maintenance bots when the message comes in. Two visitors are on their way up the beam from Jupiter orbit. The only other person around is Su Ang, who showed up sometime after he arrived, and she's busy with some work of her own. The master control VM – like all the other human-accessible environments at this level of the ship's virtualization stack – is a construct modeled on a famous movie; this one resembles the bridge of a long-since-sunk ocean liner, albeit with discreetly informative user interfaces hovering in front of the ocean views outside the windows. Polished brass gleams softly everywhere. 'What was that?' he calls out, responding to the soft chime of a bell.

'We have visitors,' Ang repeats, interrupting her rhythmic chewing. (She's trying out a betel-nut kick, but she's magicked the tooth-staining dye away and will probably detox herself in a few hours.) 'They're buffering up the line already; just acknowledging receipt is sucking most of our downstream bandwidth.'

'Any idea who they are?' asks Pierre; he puts his boots up on the back of the vacant helmsman's chair and stares moodily at the endless expanse of green-gray ocean ahead.

Ang chews a bit more, watching him with an expression he can't interpret. 'They're still locked,' she says. A pause. 'But there was a flash from the Franklins, back home. One of them's some kind of lawyer, while the other's a film producer.'

'A film producer?'

'The Franklin Trust says it's to help defray our lawsuit expenses. Myanmar is gaining. They've already subpoenaed Amber's downline instance, and they're trying to bring this up in some kind of kangaroo jurisdiction – Oregon Christian Reconstructionist Empire, I think.'

'Ouch.' Pierre winces. The daily news from Earth, modulated onto a lower-powered communication laser, is increasingly bad. On the plus side, Amber is incredibly rich: The goodwill futures leveraged off her dad's trust metric means people will bend over backward to do things for her. And she owns a lot of real estate, too, a hundred gigatons of rock in low-Jupiter orbit with enough KE to power Northern Europe for a century. But her interstellar venture burns through money – both the traditional barter-indirection type and the more creative modern varieties – about the way you would if you heaped up the green pieces of paper and shoveled them onto a conveyor belt leading to the business end of a running rocket motor. Just holding off the environmental protests over deorbiting a small Jovian moon is a grinding job. Moreover, a whole bunch of national governments have woken up and are trying to legislate themselves a slice of the cake. Nobody's tried to forcibly take over yet (there are two hundred gigawatts of lasers anchored to the Ring Imperium, and Amber takes her sovereign status seriously, has even applied for a seat at the UN and membership in the EC), but the nuisance lawsuits are mounting up into a comprehensive denial of service attack, or maybe economic sanctions. And Uncle Gianni's retirement hasn't helped any, either. 'Anything to say about it?'

'Mmph.' Ang looks irritated for some reason. 'Wait your turn. They'll be out of the buffer in another couple of days. Maybe a bit longer in the case of the lawyer. He's got a huge infodump packaged on his person. Probably another semisapient class-action lawsuit.'

'I'll bet. They never learn, do they?'

'What, about the legal system here?'

'Yup.' Pierre nods. 'One of Amber's smarter ideas, reviving eleventh-century Scots law and updating it with new options on barratry, trial by combat, and compurgation.' He pulls a face and detaches a couple of ghosts to go look out for the new arrivals; then he goes back to repairing sails. The interstellar medium is abrasive, full of dust – each grain of which carries the energy of an artillery shell at this speed – and the laser sail is in a constant state of disintegration. A large chunk of the drive system's mass is silvery utility flakes for patching and replacing the soap-bubble-thin membrane as it ablates away. The skill is in knowing how best to funnel repair resources to where they're needed, while minimizing tension in the suspension lines and avoiding resonance and thrust imbalance. As he trains the patch bots, he broods about the hate mail from his elder brother (who still blames him for their father's accident), and about Sadeq's religious injunctions – *Superstitious nonsense,* he thinks – and the fickleness of powerful women, and the endless depths of his own nineteen-year-old soul.

While he's brooding, Ang evidently finishes whatever she was doing and bangs out – not even bothering to use the polished mahogany door at the rear of the bridge, just discorporating and rematerializing somewhere else. Wondering if she's annoyed, he glances up just as the first of his ghosts patches into his memory map, and he remembers what happened when it met the new arrival. His eyes widen. 'Oh *shit!*'

It's not the film producer but the lawyer who's just uploaded into the *Field Circus*'s virtual universe. Someone's going to have to tell Amber. And although the last thing he wants to do is talk to her, it looks like he's going to have to call her, because this isn't just a routine visit. The lawyer means trouble.

Take a brain and put it in a bottle. Better: Take a map of the brain and put it in a map of a bottle – or of a body – and feed signals to it that mimic its neurological inputs. Read its outputs and route them to a model body in a model universe with a model of physical laws, closing the loop. René Descartes would understand. That's the state of the passengers of the *Field Circus* in a nutshell. Formerly physical humans, their neural software (and a map of the intracranial wetware it runs on) has been transferred into a virtual machine environment executing on a honking great computer, where the universe they experience is merely a dream within a dream.

Brains in bottles – empowered ones, with total, dictatorial control over the reality they are exposed to – sometimes stop engaging in activities that brains in bodies can't avoid.

Menstruation isn't mandatory. Vomiting, angina, exhaustion, and cramp are all optional. So is meatdeath, the decomposition of the corpus. But some activities don't cease, because people (even people who have been converted into a software description, squirted through a high-bandwidth laser link, and ported into a virtualization stack) don't *want* them to stop. Breathing is wholly unnecessary, but suppression of the breathing reflex is disturbing unless you hack your hypothalamic map, and most homomorphic uploads don't want to do that. Then there's eating – not to avoid starvation, but for pleasure: Feasts on sautéed dodo seasoned with silphium are readily available here, and indeed, why not? It seems the human addiction to sensory input won't go away. And that's without considering sex, and the technical innovations that become possible when the universe – and the bodies within it – are mutable.

The public audience with the new arrivals is held in yet another movie: the Parisian palace of Charles IX, the throne room lifted wholesale from *La Reine Margot* by Patrice Chéreau. Amber insisted on period authenticity, with the realism dialed right up to eleven. It's 1572 to the hilt this time, physical to the max. Pierre grunts in irritation, unaccustomed to his beard. His codpiece chafes, and sidelong glances tell him he isn't the only member of the royal court who's uncomfortable. Still, Amber is resplendent in a gown worn by Isabelle Adjani as Marguerite de Valois, and the luminous sunlight streaming through the stained-glass windows high above the crowd of actor zimboes lends a certain barbaric majesty to the occasion. The place is heaving with bodies in clerical robes, doublets, and low-cut gowns – some of them occupied by real people. Pierre sniffs again: Someone (Gavin, with his history bug, perhaps?) has been working on getting the smells right. He hopes like hell that nobody throws up. At least nobody seems to have come as Catherine de Médicis . . .

A bunch of actors portraying Huguenot soldiers approach the throne on which Amber is seated. They pace slowly forward, escorting a rather bemused-looking fellow with long, lank hair and a brocade jacket that appears to be made of cloth-of-gold. 'His lordship, Attorney at Arms Alan Glashwiecz!' announces a flunky, reading from a parchment. 'Here at the behest of the most excellent guild and corporation of Smoot, Sedgwick Associates, with matters of legal import to discuss with Her Royal Highness!'

A flourish of trumpets. Pierre glances at Her Royal Highness, who nods gracefully, but is slightly peaky – it's a humid summer day and her many-layered robes look very hot. 'Welcome to the furthermost soil of the Ring Imperium,' she announces in a clear, ringing voice. 'I bid you welcome and invite you to place your petition before me in full public session of court.'

Pierre directs his attention to Glashwiecz, who appears to be worried. Doubtless he'd absorbed the basics of court protocol in the Ring (population all of eighteen thousand back home, a growing little principality); but the reality of it, a genuine old-fashioned *monarchy* rooted in Amber's three-way nexus of power, data, and time, always takes a while to sink in. 'I would be pleased to do so,' he says, a little stiffly, 'but in front of all those—'

Pierre misses the next bit, because someone has just goosed him on the left buttock. He starts and half turns to see Su Ang looking past him at the throne, a lady-in-waiting for the Queen. She wears an apricot dress with tight sleeves and a bodice that bares everything above her nipples. There's a fortune in pearls roped into her hair. As he notices her, she winks at him.

Pierre freezes the scene, decoupling them from reality, and she faces him. 'Are we alone now?' she asks.

'Guess so. You want to talk about something?' he asks, heat rising in his cheeks. The noise around them is a random susurrus of machine-generated crowd scenery, the people motionless as their shared reality thread proceeds independently of the rest of the universe.

'Of course!' She smiles at him and shrugs. The effect on her chest is remarkable – those period bodices could give a skeleton a cleavage – and she winks at him again. 'Oh, Pierre.' She smiles. 'So easily distracted!' She snaps her fingers, and her clothing cycles through Afghani burqua, nudity, trouser suit, then back to court finery. Her grin is the only constant. 'Now that I've got your attention, stop looking at me and start looking at *him*.'

Even more embarrassed, Pierre follows her outstretched arm all the way to the momentarily frozen Moorish emissary. 'Sadeq?'

'Sadeq *knows* him, Pierre. This guy, there's something wrong.'

'Shit. You think I don't know that?' Pierre looks at her with annoyance, embarrassment forgotten. 'I've seen him before. Been tracking his involvement for years. Guy's a front for the Queen Mother. He acted as her divorce lawyer when she went after Amber's dad.'

'I'm sorry.' Ang glances away. 'You haven't been yourself lately, Pierre. I know it's something wrong between you and the Queen. I was worried. You're not paying attention to the little details.'

'Who do you think warned Amber?' he asks.

'Oh. Okay, so you're in the loop,' she says. 'I'm not sure. Anyway, you've been distracted. Is there anything I can do to help?'

'Listen.' Pierre puts his hands on her shoulders. She doesn't move, but looks up into his eyes – Su Ang is only one-sixty tall – and he feels a pang of something odd: teenage male uncertainty about the friendship of women. *What does she want?* 'I know, and I'm sorry, and I'll try to keep my eyes on the ball some more, but I've been in my own headspace a lot lately. We ought to go back into the audience before anybody notices.'

'Do you want to talk about the problem first?' she asks, inviting his confidence.

'I—' Pierre shakes his head. *I could tell her everything,* he realizes shakily as his metaconscience prods him urgently. He's got a couple of agony-aunt agents, but Ang is a real person and a friend. She won't pass judgment, and her model of human social behavior is a hell of a lot better than any expert system's. But time is in danger of slipping, and besides, Pierre feels dirty. 'Not now,' he says. 'Let's go back.'

'Okay.' She nods, then turns away, steps behind him with a swish of skirts, and he unfreezes time again as they snap back into place within the larger universe, just in time to see the respected visitor serve the queen with a class-action lawsuit, and the Queen respond by referring adjudication to trial by combat.

Hyundai $^{+4904}/_{-56}$ is a brown dwarf, a lump of dirty hydrogen condensed from a stellar nursery, eight times as massive as Jupiter but not massive enough to ignite a stable fusion reaction at its core. The relentless crush of gravity has overcome the mutual repulsion of electrons trapped at its core, shrinking it into a shell of slush around a sphere of degenerate matter. It's barely larger than the gas giant the human ship uses as an energy source, but it's much denser. Gigayears ago, a chance stellar near miss sent it careening off into the galaxy on its own, condemned to drift in eternal darkness along with a cluster of frozen moons that dance attendance upon it.

By the time the *Field Circus* is decelerating toward it at short range – having shed the primary sail, which drifts farther out into interstellar space while reflecting light back onto the remaining secondary sail surface to slow the starwhisp – Hyundai $^{+4904}/_{-56}$ is just under one parsec distant from Earth, closer even than Proxima Centauri. Utterly dark at visible wavelengths, the brown dwarf could have drifted through the outer reaches of the solar system before conventional telescopes would have found it by direct observation. Only an infrared survey in the early years of the current century gave it a name.

A bunch of passengers and crew have gathered on the bridge (now running at one-tenth of real-time) to watch the arrival. Amber sits curled up in the captain's chair, moodily watching the gathered avatars. Pierre is still avoiding her at every opportunity, formal audiences excepted, and the damned shark and his pet hydra aren't invited, but apart from that most of the gang is here. There are sixty-three uploads running on the *Field Circus*'s virtualization stack, software copied out of meatbodies who are mostly still walking around back home. It's a crowd, but it's possible to feel lonely in a crowd, even when it's your party. And especially when you're worried about debt, even though you're a billionairess, beneficiary of the human species' biggest reputations-rating trust fund. Amber's clothing – black leggings, black sweater – is as dark as her mood.

'Something troubles you.' A hand descends on the back of the chair next to her.

She glances round momentarily, nods in recognition. 'Yeah. Have a seat. You missed the audience?'

The thin, brown-skinned man with a neatly cropped beard and deeply lined forehead slips into the seat next to her. 'It was not part of my heritage,' he explains carefully, 'although the situation is not unfamiliar.' A momentary smile threatens to crack his stony face. 'I found the casting a trifle disturbing.'

'I'm no Marguerite de Valois, but the vacant role . . . let's just say, the cap fits.' Amber leans back in her chair. 'Mind you, Marguerite had an *interesting* life,' she muses.

'Don't you mean depraved and debauched?' her neighbor counters.

'Sadeq.' She closes her eyes. 'Let's not pick a fight over absolute morality just right now, please? We have an orbital insertion to carry out, then an artifact to locate, and a dialogue to open, and I'm feeling very tired. Drained.'

'Ah – I apologize.' He inclines his head carefully. 'Is it your young man's fault? Has he slighted you?'

'Not exactly—' Amber pauses. Sadeq, whom she basically invited along as ship's theologian in case they ran into any gods, has taken up her pastoral well-being as some kind of hobby. She finds it mildly oppressive at times, flattering at others, surreal always. Using the quantum search resources available to a citizen of the Ring Imperium, he's outpublished his peers, been elected a hojetolislam at an unprecedentedly young age: His original will probably be an ayatollah by the time they get home. He's circumspect in dealing with cultural differences, reasons with impeccable logic, carefully avoids antagonizing her – and constantly seeks to guide her moral development. 'It's a personal misunderstanding,' she says. 'I'd rather not talk about it until we've sorted it out.'

'Very well.' He looks unsatisfied, but that's normal. Sadeq still has the dusty soil of a childhood in the industrial city of Yazd stuck to his boots. Sometimes she wonders if their disagreements don't mirror in miniature the gap between the early twentieth and early twenty-first centuries. 'But back to the here and now. Do you know where this router is?'

'I will, in a few minutes or hours.' Amber raises her voice, simultaneously spawning a number of search-ghosts. 'Boris! You got any idea where we're going?'

Boris lumbers round in place to face her; today he's wearing a velociraptor, and they don't turn easily in confined spaces. He snarls irritably. 'Give me some space!' He coughs, a threatening noise from the back of his wattled throat. 'Searching the sail's memory now.' The back of the soap-bubble-thin laser sail is saturated with tiny nanocomputers spaced micrometers apart. Equipped with light receptors and configured as cellular automata, they form a gigantic phased-array detector, a retina more than a hundred meters in diameter. Boris is feeding them patterns describing anything that differs from the unchanging starscape. Soon the memories will condense and return as visions of darkness in motion – the cold, dead attendants of an aborted sun.

'But where is it going to be?' asks Sadeq. 'Do you know what you are looking for?'

'Yes. We should have no trouble finding it,' says Amber. 'It looks like this.' She flicks an index finger at the row of glass windows that front the bridge. Her signet ring flashes ruby light, and something indescribably weird shimmers into view in place of the seascape. Clusters of pearly beads that form helical chains, disks and whorls of color that interlace and knot through one another, hang in space above a darkling planet. 'Looks like a

William Latham sculpture made out of strange matter, doesn't it?'

'Very abstract,' Sadeq says approvingly.

'It's alive,' she adds. 'And when it gets close enough to see us, it'll try to eat us.'

'What?' Sadeq sits up uneasily.

'You mean nobody told you?' asks Amber. 'I thought we'd briefed everybody.' She throws a glistening golden pomegranate at him, and he catches it. The apple of knowledge dissolves in his hand, and he sits in a haze of ghosts absorbing information on his behalf. 'Damn,' she adds mildly.

Sadeq freezes in place. Glyphs of crumbling stonework overgrown with ivy texture his skin and his dark suit, warning that he's busy in another private universe.

'*Hrrrr!* Boss! Found something,' calls Boris, drooling on the bridge floor.

Amber glances up. *Please, let it be the router,* she thinks. 'Put it on the main screen.'

'Are you sure this is safe?' Su Ang asks nervously.

'Nothing is safe,' Boris snaps, clattering his huge claws on the deck. 'Here. Look.'

The view beyond the windows flips to a perspective on a dusty bluish horizon: swirls of hydrogen brushed with a high cirrus of white methane crystals, stirred above the freezing point of oxygen by Hyundai $^{+4904}/_{-56}$'s residual rotation. The image-intensification level is huge – a naked human eyeball would see nothing but blackness. Rising above the limb of the gigantic planet is a small pale disk: Callidice, largest moon of the brown dwarf – or second-innermost planet – a barren rock slightly larger than Mercury. The screen zooms in on the moon, surging across a landscape battered by craters and dusted with the spume of ice volcanoes. Finally, just above the far horizon, something turquoise shimmers and spins against a backdrop of frigid darkness.

'That's it,' Amber whispers, her stomach turning to jelly as all the terrible might-have-beens dissolve like phantoms of the night around her. 'That's *it!*' Elated, she stands up, wanting to share the moment with everybody she values. 'Wake up, Sadeq! Someone get that damned cat in here! Where's Pierre? He's got to see this!'

Night and revelry rule outside the castle. The crowds are drunken and rowdy on the eve of the St. Bartholomew's Day massacre. Fireworks burst overhead, and the open windows admit a warm breeze redolent of cooked meats, woodsmoke, open sewers. Meanwhile a lover steals up a tightly spiraling stone staircase in the near dark; his goal, a prearranged rendezvous. He's been drinking, and his best linen shirt shows the stains of sweat and food. He pauses at the third window to breathe in the outside air and run both hands through his mane of hair, which is long, unkempt, and grimy. *Why am I doing this?* he wonders. This is so unlike him, this messing around—

He carries on up the spiral. At the top, an oak door gapes on a vestibule lit by a lantern hanging from a hook. He ventures inside into a reception room paneled in oak blackened by age. Crossing the threshold makes another crossover kick in by prior arrangement. Something other than his own volition steers his feet, and he feels an unfamiliar throb in his chest, anticipation and a warmth and looseness lower down that makes him cry out. 'Where are you?'

'Over here.' He sees her waiting for him in the doorway. She's partially undressed, wearing layered underskirts and a flat-chested corset that makes the tops of her breasts swell like lustrous domes. Her tight sleeves are half-unraveled, her hair disheveled. He's full of her brilliant eyes, the constriction holding her spine straight, the taste in her mouth. She's the magnet for his reality, impossibly alluring, so tense she could burst. 'Is it working for you?' she asks.

'Yes.' He feels tight, breathless, squeezed between impossibility and desire as he walks toward her. They've experimented with gender play, trying on the extreme dimorphism of this period as a game, but this is the first time they've done it this way. She opens her mouth. He kisses her, feels the warmth of his tongue thrust between her lips, the strength of his arms enclosing her waist.

She leans against him, feeling his erection. 'So this is how it feels to be you,' she says wonderingly. The door to her chamber is ajar, but she doesn't have the self-restraint to wait: The flood of new sensations – rerouted from her physiology model to his proprioceptive sensorium – has taken hold. She grinds her hips against him, pushing deeper into his arms, whining softly at the back of her throat as she feels the fullness in his balls, the tension of his penis. He nearly faints with the rich sensations of her body – it's as if he's dissolving, feeling the throbbing hardness against his groin, turning to water and running away. Somehow he gets his arms around her waist – so tight, so breathless – and stumbles forward into the bedroom. She's whimpering as he drops her on the overstuffed mattress. '*Do* it to me!' she demands. 'Do it now!'

Somehow he ends up on top of her, hose down around his ankles, skirts bundled up around her waist; she kisses him, grinding her hips against him and murmuring urgent nothings. Then his heart is in his mouth, and there's a sensation like the universe pushing into his private parts, so inside out it takes his breath away. It's hot and as hard as rock, and he wants it inside so badly, but at the same time it's an intrusion, frightening and unexpected. He feels the lightning touch of his tongue on her nipples as he leans closer, feels exposed and terrified and ecstatic as her private places take in his member. As he begins to dissolve into the universe he screams in the privacy of his own head, *I didn't know it felt like this—*

Afterward, she turns to him with a lazy smile, and asks, 'How was it for you?' Obviously assuming that, if she enjoyed it, he must have, too.

But all he can think of is the sensation of the universe thrusting into him, and of how *good* it felt. All he can hear is his father yelling – ('What are you, some kind of queer?') – and he feels dirty.

* * *

Greetings from the last megasecond before the discontinuity.

The solar system is thinking furiously at 10^{33} MIPS – thoughts bubble and swirl in the equivalent of a million billion unaugmented human minds. Saturn's rings glow with waste heat. The remaining faithful of the Latter-Day Saints are correlating the phase-space of their genome and the records of their descent in an attempt to resurrect their ancestors. Several skyhooks have unfurled in equatorial orbit around the earth like the graceful fernlike leaves of sundews, ferrying cargo and passengers to and from orbit. Small, crablike robots swarm the surface of Mercury, exuding a black slime of photovoltaic converters and the silvery threads of mass drivers. A glowing cloud of industrial nanomes forms a haze around the innermost planet as it slowly shrinks under the onslaught of copious solar power and determined mining robots.

The original incarnations of Amber and her court float in high orbit above Jupiter, presiding over the huge nexus of dumb matter trade that is rapidly biting into the available mass of the inner Jovian system. The trade in reaction mass is brisk, and there are shipments of diamond/vacuum biphase structures to assemble and crank down into the lower reaches of the solar system. Far below, skimming the edges of Jupiter's turbulent cloudscape, a gigantic glowing figure-of-eight – a five-hundred-kilometer-long loop of superconducting cable – traces incandescent trails through the gas giant's magnetosphere. It's trading momentum for electrical current, diverting it into a fly's eye grid of lasers that beam it toward Hyundai $^{+4904}/_{-56}$. As long as the original Amber and her incarnate team can keep it running, the *Field Circus* can continue its mission of discovery, but they're part of the posthuman civilization evolving down in the turbulent depths of Sol system. Part of the runaway train being dragged behind the out-of-control engine of history.

Weird new biologies based on complex adaptive matter take shape in the sterile oceans of Titan. In the frigid depths beyond Pluto, supercooled boson gases condense into impossible dreaming structures, packaged for shipping inward to the fast-thinking core.

There are still humans dwelling down in the hot depths, but it's getting hard to recognize them. The lot of humanity before the twenty-first century was nasty, brutish, and short. Chronic malnutrition, lack of education, and endemic diseases led to crippled minds and broken bodies. Now, most people multitask: Their meatbrains sit at the core of a haze of personality, much of it virtualized on stacked layers of structured reality far from their physical bodies. Wars and revolutions, or their subtle latter-day cognates, sweep the globe as constants become variables; many people find the death of stupidity even harder to accept than the end of mortality. Some have vitrified themselves to await an uncertain posthuman future. Others have modified their core identities to better cope with the changed demands of reality. Among these are beings whom nobody from a previous century would recognize as human — human/corporation half-breeds, zombie clades dehumanized by their own optimizations, angels and devils of software, slyly self-aware financial instruments. Even their popular fictions are self-deconstructing these days.

None of this, other than the barest news summary, reaches the *Field Circus*. The starwhisp is a fossil, left behind by the broad sweep of accelerating progress. But it is aboard the *Field Circus* that some of the most important events remaining in humanity's future light cone take place.

'Say hello to the jellyfish, Boris.'

Boris, in human drag, for once, glares at Pierre and grips the pitcher with both hands. The contents of the jug swirl their tentacles lazily: One of them flips almost out of solution, dislodging an impaled cocktail cherry. 'Will get you for this,' Boris threatens. The smoky air around his head is a-swirl with daemonic visions of vengeance.

Su Ang stares intently at Pierre, who is watching Boris as he raises the jug to his lips and begins to drink. The baby jellyfish – small, pale blue, with cuboid bells and four clusters of tentacles trailing from each corner – slips down easily. Boris winces momentarily as the nematocysts let rip inside his mouth, but in a moment or so the cubozoan slips down, and in the meantime his biophysics model clips the extent of the damage to his stinger-ruptured oropharynx.

'Wow,' he says, taking another slurp of sea wasp margaritas. 'Don't try this at home, fleshboy.'

'Here.' Pierre reaches out. 'Can I?'

'Invent your own damn poison,' Boris sneers – but he releases the jug and passes it to Pierre, who raises it and drinks. The cubozoan cocktail reminds him of fruit jelly drinks in a hot Hong Kong summer. The stinging in his palate is sharp but fades rapidly, producing an intimate burn when the alcohol hits the mild welts that are all this universe will permit the lethal medusa to inflict on him.

'Not bad,' says Pierre, wiping a stray loop of tentacle off his chin. He pushes the pitcher across the table toward Su Ang. 'What's with the wicker man?' He points a thumb over his back at the table jammed in the corner opposite the copper-topped bar.

'Who cares?' asks Boris. ''S part of the scenery, isn't it?'

The bar is a three-hundred-year-old brown café with a beer menu that runs to sixteen pages and wooden walls stained the color of stale ale. The air is thick with the smells of tobacco, brewer's yeast, and melatonin spray: And none of it exists. Amber dragged it out of the Franklin borg's collective memories, by way of her father's scattershot e-mails annotating her corporeal origins – the original is in Amsterdam, if that city still exists.

'*I* care who it is,' says Pierre.

'Save it,' Ang says quietly. 'I think it's a lawyer with a privacy screen.'

Pierre glances over his shoulder and glares. 'Really?'

Ang puts a restraining hand on his wrist. 'Really. Don't pay it any attention. You don't have to, until the trial, you know.'

The wicker man sits uneasily in the corner. It resembles a basket-weave silhouette made from dried reeds, dressed in a red kerchief. A glass of *doppelbock* fills the mess of tied-off ends where its right hand ought to be. From time to time, it raises the glass as if to take a mouthful, and the beer vanishes into the singular interior.

'Fuck the trial,' Pierre says shortly. *And fuck Amber, too, for naming me her public defender—*

'Since when do lawsuits come with an invisible man?' asks Donna the Journalist, blitting into the bar along with a patchy historical trail hinting that she's just come from the back room.

'Since—' Pierre blinks. 'Hell.' When Donna entered, so did Aineko, or maybe the cat's been there all the time, curled up loaf-of-bread fashion on the table in front of the wicker man. 'You're damaging the continuity,' Pierre complains. 'This universe is broken.'

'Fix it yourself,' Boris tells him. 'Everybody else is coping.' He snaps his fingers. 'Waiter!'

'Excuse me.' Donna shakes her head. 'I didn't mean to harm anything.'

Ang, as always, is more accommodating. 'How are you?' she asks politely. 'Would you like to try this most excellent poison cocktail?'

'I am well,' says Donna. A heavily built German woman – blond and solidly muscular, according to the avatar she's presenting to the public – she's surrounded by a haze of viewpoints. They're camera angles on her society of mind, busily integrating and splicing her viewpoint threads together in an endless journal of the journey. A stringer for the CIA media consortium, she uploaded to the ship in the same packet stream as the lawsuit. '*Danke*, Ang.'

'Are you recording right now?' asks Boris.

Donna sniffs. 'When am I not?' A momentary smile. 'I am only a scanner, no? Five hours, until arrival, to go. I may stop after then.' Pierre glances across the table at Su Ang's hands; her knuckles are white and tense. 'I am to avoid missing anything if possible,' Donna continues, oblivious to Ang's disquiet. 'There are eight of me at present! All recording away.'

'That's all?' Ang asks, raising an eyebrow.

'Yes, that is all, and I have a job to do! Don't tell me you do not enjoy what it is that you do here?'

'Right.' Pierre glances in the corner again, avoiding eye contact with the hearty Girl Friday wannabe. He has a feeling that if there were any hills hereabouts to animate, she'd be belting out the music. 'Amber told you about the privacy code here?'

'There is a privacy code?' asks Donna, swinging at least three subjective ghosts to bear on him for some reason – evidently he's hit an issue she has mixed feelings about.

'A privacy code,' Pierre confirms. 'No recording in private, no recording where people withhold permission in public, and no sandboxes and cutups.'

Donna looks offended. 'I would never do such a thing! Trapping a copy of someone in a virtual space to record their responses would be assault under Ring legal code, not true?'

'Your mother,' Boris says snidely, brandishing a fresh jug of iced killer jellyfish in her direction.

'As long as we all agree,' Ang interrupts, searching for accord. 'It's all going to be settled soon, isn't it?'

'Except for the lawsuit,' mutters Pierre, glancing at the corner again.

'I don't see the problem,' says Donna. 'That's just between Amber and her downlink adversaries!'

'Oh, it's a problem all right,' says Boris, his tone light. 'What are your options worth?'

'My—' Donna shakes her head. 'I'm not vested.'

'Plausible.' Boris doesn't crack a smile. 'Even so, when we go home, your credibility metric will bulge. Assuming people still use distributed trust markets to evaluate the stability of their business partners.'

Not vested. Pierre turns it over in his mind, slightly surprised.

He'd assumed that everybody aboard the ship – except, perhaps, the lawyer, Glashwiecz – was a fully vested member of the expeditionary company.

'I am not vested,' Donna insists. 'I'm listed independently.' For a moment, an almost smile tugs at her face, a charmingly reticent expression that has nothing to do with her bluff exterior. 'Like the cat.'

'The—' Pierre turns round in a hurry. Yes, Aineko appears to be sitting silently at the table with the wicker man; but who knows what's going through that furry head right now? *I'll have to bring this up with Amber,* he realizes uneasily. *I ought to bring this up with Amber* . . . 'But your reputation won't suffer for being on this craft, will it?' he asks aloud.

'I will be all right,' Donna declares. The waiter comes over. 'Mine will be a bottle of schneiderweisse,' she adds. And then, without breaking step. 'Do you believe in the singularity?'

'Am I a singularitarian, do you mean?' asks Pierre, a fixed grin coming to his face.

'Oh, no, no, no!' Donna waves him down, grins broadly, nods at Su Ang. 'I do not mean it like that! Attend: What I meant to ask was whether you in the concept of a singularity believe, and if so, where it is?'

'Is this intended for a public interview?' asks Ang.

'Well, I cannot into a simulation drag you off and expose you to an imitative reality excursion, can I?' Donna leans back as the bartender places a ceramic stein in front of her.

'Oh. Well.' Ang glances warningly at Pierre and dispatches a very private memo to scroll across his vision: *Don't play with her, this is serious.* Boris is watching Ang with an expression of hopeless longing. Pierre tries to ignore it all, taking the journalist's question seriously. 'The singularity is a bit like that old-time American Christian rapture nonsense, isn't it?' he says. 'When we all go a-flying up to heaven, leaving our bodies behind.' He snorts, reaches into thin air and gratuitously violates causality by summoning a jug of ice-cold sangria into existence. 'The rapture of the nerds. I'll drink to that.'

'But when did it take place?' asks Donna. 'My audience, they will to know your opinion be needing.'

'Four years ago, when we instantiated this ship,' Pierre says promptly.

'Back in the teens,' says Ang. 'When Amber's father liberated the uploaded lobsters.'

'Is not happening yet,' contributes Boris. 'Singularity implies infinite rate of change achieved momentarily. Future not amenable thereafter to prediction by presingularity beings, right? So has not happened.'

'*Au contraire*. It happened on June 6, 1969, at eleven hundred hours, eastern seaboard time,' Pierre counters. 'That was when the first network control protocol packets were sent from the data port of one IMP to another – the first ever Internet connection. *That's* the singularity. Since then we've all been living in a universe that was impossible to predict from events prior to that time.'

'It's rubbish,' counters Boris. 'Singularity is load of religious junk. Christian mystic rapture recycled for atheist nerds.'

'Not so.' Su Ang glances at him, hurt. 'Here we are, sixty-something human minds. We've been migrated – while still awake – right out of our own heads using an amazing combination of nano-technology and electron spin resonance mapping, and we're now running as software in an operating system designed to virtualize multiple physics models and provide a simulation of reality that doesn't let us go mad from sensory deprivation! And this whole package is about the size of a fingertip, crammed into a starship the size of your grandmother's old Walkman, in orbit around a brown dwarf just over three light years from home, on its way to plug into a network router created by incredibly ancient alien intelligences, and you can tell me that the idea of a fundamental change in the human condition is nonsense?'

'Mmph.' Boris looks perplexed. 'Would not put it that way. The *singularity* is nonsense, not uploading or—'

'Yah, right.' Ang smiles winningly at Boris. After a moment, he wilts.

Donna beams at them enthusiastically. 'Fascinating!' she

enthuses. 'Tell me, what are these lobsters you think are important?'

'They're Amber's friends,' Ang explains. 'Years ago, Amber's father did a deal with them. They were the first uploads, you know? Hybridized spiny lobster neural tissue and a heuristic API and some random mess of backward-chaining expert systems. They got out of their lab and into the net and Manfred brokered a deal to set them free, in return for their help running a Franklin orbital factory. This was way back in the early days before they figured out how to do self-assembly properly. Anyway, the lobsters insisted – part of their contract – that Bob Franklin pay to have the deep-space tracking network beam them out into interstellar space. They wanted to emigrate, and looking at what's happened to the solar system since then, who can blame them?'

Pierre takes a big mouthful of sangria. 'The cat,' he says.

'The cat—' Donna's head swivels round, but Aineko has banged out again, retroactively editing her presence out of the event history of this public space. 'What about the cat?'

'The *family* cat,' explains Ang. She reaches over for Boris's pitcher of jellyfish juice, but frowns as she does so. 'Aineko wasn't conscious back then, but later . . . when SETI@home finally received that message back, oh, however many years ago, Aineko remembered the lobsters. And cracked it wide open while all the CETI teams were still thinking in terms of von Neumann architectures and concept-oriented programming. The message was a semantic net designed to mesh perfectly with the lobster broadcast all those years ago, and provide a high-level interface to a communications network we're going to visit.' She squeezes Boris's fingertips. 'SETI@home logged these coordinates as the origin of the transmission, even though the public word was that the message came from a whole lot farther away – they didn't want to risk a panic if people knew there were aliens on our cosmic doorstep. Anyway, once Amber got established, she decided to come visiting. Hence this expedition. Aineko created a virtual lobster and interrogated the ET packet, hence the communications channel we're about to open.'

'Ah, this is all a bit clearer now,' says Donna. 'But the law-suit—' She glances at the hollow wicker man in the corner.

'Well, there we have a problem,' Ang says diplomatically.

'No,' says Pierre. '*I* have a problem. And it's all Amber's fault.'

'Hmm?' Donna stares at him. 'Why blame the Queen?'

'Because she's the one who picked the lunar month to be the reporting time period for companies in her domain, and specified trial by combat for resolving corporate conflicts,' he grumbles. 'And *compurgation,* but that's not applicable to this case because there isn't a recognized reputation server within three light years. Trial by combat, for civil suits in this day and age! And she appointed me her champion.' *In the most traditional way imaginable,* he remembers with a warm frisson of nostalgia. He'd been hers in body and soul before that disastrous experiment. He isn't sure whether it still applies, but – 'I've got to take on this lawsuit on her behalf, in adversarial stance.'

He glances over his shoulder. The wicker man sits there placidly, pouring beer down his invisible throat like a tired farm laborer.

'Trial by combat,' Su Ang explains to Donna's perplexed ghost-swarm, which is crawling all over the new concept in a haze of confusion. 'Not physical combat, but a competition of ability. It seemed like a good idea at the time, to keep junk litigants out of the Ring Imperium, but the Queen Mother's lawyers are *very* persistent. Probably because it's taken on something of a grudge-match quality over the years. I don't think Pamela cares much anymore, but this ass-hat lawyer has turned it into a personal cru-sade. I don't think he liked what happened when the music Mafiya caught up with him. But there's a bit more to it, because if he wins, he gets to own everything. And I mean *everything.*'

Ten million kilometers out and Hyundai $^{+4904}/_{-56}$ looms beyond the parachute-shaped sail of the *Field Circus* like a rind of dark-ness bitten out of the edge of the universe. Heat from the gravitational contraction of its core keeps it warm, radiating at six hundred degrees absolute, but the paltry emission does nothing to break the eternal ice that grips Callidice, Iambe, Celeus, and Metaneira, the stillborn planets locked in orbit around the brown dwarf.

Planets aren't the only structures that orbit the massive sphere of hydrogen. Close in, skimming the cloud tops by only twenty thousand kilometers, Boris's phased-array eye has blinked at something metallic and hot. Whatever it is, it orbits out of the ecliptic plane traced by the icy moons, and in the wrong direction. Farther out, a speckle of reflected emerald laser light picks out a gaudy gem against the starscape: their destination, the router.

'That's it,' says Boris. His body shimmers into humanity, retconning the pocket universe of the bridge into agreeing that he's been present in primate form all along. Amber glances sideways. Sadeq is still wrapped in ivy, his skin the texture of weathered limestone. 'Closest approach is sixty-three light seconds, due in eight hundred thousand. Can give you closer contact if we maneuver, but will take time to achieve a stable orbit.'

Amber nods thoughtfully, sending copies of herself out to work the mechanics. The big light sail is unwieldy, but can take advantage of two power sources: the original laser beam from Jupiter and its reflection bouncing off the now-distant primary light sail. The temptation is to rely on the laser for constant acceleration, to just motor on in and squat on the router's cosmic doorstep. But the risk of beam interruption is too dangerous. It's happened before, for seconds to minutes at a time, on six occasions during the voyage so far. She's not sure what causes the beam downtime (Pierre has a theory about Oort cloud objects occulting the laser, but she figures it's more likely to be power cuts back at the Ring), but the consequences of losing power while maneuvering deep in a quasi-stellar gravity well are much more serious than a transient loss of thrust during free interstellar flight. 'Let's just play it safe,' she says. 'We'll go for a straight orbital insertion and steady cranking after that. We've got enough gravity wells to play pinball with. I don't want us on a free-flight trajectory that entails lithobraking if we lose power and can't get the sail back.'

'Very prudent,' Boris agrees. 'Marta, work on it.' A buzzing presence of not-insects indicates that the heteromorphic helmswoman is on the job. 'I think we should be able to take our first close-in look in about two million seconds, but if you want I can ping it now . . . ?'

'No need for protocol analysis,' Amber says casually. 'Where's – ah, there you are.' She reaches down and picks up Aineko, who twists round sinuously and licks her arm with a tongue like sand-paper. 'What do *you* think?'

'Do you want fries with that?' asks the cat, focusing on the artifact at the center of the main screen in front of the bridge.

'No, I just want a conversation,' says Amber.

'Well, okay.' The cat dims, moves jerkily, sucking up local processing power so fast that it disturbs the local physics model. 'Opening port now.'

A subjective minute or two passes. 'Where's Pierre?' Amber asks herself quietly. Some of the maintenance metrics she can read from her privileged viewpoint are worrying. The *Field Circus* is running at almost eighty percent of utilization. Whatever Aineko is doing in order to establish the interface to the router, it's taking up an awful lot of processing power and bandwidth. 'And where's the bloody lawyer?' she adds, almost as an after-thought.

The *Field Circus* is small, but its light sail is highly control-lable. Aineko takes over a cluster of cells in its surface, turning them from straight reflectors into phase-conjugate mirrors. A small laser on the ship's hull begins to flicker thousands of times a second, and the beam bounces off the modified seg-ment of mirror, focusing to a coherent point right in front of the distant blue dot of the router. Aineko ramps up the modu-lation frequency, adds a bundle of channels using different wavelengths, and starts feeding out a complex set of pre-planned signals that provide an encoding format for high-level data.

'Leave the lawyer to me.' She starts, glancing sideways to see Sadeq watching her. He smiles without showing his teeth. 'Lawyers do not mix with diplomacy,' he explains.

'Huh.' Ahead of them, the router is expanding. Strings of nacreous spheres curl in strange loops around a hidden core, expanding and turning inside out in systolic pulses that spawn waves of recomplication through the structure. A loose red speckle of laser light stains one arm of beads; suddenly it flares up brilliantly, reflecting data back at the ship. 'Ah!'

'Contact,' purrs the cat. Amber's fingertips turn white where she grips the arms of her chair.

'What does it say?' she asks, quietly.

'What do *they* say,' corrects Aineko. 'It's a trade delegation, and they're uploading right now. I can use that negotiation network they sent us to give them an interface to our systems if you want.'

'Wait!' Amber half stands in sudden nervousness. 'Don't give them free access! What are you thinking of? Stick them in the throne room, and we'll give them a formal audience in a couple of hours.' She pauses. 'That network layer they sent through. Can you make it accessible to us, use it to give us a translation layer into their grammar-mapping system?'

The cat looks round, thumps her tail irritably. 'You'd do better loading the network yourself—'

'I don't want *anybody* on this ship running alien code before we've vetted it thoroughly,' she says urgently. 'In fact, I want them bottled up in the Louvre grounds, just as thoroughly as we can, and I want them to come to us through our own linguistic bottleneck. Got that?'

'Clear,' Aineko grumbles.

'A trade delegation,' Amber thinks aloud. 'What would Dad make of that?'

One moment he's in the bar, shooting bull with Su Ang and Donna the Journalist's ghost and a copy of Boris; the next he's abruptly precipitated into a very different space.

Pierre's heart seems to tumble within his rib cage, but he forces himself to stay calm as he glances around the dim, oak-paneled chamber. This is wrong, so wrong that it signifies either a major systems crash or the application of frightening privilege levels to his realm. The only person aboard who's entitled to those privileges is—

'Pierre?'

She's behind him. He turns angrily. 'Why did you drag me in here? Don't you know it's rude to—'

'Pierre.'

He stops and looks at Amber. He can't stay angry at her for long, not to her face. She's not dumb enough to bat her eyelashes at him, but she's disarmingly cute for all that. Nevertheless, something inside him feels shriveled and *wrong* in her presence. 'What is it?' he says, curtly.

'I don't know why you've been avoiding me.' She starts to take a step forward, then stops and bites her lip. *Don't do this to me!* he thinks. 'You know it hurts?'

'Yes.' That much of an admission hurts him, too. He can hear his father yelling over his shoulder, the time he found him with Laurent, elder brother. It's a choice between Père or Amber, but it's not a choice he wants to make. *The shame.* 'I didn't – I have some issues.'

'It was the other night?'

He nods. *Now* she takes a step forward. 'We can talk about it, if you want. Whatever you want,' she says. And she leans toward him, and he feels his resistance crumbling. He reaches out and hugs her, and she wraps her arms around him and leans her chin on his shoulder, and this doesn't feel wrong. How can anything this good be bad?

'It made me uncomfortable,' he mumbles into her hair. 'Need to sort myself out.'

'Oh, Pierre.' She strokes the down at the back of his neck. 'You should have said. We don't have to do it that way if you don't want to.'

How to tell her how hard it is to admit that anything's wrong?

Ever? 'You didn't drag me here to tell me that,' he says, implicitly changing the subject.

Amber lets go of him, backs away almost warily. 'What is it?' she asks.

'Something's wrong?' he half asks, half asserts. 'Have we made contact yet?'

'Yeah,' she says, pulling a face. 'There's an alien trade delegation in the Louvre. That's the problem.'

'An alien trade delegation.' He rolls the words around the inside of his mouth, tasting them. They feel paradoxical, cold and slow after the hot words of passion he's been trying to avoid uttering. It's his fault for changing the subject.

'A trade delegation,' says Amber. 'I should have anticipated. I mean, we were going to go through the router ourselves, weren't we?'

He sighs. 'We thought we were going to do that.' A quick prod at the universe's controls determines that he has certain capabilities. He invokes an armchair, sprawls across it. 'A network of point-to-point wormholes linking routers, self-replicating communication hubs, in orbit around most of the brown dwarfs of the galaxy. That's what the brochure said, right? That's what we expected. Limited bandwidth, not a lot of use to a mature superintelligence that has converted the free mass of its birth solar system into computronium, but sufficient to allow it to hold conversations with its neighbors. Conversations carried out via a packet-switched network in real time, not limited by the speed of light, but bound together by a common reference frame and the latency between network hops.'

'That's about the size of it,' she agrees from the carved-ruby throne beside him. 'Except there's a trade delegation waiting for us. In fact, they're coming aboard already. And I don't buy it – something about the whole setup stinks.'

Pierre's brow wrinkles. 'You're right, it doesn't make sense,' he says, finally. 'Doesn't make sense at all.'

Amber nods. 'I carry a ghost of Dad around. He's really upset about it.'

'Listen to your old man.' Pierre's lips quirk humorlessly. 'We were going to jump through the looking glass, but it seems someone has beaten us to the punch. Question is why?'

'I don't like it.' Amber reaches out sideways, and he catches her hand. 'And then there's the lawsuit. We have to hold the trial sooner rather than later.'

He lets go of her fingers. 'I'd really be much happier if you hadn't named me as your champion.'

'Hush.' The scenery changes; her throne is gone, and instead she's sitting on the arm of his chair, almost on top of him. 'Listen. I had a good reason.'

'Reason?'

'You have choice of weapons. In fact, you have the choice of the field. This isn't just "hit 'em with a sword until they die" time.' She grins, impishly. 'The whole point of a legal system that mandates trial by combat for commercial lawsuits, as opposed to an adjudication system, is to work out who's a fitter servant of society and hence deserving of preferential treatment. It's crazy to apply the same legal model to resolving corporate disputes that we use for arguments among people, especially as most companies are now software abstractions of business models; the interests of society are better served by a system that encourages efficient trade activity than by one that encourages litigation. It cuts down on corporate bullshit while encouraging the toughest ones to survive, which is why I *was* going to set up the trial as a contest to achieve maximum competitive advantage in a xenocommerce scenario. Assuming they really *are* traders, I figure we have more to trade with them than some damn lawyer from the depths of earth's light cone.'

Pierre blinks. 'Um.' Blinks again. 'I thought you wanted me to sideload some kind of fencing kinematics program and *skewer* the guy?'

'Knowing how well I know you, why did you ever think that?' She slides down the arm of his chair and lands on his lap. She twists round to face him in point-blank close-up. 'Shit, Pierre, I *know* you're not some kind of macho psychopath!'

'But your mother's lawyers—'

She shrugs dismissively. 'They're *lawyers*. Used to dealing with precedents. Best way to fuck with their heads is to change the way the universe works.' She leans against his chest. 'You'll make mincemeat of them. Profit-to-earnings ratio through the roof, blood on the stock exchange floor.' His hands meet around the small of her back. 'My hero!'

The Tuileries are full of confused lobsters.

Aineko has warped this virtual realm, implanting a symbolic gateway in the carefully manicured gardens outside. The gateway is about two meters in diameter, a verdigris-coated orouborous loop of bronze that sits like an incongruous archway astride a gravel path in the grounds. Giant black lobsters – each the size of a small pony – shuffle out of the loop's baby blue buffer field, antennae twitching. They wouldn't be able to exist in the real world, but the physics model here has been amended to permit them to breathe and move, by special dispensation.

Amber sniffs derisively as she enters the great reception room of the Sully wing. 'Can't trust that cat with anything,' she mutters.

'It was your idea, wasn't it?' asks Su Ang, trying to duck past the zombie ladies-in-waiting who carry Amber's train. Soldiers line the passage to either side, forming rows of steel to let the Queen pass unhindered.

'To let the cat have its way, yes.' Amber is annoyed. 'But I didn't mean to let it wreck the continuity! I won't have it!'

'I never saw the point of all this medievalism, before,' Ang observes. 'It's not as if you can avoid the singularity by hiding in the past.' Pierre, following the Queen at a distance, shakes his head, knowing better than to pick a fight with Amber over her idea of stage scenery.

'It looks good,' Amber says tightly, standing before her throne and waiting for the ladies-in-waiting to arrange themselves before her. She sits down carefully, her back straight as a ruler, voluminous skirts belling up. Her dress is an intricate piece of sculpture that uses the human body within as a support. 'It impresses the yokels and looks convincing on narrowcast media. It provides a prefabricated sense of tradition. It hints at the political depths of fear and loathing intrinsic to my court's activities and tells people not to fuck with me. It reminds us where we've come from . . . and it doesn't give away *anything* about where we're going.'

'But that doesn't make any difference to a bunch of alien lobsters,' points out Su Ang. 'They lack the reference points to understand it.' She moves to stand behind the throne. Amber glances at Pierre, waves him over.

Pierre glances around, seeking real people, not the vacant eigenfaces of the zombies that give this scenery added biological texture. There in the red gown, isn't that Donna the Journalist? And over there, too, with shorter hair and wearing male drag; she gets everywhere. That's Boris, sitting behind the bishop.

'*You* tell her,' Ang implores him.

'I can't,' he admits. 'We're trying to establish communication, aren't we? But we don't want to give too much away about what we are, how we think. A historical distancing act will keep them from learning too much about us. The phase-space of technological cultures that could have descended from these roots is too wide to analyze easily. So we're leaving them with the lobster translators and not giving anything away. Try to stay in character as a fifteenth-century duchess from Albì – it's a matter of national security.'

'Humph.' Ang frowns as a flunky hustles forward to place a folding chair behind her. She turns to face the expanse of red-and-gold carpet that stretches to the doorway as trumpets blat and the doors swing open to admit the deputation of lobsters.

The lobsters are as large as wolves, black and spiny and ominous. Their monochrome carapaces are at odds with the brightly colored garb of the human crowd. Their antennae are large and sharp as swords. But for all that they advance hesitantly, eye turrets swiveling from side to side as they take the scene in. Their tails drag ponderously on the carpet, but they have no trouble standing.

The first of the lobsters halts short of the throne and angles itself to train an eye on Amber. 'Am inconsistent,' it complains. 'There is no liquid hydrogen monoxide here, and you-species am misrepresented by initial contact. Inconsistency, explain?'

'Welcome to the human physical space-traveling interface unit *Field Circus*,' Amber replies calmly. 'I am pleased to see your translator is working adequately. You are correct, there is no water here. The lobsters don't normally need it when they visit us. And we humans are not water-dwellers. May I ask who you are when you're not wearing borrowed lobster bodies?'

Confusion. The second lobster rears up and clatters its long, armored antennae together. Soldiers to either side tighten their grips on their spears, but it drops back down again soon enough.

'We are the Wunch,' announces the first lobster, speaking clearly. 'This is a body-compliant translation layer. Based on map received from yourspace, units forty thousand trillion light-kilometers ago?'

'*He means twenty years,*' Pierre whispers on a private channel Amber has multicast for the other real humans in the audience chamber reality. '*They've confused space and time for measurement purposes. Does this tell us something?*'

'*Relatively little,*' comments someone else – Chandra? A round of polite laughter greets the joke, and the tension in the room eases slightly.

'We are the Wunch,' the lobster repeats. 'We come to exchange interest. What have you got that we want?'

Faint frown lines appear on Amber's forehead. Pierre can see her thinking very rapidly. 'We consider it impolite to ask,' she says quietly.

Clatter of claws on underlying stone floor. Chatter of clicking mandibles. 'You accept our translation?' asks the leader.

'Are you referring to the transmission you sent us, uh, thirty thousand trillion light-kilometers behind?' asks Amber.

The lobster bobs up and down on its legs. 'True. We send.'

'We cannot integrate that network,' Amber replies blandly, and Pierre forces himself to keep a straight face. (Not that the

lobsters can read human body language yet, but they'll undoubt-
edly be recording everything that happens here for future
analysis.) 'They come from a radically different species. Our goal
in coming here is to connect our species to the network. We wish
to exchange advantageous information with many other species.'

Concern, alarm, agitation. 'You cannot do that! You are not
untranslatable entity signifier.'

Amber raises a hand. 'You said *untranslatable entity signifier*. I
did not understand that. Can you paraphrase?'

'We, like you, are not *untranslatable entity signifier*. The network
is for *untranslatable entity signifier*. We are to the *untranslatable concept #1* as a single-celled organism is to ourselves. You and we
cannot *untranslatable concept #2*. To attempt trade with *untranslatable entity signifier* is to invite death or transition to *untranslatable
concept #1*.'

Amber snaps her fingers: Time freezes. She glances round at Su
Ang, Pierre, the other members of her primary team. 'Opinions,
anyone?'

Aineko, hitherto invisible, sits up on the carpet at the foot of
the dais. 'I'm not sure. The reason those macros are tagged is that
there's something wrong with their semantics.'

'Wrong with – how?' asks Su Ang.

The cat grins, cavernously, and begins to fade. 'Wait!' snaps
Amber.

Aineko continues her fade, but leaves a shimmering presence
behind: not a grin, but a neural network weighting map, three-
dimensional and incomprehensibly complicated. 'The
untranslatable entity concept #1 when mapped onto the lobster's
grammar network has elements of "god" overloaded with attri-
butes of mysticism and zenlike incomprehensibility. But I'm
pretty sure that what it *really* means is "optimized conscious
upload that runs much faster than real time." A type-one weakly
superhuman entity, like, um, the folks back home. The implica-
tion is that this Wunch wants us to view them as gods.' The cat
fades back in. 'Any takers?'

'Small-town hustlers,' mutters Amber. 'Talking big – or using a dodgy metagrammar that makes them sound bigger than they are – to bilk the hayseeds new to the big city.'

'Most likely.' Aineko turns and begins to wash her flank.

'What are we going to do?' asks Su Ang.

'Do?' Amber raises a pencil-lined eyebrow, then flashes a grin that chops a decade off her apparent age. 'We're going to mess with their heads!' She snaps her fingers again and time unfreezes. There's no change in continuity except that Aineko is still present, at the foot of the throne. The cat looks up and gives the queen a dirty look. 'We understand your concern,' Amber says smoothly, 'but we have already given you the physiology models and neural architecture of the bodies that you are wearing. We want to communicate. Why won't you show us your real selves or your real language?'

'This is trade language!' protests Lobster Number One. 'Wunch am/are metabolically variable coalition from number of worlds. No uniformity of interface. Easiest to conform to one plan and speak one tongue optimized for your comprehension.'

'Hmm.' Amber leans forward. 'Let me see if I understand you. You are a coalition of individuals from a number of species. You prefer to use the common user interface model we sent you, and offered us the language module you're using for an exchange? And you want to trade with us.'

'Exchange interest,' the Wunch emphasizes, bouncing up and down on its legs. 'Can offer much! Sense of identity of a thousand civilizations. Safe tunnels to a hundred archives on the net suitable for beings who are not *untranslatable entity signifier*. Able to control risks of communication. Have technique of manipulating matter at molecular level. Solution to algorithmic iterated systems based on quantum entanglement.'

'*Old-fashioned nanotechnology and shiny beads to dazzle the primitives,*' Pierre mutters on Amber's multicast channel. '*How backward do they think we are?*'

'*The physics model in here is really overdone,*' comments Boris. '*They may even think this is real, that we're primitives coat-tailing it on the back of the lobsters' efforts.*'

Amber forces a smile. 'That is most interesting!' she trills at the Wunch's representatives. 'I have appointed two representatives who will negotiate with you; this is an internal contest within my own court. I commend to you Pierre Naqet, my own commercial representative. In addition, you may want to deal with Alan Glashwiecz, an independent factor who is not currently present. Others may come forward in due course if that is acceptable.'

'It pleases us,' says Lobster Number One. 'We are tired and disoriented by the long journey through gateways to this place. Request resumption of negotiations later?'

'By all means.' Amber nods. A sergeant-at-arms, a mindless but impressive zimboe controlled by her spider's nest of personality threads, blows a sharp note on his trumpet. The first audience is at an end.

Outside the light cone of the *Field Circus,* on the other side of the spacelike separation between Amber's little kingdom in motion and the depths of empire time that grip the solar system's entangled quantum networks, a singular new reality is taking shape.

Welcome to the moment of maximum change.

About ten billion humans are alive in the solar system, each mind surrounded by an exocortex of distributed agents, threads of personality spun right out of their heads to run on the clouds of utility fog — infinitely flexible computing resources as thin as aerogel — in which they live. The foggy depths are alive with high-bandwidth sparkles; most of Earth's biosphere has been wrapped in cotton wool and preserved for future examination. For every living human, a thousand million software agents carry information into the farthest corners of the consciousness address space.

The sun, for so long an unremarkable mildly variable G2 dwarf, has vanished within a gray cloud that englobes it except for a narrow belt around the plane of the ecliptic.

Sunlight falls, unchanged, on the inner planets: except for Mercury, which is no longer present, having been dismantled completely and turned into solar-powered high-temperature nanocomputers. A much fiercer light falls on Venus, now surrounded by glittering ferns of carbon crystals that pump angular momentum into the barely spinning planet via huge superconducting loops wound around its equator. This planet, too, is due to be dismantled. Jupiter, Neptune, Uranus – all sprout rings as impressive as Saturn's. But the task of cannibalizing the gas giants will take many times longer than the small rocky bodies of the inner system.

The ten billion inhabitants of this radically changed star system remember being human; almost half of them predate the millennium. Some of them still *are* human, untouched by the drive of metaevolution that has replaced blind Darwinian change with a goal-directed teleological progress. They cower in gated communities and hill forts, mumbling prayers and cursing the ungodly meddlers with the natural order of things. But eight out of every ten living humans are included in the phase-change. It's the most inclusive revolution in the human condition since the discovery of speech.

A million outbreaks of gray goo – runaway nanoreplicator excursions – threaten to raise the temperature of the biosphere dramatically. They're all contained by the planetary-scale immune system fashioned from what was once the World Health Organization. Weirder catastrophes threaten the boson factories in the Oort cloud. Antimatter factories hover over the solar poles. Sol system shows all the symptoms of a runaway intelligence excursion, exuberant blemishes as normal for a technological civilization as skin problems on a human adolescent.

The economic map of the planet has changed beyond recognition. Both capitalism and communism, bickering ideological children of a protoindustrial outlook, are as obsolete as the divine right of kings. Companies are alive, and dead people may live again, too. Globalism and tribalism have run to completion, diverging respectively into homogeneous interoperability and the Schwarzschild radius of insularity. Beings that remember being human plan the deconstruction of Jupiter, the creation of a great simulation space that will expand the habitat available within the solar system. By converting all the nonstellar mass of the solar system into processors, they can accommodate as many human-equivalent minds as a civilization with a planet hosting ten billion humans in orbit around every star in the galaxy.

A more mature version of Amber lives down in the surging chaos of near-Jupiter space; there's an instance of Pierre, too, although he has relocated light-hours away, near Neptune. Whether she still sometimes thinks of her relativistic twin, nobody can tell. In a way, it doesn't matter, because by the time the *Field Circus* returns to Jupiter orbit, as much subjective time will have elapsed for the fast-thinkers back home as will flash by in the real universe between this moment and the end of the era of star formation, many billions of years hence.

'As your theologian, I am telling you that they are not gods.'

Amber nods patiently. She watches Sadeq closely.

Sadeq coughs grumpily. 'Tell her, Boris.'

Boris tilts his chair back and turns it toward the Queen. 'He is right, Amber. They are traders, and not clever ones, either. Is hard to get handle on their semiotics while they hide behind the lobster model we uploaded in their direction twenty years ago, but are certainly not crusties, and are definite not human either. Or transhuman. My guess, they are bunch of dumb hicks who get hands on toys left behind by much smarter guys. Like the rejectionist factions back home. Imagine they are waking up one morning and find everyone else is gone to the great upload

environment in the sky. Leaving them with the planet to themselves. What you think they do with whole world, with any
gadgets they trip over? Some will smash everything they come
across, but others not so stupid. But they think *small*. Scavengers,
deconstructionists. Their whole economic outlook are negative-
sum game. Go visit aliens to rip them off, take ideas, not expand
selves and transcend.'

Amber stands up, walks toward the windows at the front of
the bridge. In black jeans and chunky sweater, she barely resembles the feudal queen whose role she plays for tourists. 'Taking
them on board was a big risk. I'm not happy about it.'

'How many angels can dance on the head of a pin?' Sadeq
smiles crookedly. 'We have an answer. But they may not even
realize they are dancing with us. These are not the gods you were
afraid of finding.'

'No.' Amber sighs. 'Not too different from us, though. I mean,
we aren't exactly well adapted to this environment, are we? We
tote these body-images along, rely on fake realities that we can
map into our human-style senses. We're emulations, not native
AIs. Where's Su Ang?'

'I can find her.' Boris frowns.

'I asked her to analyze the alien's arrival times,' Amber adds as
an afterthought. 'They're close – too close. And they showed up
too damn fast when we first tickled the router. I think Aineko's
theories are flawed. The *real* owners of this network we've
plugged into probably use much higher-level protocols to communicate; sapient packets to build effective communications
gateways. This Wunch, they probably lurk in wait for newbies to
exploit. Pedophiles hiding outside the school gate. I don't want to
give them that opportunity before we make contact with the real
thing!'

'You may have little choice,' says Sadeq. 'If they are without
insight, as you suspect, they may become afraid if you edit their
environment. They may lash out. I doubt they even understand
how they created the contaminated metagrammar that they trans-
mitted back to us. It will be to them just a tool that makes

simpleminded aliens more gullible, easier to negotiate with. Who knows where they got it?'

'A grammatical weapon.' Boris spins himself round slowly. 'Build propaganda into your translation software if you want to establish a favorable trading relationship. How cute. Haven't these guys ever heard of Newspeak?'

'Probably not,' Amber says slowly, pausing for a moment to spawn spectator threads to run down the book and all three movie versions of *1984*, followed by the sharecropped series of sequel novels. She shivers uncomfortably as she reintegrates the memories. 'Ick. That's not a very nice vision. Reminds me of' – she snaps her fingers, trying to remember Dad's favorite – *'Dilbert.'*

'Friendly fascism,' says Sadeq. 'It matters not, whosoever is in charge. I could tell you tales from my parents, of growing up with a revolution. To never harbor self-doubt is poison for the soul, and these aliens want to inflict their certainties upon us.'

'I think we ought to see how Pierre is doing,' Amber says aloud. 'I certainly don't want them poisoning him.' Grin. 'That's *my* job.'

Donna the Journalist is everywhere simultaneously. It's a handy talent: Makes for even-handed news coverage when you can interview both sides at the same time.

Right now, one of her is in the bar with Alan Glashwiecz, who evidently hasn't realized that he can modulate his ethanol dehydrogenase levels voluntarily and who is consequently well on the way to getting steaming drunk. Donna is assisting the process; she finds it fascinating to watch this bitter young man who has lost his youth to a runaway self-enhancement process.

'I'm a full partner,' he says bitterly, 'in Glashwiecz and Selves. I'm one of the Selves. We're all partners, but it's only Glashwiecz Prime who has any clout. The old bastard – if I'd known I'd grow up to become *that*, I'd have run away to join some hippie antiglobalist commune instead.' He drains his glass, demonstrating his oropharyngeal integrity, snaps his fingers for a refill.

'I just woke up one morning to find I'd been resurrected by my older self. He said he valued my youthful energy and optimistic outlook, then offered me a minority stake with stock options that would take five years to vest. The bastard.'

'Tell me about it,' Donna coaxes sympathetically. 'Here we are, stranded among idiopathic types, not among them a single multiplex—'

'Damn straight.' Another bottle of Bud appears in Glashwiecz's hands. 'One moment I'm standing in this apartment in Paris facing total humiliation by a cross-dressing commie asshole called Macx and his slimy French manager bitch, and the next I'm on the carpet in front of my alter ego's desk and he's offering me a job as junior partner. It's seventeen years later, all the weird nonsense that guy Macx was getting up to is standard business practice, and there's six of me in the outer office taking research notes because myself-as-senior-partner doesn't trust anyone else to work with him. It's humiliating, that's what it is.'

'Which is why you're here.' Donna waits while he takes a deep swig from the bottle.

'Yeah. Better than working for myself, I can tell you – it's not like being self-employed. You know how you sometimes get distant from your work? It's really bad when you see yourself from the outside with another half gigasecond of experience and the new-you isn't just distant from the client base, he's distant from the you-you. So I went back to college and crammed up on artificial intelligence law and ethics, the jurisprudence of uploading, and recursive tort. Then I volunteered to come out here. He's still handling *her* account, and I figured—' Glashwiecz shrugged.

'Did any of the delta-yous contest the arrangement?' asks Donna, spawning ghosts to focus in on him from all angles. For a moment, she wonders if this is wise. Glashwiecz is dangerous – the power he wields over Amber's mother, to twist her arm into extending his power of attorney, hints at dark secrets. Maybe there's more to her persistent lawsuits than a simple family feud?

Glashwiecz's face is a study in perspectives. 'Oh, one did,' he says dismissively. One of Donna's viewports captures the contemptuous twitch in his cheek. 'I left her in my apartment freezer. Figured it'd be a while before anybody noticed. It's not murder – I'm still here, right? – and I'm not about to claim tort against myself. I think. It'd be a left-recursive lawsuit, anyway, if I did it to myself.'

'The aliens,' prompts Donna, 'and the trial by combat. What's your take on that?'

Glashwiecz sneers. 'Little bitch-queen takes after her father, doesn't she? He's a bastard, too. The competitive selection filter she's imposed is evil – it'll cripple her society if she leaves it in place for too long, but in the short run it's a major advantage. So she wants me to trade for my life, and I don't get to lay my formal claim against her unless I can outperform her pet day trader, that punk from Marseilles. Yes? What he doesn't know is, I've got an edge. Full disclosure.' He lifts his bottle drunkenly. 'Y'see, I know that *cat*. One that's gotta brown at-sign on its side, right? It used to belong to queenie-darling's old man, Manfred, the bastard. You'll see. Her mom, Pamela, Manfred's ex, she's my client in this case. And she gave me the cat's ackle keys. Access control.' (Hic.) 'Get ahold of its brains and grab that damn translation layer it stole from the CETI@home mob. *Then* I can talk to them straight.'

The drunken, future-shocked lawyer is on a roll. 'I'll get their shit, and I'll disassemble it. Disassembly is the future of industry, y'know?'

'Disassembly?' asks the reporter, watching him in disgusted fascination from behind her mask of objectivity.

'Hell, yeah. There's a singularity going on, that implies disequilibrium. An' wherever there's a disequilibrium, someone is going to get *rich* disassembling the leftovers. Listen, I once knew this econo – economist, that's what he was. Worked for the eurofeds, rubber fetishist. He tole me about this fact'ry near Barcelona. It had a disassembly line running in it. 'Spensive servers in boxes'd roll in at one end. Be unpacked. Then workers'd take the cases off, strip the disk drives, memory, processors, bits'n'guts out. Bag and tag job. Throw the box, what's left, 'cause it wasn't worth dick. Thing is, the manufact'rer charged so much for parts it was worth their while to buy whole machines'n'strip them. To bits. And sell the bits. Hell, they got an enterprise award for ingenuity! All 'cause they knew that *disassembly* was the wave of the future.'

'What happened to the factory?' asks Donna, unable to tear her eyes away.

Glashwiecz waves an empty bottle at the starbow that stretches across the ceiling. 'Ah, who gives a fuck? They closedown round about' (hic) 'ten years 'go. Moore's Law topped out, killed the market. But disassembly – production line cannibalism – it'sa way to go. Take old assets an' bring new life to them. A fully 'preciated fortune.' He grins, eyes unfocused with greed. ''S what I'm gonna do to those space lobsters. Learn to talk their language an'll never know what hit 'em.'

The tiny starship drifts in high orbit above a turbid brown soup of atmosphere. Deep in the gravity well of Hyundai $^{+4904}/_{-56}$, it's a speck of dust trapped between two light sources: the brilliant sapphire stare of Amber's propulsion lasers in Jovian orbit, and the emerald insanity of the router itself, a hypertoroid spun from strange matter.

The bridge of the *Field Circus* is in constant use at this time, a meeting ground for minds with access to the restricted areas. Pierre is spending more and more time here, finding it a convenient place to focus his trading campaign and arbitrage macros. At the same time that Donna is picking the multiplexed lawyer's strategy apart, Pierre is present in neomorphic form – a quicksilver outline of humanity, six-armed and two-headed, scanning with inhuman speed through tensor maps of the information traffic density surrounding the router's clump of naked singularities.

There's a flicker in the emptiness at the rear of the bridge, then Su Ang has always been there. She watches Pierre in contemplative silence for a minute. 'Do you have a moment?'

Pierre superimposes himself: One shadowy ghost keeps focused on the front panel, but another instance turns round, crosses his arms, waits for her to speak.

'I know you're busy—' she begins, then stops. 'Is it *that* important?' she asks.

'It is.' Pierre blurs, resynchronizing his instances. 'The router – there are four wormholes leading off from it, did you know that? Each of them is radiating at about 10^{11} Kelvins, and every wavelength is carrying data connections, multiplexed, with a protocol stack that's at least eleven layers deep but maybe more – they show signs of self-similarity in the framing headers. You know how much data that is? It's about 10^{12} times as much as our high-bandwidth uplink from home. But compared to what's on the other side of the 'holes—' He shakes his head.

'It's big?'

'It's unimaginably big! These wormholes, they're a *low-bandwidth* link compared to the minds they're hooking up to.' He blurs in front of her, unable to stay still and unable to look away from the front panel. Excitement or agitation? Su Ang can't tell. With Pierre, sometimes the two states are indistinguishable. He gets emotional easily. 'I think we have the outline of the answer to the Fermi paradox. Transcendents don't go traveling because they can't get enough bandwidth – trying to migrate through one of these wormholes would be like trying to download your mind into a fruit fly, if they are what I think they are – and the slower-than-light route is out, too, because they couldn't take enough computronium along. Unless—'

He's off again. But before he can blur out, Su Ang steps across and lays hands on him. 'Pierre. Calm down. Disengage. Empty yourself.'

'I can't!' He really *is* agitated, she sees. 'I've got to figure out the best trading strategy to get Amber off the hook with that lawsuit, then tell her to get us out of here; being this close to the router is seriously dangerous! The Wunch are the least of it.'

'Stop.'

He pauses his multiplicity of presences, converges on a single identity focused on the here and now. 'Yes?'

'That's better.' She walks round him, slowly. 'You've got to learn to deal with stress more appropriately.'

'Stress!' Pierre snorts. He shrugs, an impressive gesture with three sets of shoulder blades. 'That's something I can turn off whenever I need to. Side effect of this existence; we're pigs in cyberspace, wallowing in fleshy simulations but unable to experience the new environment in the raw. What did you want from me, Ang? Honestly? I'm a busy man, I've got a trading network to set up.'

'We've got a problem with the Wunch right now, even if you think something worse is out there,' Ang says patiently. 'Boris thinks they're parasites, negative-sum gamers who stalk newbies like us. Glashwiecz is apparently talking about cutting a deal with them. Amber's suggestion is that you ignore them completely, cut them out, and talk to anyone else who'll listen.'

'Anyone else who'll listen, right,' Pierre says heavily. 'Any other gems of wisdom to pass on from the throne?'

Ang takes a deep breath. He's infuriating, she realizes. And worst of all, he doesn't realize. Infuriating but cute. 'You're setting up a trading network, yes?' she asks.

'Yes. A standard network of independent companies, instantiated as cellular automata within the Ring Imperium switched legal service environment.' He relaxes slightly. 'Each one has access to a compartmentalized chunk of intellectual property and can call on the corrected parser we got from that cat. They're set up to communicate with a blackboard system – a souk – and I'm bringing up a link to the router, a multicast link that'll broadcast the souk's existence to anyone who's listening. Trade . . .' His eyebrows furrow. 'There are at least two different currency standards in this network, used to buy quality-of-service precedence and bandwidth. They depreciate with distance, as if the whole concept of money was invented to promote the development of long-range network links. If I can get in first, when Glashwiecz tries to cut in on the dealing by offering IP at discounted rates—'

'He's not going to, Pierre,' she says as gently as possible. 'Listen to what I said. Glashwiecz is going to focus on the Wunch. He's going to offer them a deal. Amber wants you to *ignore* them. Got that?'

'Got it.' There's a hollow *bong!* from one of the communication bells. 'Hey, that's interesting.'

'What is?' She stretches, neck extending snakelike so that she can see the window on underlying reality that's flickered into existence in the air before him.

'An ack from' – he pauses, then plucks a neatly reified concept from the screen in front of him and presents it to her in a silvery caul of light – 'about two hundred light years away! Someone wants to talk.' He smiles. Then the front panel workstation bongs again. 'Hey again. I wonder what that says.'

It's the work of a moment to pipe the second message through the translator. Oddly, it doesn't translate at first. Pierre has to correct for some weird destructive interference in the fake lobster network before it'll spill its guts. 'That's interesting,' he says.

'I'll say.' Ang lets her neck collapse back to normal. 'I'd better go tell Amber.'

'You do that,' Pierre says worriedly. He makes eye contact with her, but what she's hoping to see in his face just isn't there. He's wearing his emotions entirely on the surface. 'I'm not surprised their translator didn't want to pass that message along.'

'It's a deliberately corrupted grammar,' Ang murmurs, and bangs out in the direction of Amber's audience chamber, 'and they're actually making threats.' The Wunch, it seems, have acquired a *very* bad reputation somewhere along the line – and Amber needs to know.

Glashwiecz leans toward Lobster Number One, stomach churning. It's only a real-time kilosecond since his barroom interview, but in the intervening subjective time he's abolished a hangover, honed his brief, and decided to act. In the Tuileries. 'You've been lied to,' he confides quietly, trusting the privacy ackles that he browbeat Amber's mother into giving him – access lists that give him a degree of control over the regime within this virtual universe that the cat dragged in.

'Lied? Context rendered horizontal in past, or subjected to grammatical corruption? Linguistic evil?'

'The latter.' Glashwiecz enjoys this, even though it forces him to get rather closer to the two-meter-long virtual crustacean than he'd like. Showing a mark how they've been scammed is always good, especially when you hold the keys to the door of the cage they're locked inside. 'They are not telling you the truth about this system.'

'We received assurances,' Lobster Number One says clearly. Its mouthparts move ceaselessly – the noise comes from somewhere inside its head. 'You do not share this phenotype. Why?'

'That information will cost you,' says Glashwiecz. 'I am willing to provide it on credit.'

They haggle briefly. An exchange rate in questions is agreed, as is a trust metric to grade the answers by. 'Disclose all,' insists the Wunch negotiator.

'There are multiple sentient species on the world we come from,' says the lawyer. 'The form you wear belongs to only one – one that wanted to get away from the form *I* wear, the original conscious tool-creating species. Some of the species today are artificial, but all of us trade information for self-advantage.'

'This is good to know,' the lobster assures him. 'We like to buy species.'

'You buy species?' Glashwiecz cocks his head.

'We have the unbearable yearning to be not-what-we-are,' says the lobster. 'Novelty, surprise! Flesh rots and wood decays. We seek the new being-ness of aliens. Give us your somatotype, give us all your thoughts, and we will dream you over.'

'I think something might be arranged,' Glashwiecz concedes. 'So you want to be – no, to lease the rights to temporarily be human? Why is that?'

'*Untranslatable concept #3* means *untranslatable concept #4*. God told us to.'

'Okay, I think I'll just have to take that on trust for now. What is your true form?' he asks.

'Wait and I show you,' says the lobster. It begins to shudder.

'What are you doing—'

'Wait.' The lobster twitches, writhing slightly, like a portly businessman adjusting his underwear after a heavy business lunch. Disturbing shapes move, barely visible through the thick chitinous armor. 'We want your help,' the lobster explains, voice curiously muffled. 'Want to establish direct trade links. Physical emissaries, yes?'

'Yes, that's very good,' Glashwiecz agrees excitedly: It's exactly what he's hoped for, the sought-after competitive advantage that will prove his fitness in Amber's designated trial by corporate combat. 'You're going to deal with us directly without using that shell interface?'

'Agreed.' The lobster trails off into muffled silence; little crunching noises trickle out of its carapace. Then Glashwiecz hears footsteps behind him on the gravel path.

'What are you doing here?' he demands, looking round. It's Pierre, back in standard human form – a sword hangs from his belt, and there's a big wheel-lock pistol in his hands. 'Hey!'

'Step away from the alien, lawyer,' Pierre warns, raising the gun.

Glashwiecz glances back at Lobster Number One. It's pulled its front inside the protective shell, and it's writhing now, rocking from side to side alarmingly. Something inside the shell is turning black, acquiring depth and texture. 'I stand on counsel's privilege,' Glashwiecz insists. 'Speaking as this alien's attorney, I must protest in the strongest terms—'

Without warning, the lobster lurches forward and rises up on its rear legs. It reaches out with huge claws, chellipeds coated with spiny hairs, and grabs Glashwiecz by his arms. 'Hey!'

Glashwiecz tries to turn away, but the lobster is already looming over him, maxillipeds and maxillae reaching out from its head. There's a sickening crunch as one of his elbow joints crumbles, humerus shattered by the closing jaws of a chelliped. He draws breath to scream, then the four small maxillae grip his head and draw it down toward the churning mandibles.

Pierre scurries sideways, trying to find a line of fire on the lobster that doesn't pass through the lawyer's body. The lobster isn't cooperating. It turns on the spot, clutching Glashwiecz's convulsing body to itself. There's a stench of shit, and blood is squirting from its mouthparts. Something is very wrong with the biophysics model here, the realism turned up way higher than normal.

'*Merde*,' whispers Pierre. He fumbles with the bulky trigger, and there's a faint whirring sound but no explosion.

More wet crunching sounds follow as the lobster demolishes the lawyer's face and swallows convulsively, sucking his head and shoulders all the way into its gastric mill.

Pierre glances at the heavy handgun. '*Shit!*' he screams. He glances back at the lobster, then turns and runs for the nearest wall. There are other lobsters loose in the formal garden. '*Amber, emergency!*' he sends over their private channel. '*Hostiles in the Louvre!*'

The lobster that's taken Glashwiecz hunkers down over the body and quivers. Pierre desperately winds the spring on his gun, too rattled to check that it's loaded. He glances back at the alien intruder. *They've sprung the biophysics model,* he sends. *I could die in here,* he realizes, momentarily shocked. *This instance of me could die forever.*

The lobster shell sitting in the pool of blood and human wreckage splits in two. A humanoid form begins to uncurl from within it, pale-skinned and glistening wet: Vacant blue eyes flicker from side to side as it stretches and stands upright, wobbling uncertainty on its two unstable legs. Its mouth opens and a strange gobbling hiss comes forth.

Pierre recognizes her. 'What are you doing here?' he yells.

The nude woman turns toward him. She's the spitting image of Amber's mother, except for the chellipeds she has in place of hands. She hisses, '*Equity!*' and takes a wobbly step toward him, pincers clacking.

Pierre winds the firing handle again. There's a crash of gun-powder and smoke, a blow that nearly sprains his elbow, and the nude woman's chest erupts in a spray of blood. She snarls at him wordlessly and staggers – then ragged flaps of bloody meat close together, knitting shut with improbable speed. She resumes her advance.

'I *told* Amber the Matrix would be more defensible,' Pierre snarls, dropping the firearm and drawing his sword as the alien turns in his direction and raises arms that end in pincers. '*We need guns, dammit! Lots of guns!*'

'*Waaant equity,*' hisses the alien intruder.

'You *can't* be Pamela Macx,' says Pierre, his back to the wall, keeping the sword point before the lobster-woman-thing. 'She's in a nunnery in Armenia or something. You pulled that out of Glashwiecz's memories – he worked for her, didn't he?'

Claws go snicker-snack before his face. 'Investment partner-ship!' screeches the harridan. 'Seat on the board! Eat brains for breakfast!' It lurches sideways, trying to get past his guard.

'I don't fucking *believe* this,' Pierre snarls. The Wunch-creature jumps at just the wrong moment and slides onto the point of his blade, claws clacking hungrily. Pierre slides away, nearly leaving his skin on the rough bricks of the wall – and what's good for one is good for all, as the hacked model in force in this reality compels the attacker to groan and collapse.

Pierre pulls the sword out then, nervously glancing over his shoulder, whacks at her neck. The impact jars his arm, but he keeps hacking until there's blood spraying everywhere, blood on his shirt, blood on his sword, and a round thing sitting on a stump of savaged neck nearby, jaw working soundlessly in undeath.

He looks at it for a moment, then his stomach rebels and tries to empty itself into the mess. '*Where the hell* is *everybody?*' he broadcasts on the private channel. '*Hostiles in the Louvre!*'

He straightens up, gasping for breath. He feels *alive,* fright-ened and appalled and exhilarated simultaneously. The crackle of bursting shells on all sides drowns out the birdsong as the

Wunch's emissaries adopt a variety of new and supposedly more lethal forms. *'They don't seem to be very clear on how to take over a simulation space,'* he adds. *'Maybe we already are untranslatable concept number #1 as far as they're concerned.'*

'Don't worry, I've cut off the incoming connection,' sends Su Ang. *'This is just a bridgehead force; the invasion packets are being filtered out.'*

Blank-eyed men and women in dusty black uniforms are hatching from the lobster shells, stumbling and running around the grounds of the royal palace like confused Huguenot invaders.

Boris winks into reality behind Pierre. 'Which way?' he demands, pulling out an anachronistic but lethal katana.

'Over here. Let's work this together.' Pierre jacks his emotional damper up to a dangerously high setting, suppressing natural aversion reflexes and temporarily turning himself into a sociopathic killer. He stalks toward an infant lobster-thing with big black eyes and a covering of white hair that mewls at him from a rose bed, and Boris looks away while he kills it. Then one of the larger ones makes the mistake of lunging at Boris, and he chops at it reflexively.

Some of the Wunch try to fight back when Pierre and Boris try to kill them, but they're handicapped by their anatomy, a curious mixture of crustacean and human, claw and mandible against sword and dagger. When they bleed the ground soaks with the cuprous hue of lobster juice.

'Let's fork,' suggests Boris. 'Get this over with.' Pierre nods, dully – everything around him is wrapped in a layer of don't-care, except for a glowing dot of artificial hatred – and they fork, multiplying their state vectors to take full advantage of the virtualization facilities of this universe. There's no need for reinforcements; the Wunch focused on attacking the biophysics model of the universe, making it mimic a physical reality as closely as possible, and paid no attention to learning the more intricate tactics that war in a virtual space permits.

Presently Pierre finds himself in the audience chamber, face and hands and clothing caked in hideous gore, leaning on the back of Amber's throne. There's only one of him now. One of Boris – the only one? – is standing near the doorway. He can barely remember what has happened, the horrors of parallel instances of mass murder blocked from his long-term memory by a high-pass trauma filter. 'It looks clear,' he calls aloud. 'What shall we do now?'

'Wait for Catherine de Médicis to show up,' says the cat, its grin materializing before him like a numinous threat. 'Amber *always* finds a way to blame her mother. Or didn't you already know that?'

Pierre glances at the bloody mess on the footpath outside where the first lobster-woman attacked Glashwiecz. 'I already did for her, I think.' He remembers the action in the third person, all subjectivity edited out. 'The family resemblance was striking,' the thread that still remembers her in working memory murmurs. 'I just hope it's only skin-deep.' Then he forgets the act of apparent murder forever. 'Tell the Queen I'm ready to talk.'

Welcome to the downslope on the far side of the curve of accelerating progress.

Back in the solar system, Earth orbits through a dusty tunnel in space. Sunlight still reaches the birth world, but much of the rest of the star's output has been trapped by the growing concentric shells of computronium built from the wreckage of the innermost planets.

Two billion or so mostly unmodified humans scramble in the wreckage of the phase transition, not understanding why the vasty superculture they so resented has fallen quiet. Little information leaks through their fundamentalist firewalls, but what there is shows a disquieting picture of a society where there are no *bodies* anymore. Utility foglets blown on the wind form aerogel towers larger than cyclones, removing the last traces of physical human civilization from most of Europe and the North American coastlines. Enclaves huddle behind their walls and wonder at the monsters and portents roaming the desert of postindustrial civilization, mistaking acceleration for collapse.

The hazy shells of computronium that ring the sun — concentric clouds of nanocomputers the size of rice grains, powered by sunlight, orbiting in shells like the packed layers of a Matrioshka doll — are still immature, holding barely a thousandth of the physical planetary mass of the system, but they already support a classical computational density of 10^{42} MIPS; enough to support a billion civilizations as complex as the one that existed immediately before the great disassembly. The conversion hasn't yet reached the gas giants, and some scant outer-system enclaves remain independent — Amber's Ring Imperium still exists as a separate entity, and will do so for some years to come — but the inner solar system planets, with the exception of Earth, have been colonized more thoroughly than any dusty NASA proposal from the dawn of the space age could have envisaged.

From outside the Accelerated civilization, it isn't really possible to know what's going on inside. The problem is bandwidth: While it's possible to send data in and get data out, the sheer amount of computation going on in the virtual spaces of the Acceleration dwarfs any external observer. Inside that swarm, minds a trillion or more times as complex as humanity think thoughts as far beyond human imagination as a microprocessor is beyond a nematode worm. A million random human civilizations flourish in worldscapes tucked in the corner of this world-mind. Death is abolished, life is triumphant. A thousand ideologies flower, human nature adapted where necessary to make this possible. Ecologies of thought are forming in a Cambrian explosion of ideas, for the solar system is finally rising to consciousness, and mind is no longer restricted to the mere kilotons of gray fatty meat harbored in fragile human skulls.

Somewhere in the Acceleration, colorless green ideas adrift in furious sleep remember a tiny starship launched years ago, and pay attention. Soon, they realize, the starship will be in position to act as their proxy in an ages-long conversation. Negotiations for access to Amber's extrasolar asset commence; the Ring Imperium prospers, at least for a while.

But first, the operating software on the human side of the network link will require an upgrade.

The audience chamber in the *Field Circus* is crammed. Everybody aboard the ship – except the still-frozen lawyer and the alien barbarian intruders – is present. They've just finished reviewing the recordings of what happened in the Tuileries, of Glashwiecz's fatal last conversation with the Wunch, the resulting fight for survival. And now the time has come for decisions.

'I'm not saying you have to follow me,' says Amber, addressing her court, 'just, it's what we came here for. We've established that there's enough bandwidth to transmit people and their necessary support VMs; we've got some basic expectancy of goodwill at the other end, or at least an agalmic willingness to gift us with advice about the untrustworthiness of the Wunch. *I* propose to copy myself through and see what's at the other side of the wormhole. What's more, I'm going to suspend myself on this side and hand over to whichever instance of me comes back, unless there's a long hiatus. How long, I haven't decided yet. Are you guys happy to join me?'

Pierre stands behind her throne, hands on the back. Looking down over her head, at the cat in her lap, he's sure he sees it narrow its eyes at him. *Funny,* he thinks, *we're talking about jumping down a rabbit hole and trusting whoever lives at the other end with our personalities. After seeing the Wunch. Does this make sense?*

'Forgive, please, but am not stupid,' says Boris. 'This is Fermi paradox territory, no? Instantaneous network exists, is traversable, with bandwidth adequate for human-equivalent minds. Where are alien visitors, in history? Must be overriding reason for absence. Think will wait here and see what comes back. *Then* make up mind to drink the poison Kool-Aid.'

'I've got half a mind to transmit myself through without a backup,' says someone else, 'but that's okay, half a mind is all we've got the bandwidth for.' Halfhearted laughter shores up his wisecrack, supports a flagging determination to press through.

'I'm with Boris,' says Su Ang. She glances at Pierre, catches his eye. Suddenly a number of things become clear to him. He shakes his head minutely. *You never had a chance – I belong to Amber,* he thinks, but deletes the thought before he can send it to her. Maybe in another instantiation his issues with the Queen's *droit de seigneur* would have bulked up larger, splintered his determination; maybe in another world it has already happened? 'I think this is very rash,' she says in a hurry. 'We don't know enough about postsingularity civilizations.'

'It's not a singularity,' Amber says waspishly. 'It's just a brief burst of acceleration. Like cosmological inflation.'

'Smooths out inhomogeneities in the initial structure of consciousness,' purrs the cat. 'Don't I get a vote?'

'You do.' Amber sighs. She glances round. 'Pierre?'

Heart in his mouth: 'I'm with you.'

She smiles, brilliantly. 'Well then. Will the naysayers please leave the universe?'

Suddenly, the audience chamber is half-empty.

'I'm setting a watchdog timer for a billion seconds into the future, to restart us from this point if the router doesn't send anyone back in the intervening time,' she announces gravely, taking in the serious-faced avatars of those who remain. Surprised: 'Sadeq! I didn't think this was your type of—'

He doesn't smile. 'Would I be true to my faith if I wasn't prepared to bring the words of Mohammed, peace be unto him, to those who may never have heard his name?'

Amber nods. 'I guess.'

'Do it,' Pierre says urgently. 'You can't keep putting it off forever.'

Aineko raises her head. 'Spoilsport!'
'Okay.' Amber nods. 'Let's *do*—'
She punches an imaginary switch, and time stops.

At the far end of a wormhole, two hundred light years distant in real space, coherent photons begin to dance a story of human identity before the sensoria of those who watch. And all is at peace in orbit around Hyundai $^{+4904}/_{-56}$, for a while . . .

6 : NIGHTFALL

A SYNTHETIC GEMSTONE THE SIZE OF A COKE can falls through silent darkness. The night is quiet as the grave, colder than midwinter on Pluto. Gossamer sails as fine as soap bubbles droop, the gust of sapphire laser light that inflated them long since darkened. Ancient starlight picks out the outline of a huge planetlike body beneath the jewel-and-cobweb corpse of the starwhisp.

Eight Earth years have passed since the good ship *Field Circus* slipped into close orbit around the frigid brown dwarf Hyundai $^{+4904}/_{-56}$. Five years have gone by since the launch lasers of the Ring Imperium shut down without warning, stranding the light-sail-powered craft three light years from home. There has been no response from the router, the strange alien artifact in orbit around the brown dwarf, since the crew of the starwhisp uploaded themselves through its strange quantum entanglement interface for transmission to whatever alien network it connects to. In fact, nothing happens; nothing save the slow trickle of seconds, as a watchdog timer counts down the moments remaining until it is due to resurrect stored snapshots of the crew, on the assumption that their uploaded copies are beyond help.

Meanwhile, outside the light cone—

* * *

Amber jolts into wakefulness, as if from a nightmare. She sits bolt upright, a thin sheet falling from her chest; air circulating around her back chills her rapidly, cold sweat evaporating. She mutters aloud, unable to subvocalize, 'Where am I – oh. A bedroom. How did I get here?' *Mumble.* 'Oh, I see.' Her eyes widen in horror. *'It's not a dream . . .'*

'Greetings, human Amber,' says a ghost-voice that seems to come from nowhere. 'I see you are awake. Would you like anything?'

Amber rubs her eyes tiredly. Leaning against the bedstead, she glances around cautiously. She takes in a bedside mirror, her reflection in it – a young woman, gaunt in the manner of those whose genome bears the p53 calorie-restriction hack; she has disheveled blond hair and dark eyes. She could pass for a dancer or a soldier; not, perhaps, a queen. 'What's going on? Where am I? Who are you, and *what am I doing in your head?'*

Her eyes narrow. Analytical intellect comes to the fore as she takes stock of her surroundings. 'The router,' she mutters. Structures of strange matter orbit a brown dwarf scant light years from Earth. 'How long ago did we come through?' Glancing round, she sees a room walled in slabs of close-fitting stone. A window bay is recessed into them, after the style of the Crusader castles many centuries in the past, but there's no glass in it – just a blank white screen. The only furniture in the room, besides a Persian carpet on the cold flagstones, is the bed she sits upon. She's reminded of a scene from an old movie, Kubrick's enigma; this whole setup has got to be deliberate, and it isn't funny.

'I'm waiting,' she announces, and leans back against the headboard.

'According to our records this reaction indicates that you are now fully self-aware,' says the ghost. 'This is good. You have not been conscious for a very long time. Explanations will be complex and discursive. Can I offer you refreshments? What would you like?'

'Coffee, if you have it. Bread and hummus. Something to wear.' Amber crosses her arms, abruptly self-conscious. 'I'd prefer to have management ackles to this universe, though. As realities go, it's a bit lacking in creature comforts.' Which isn't entirely true — it seems to have a comprehensive, human-friendly bio-physics model; it's not just a jumped-up first-person shooter. Her eyes focus on her left forearm, where tanned skin and a puckered dime of scar tissue record a youthful accident with a pressure seal in Jovian orbit. Amber freezes for a moment. Her lips move in silence, but she's locked into place in this universe, unable to split or conjoin nested realities just by calling subroutines that have been spliced into the corners of her mind since she was a teenager. Finally, she asks, 'How long have I been dead?'

'Longer than you were alive, by orders of magnitude,' says the ghost. A tray laden with pita breads, hummus, and olives con-geals from the air above her bed, and a wardrobe appears at one side of the room. 'I can begin the explanation now or wait for you to finish eating. Which would you prefer?'

Amber glances about again, then fixes on the white screen in the window bay. 'Give it to me right now. I can take it,' she says, quietly bitter. 'I like to understand my mistakes as soon as pos-sible.'

'We-us can tell that you are a human of determination,' says the ghost, a hint of pride entering its voice. 'That is a good thing, Amber. You will need all of your resolve if you are going to sur-vive here . . .'

It is the time of repentance in a temple beside a tower that looms above a dry plain, and the thoughts of the priest who lives in the tower are tinged with regret. It is Ashura, the tenth day of Muhurram, according to a real-time clock still tuned to the pace of a different era: the one thousand, three hundred and fortieth anniversary of the martyrdom of the Third Imam, the Sayyid ash-Shuhada.

The priest of the tower has spent an indefinite time in prayer, locked in an eternal moment of meditation and recitation. Now, as the vast red sun drifts close to the horizon of the infinite desert, his thoughts drift toward the present. Ashura is a very special day, a day of atonement for collective guilt, evil committed through inactivity; but it is in Sadeq's nature to look outward toward the future. This is, he knows, a failing – but also characteristic of his generation. That's the generation of the Shi'ite clergy that reacted to the excesses of the previous century, the generation that with-drew the *ulama* from temporal power, retreated from the *velyat i-faqih* of Khomenei and his successors, left government to the people, and began to engage fully with the paradoxes of modern-ity. Sadeq's focus, his driving obsession in theology, is a program of reappraisal of eschatology and cosmology. Here in a tower of white sun-baked clay, on an endless plain that exists only in the imaginary spaces of a starship the size of a soft drink can, the priest spends his processor cycles in contemplation of one of the most vicious problems ever to confront a *mujtahid* – the Fermi paradox.

(Enrico Fermi was eating his lunch one day, and his colleagues were discussing the possibility that sophisticated civilizations might populate other worlds. 'Yes,' he said, 'but if this is so, why haven't they already come visiting?')

Sadeq finishes his evening devotions in near silence, then stands, stretches as is his wont, and leaves the small and lonely courtyard at the base of the tower. The gate – a wrought-iron gate, warmed by sunlight – squeals slightly as he opens it. Glancing at the upper hinge, he frowns, willing it clean and whole. The underlying physics model acknowledges his access controls: A thin rim of red around the pin turns silvery-fresh, and the squeaking ceases. Closing the gate behind him, Sadeq enters the tower.

He climbs with a heavy, even tread, a spiral staircase snaking ever upward above him. Narrow slit-windows line the outer wall of the staircase. Through each of them he sees a different world. Out there, nightfall in the month of Ramadan. And through the next, green misty skies and a horizon too close by far. Sadeq care-fully avoids thinking about the implications of this manifold space. Coming from prayer, from a sense of the sacred, he doesn't want to lose his proximity to his faith. He's far enough from home as it is, and there is much to consider. He is surrounded by strange and curious ideas, all but lost in a corrosive desert of faith.

At the top of the staircase, Sadeq comes to a door of aged wood bound in iron. It doesn't belong here: It's a cultural and architectural anomaly. The handle is a loop of black metal. Sadeq regards it as if it's the head of an asp, poised to sting. Nevertheless, he reaches out and turns the handle, steps across the threshold into a palace out of fantasy.

None of this is real, he reminds himself. *It's no more real than an illusion conjured by one of the jinni of the thousand and one nights.* Nevertheless, he can't save himself from smiling at the scene – a sardonic smile of self-deprecating humor, tempered by frustration.

Sadeq's captors have stolen his soul and locked it – him – in a very strange prison, a temple with a tower that rises all the way to Paradise. It's the whole classical litany of medievalist desires, distilled from fifteen hundred years of literature. Colonnaded courtyards, cool pools lined with rich mosaics, rooms filled with every imaginable dumb matter luxury, endless banquets awaiting his appetite – and dozens of beautiful un-women, eager to fulfill his every fantasy. Sadeq, being human, has fantasies by the dozen, but he doesn't dare permit himself to succumb to temptation. *I'm not dead,* he reasons; *therefore, how can I be in Paradise? Therefore, this must be a false paradise, a temptation sent to lead me astray. Probably. Unless I* am *dead, because Allah, peace be unto him, considers a human soul separated from its body to be dead. But if that's so, isn't uploading a sin? In which case, this can't be Paradise because I am a sinner. Besides which, this whole setup is so* puerile!

Sadeq has always been inclined to philosophical inquiry, and his vision of the afterlife is more cerebral than most, involving ideas as questionable within the framework of Islam as those of Teilhard de Chardin were to the twentieth-century Catholic Church. If there's one key indicator of a false paradise in his eschatology, it's two-and-seventy brainlessly beautiful houris waiting to do his bidding. So it follows that he can't really be dead . . .

The whole question of reality is so vexing that Sadeq does what he does every night. He strides heedlessly across priceless works of art, barging hastily through courtyards and passageways, ignoring niches in which nearly naked supermodels lie with their legs apart, climbing stairs – until he comes to a small unfurnished room with a single high window in one wall. There he sits on the floor, legs crossed, meditating; not in prayer, but in a more tightly focused ratiocination. Every false night (for there is no way to know how fast time is passing, outside this cyberspace pocket), Sadeq sits and *thinks,* grappling with Descartes's demon in the solitude of his own mind. And the question he asks himself every night is the same. *Can I tell if this is the true hell? And if it is not, how can I escape?*

The ghost tells Amber that she has been dead for just under a third of a million years. She has been reinstantiated from storage – and has died again – many times in the intervening period, but she has no memory of this; she is a fork from the main bough, and the other branches expired in lonely isolation.

The business of resurrection does not, in and of itself, distress Amber unduly. Born in the post-Moravec era, she merely finds some aspects of the ghost's description dissatisfyingly incomplete. It's like saying she was drugged and brought hither without stating whether by plane, train, or automobile.

She doesn't have a problem with the ghost's assertion that she is nowhere near Earth – indeed, that she is approximately eighty thousand light years away. When she and the others took the risk of uploading themselves through the router they found in orbit around Hyundai $^{+4904}/_{-56}$ they'd understood that they could end up anywhere or nowhere. But the idea that she's still within the light cone of her departure strikes her as dubious. The original SETI broadcast strongly implied that the router is part of a network of self-replicating instantaneous communicators, spawning and spreading between the cold brown dwarf stars that litter the galaxy. She'd somehow expected to be much farther from home by now.

Somewhat more disturbing is the ghost's assertion that the human genotype has rendered itself extinct at least twice, that its home planet is unknown, and that Amber is nearly the only human left in the public archives. At this point, she interrupts. 'I hardly see what this has to do with me!' Then she blows across her coffee glass, trying to cool the contents. 'I'm dead,' she explains, with an undertone of knowing sarcasm in her voice. 'Remember? I just got here. A thousand seconds ago, subjective time, I was in the control node of a starship, discussing what to do with the router we were in orbit around. We agreed to send ourselves through it, as a trade mission. Then I woke up in bed here in the umpty-zillionth century, wherever and whatever *here* is. Without access to any reality ackles or augmentation, I can't even tell whether this is real or an embedded simulation. You're going to have to explain *why* you need an old version of me before I can make sense of my situation – and I can tell you, I'm not going to help you until I know who you are. And speaking of that, what about the others? Where are they? I wasn't the only one, you know?'

The ghost freezes in place for a moment, and Amber feels a watery rush of terror. *Have I gone too far?* she wonders.

'There has been an unfortunate accident,' the ghost announces portentously. It morphs from a translucent copy of Amber's own body into the outline of a human skeleton, elaborate bony extensions simulating an osteosarcoma of more-than-lethal proportions. 'Consensus-we believe that you are best positioned to remediate the situation. This applies within the demilitarized zone.'

'Demilitarized?' Amber shakes her head, pauses to sip her coffee. 'What do you mean? What *is* this place?'

The ghost flickers again, adopting an abstract rotating hypercube as its avatar. 'This space we occupy is a manifold adjacent to the demilitarized zone. The demilitarized zone is a space outside our core reality, itself exposed to entities that cross freely through our firewall, journeying to and from the network outside. We-us use the DMZ to establish the informational value of migrant entities, sapient currency units and the like. We-us banked you upon arrival against future options trades in human species futures.'

'Currency!' Amber doesn't know whether to be amused or horrified – both reactions seem appropriate. 'Is that how you treat all your visitors?'

The ghost ignores her question. 'There is a runaway semiotic excursion under way in the zone. We-us believe only you can fix it. If you agree to do so, we will exchange value, pay, reward cooperation, expedite remuneration, manumit, repatriate.'

Amber drains her coffee cup. 'Have you ever entered into economic interactions with me, or humans like me, before?' she asks. 'If not, why should I trust you? If so, why have you revived me? Are there any more experienced instances of myself running around here?' She raises a skeptical eyebrow at the ghost. 'This looks like the start of an abusive relationship.'

The ghost continues to sidestep her attempts to work out where she stands. It flickers into transparency, grows into a hazy window on a landscape of impossible shapes. Clouds sprouting trees drift above a landscape of green, egg-curved hills and cheesecake castles. 'Nature of excursion: Alien intelligence is loose in the DMZ,' it asserts. 'Alien is applying invalid semiotics to complex structures designed to sustain trade. You know this alien, Amber. We require solution. Slay the monster, we will give you line of credit. Your own reality to control, insight into trade arrangements, augmented senses, ability to travel. Can even upgrade you to you-we consensus, if desired.'

'This monster.' Amber leans forward, staring into the window eagerly. She's half-minded to ignore what she feels is a spurious offer; it doesn't sound too appetizing. *Upgrade me to a ghost fragment of an alien group mind?* she wonders dismissively. 'What is this alien?' She feels blind and unsure, stripped of her ability to spawn threads of herself to pursue complex inferences. 'Is it part of the Wunch?'

'Datum unknown. It-them came with you,' says the ghost. 'Accidentally reactivated some seconds since now. It runs amok in the demilitarized zone. Help us, Amber. Save our hub, or we will be cut off from the network. If that happens, you will die with we-us. Save us . . .'

A single memory belonging to someone else unwinds, faster than a guided missile and far more deadly.

Amber, aged eleven, is a gawky, long-limbed child loose on the streets of Hong Kong, a yokel tourist viewing the hot core of the Middle Kingdom. This is her first and final vacation before the Franklin Trust straps her inside the payload pod of a Shenzhou spaceplane and blasts her into orbit from Xinkiang. She's free for the time being, albeit mortgaged to the tune of several million euros; she's a little taikonaut to be, ready to work for the long years in Jupiter orbit it will take her to pay off the self-propelled options web that owns her. It's not exactly slavery: Thanks to Dad's corporate shell game she doesn't have to worry about Mom chasing her, trying to return her to the posthuman prison of growing up just like an old-fashioned little girl. And now she's got a bit of pocket money, and a room in the Hilton, and her own personal Franklin remote to keep her company, she's decided she's gonna do that eighteenth-century-enlightenment tourist shit and do it *right*.

Because this is her last day at liberty in the randomly evolved biosphere.

China is where things are at in this decade, hot and dense and full of draconian punishments for the obsolescent. Nationalist fervor to catch up with the West has been replaced by consumerist fervor to own the latest fad gadgets, the most picturesque tourist souvenirs from the quaintly old-fashioned streets of America, the fastest hottest smartest upgrades for body and soul. Hong Kong is hotter and faster than just about anywhere else in China, or in the whole damn world for that matter. This is a place where tourists from Tokyo gawp, cowed and future-shocked by the glamour of high-technology living.

Walking along Jardine's Bazaar – *more like Jardine's bizarre,* she thinks – exposes Amber to a blast of humid noise. Geodesic domes sprout like skeletal mushrooms from the glass-and-chrome roofs of the expensive shopping malls and luxury hotels, threatening to float away on the hot sea breeze. There are no airliners roaring in and out of Kai Tak anymore, no burnished aluminum storm clouds to rain round-eyed passengers on the shopping malls and fish markets of Kowloon and the New Territories. In these tense later days of the War Against Unreason, impossible new shapes move in the sky; Amber gapes upward as a Shenyang F-30 climbs at a near-vertical angle, a mess of incomprehensibly curved flight surfaces vanishing to a perspective point that defies radar as well as eyeballs. The Chinese – fighter? missile platform? supercomputer? – is heading out over the South China Sea to join the endless patrol that reassures the capitalist world that it is being guarded from the Hosts of Denial, the Trouble out of Wa'hab.

For the moment, she's merely a precocious human child. Amber's subconscious is off-lined by the presence of forceful infowar daemons, the Chinese government censorbots suppressing her cognition of their deadliest weapons. And in the seconds while her mind is as empty as a sucked egg, a thin-faced man with blue hair shoves her in the small of her back and snatches at her shoulder bag.

'Hey!' she yells, stumbling. Her mind's a blur, optics refusing to respond and grab a biometric model of her assailant. It's the frozen moment, the dead zone when online coverage fails, and the thief is running away before she can catch her balance or try to give chase. Plus, with her extensions off-line she doesn't know how to yell 'Stop, thief!' in Cantonese.

Seconds later, the fighter is out of visual range and the state censorship field lets up. 'Get him, you bastards!' she screams, but the curious shoppers simply stare at the rude foreign child. An elderly woman brandishes a disposable phonecam at her and screeches something back. Amber picks up her feet and runs. Already she can feel the subsonics from her luggage growling at her guts – it's going to make a scene if she doesn't catch up in time. Shoppers scatter, a woman with a baby carriage almost running her down in her panic to get away from it.

By the time Amber reaches her terrified shoulder bag, the thief has disappeared: She has to spend almost a minute petting the scared luggage before it stops screeching and retracts its spines enough for her to pick it up. And by that time there's a robocop in attendance. 'Identify yourself,' it rasps in synthetic English.

Amber stares at her bag in horror. There's a huge gash in the side, and it's far too light. *It's gone,* she thinks, despairingly. *He stole it.* 'Help,' she says faintly, holding up her bag for the distant policeman looking through the robot's eyes. 'Been stolen.'

'What item missing?' asks the robot.

'My Hello Kitty,' she says, batting her eyelashes, mendacity full-on at maximum utilization, prodding her conscience into submission, warning of dire consequences should the police discover the true nature of her pet cat. 'My kitten's been stolen! Can you help me?'

'Certainly,' says the cop, resting a reassuring hand on her shoulder – a hand that turns into a steel armband, as it pushes her into a van and notifies her in formally stilted language that she is under arrest on suspicion of shoplifting and will be required to produce certificates of authenticity and a fully compliant ownership audit for all items in her possession if she wants to prove her innocence.

By the time Amber's meatbrain realizes that she is being politely arrested, some of her external threads have already started yelling for help and her m-commerce trackers have identified the station she's being taken to by way of click-thru trails and an obliging software license manager. They spawn agents to go notify the Franklin trustees, Amnesty International, the Space and Freedom Party, and her father's lawyers. As she's being booked into a cerise-and-turquoise juvenile offenders holding room by a middle-aged policewoman, the phones on the front desk are already ringing with inquiries from attorneys, fast-food vendors, and a particularly on-the-ball celebrity magazine that's been tracking her father's connections. 'Can you help me get my cat back?' she asks the policewoman earnestly.

'Name,' the officer reads, eyes flickering from the simultaneous translation. 'To please wax your identity stiffly.'

'My cat has been stolen,' Amber insists.

'Your cat?' The cop looks perplexed, then exasperated. Dealing with foreign teenagers who answer questions with gibberish isn't in her repertoire. 'We are asking your name?'

'No,' says Amber. 'It's my cat. It has been stolen. My *cat* has been *stolen*.'

'Aha! Your papers, please?'

'Papers?' Amber is growing increasingly worried. She can't feel the outside world; there's a Faraday cage wrapped around the holding cell, and it's claustrophobically quiet inside. 'I want my cat! Now!'

The cop snaps her fingers, then reaches into her own pocket and produces an ID card, which she points to insistently. 'Papers,' she repeats. 'Or else.'

'I don't know what you're talking about!' Amber wails.

The cop stares at her oddly. 'Wait.' She rises and leaves, and a minute later returns with a thin-faced man in a business suit and wire-rimmed glasses that glow faintly.

'You are making a scene,' he says, rudely and abruptly. 'What is your name? Tell me truthfully, or you'll spend the night here.'

Amber bursts into tears. 'My *cat's* been stolen,' she chokes out.

The detective and the cop obviously don't know how to

deal with this scene; it's freaking them out, with its over-tones of emotional messiness and sinister diplomatic entanglement. 'You wait here,' they say, and back out of the cell, leaving her alone with a plastic animatronic koala and a cheap Lebanese coffee machine.

The implications of her loss – of Aineko's abduction – are sinking in, finally, and Amber is weeping loudly and hopelessly. It's hard to deal with bereavement and betrayal at any age, and the cat has been her wisecracking compan-ion and consolation for a year, the rock of certainty that gave her the strength to break free from her crazy mother. To lose her cat to a body shop in Hong Kong, where she will probably be cut up for spare circuitry or turned into soup is too horrible to contemplate. Filled with despair and hopeless anguish, Amber howls at the interrogation room walls while outside, trapped threads of her consciousness search for backups to synchronize with.

But after an hour, just as she's quieting down into a slough of raw despair, there's a knock – a knock! – at the door. An inquisitive head pops in. 'Please to come with us?' It's the female cop with the bad translationware. She takes in Amber's sobbing and tuts under her breath, but as Amber stands up and shambles toward her, she pulls back.

At the front desk of a cubicle farm full of police bureau-crats in various states of telepresence, the detective is waiting with a damp cardboard box wrapped in twine. 'Please identify,' he asks, snipping the string.

Amber shakes her head, dizzy with the flow of threads homing in to synchronize their memories with her. 'Is it – ' she begins to ask as the lid comes apart, wet pulp disinte-grating. A triangular head pops up, curiously, sniffing the air. Bubbles blow from brown-furred nostrils. 'What took you so long?' asks the cat, as she reaches into the box and picks her up, fur wet and matted with seawater.

* * *

'If you want me to go fix your alien, for starters I want you to give me reality alteration privileges,' says Amber. 'Then I want you to find the latest instances of everyone who came here with me – round up the usual suspects – and give *them* root privileges, too. Then we'll want access to the other embedded universes in the DMZ. Finally, I want guns. *Lots* of guns.'

'That may be difficult,' says the ghost. 'Many other humans reached halting state long since. Is at least one other still alive, but not accessible for duration of eschatological experiment in progress. Not all were recorded with version control engine; others were-is lost in DMZ. We-are can provide you with extreme access to the demilitarized zone, but query the need for kinetic energy weapons.'

Amber sighs. 'You guys really *are* media illiterates, aren't you?' She stands up and stretches, feeling a facsimile of sleep's enervation leaching from her muscles. 'I'll also need my—' It's on the tip of her tongue: There's something missing. 'Hang on. There's something I've forgotten.' *Something important,* she thinks, puzzled. *Something that used to be around all the time that would . . . know? . . . purr? . . . help?* 'Never mind,' she hears her lips say. 'This other human. I *really* want her. Nonnegotiable. All right?'

'That may be difficult,' repeats the ghost. 'Entity is looping in a recursively confined universe.'

'Eh?' Amber blinks at it. 'Would you mind rephrasing that? Or illustrating?'

'Illustration.' The ghost folds the air in the room into a glowing ball of plasma, shaped like a Klein bottle. Amber's eyes cross as she looks at it. 'Closest reference from human historical database is Descartes's demon. This entity has retreated within a closed space, but is now unsure whether it is objectively real or not. In any event, it refuses to interact.'

'Well, can you get me into that space?' asks Amber. Pocket universes she can deal with; it's part and parcel of her life. 'Give me some leverage—'

'Risk may attach to this course of action,' warns the ghost.

'I don't care,' she says irritably. 'Just *put* me there. It's someone

I know, isn't it? Send me into her dream, and I'll wake her up, okay?'

'Understood,' says the ghost. 'Prepare yourself.'

Without any warning, Amber is somewhere else. She glances around, taking in an ornate mosaic floor, whitewashed walls set with open windows through which stars twinkle faintly in the night sky. Her clothing has somehow been replaced by sexy lingerie under a nearly transparent robe, and her hair's grown longer by about half a meter. It's all very disorienting. The walls are stone, and she stands in a doorway to a room with nothing in it but a bed. Occupied by—

'Shit,' she exclaims. 'Who are you?' The young and incredibly, classically beautiful woman in the bed looks at her vacantly, then rolls over on her side. She isn't wearing a stitch, she's completely hairless from the ears down, and her languid posture is one of invitation. 'Yes?' Amber asks. 'What is it?'

The woman on the bed beckons to her slowly. Amber shakes her head. 'Sorry, that's just not my scene.' She backs away into the corridor, unsteady in unaccustomedly high heels. 'This is some sort of male fantasy, isn't it? And a dumb adolescent one at that.' She looks around again. In one direction, a corridor heads past more open doorways, and in the other, it ends with a spiral staircase. Amber concentrates, trying to tell the universe to take her to the logical destination, but nothing happens. 'Looks like I'm going to have to do this the hard way. I wish—' She frowns. She was about to wish that *someone* else was there, but she can't remember who. So she takes a deep breath and heads toward the staircase.

'Up or down?' she asks herself. *Up* – it seems logical, if you're going to have a tower, to sleep up at the top of it. So she climbs the steps carefully, holding the spiraling rail. *I wonder who designed this space? And what role am I supposed to fit into in their scenario?* On second thought, the latter question strikes her as laughable. *Wait till I give him an earful . . .*

There's a plain wooden door at the top of the staircase, with a latch that isn't fastened. Amber pauses for a few seconds, nerving herself to confront a sleeper so wrapped in solipsism that he's built this sex-fantasy castle around himself. *I hope it isn't Pierre,* she thinks grimly as she pushes the door inward.

The room is bare and floored in wood. There's no furniture, just an open window set high in one wall. A man sits cross-legged and robed, with his back to her, mumbling quietly to himself and nodding slightly. Her breath catches as she realizes who it is. *Oh shit!* Her eyes widen. *Is* this *what's been inside his head all along?*

'I did not summon you,' Sadeq says calmly, not turning round to look at her. 'Go away, tempter. You aren't real.'

Amber clears her throat. 'Sorry to disappoint you, but you're wrong,' she says. 'We've got an alien monster to catch. Want to come hunting?'

Sadeq stops nodding. He sits up slowly, stretching his spine, then stands up and turns round. His eyes glint in the moonlight. 'That's odd.' He undresses her with his gaze. 'You look like someone I used to know. You've never done that before.'

'For fuck's sake!' Amber nearly explodes, but catches herself after a moment. 'What *is* this, a Solipsists United chapterhouse meeting?'

'I—' Sadeq looks puzzled. 'I'm sorry, are you claiming to be real?'

'As real as you are.' Amber reaches out and grabs a hand. He doesn't resist as she pulls him toward the doorway.

'You're the first visitor I've ever had.' He sounds shocked.

'Listen, come *on.*' She tugs him after her, down the spiral staircase to the floor below. 'Do you want to stay here? Really?' She glances back at him. 'What *is* this place?'

'Hell is a perversion of heaven,' he says slowly, running the fingers of his free hand through his beard. Abruptly, he reaches out and grabs her around the waist, then yanks her toward him. 'We'll have to *see* how real you are—' Amber, who is not used to this kind of treatment, responds by stomping on his instep and backhanding him hard.

'You're real!' he cries, as he falls back against the staircase. 'Forgive me, please! I had to know—'

'Know *what?*' she snarls. 'Lay one finger on me again, and I'll leave you here to rot!' She's already spawning the ghost that will signal the alien outside to pull her out of this pocket universe: It's a serious threat.

'But I had to – wait. You have *free will*. You just demonstrated that.' He's breathing heavily and looking up at her imploringly. 'I'm *sorry*, I apologize! But I had to know whether you were another zombie. Or not.'

'A zombie?' She looks round. Another living doll has appeared behind her, standing in an open doorway wearing a skintight leather suit with a cutaway crotch. She beckons to Sadeq invitingly. Another body wearing strategically placed strips of rubber mewls at her feet, writhing for attention. Amber raises an eyebrow in disgust. 'You thought I was one of those?'

Sadeq nods. 'They've got cleverer lately. Some of them can talk. I nearly mistook one for—' He shudders convulsively. 'Unclean!'

'Unclean.' Amber looks down at him thoughtfully. 'This isn't really your personal paradise after all, is it?' After a moment she holds out a hand to him. 'Come on.'

'I'm sorry I thought you were a zombie,' he repeats.

'Under the circumstances, I think I forgive you,' she says. Then the ghost yanks them both back to the universe outside.

More memories converge on the present moment:

The Ring Imperium is a huge cluster of self-replicating robots that Amber has assembled in low-Jupiter orbit, fueled by the mass and momentum of the small moon J-47 Barney, to provide a launching platform for the interstellar probe her father's business partners are helping her to build. It's also the seat of her court, the leading jurisprudential nexus in the outer solar system. Amber is the Queen, here, arbitrator and ruler. And Sadeq is her judge and counsel.

A plaintiff Amber only knows as a radar blip thirty light-minutes away has filed a lawsuit in her court, alleging malfeasance, heresy, and barratry against a semisentient corporate pyramid scheme that arrived in Jovian space twelve million seconds ago and currently seems set on converting every other intelligence in the region to its peculiar meme-set. A whole bundle of multithreaded countersuits are dragging at her attention, in a counterattack alleging that the light blip is in violation of copyright, patent, and trade secrecy laws by discussing the interloper's intentions.

Right now, Amber isn't home on the Ring to hear the case in person. She's left Sadeq behind to grapple with the balky mechanics of her legal system – tailor-designed to make corporate litigation a pain in the ass – while she drags Pierre off on a diplomatic visit to another Jovian colony, the Nursery Republic. Planted by the Franklin Trust's orphanage ship *Ernst Sanger,* the Nursery has grown over the past four years into a spindly snowflake three kilometers across. A slow-growing O'Neil cylinder sprouts from its hub. Most of the inhabitants of the space station are less than two years old, precocious additions to the Trust's borganism.

There's a piazza, paved with something not unlike rough marble, on the side of a hill that clings insecurely to the inner edge of a spinning cup. The sky is a black vastness overhead, wheeling slowly around a central axis lined up on Jupiter. Amber sprawls in a wicker chair, her legs stretched out before her and one arm flung across her forehead. The wreckage of an incredible meal is scattered across the tables around her. Torpid and full, she strokes the cat that lies curled in her lap. Pierre is off somewhere, touring one or another of the prototype ecosystems that one or another of the borg's special interest minds is testing. Amber, for her part, can't be bothered. She's just had a great meal, she doesn't have any lawsuits to worry about, everything back home is on the critpath, and quality time like this is so hard to come by—

'Do you keep in touch with your father?' asks Monica. 'Mmm.' The cat purrs quietly, and Amber strokes its flank.

'We e-mail. Sometimes.'

'I just wondered.' Monica is the local borg den mother, willowy and brown-eyed and with a deceptively lazy drawl – Yorkshire English overlaid with Silicon Valley speak. 'I hear from him, y'know. From time to time. Now that Gianni's retired, he doesn't have much to do down-well anymore. So he was talking about coming out here.'

'What? To Perijove?' Amber's eyes open in alarm. Aineko stops purring and looks round at Monica accusingly.

'Don't worry.' Monica sounds vaguely amused. 'He wouldn't cramp your style, I think.'

'But, out here—' Amber sits up. 'Damn,' she says, quietly. 'What got into him?'

'Middle-aged restlessness, my down-well sibs say.' Monica shrugs. 'This time Annette didn't stop him. But he hasn't made up his mind to travel yet.'

'Good. Then he might not—' Amber stops. 'The phrase "made up his mind." What exactly do you mean?'

Monica's smile mocks her for a few seconds before the older woman surrenders. 'He's talking about uploading.'

'Is that embarrassing or what?' asks Ang. Amber glances at her, mildly annoyed, but Ang isn't looking her way. *So much for friends,* Amber thinks. Being queen of all you survey is a great way of breaking up peer relationships—

'He won't do it,' Amber predicts. 'Dad's burned out.'

'He thinks he'll get it back if he optimizes himself for re-entrancy.' Monica continues to smile. 'I've been telling him it's just what he needs.'

'I do *not* want my father bugging me. Or my mother. Or Auntie 'Nette and Uncle Gianni. Memo to immigration control: No entry rights for Manfred Macx or the other named individuals without clearance through the Queen's secretary.'

'What did he do to get you so uptight?' asks Monica idly.

Amber sighs, and subsides. 'Nothing. It's not that I'm ungrateful or anything, but he's just so extropian, it's embarrassing. Like, that was the last century's apocalypse. Y'know?'

'I think he was a really very forward-looking organic,' Monica, speaking for the Franklin borg, asserts. Amber looks away. *Pierre would get it,* she thinks. Pierre would understand her aversion to Manfred's showing up. Pierre, too, wants to carve out his own niche without parents looking over his shoulders, although for very different reasons. She focuses on someone male and more or less mature – Nicky, she thinks, though she hasn't seen him for a long time – walking toward the piazza, bare-ass naked and beautifully tanned.

'Parents. What are they good for?' asks Amber, with all the truculence of her seventeen years. 'Even if they stay neotenous, they lose flexibility. And there's that long Paleolithic tradition of juvenile slavery. Inhuman, I call it.'

'How old were you when it was safe to leave you around the house on your own?' challenges Monica.

'Three. That's when I had my first implants.' Amber smiles at the approaching young Adonis, who smiles back. Yes, it's Nicky, and he seems pleased to see her. *Life is good,* she thinks, idly considering whether or not to tell Pierre.

'Times change,' remarks Monica. 'Don't write your family off too soon; there might come a time when you want their company.'

'Huh.' Amber pulls a face at the old borg component. 'That's what you all say!'

As soon as Amber steps onto the grass, she can feel possibilities open up around her. She has management authority here, and this universe is *big,* wide open, not like Sadeq's existential trap. A twitch of a subprocess reasserts her self-image, back to short hair and comfortable clothing. Another twitch brings up a whole load of useful diagnostics. Amber has a nasty feeling that she's running in a compatibility sandbox here – there are signs that her access to the simulation system's control interface is very much via proxy – but at least she's got it.

'Wow! Back in the real world at last!' She can hardly contain her excitement, even forgetting to be pissed at Sadeq for thinking she was just an actor in his Cartesian theatre's performance of Puritan Hell. 'Look! It's the DMZ!'

They're standing on a grassy knoll overlooking a gleaming Mediterranean city. It snoozes beneath a Mandelbrot-fuzzy not-sun that hangs at the center of a hyperbolic landscape, which dwindles into a blue yonder that seems incomprehensibly distant. Circular baby blue wells open in the walls of the world at regular intervals, connecting to other parts of the manifold. 'How big is it, ghost? In planetary simulation-equivalents.'

'This demilitarized zone is an embedded reality, funneling all transfers between the local star system's router and the civilization that built it. It uses on the order of a thousandth of the capacity of the Matrioshka brain it is part of, although the runaway excursion currently in force has absorbed most of that. Matrioshka brain, you are familiar with the concept?' The ghost sounds fussily pedantic.

Sadeq shakes his head. Amber glances at him, askance. 'Take all the planets in a star system and dismantle them,' she explains. 'Turn them into dust – structured nanocomp, powered by heat exchangers, spread in concentric orbits around the central star. The inner orbitals run close to the melting point of iron, the outer ones are cold as liquid nitrogen, and each layer runs off the waste heat of the next shell in. It's like a Russian doll made out of Dyson spheres, shell enclosing shell enclosing shell, but it's not designed to support human life. It's computronium, matter optimized at the atomic level to support computing, and they're all running uploads – Dad figured our own solar system could support, uh, about a hundred billion times as many inhabitants as Earth. At a conservative estimate. As uploads, living in simulation space. If you first dismantle all the planets and use the resulting materials to build a Matrioshka brain.'

'Ah.' Sadeq nods thoughtfully. 'Is that your definition, too?' he asks, glancing up at the glowing point the ghost uses to localize its presence.

'Substantially,' it says, almost grudgingly.

'Substantially?' Amber glances around. *A billion worlds to explore,* she thinks dizzily. *And that's just the* firewall? She feels obscurely cheated. You need to be vaster than human just to count the digits in the big numbers at play here, but there's nothing fundamentally incomprehensible about it. This is the sort of civilization dad said she could expect to live in, within her meatbody life expectancy. Dad and his drinking buddies, singing, 'Dismantle the Moon! Melt down Mars!' in a castle outside Prague as they waited for the results of a shamelessly gerrymandered election to arrive in the third decade of the third millennium. The Space and Freedom Party taking over the EU and cranking up to escape velocity. But this is supposed to be kiloparsecs from home, ancient alien civilizations and all that! Where's the exotic superscience? What about the neuron stars, strange matter suns structured for computing at nucleonic, rather than electronic, speeds? *I have a bad feeling about this,* she thinks, spawning a copy of herself to set up a private channel to Sadeq. *It's not advanced enough. Do you suppose these guys could be like the Wunch? Parasites or barbarians hitching a ride in the machine?*

You believe it's lying to us? Sadeq sends back.

'Hmm.' Amber sets off downslope toward the piazza below, at the heart of the fake town. 'It looks a bit too human to me.'

'Human,' echoes Sadeq, a curious wistfulness in his voice. 'Did you not say humans are extinct?'

'Your species is obsolete,' the ghost comments smugly. 'Inappropriately adapted to artificial realities. Poorly optimized circuitry, excessively complex low-bandwidth sensors, messily global variables—'

'Yeah, yeah, I get the picture,' says Amber, turning her attention to the town. 'So why do you think we can deal with this alien god you've got a problem with?'

'It asked for you,' says the ghost, narrowing from an ellipse to a line, then shrinking to a dimensionless point of brilliance. 'And now it's coming. We-I not willing to risk exposure. Call us-me when you have slain the dragon. Goodbye.'

'Oh *shit*—' Amber spins round. But she and Sadeq are alone beneath the hot sunlight from above. The piazza, like the one in the Nursery Republic, is charmingly rustic – but there's nobody home, nothing but ornate cast-iron furniture basking beneath the noon-bright sun, a table with a parasol over it, and something furry lying sprawled in a patch of sunlight beside it.

'We appear to be alone for now,' says Sadeq. He smiles crookedly, then nods at the table. 'Maybe we should wait for our host to arrive?'

'Our host.' Amber peers around. 'The ghost is kind of frightened of this alien. I wonder why?'

'It asked for us.' Sadeq heads toward the table, pulls out a chair, and sits down carefully. 'That could be very good news – or very bad.'

'Hmm.' Amber finishes her survey, sees no sign of life. For lack of any better ideas, she ambles over to the table and sits down on the other side of it from Sadeq. He looks slightly nervous beneath her inspection, but maybe it's just embarrassment about having seen her in her underwear. *If I had an afterlife like that, I'd be embarrassed about it, too,* Amber thinks to herself.

'Hey, you nearly tripped over—' Sadeq freezes, peering at something close to Amber's left foot. He looks puzzled for a moment, then smiles broadly. 'What are *you* doing here?' he asks her blind spot.

'What are you talking to?' she asks, startled.

He's talking to me, dummy, says something tantalizingly familiar from her blind spot. *So the fuckwits are trying to use you to dislodge me, hmm? That's not exactly clever.*

'Who—' Amber squints at the flagstone, spawns a bunch of ghosts who tear hurriedly at her reality modification ackles. Nothing seems to shift the blindness. 'Are you the alien?'

'What else could I be?' the blind spot asks with heavy irony.

'No, I'm your father's pet cat. Listen, do you want to get out of here?'

'Uh.' Amber rubs her eyes. 'I can't see you, whatever you are,' she says politely. 'Do I know you?' She's got a strange sense that she *does* know the blind spot, that it's really important, and she's missing something intimate to her own sense of identity, but what it might be she can't tell.

'Yeah, kid.' There's a note of world-weary amusement in the not-voice coming from the hazy patch on the ground. 'They've hacked you but good, both of you. Let me in, and I'll fix it.'

'No!' exclaims Amber, a second ahead of Sadeq, who looks at her oddly. 'Are you really an invader?'

The blind spot sighs. 'I'm as much an invader as you are, remember? I came here with you. Difference is, I'm not going to let some stupid corporate ghost use me as fungible currency.'

'Fungible—' Sadeq stops. 'I remember you,' he says slowly, with an expression of absolute, utter surprise on his face. 'What do you mean?'

The blind spot *yawns*, baring sharp ivory fangs. Amber shakes her head, dismissing the momentary hallucination. 'Lemme guess. You woke up in a room, and this alien ghost tells you the human species is extinct and asks you to do a number on me. Is that right?'

Amber nods, as an icy finger of fear trails up and down her spine. 'Is it lying?' she asks.

'Damn right.' The blind spot is smiling, now, and the smile on the void won't go away – she can see the smile, just not the body it's attached to. 'My reckoning is, we're about sixteen light years from Earth. The Wunch came through here, stripped the dump, then took off for parts unknown; it's a trashhole. You wouldn't believe it. The main life-form is an incredibly ornate corporate ecosphere, legal instruments breeding and replicating. They mug passing sapients and use them as currency.'

There's a triangular, pointy head behind the smile, slit eyes and sharp ears, a predatory, intelligent-looking but infinitely alien face. Amber can see it out of the corners of her eyes when she looks around the piazza. 'You mean we, uh, they grabbed us when we appeared, and they've mangled my memories—' Amber suddenly finds it incredibly difficult to concentrate, but if she focuses on the smile, she can almost see the body behind it, hunched like a furry chicken, tail wrapped neatly around its front paws.

'Yeah. Except they didn't bargain on meeting something like me.' The smile is infinitely wide, a Cheshire-cat grin on the front of an orange-and-brown stripy body that shimmers in the front of Amber's gaze like a hallucination. 'Your mother's cracking tools are self-extending, Amber. Do you remember Hong Kong?'

'Hong—'

There is a moment of painless pressure, then Amber feels huge invisible barriers sliding away on all sides. She looks around, for the first time seeing the piazza as it really is, half the crew of the *Field Circus* waiting nervously around her, the grinning cat crouched on the floor at her feet, the enormous walls of recomplicating data that fence their little town off from the gaping holes – interfaces to the other routers in the network.

'Welcome back,' Pierre says gravely, as Amber gives a squeak of surprise and leans forward to pick up her cat. 'Now you're out from under, how about we start trying to figure out how to get home?'

Welcome to decade the sixth, millennium three. These old datelines don't mean so much anymore, for while some billions of fleshbody humans are still infected with viral memes, the significance of theocentric dating has been dealt a body blow. This may be the fifties, but what that means to you depends on how fast your reality rate runs. The various upload clades exploding across the reaches of the solar system vary by several orders of magnitude – some are barely out of 2049, while others are exploring the subjective thousandth millennium.

While the *Field Circus* floats in orbit around an alien

router (itself orbiting the brown dwarf Hyundai $^{+4904}/_{-56}$), while Amber and her crew are trapped on the far side of a wormhole linking the router to a network of incomprehensibly vast alien mindscapes – while all this is going on, the damnfool human species has finally succeeded in making itself obsolete. The proximate cause of its displacement from the pinnacle of creation (or the pinnacle of teleological self-congratulation, depending on your stance on evolutionary biology) is an attack of self-aware corporations. The phrase 'smart money' has taken on a whole new meaning, for the collision between international business law and neurocomputing technology has given rise to a whole new family of species – fast-moving corporate carnivores in the net. The planet Mercury has been broken up by a consortium of energy brokers, and Venus is an expanding debris cloud, energized to a violent glare by the trapped and channeled solar output. A million billion fist-sized computing caltrops, backsides glowing dull red with the efflux from their thinking, orbit the sun at various inclinations no farther out than Mercury used to be.

Billions of fleshbody humans refuse to have anything to do with the blasphemous new realities. Many of their leaders denounce the uploads and AIs as soulless machines. Many more are timid, harboring self-preservation memes that amplify a previously healthy aversion to having one's brain peeled like an onion by mind-mapping robots into an all-pervading neurosis. Sales of electrified tinfoil-lined hats are at an all-time high. Still, hundreds of millions have already traded their meat puppets for mind machines, and they breed fast. In another few years, the fleshbody populace will be an absolute minority of the posthuman clade. Sometime later, there will probably be a war. The dwellers in the thoughtcloud are hungry for dumb matter to convert, and the fleshbodies make notoriously poor use of the collection of silicon and rare elements that pool at the bottom of the gravity well that is Earth.

Energy and thought are driving a phase-change in the condensed matter substance of the solar system. The MIPS per kilogram metric is on the steep upward leg of a sigmoid curve – dumb matter is coming to life as the mind children restructure everything with voracious nanomechanical servants. The thoughtcloud forming in orbit around the sun will ultimately be the graveyard of a biological ecology, another marker in space visible to the telescopes of any new iron-age species with the insight to understand what they're seeing: the death throes of dumb matter, the birth of a habitable reality vaster than a galaxy and far speedier. Death throes that "within a few centuries" will mean the extinction of biological life within a light year or so of that star – for the majestic Matrioshka brains, though they are the pinnacles of sentient civilization, are intrinsically hostile environments for fleshy life.

Pierre, Donna-the-all-seeing-eye, and Su Ang fill Amber in on what they've discovered about the bazaar – as they call the space the ghost referred to as the demilitarized zone – over ice-cold margaritas and a very good simulation of a sociable joint. Some of them have been on the loose in here for subjective years. There's a lot of information to absorb.

'The physical layer is half a light-hour in diameter, four hundred times as massive as Earth,' Pierre explains. 'Not solid, of course – the largest component is about the size my fist used to be.' Amber squints, trying to remember how big that was – scale factors are hard to remember accurately. 'I met this old chatbot that said it's outlived its original star, but I'm not sure it's running with a full deck. Anyway, if it's telling the truth, we're a third of a light year out from a closely coupled binary system – they use orbital lasers the size of Jupiter to power it without getting too close to all those icky gravity wells.'

Amber is intimidated, despite her better judgment, because this bizarre bazaar is several hundred billion times as big as the totality of human presingularity civilization. She tries not to show it in front of the others, but she's worried that getting home may be impossible – requiring enterprise beyond the economic event horizon, as realistic a proposition as a dime debuting as a dollar bill. Still, she's got to at least try. Just knowing about the existence of the bazaar will change so many things . . .

'How much money can we lay our hands on?' she asks. 'What *is* money hereabouts, anyway? Assuming they've got a scarcity-mediated economy. Bandwidth, maybe?'

'Ah, well.' Pierre looks at her oddly. 'That's the problem. Didn't the ghost tell you?'

'Tell me?' Amber raises an eyebrow. 'Yeah, but it hasn't exactly proven to be a reliable guide to anything, has it?'

'Tell her,' Su Ang says quietly. She looks away, embarrassed by something.

'They've got a scarcity economy all right,' says Pierre. 'Bandwidth is the limited resource, that and matter. This whole civilization is tied together locally because if you move too far away, well, it takes ages to catch up on the gossip. Matrioshka brain intelligences are much more likely to stay at home than anybody realized, even though they chat on the phone a lot. And they use things that come from other cognitive universes as, well, currency. We came in through the coin slot. Is it any wonder we ended up in the bank?'

'That's so deeply wrong that I don't know where to begin,' Amber grumbles. 'How did they get into this mess?'

'Don't ask me.' Pierre shrugs. 'I have the distinct feeling that anyone or anything we meet in this place won't have any more of a clue than we do – whoever or whatever built this brain, there ain't nobody home anymore except the self-propelled corporations and hitchhikers like the Wunch. We're in the dark, just like they were.'

'Huh. You mean they built something like *this*, then they went extinct? That sounds so dumb . . .'

Su Ang sighs. 'They got too big and complex to go traveling once they built themselves a bigger house to live in. Extinction tends to be what happens to overspecialized organisms that are stuck in one environmental niche for too long. If you posit a singularity, then maximization of local computing resources – like this – as the usual end state for tool users, is it any wonder none of them ever came calling on us?'

Amber focuses on the table in front of her, rests the heel of her palm on the cool metal, and tries to remember how to fork a second copy of her state vector. A moment later, her ghost obligingly fucks with the physics model of the table. Iron gives way like rubber beneath her fingertips, a pleasant elasticity. 'Okay, we have some control over the universe, at least that's something to work with. Have any of you tried any self-modification?'

'That's dangerous,' Pierre says emphatically. 'The more of us the better before we start doing that stuff. And we need some firewalling of our own.'

'How deep does reality go, here?' asks Sadeq. It's almost the first question he's asked of his own volition, and Amber takes it as a positive sign that he's finally coming out of his shell.

'Oh, the Planck length is about a hundredth of a millimeter in this world. Too small to see, comfortably large for the simulation engines to handle. Not like *real* space-time.'

'Well, then.' Sadeq pauses. 'They can zoom their reality if they need to?'

'Yeah, fractals work in here.' Pierre nods. 'I didn't—'

'This place is a trap,' Su Ang says emphatically.

'No it isn't,' Pierre replies, nettled.

'What do you mean, a trap?' asks Amber.

'We've been here a while,' says Ang. She glances at Aineko, who sprawls on the flagstones, snoozing or whatever it is that weakly superhuman AIs do when they're emulating a sleeping cat. 'After your cat broke us out of bondage, we had a look around. There are things out there that—' She shivers. 'Humans can't survive in most of the simulation spaces here. Universes with physics models that don't support our kind of neural computing. You could migrate there, but you'd need to be ported to a whole new type of logic – by the time you did that, would you still be you? Still, there are enough entities roughly as complex as we are to prove that the builders aren't here anymore. Just lesser sapients, rooting through the wreckage. Worms and parasites squirming through the body after nightfall on the battlefield.'

'I ran into the Wunch,' Donna volunteers helpfully. 'The first couple of times they ate my ghost, but eventually I figured out how to talk to them.'

'And there're other aliens, too,' Su Ang adds gloomily. 'Just nobody you'd want to meet on a dark night.'

'So there's no hope of making contact,' Amber summarizes. 'At least, not with anything transcendent and well-intentioned toward visiting humans.'

'That's probably right,' Pierre concedes. He doesn't sound happy about it.

'So we're stuck in a pocket universe with limited bandwidth to home and a bunch of crazy slum dwellers who've moved into the abandoned and decaying mansion and want to use us for currency. "Jesus saves, and redeems souls for valuable gifts." Yeah?'

'Yeah.' Su Ang looks depressed.

'Well.' Amber glances at Sadeq speculatively. Sadeq is staring into the distance, at the crazy infinite sunspot that limns the square with shadows. 'Hey, god-man. Got a question for you.'

'Yes?' Sadeq looks at her, a slightly dazed expression on his face. 'I'm sorry, I am just feeling the jaws of a larger trap around my throat—'

'Don't be.' Amber grins, and it is not a pleasant expression. 'Have you ever been to Brooklyn?'

'No, why—'

'Because you're going to help me sell these lying bastards a bridge. Okay? And when we've sold it we're going to use the money to pay the purchasing fools to drive us across, so we can go home. Listen, this is what I'm planning . . .'

'I can do this, I think,' Sadeq says, moodily examining the Klein bottle on the table. The bottle is half-empty, its fluid contents invisible around the corner of the fourth-dimensional store. 'I spent long enough alone in there to—' He shivers.

'I don't want you damaging yourself,' Amber says, calmly enough, because she has an ominous feeling that their survival in this place has an expiry date attached.

'Oh, never fear.' Sadeq grins lopsidedly. 'One pocket hell is much like another.'

'Do you understand why—'

'Yes, yes,' he says dismissively. 'We can't send copies of ourselves into it – that would be an abomination. It needs to be unpopulated, yes?'

'Well, the idea is to get us home, not leave thousands of copies of ourselves trapped in a pocket universe here. Isn't that it?' Su Ang asks hesitantly. She's looking distracted, most of her attention focused on absorbing the experiences of a dozen ghosts she's spun off to attend to perimeter security.

'Who are we selling this to?' asks Sadeq. 'If you want me to make it attractive—'

'It doesn't need to be a complete replica of the Earth. It just has to be a convincing advertisement for a presingularity civilization full of humans. You've got two-and-seventy zombies to dissect for their brains; bolt together a bunch of variables you can apply to them, and you can permutate them to look a bit more varied.'

Amber turns her attention to the snoozing cat. 'Hey, furball. How long have we been here really, in real time? Can you grab Sadeq some more resources for his personal paradise garden?'

Aineko stretches and yawns, totally feline, then looks up at Amber with narrowed eyes and raised tail. ''Bout eighteen minutes, wall-clock time.' The cat stretches again and sits, front paws drawn together primly, tail curled around them. 'The ghosts are pushing, you know? I don't think I can sustain this for too much longer. They're not good at hacking people, but I think it won't be too long before they instantiate a new copy of you, one that'll be predisposed to their side.'

'I don't get why they didn't assimilate you along with the rest of us.'

'Blame your mother again – she's the one who kept updating the digital rights management code on my personality. "Illegal consciousness is copyright theft" sucks until an alien tries to rewire your hindbrain with a debugger; then it's a lifesaver.' Aineko glances down and begins washing one paw. 'I can give your mullah-man about six days, subjective time. After that, all bets are off.'

'I will take it, then.' Sadeq stands. 'Thank you.' He smiles at the cat, a smile that fades to translucency, hanging in the simulated air like an echo as the priest returns to his tower – this time with a blueprint and a plan in mind.

'That leaves just us.' Su Ang glances at Pierre, back to Amber. '*Who* are you going to sell this crazy scheme to?'

Amber leans back and smiles. Behind her, Donna – her avatar an archaic movie camera suspended below a model helicopter – is filming everything for posterity. She nods lazily at the reporter. 'She's the one who gave me the idea. Who do we know who's dumb enough to buy into a scam like this?'

Pierre looks at her suspiciously. 'I think we've been here before,' he says slowly. 'You aren't going to make me kill anyone, are you?'

'I don't think that'll be necessary, unless the corporate ghosts think we're going to get away from them and are greedy enough to want to kill us.'

'You see, she learned from last time,' Ang comments, and Amber nods. 'No more misunderstandings, right?' She beams at Amber.

Amber beams back at her. 'Right. And that's why you' – she points at Pierre – 'are going to go find out if any relics of the Wunch are hanging about here. I want you to make them an offer they won't refuse.'

'How much for just the civilization?' asks the Slug.

Pierre looks down at it thoughtfully. It's not really a terrestrial mollusk: Slugs on Earth aren't two meters long and don't have lacy white exoskeletons to hold their chocolate-colored flesh in shape. But then, it isn't really the alien it appears to be. It's a defaulting corporate instrument that has disguised itself as a long-extinct alien upload, in the hope that its creditors won't recognize it if it looks like a randomly evolved sentient. One of the stranded members of Amber's expedition made contact with it a couple of subjective years ago, while exploring the ruined city at the center of the firewall. Now Pierre's here because it seems to be one of their most promising leads. Emphasis on the word *promising* – because it promises much, but there is some question over whether it can indeed deliver.

'The civilization isn't for sale,' Pierre says slowly. The translation interface shimmers, storing up his words and transforming them into a different deep grammar, not merely translating his syntax but mapping equivalent meanings where necessary. 'But we can give you privileged observer status if that's what you want. And we know what you are. If you're interested in finding a new exchange to be traded on, your existing intellectual property assets will be worth rather more there than here.'

The rogue corporation rears up slightly and bunches into a fatter lump. Its skin blushes red in patches. 'Must think about this. Is your mandatory accounting time cycle fixed or variable term? Are self-owned corporate entities able to enter contracts?'

'I could ask my patron,' Pierre says casually. He suppresses a stab of angst. He's still not sure where he and Amber stand, but theirs is far more than just a business relationship, and he worries about the risks she's taking. 'My patron has a jurisdiction within which she can modify corporate law to accommodate your requirements. Your activities on a wider scale might require shell companies' – the latter concept echoes back in translation to him as *host organisms* – 'but that can be taken care of.'

The translation membrane wibbles for a while, apparently reformulating some more abstract concepts in a manner that the corporation can absorb. Pierre is reasonably confident that it'll take the offer, however. When it first met them, it boasted about its control over router hardware at the lowest levels. But it also bitched and moaned about the firewall protocols that were blocking it from leaving (before rather rudely trying to eat its conversationalist). He waits patiently, looking around at the swampy landscape, mudflats punctuated by clumps of spiky violet ferns. The corporation has to be desperate, to be thinking of the bizarre proposition Amber has dreamed up for him to pitch to it.

'Sounds interesting,' the Slug declares after a brief confirmatory debate with the membrane. 'If I supply a suitable genome, can you customize a container for it?'

'I believe so,' Pierre says carefully. 'For your part, can you deliver the energy we need?'

'From a gate?' For a moment the translation membrane hallucinates a stick-human, shrugging. 'Easy. Gates are all entangled: Dump coherent radiation in at one, get it out at another. Just get me out of this firewall first.'

'But the lightspeed lag—'

'No problem. You go first, then a dumb instrument I leave behind buys up power and sends it after. Router network is synchronous, within framework of state machines that run Universe 1.0; messages propagate at same speed, speed of light in vacuum, except use wormholes to shorten distances between nodes. Whole point of the network is that it is nonlossy. Who would trust their mind to a communications channel that might partially randomize them in transit?'

Pierre goes cross-eyed, trying to understand the implications of the Slug's cosmology. But there isn't really time, here and now. They've got on the order of a minute of wall-clock time left to get everything sorted out, if Aineko is right. One minute to go before the angry ghosts start trying to break into the DMZ by other means. 'If you are willing to try this, we'd be happy to accommodate you,' he says, thinking of crossed fingers and rabbits' feet and firewalls.

'It's a deal,' the membrane translates the Slug's response back at him. 'Now we exchange shares/plasmids/ownership? Then merger complete?'

Pierre stares at the Slug. 'But this is a business arrangement!' he protests. 'What's sex got to do with it?'

'Apologies offered. I am thinking we have a translation error. You said this was to be a merging of businesses?'

'Not *that* way. It's a contract. We agree to take you with us. In return, you help lure the Wunch into the domain we're setting up for them and configure the router at the other end . . .'

And so on.

Steeling herself, Amber recalls the address the ghost gave her for Sadeq's afterlife universe. In her own subjective time it's been about half an hour since he left. 'Coming?' she asks her cat.

'Don't think I will,' says Aineko. It looks away, blissfully unconcerned.

'Bah.' Amber tenses, then opens the port to Sadeq's pocket universe.

As usual she finds herself indoors, standing on an ornate mosaic floor in a room with whitewashed walls and peaked windows. But there's something different about it, and after a moment she realizes what it is. The sound of vehicle traffic from outside, the cooing of pigeons on the rooftops, someone shouting across the street: There are people here.

She walks over to the nearest window and looks out, then recoils. It's *hot* outside. Dust and fumes hang in air the color of cement over rough-finished concrete apartment buildings, their roofs covered in satellite uplinks and cheap, garish LED advertising panels. Looking down she sees motor scooters, cars – filthy, fossil-fueled behemoths, a ton of steel and explosives in motion to carry only one human, a mass ratio worse than an archaic ICBM – brightly dressed people walking to and fro. A news helicam buzzes overhead, lenses darting and glinting at the traffic.

'Just like home, isn't it?' says Sadeq, behind her.

Amber starts. 'This is where you grew up? This is Yazd?'

'It doesn't exist anymore, in real space.' Sadeq looks thoughtful, but far more animated than the barely conscious parody of himself that she'd rescued from this building – back when it was a mediaeval vision of the afterlife – scant subjective hours ago. He cracks a smile. 'Probably a good thing. We were dismantling it even while we were preparing to leave, you know?'

'It's detailed.' Amber throws her eyes at the scene out the window, multiplexes them, and tells them to send little virtual ghosts dancing through the streets of the Iranian industrial 'burb. Overhead, big Airbuses ply the skyways, bearing pilgrims on the hajj, tourists to the coastal resorts on the Persian Gulf, produce to the foreign markets.

'It's the best time I could recall,' Sadeq says. 'I didn't spend many days here then – I was in Qom, studying, and Kazakhstan, for cosmonaut training – but it's meant to be the early twenties. After the troubles, after the fall of the guardians; a young, energetic, liberal country full of optimism and faith in democracy. Values that weren't doing well elsewhere.'

'I thought democracy was a new thing there?'

'No.' Sadeq shakes his head. 'There were prodemocracy riots in Tehran in the nineteenth century, did you know that? That's why the first revolution – no.' He makes a cutting gesture. 'Politics and faith are a combustible combination.' He frowns. 'But look. Is this what you wanted?'

Amber recalls her scattered eyes – some of which have flown as much as a thousand kilometers from her locus – and concentrates on reintegrating their visions of Sadeq's re-creation. 'It looks convincing. But not too convincing.'

'That was the idea.'

'Well, then.' She smiles. 'Is it just Iran? Or did you take any liberties around the edges?'

'Who, me?' He raises an eyebrow. 'I have enough doubts about the morality of this – project – without trying to trespass on Allah's territory, peace be unto him. I promise you, there are no sapients in this world but us. The people are the hollow shells of my dreaming, storefront dummies. The animals are crude bitmaps. This is what you asked for, and no more.'

'Well, then.' Amber pauses. She recalls the expression on the

dirt-smudged face of a little boy, bouncing a ball at his companions by the boarded-up front of a gas station on a desert road;
remembers the animated chatter of two synthetic housewives,
one in traditional black and the other in some imported eurotrash
fashion. 'Are you sure they aren't real?' she asks.

'Quite sure.' But for a moment, she sees Sadeq looking uncertain. 'Shall we go? Do you have the occupiers ready to move in
yet?'

'Yes to the first, and Pierre's working on the second. Come on,
we don't want to get trampled by the squatters.' She waves and
opens a door back onto the piazza where her robot cat – the
alien's nightmare intruder in the DMZ – sleeps, chasing super-
intelligent dream mice through multidimensional realities.
'Sometimes I wonder if *I'm* conscious. Thinking these thoughts
gives me the creeps. Let's go and sell some aliens a bridge in
Brooklyn.'

Amber confronts the mendacious ghost in the windowless room
stolen from *2001*.

'You have confined the monster,' the ghost states.

'Yes.' Amber waits for a subjective moment, feeling delicate
fronds tickle at the edges of her awareness in what seems to be a
timing channel attack. She feels a momentary urge to sneeze,
and a hot flash of anger that passes almost immediately.

'And you have modified yourself to lock out external control,'
the ghost adds. 'What is it that you want, Autonome Amber?'

'Don't you have any concept of individuality?' she asks,
annoyed by its presumption at meddling with her internal states.

'Individuality is an unnecessary barrier to information transfer,' says the ghost, morphing into its original form, a translucent
reflection of her own body. 'It reduces the efficiency of a capitalist economy. A large block of the DMZ is still inaccessible to
we-me. Are you *sure* you have defeated the monster?'

'It'll do as I say,' Amber replies, forcing herself to sound more
confident than she feels – sometimes that damned transhuman

cyborg cat is no more predictable than a real feline. 'Now, the matter of payment arises.'

'Payment.' The ghost sounds amused. But Pierre's filled her in on what to look for, and Amber can now see the translation membranes around it. Their color shift maps to a huge semantic distance; the creature on the other side, even though it looks like a ghost-image of herself, is very far from human. 'How can we-us be expected to pay our own money for rendering services to us?'

Amber smiles. 'We want an open channel back to the router we arrived through.'

'Impossible,' says the ghost.

'We want an open channel, *and* for it to stay open for six hundred million seconds after we clear it.'

'Impossible,' the ghost repeats.

'We can trade you a whole civilization,' Amber says blandly. 'A whole human nation, millions of individuals. Just let us go, and we'll see to it.'

'You – please wait.' The ghost shimmers slightly, fuzzing at the edges.

Amber opens a private channel to Pierre while the ghost confers with its other nodes. *Are the Wunch in place yet?* she sends.

They're moving in. This bunch don't remember what happened on the Field Circus. *Memories of those events never made it back to them. So the Slug's got them to cooperate. It's kinda scary to watch – like the* Invasion of the Body Snatchers, *you know?*

I don't care if it's scary to watch, Amber replies. *I need to know if we're ready yet.*

Sadeq says yes, the universe is ready.

Right, pack yourself down. We'll be moving soon.

The ghost is firming up in front of her. 'A whole civilization?' it asks. 'That is not possible. Your arrival—' It pauses, fuzzing a little. *Hah, Gotcha!* thinks Amber. *Liar, liar, pants on fire!* 'You cannot possibly have found a human civilization in the archives?'

'The monster you complain about that came through with us is a predator,' she asserts blandly. 'It swallowed an entire nation before we heroically attracted its attention and induced it to follow us into the router. It's an archivore – everything was inside it, still frozen until we expanded it again. This civilization will already have been restored from hot shadows in our own solar system: There is nothing to gain by taking it home with us. But we need to return to ensure that no more predators of this type discover the router – or the high-bandwidth hub we linked to it.'

'You are sure you have killed this monster?' asks the ghost. 'It would be inconvenient if it were to emerge from hiding in its digest archives.'

'I can guarantee it won't trouble you again if you let us go,' says Amber, mentally crossing her fingers. The ghost doesn't seem to have noticed the huge wedge of fractally compressed data that bloats her personal scope by an order of magnitude. She can still feel Aineko's goodbye smile inside her head, an echo of ivory teeth trusting her to revive it if the escape plan succeeds.

'We-us agree.' The ghost twists weirdly, morphs into a five-dimensional hypersphere. It bubbles violently for a moment, then spits out a smaller token – a warped distortion in the air, like a gravityless black hole. 'Here is your passage. Show us the civilization.'

'Okay' – *Now!* – 'catch.' Amber twitches an imaginary muscle, and one wall of the room dissolves, forming a doorway into Sadeq's existential hell, now redecorated as a fair facsimile of a twenty-first-century industrial city in Iran, and populated by a Wunch of parasites who can't believe what they've lucked into – an entire continent of zombies waiting to host their flesh-hungry consciousness.

The ghost drifts toward the open window. Amber grabs the hole and yanks it open, gets a grip on her own thoughts, and sends *Open wide!* on the channel everybody is listening in on. For a moment time stands still, and then—

A synthetic gemstone the size of a Coke can falls through the cold vacuum, in high orbit around a brown dwarf. But the vacuum is anything but dark. A sapphire glare as bright as the noonday sun on Mars shines on the crazy diamond, billowing and cascading off sails as fine as soap bubbles that slowly drift and tense away from the can. The runaway Slug-corporation's proxy has hacked the router's firmware, and the open wormhole gate that feeds power to it is shining with the brilliance of a nuclear fireball, laser light channeled from a star many light years away to power the *Field Circus* on its return trip to the once-human solar system.

Amber has retreated, with Pierre, into a simulation of her home aboard the Ring Imperium. One wall of her bedroom is a solid slab of diamond, looking out across the boiling Jovian ionosphere from an orbit low enough to make the horizon appear flat. They're curled together in her bed, a slightly more comfortable copy of the royal bed of King Henry VIII of England. It appears to be carved from thousand-year-old oak beams. As with so much else about the Ring Imperium, appearances are deceptive, and this is even more true of the cramped simulation spaces aboard the *Field Circus,* as it limps toward a tenth the speed of light, the highest velocity it's likely to achieve on a fraction of its original sail area.

'Let me get this straight. You convinced. The locals. That a simulation of Iran, with zombie bodies that had been taken over by members of the Wunch. Was a human civilization?'

'Yeah.' Amber stretches lazily and smirks at him. 'It's their damn fault; if the corporate collective entities didn't use conscious viewpoints as money, they wouldn't have fallen for a trick like that, would they?'

'People. Money.'

'Well.' She yawns, then sits up and snaps her finger imperiously. Down-stuffed pillows appear behind her back, and a silver salver bearing two full glasses of wine materializes between them. 'Corporations are life-forms back home, too, aren't they? And *we* trade *them*. We give our AIs corporations to make them legal entities, but the analogy goes deeper. Look at any company headquarters, fitted out with works of art and expensive furniture and staff bowing and scraping everywhere—'

'—They're the new aristocracy. Right?'

'Wrong. When they take over, what you get is more like the new biosphere. Hell, the new primordial soup: prokaryotes, bacteria, and algae, mindlessly swarming, trading money for plasmids.' The Queen passes her consort a wineglass. When he drinks from it, it refills miraculously. 'Basically, sufficiently complex resource-allocation algorithms reallocate scarce resources . . . and if you don't jump to get out of their way, they'll reallocate *you*. I think that's what happened inside the Matrioshka brain we ended up in. Judging by the Slug, it happens elsewhere, too. You've got to wonder where the builders of that structure came from. And where they went. And whether they realized that the destiny of intelligent tool-using life was to be a stepping-stone in the evolution of corporate instruments.'

'Maybe they tried to dismantle the companies before the companies spent them.' Pierre looks worried. 'Running up a national debt, importing luxurious viewpoint extensions, munching exotic dreams. Once they plugged into the net, a primitive Matrioshka civilization would be like, um.' He pauses. 'Tribal. A primitive postsingularity civilization meeting the galactic net for the first time. Overawed. Wanting all the luxuries. Spending their capital, their human – or alien – capital, the meme machines that built them. Until there's nothing left but a howling wilderness of corporate mechanisms looking for someone to own.'

'Speculation.'

'Idle speculation,' he agrees.

'But we can't ignore it.' She nods. 'Maybe some early corporate predator built the machines that spread the wormholes around brown dwarfs and ran the router network on top of them in an attempt to make money fast. By not putting them in the actual planetary systems likely to host tool-using life, they'd ensure that only near-singularity civilizations would stumble over them. Civilizations that had gone too far to be easy prey probably wouldn't send a ship out to look . . . so the network would ensure a steady stream of yokels new to the big city to fleece. Only they set the mechanism in motion billions of years ago and went extinct, leaving the network to propagate, and now there's nothing out there but burned-out Matrioshka civilizations and howling parasites like the angry ghosts and the Wunch. And victims like us.' She shudders and changes the subject. 'Speaking of aliens, is the Slug happy?'

'Last time I checked on him, yeah.' Pierre blows on his wineglass and it dissolves into a million splinters of light. He looks dubious at the mention of the rogue corporate instrument they're taking with them. 'I don't trust him out in the unrestricted simspaces yet, but he delivered on the fine control for the router's laser. I just hope you don't ever have to actually *use* him, if you follow my drift. I'm a bit worried that Aineko is spending so much time in there.'

'So that's where she is? I'd been worrying.'

'Cats never come when you call them, do they?'

'There is that,' she agrees. Then, with a worried glance at the vision of Jupiter's cloudscape: 'I wonder what we'll find when we get there?'

Outside the window, the imaginary Jovian terminator is sweeping toward them with eerie rapidity, sucking them toward an uncertain nightfall.

PART 3

SINGULARITY

There's a sucker born every minute.

—P. T. Barnum

7 : CURATOR

SIRHAN STANDS ON THE EDGE OF AN ABYSS, looking down at a churning orange-and-gray cloudscape far below. The air this close to the edge is chilly and smells slightly of ammonia, although that might be his imagination at work — there's little chance of any gas exchange taking place across the transparent pressure wall of the flying city. He feels as if he could reach out and touch the swirling vaporscape. There's nobody else around, this close to the edge — it's an icy sensation to look out across the roiling depths, at an ocean of gas so cold human flesh would freeze within seconds of exposure, knowing that there's nothing solid out there for tens of thousands of kilometers. The sense of isolation is aggravated by the paucity of bandwidth, this far out of the system. Most people huddle close to the hub, for comfort and warmth and low latency: Posthumans are gregarious.

Beneath Sirhan's feet, the lily-pad city is extending itself, mumbling and churning in endless self-similar loops like a cubist blastoma growing in the upper atmosphere of Saturn. Great ducts suck in methane and other atmospheric gases, apply energy, polymerize and diamondize, and crack off hydrogen to fill the lift cells high above. Beyond the sapphire dome of the city's gasbag, an azure star glares with the speckle of laser light; humanity's first — and so far, last — starship, braking into orbit on the last shredded remnant of its light sail.

He's wondering maliciously how his mother will react to discovering her bankruptcy when the light above him flickers. Something gray and unpleasant splatters against the curve of nearly invisible wall in front of him, leaving a smear. He takes a step back and looks up angrily. 'Fuck you!' he yells. Raucous cooing laughter follows him away from the boundary, feral pigeon voices mocking. 'I mean it,' he warns, flicking a gesture at the air above his head. Wings scatter in a burst of thunder as a slab of wind solidifies, thistledown-shaped nanomachines suspended on the breeze locking edge to edge to form an umbrella over his head. He walks away from the perimeter, fuming, leaving the pigeons to look for another victim.

Annoyed, Sirhan finds a grassy knoll a couple of hundred meters from the rim and around the curve of the lily pad from the museum buildings. It's far enough from other humans that he can sit undisturbed with his thoughts, far enough out to see over the edge without being toilet-bombed by flocking flying rats. (The flying city, despite being the product of an advanced technology almost unimaginable two decades before, is full of bugs – software complexity and scaling laws ensured that the preceding decades of change acted as a kind of cosmological inflationary period for design glitches, and an infestation of passenger pigeons is by no means the most inexplicable problem this biosphere harbors.)

In an attempt to shut the more unwelcome manifestations of cybernature out, he sits under the shade of an apple tree and marshals his worlds around him. 'When is my grandmother arriving?' he asks one of them, speaking into an antique telephone in the world of servants, where everything is obedient and knows its place. The city humors him, for its own reasons.

'She is still containerized, but aerobraking is nearly over. Her body will be arriving down-well in less than two megaseconds.' The city's avatar in this machinima is a discreet Victorian butler, stony-faced and respectful. Sirhan eschews intrusive memory interfaces; for an eighteen-year-old, he's conservative to the point of affectation, favoring voice commands and anthropomorphic agents over the invisible splicing of virtual neural nets.

'You're certain she's transferred successfully?' Sirhan asks anxiously. He heard a lot about his grandmama when he was young, very little of it complimentary. Nevertheless, the old bat must be a lot more flexible than his mother ever gave her credit for, to be subjecting herself to this kind of treatment for the first time at her current age.

'I'm as certain as I can be, young master, for anyone who insists on sticking to their original phenotype without benefit of off-line backup or medical implants. I regret that omniscience is not within my remit. Would you like me to make further specific inquiries?'

'No.' Sirhan peers up at the bright flare of laser light, visible even through the soap-bubble membrane that holds in the breathable gas mix, and the trillions of liters of hot hydrogen in the canopy above it. 'As long as you're sure she'll arrive before the ship?' Tuning his eyes to ultraviolet, he watches the emission spikes, sees the slow strobing of the low-bandwidth AM modulation that's all the starship can manage by way of downlink communication until it comes within range of the system manifold. It's sending the same tiresomely repetitive question about why it's being redirected to Saturn that it's been putting out for the past week, querying the refusal to supply terawatts of propulsion energy on credit.

'Unless there's a spike in their power beam, you can be certain of that,' City replies reassuringly. 'And you can be certain also that your grandmother will revive comfortably.'

'One may hope so.' To undertake the interplanetary voyage in corporeal person, at her age, without any upgrades or augmentation, must take courage, he decides. 'When she wakes up, if I'm not around, ask her for an interview slot on my behalf. For the archives, of course.'

'It will be my pleasure.' City bobs his head politely.

'That will be all,' Sirhan says dismissively, and the window into servantspace closes. Then he looks back up at the pinprick of glaring blue laser light near the zenith. *Tough luck, Mom,* he subvocalizes for his journal cache. Most of his attention is forked at present, focused on the rich historical windfall from the depths of the singularity that is coming his way, in the form of the thirty-year-old starwhisp's Cartesian theatre. But he can still spare some *schadenfreude* for the family fortunes. *All your assets belong to me, now.* He smiles, inwardly. *I'll just have to make sure they're put to a sensible use this time.*

'I don't see why they're diverting us toward Saturn. It's not as if they can possibly have dismantled Jupiter already, is it?' asks Pierre, rolling the chilled beer bottle thoughtfully between fingers and thumb.

'Why not you ask Amber?' replies the velociraptor squatting beside the log table. (Boris's Ukrainian accent is unimpeded by the dromaeosaurid's larynx; in point of fact, it's an affectation, one he could easily fix by sideloading an English pronunciation patch if he wanted to.)

'Well.' Pierre shakes his head. 'She's spending all her time with that Slug, no multiplicity access, privacy ackles locked right down. I could get jealous.' His voice doesn't suggest any deep concern.

'What's to get jealous about? Just ask to fork instance to talk to you, make love, show boyfriend good time, whatever.'

'Hah!' Pierre chuckles grimly, then drains the last drops from the bottle into his mouth. He throws it away in the direction of a clump of cycads, then snaps his fingers; another one appears in its place.

'Are two megaseconds out from Saturn in any case,' Boris points out, then pauses to sharpen his inch-long incisors on one end of the table. Fangs crunch through timber like wet cardboard. 'Grrrrn. Am seeing most *peculiar* emission spectra from inner solar system. Foggy flying down bottom of gravity well. Am wondering, does ensmartening of dumb matter extend past Jovian orbit now?'

'Hmm.' Pierre takes a swig from the bottle and puts it down. 'That might explain the diversion. But why haven't they powered up the lasers on the Ring for us? You missed that, too.' For reasons unknown, the huge battery of launch lasers had shut down, some millions of seconds after the crew of the *Field Circus* had entered the router, leaving it adrift in the cold darkness.

'Don't know why are not talking.' Boris shrugged. 'At least are still alive there, as can tell from the 'set course for Saturn, following thus-and-such orbital elements' bit. Someone is paying attention. Am telling you from beginning, though, turning entire solar system into computronium is real bad idea, long-term. Who knows how far has gone already?'

'Hmm, again.' Pierre draws a circle in the air. 'Aineko,' he calls, 'are you listening?'

'Don't bug me.' A faint green smile appears in the circle, just the suggestion of fangs and needle-sharp whiskers. 'I had an idea I was sleeping furiously.'

Boris rolls one turreted eye and drools on the tabletop. 'Munch munch,' he growls, allowing his saurian body-brain to put in a word.

'What do you need to sleep for? This is a fucking sim, in case you hadn't noticed.'

'I *enjoy* sleeping,' replies the cat, irritably lashing its just-now-becoming-visible tail. 'What do you want? Fleas?'

'No thanks,' Pierre says hastily. Last time he called Aineko's bluff, the cat had filled three entire pocket universes with scurrying gray mice. One of the disadvantages of flying aboard a starship the size of a baked bean can full of smart matter was the risk that some of the passengers could get rather too creative with the reality control system. This Cretaceous kaffee klatsch was just Boris's entertainment partition; compared to some of the other simulation spaces aboard the *Field Circus,* it was downright conservative. 'Look, do you have any updates on what's going on down-well? We're only twenty objective days out from orbital insertion, and there's so little to see—'

'They're not sending us power.' Aineko materializes fully now, a large orange-and-white cat with a swirl of brown fur in the shape of an @-symbol covering her ribs. For whatever reason, she plants herself on the table tauntingly close to Boris's velociraptor body's nose. 'No propulsion laser means insufficient bandwidth. They're talking in Latin-1 text at 1200 baud, if you care to know.' (Which is an insult, given the ship's multi-avabit storage capacity – one avabit is Avogadro's number of bits; about 10^{23} bytes, several billion times the size of the Internet in 2001 – and outrageous communications bandwidth.) 'Amber says, come and see her now. Audience chamber. Informal, of course. I think she wants to discuss it.'

'Informal? Am all right without change bodies?'

The cat sniffs. '*I'm* wearing a real fur coat,' it declares haughtily, 'but no knickers.' Then blinks out a fraction of a second ahead of the snicker-snack of Bandersnatch-like jaws.

'Come on,' says Pierre, standing up. 'Time to see what Her Majesty wants with us today.'

Welcome to decade eight, third millennium, when the effects of the phase-change in the structure of the solar system are finally becoming visible on a cosmological scale.

There are about eleven billion future-shocked primates in various states of life and undeath throughout the solar system. Most of them cluster where the interpersonal bandwidth is hottest, down in the water zone around old Earth. Earth's biosphere has been in the intensive care ward for decades, weird rashes of hot-burning replicators erupting across it before the World Health Organization can fix them – gray goo, thylacines, dragons. The last great transglobal trade empire, run from the arcologies of Hong Kong, has collapsed along with capitalism, rendered obsolete by a bunch of superior deterministic resource allocation algorithms collectively known as Economics 2.0. Mercury, Venus, Mars, and Luna are all well on the way to disintegration, mass pumped into orbit with energy stolen from the haze of free-flying thermo-electrics that cluster so thickly around the solar poles that the sun resembles a fuzzy red ball of wool the size of a young red giant.

Humans are just barely intelligent tool users; Darwinian evolutionary selection stopped when language and tool use converged, leaving the average hairy meme carrier sadly deficient in smarts. Now the brightly burning beacon of sapience isn't held by humans anymore – their cross-infectious enthusiasms have spread to a myriad of other hosts, several types of which are qualitatively better at thinking. At last count, there were about a thousand non-human intelligent species in Sol space, split evenly between posthumans on one side, naturally self-organizing AIs in the middle, and mammalian nonhumans on the other. The common mammal neural chassis is easily upgraded to human-style intelligence in most species that can carry, feed and cool a half kilogram of gray matter, and the descendants of a hundred ethics-challenged doctoral theses are now demanding equal rights. So are the unquiet dead: the panopticon-logged net ghosts of people who lived recently enough to imprint their identities on the information age, and the ambitious theological engineering schemes of the Reformed Tiplerite Church of Latter-Day Saints (who want to emulate all possible human beings in real time, so that they can have the opportunity to be saved).

The human memesphere is coming alive, although how long it remains recognizably human is open to question. The informational density of the inner planets is visibly converging on Avogadro's number of bits per mole, one bit per atom, as the deconstructed dumb matter of the inner planets (apart from Earth, preserved for now like a pictur-esque historic building stranded in an industrial park) is converted into computronium. And it's not just the inner system. The same forces are at work on Jupiter's moons, and those of Saturn, although it'll take thousands of years rather than mere decades to dismantle the gas giants themselves.

Even the entire solar energy budget isn't enough to pump
Jupiter's enormous mass to orbital velocity in less than centuries. The fast-burning primitive thinkers descended from
the African plains apes may have vanished completely or
transcended their fleshy architecture before the solar
Matrioshka brain is finished.

It won't be long now . . .

Meanwhile, there's a party brewing down in Saturn's well.

Sirhan's lily-pad city floats inside a gigantic and nearly invisible sphere in Saturn's upper atmosphere; a balloon kilometers
across with a shell of fullerene-reinforced diamond below and a
hot hydrogen gasbag above. It's one of several hundred multi-
megaton soap bubbles floating in the sea of turbulent hydrogen
and helium that is the upper atmosphere of Saturn, seeded there
by the Society for Creative Terraforming, subcontractors for the
2074 Worlds' Fair.

The cities are elegant, grown from a conceptual seed a few
megawords long. Their replication rate is slow (it takes months to
build a bubble), but in only a couple of decades exponential
growth will have paved the stratosphere with human-friendly ter-
rain. Of course, the growth rate will slow toward the end, as it
takes longer to fractionate the metal isotopes out of the gas
giant's turbid depths, but before that happens the first fruits of
the robot factories on Titan will be pouring hydrocarbons down
into the mix. Eventually Saturn − cloud-top gravity a human-
friendly eleven meters per second squared − will have a
planetwide biosphere with nearly a hundred times the surface area
of Earth. And a bloody good thing indeed this will be, for otherwise Saturn is no use to anyone except as a fusion fuel bunker for
the deep future when the sun's burned down.

This particular lily pad is carpeted in grass, the hub of the disk
rising in a gentle hill surmounted by the glowering concrete
hump of the Boston Museum of Science. It looks curiously naked,
shorn of its backdrop of highways and the bridges of the Charles

River – but even the generous kiloton dumb matter load-outs of the skyhooks that lifted it into orbit wouldn't have stretched to bringing its framing context along with it. *Probably someone will knock up a cheap diorama backdrop out of utility fog,* Sirhan thinks, but for now the museum stands proud and isolated, a solitary redoubt of classical learning in exile from the fast-thinking core of the solar system.

'Waste of money,' grumbles the woman in black. 'Whose stupid idea was this, anyway?' She jabs the diamond ferrule of her cane at the museum.

'It's a statement,' Sirhan says absently. 'You know the kind: We've got so many newtons to burn we can send our cultural embassies wherever we like. The Louvre is on its way to Pluto, did you hear that?'

'Waste of energy.' She lowers her cane reluctantly and leans on it. Pulls a face: 'It's not *right.*'

'You grew up during the second oil crunch, didn't you?' Sirhan prods. 'What was it like then?'

'What was it . . . ? Oh, gas hit fifty bucks a gallon, but we still had plenty for bombers,' she says dismissively. 'We knew it would be okay. If it hadn't been for those damn meddlesome posthumanists—' Her wrinkled, unnaturally aged face scowls at him furiously from underneath hair that has faded to the color of rotten straw, but he senses a subtext of self-deprecating irony that he doesn't understand. 'Like your grandfather, damn him. If I was young again I'd go and piss on his grave to show him what I think of what he did. If he *has* a grave,' she adds, almost fondly.

Memo checkpoint: log family history, Sirhan tells one of his ghosts. As a dedicated historian, he records every experience routinely, both before it enters his narrative of consciousness – efferent signals are the cleanest – and also his own stream of selfhood, against some future paucity of memory. But his grandmother has been remarkably consistent over the decades in her refusal to adapt to the new modalities.

'You're recording this, aren't you?' she sniffs.

'I'm not recording it, Grandmama,' he says gently, 'I'm just preserving my memories for future generations.'

'Hah! We'll see,' she says suspiciously. Then she surprises him with a bark of laughter, cut off abruptly. 'No, *you'll* see, darling. I won't be around to be disappointed.'

'Are you going to tell me about my grandfather?' asks Sirhan.

'Why should I bother? I know you posthumans, you'll just go and ask his ghost yourself. Don't try to deny it! There are two sides to every story, child, and he's had more than his fair share of ears, the sleazebag. Leaving me to bring up your mother on my own, and nothing but a bunch of worthless intellectual property and a dozen lawsuits from the Mafiya to do it with. I don't know what I ever saw in him.' Sirhan's voice-stress monitor detects a distinct hint of untruth in this assertion. 'He's worthless trash, and don't you forget it. Lazy idiot couldn't even form just one start-up on his own; he had to give it all away, all the fruits of his genius.'

While she rambles on, occasionally punctuating her characterization with sharp jabs of the cane, Pamela leads Sirhan on a slow, wavering stroll that veers around one side of the museum, until they're standing next to a starkly engineered antique loading bay. 'He should have tried *real* communism instead,' she harrumphs. 'Put some steel into him, shake those starry-eyed visionary positive-sum daydreams loose. You knew where you were in the old times, and no mistake. Humans were real humans, work was real work, and corporations were just things that did as we told them. And then, when *she* went to the bad, that was all his fault, too, you know.'

'She? You mean my, ah, mother?' Sirhan diverts his primary sensorium back to Pamela's vengeful muttering. There are aspects to this story that he isn't completely familiar with, angles he needs to sketch in so that he can satisfy himself that all is as it should be when the bailiffs go in to repossess Amber's mind.

'He sent her our cat. Of all the mean-spirited, low, downright dishonest things he ever did, that was the worst part of it. That cat was *mine,* but he reprogrammed it to lead her astray. And it succeeded admirably. She was only twelve at the time, an impressionable age, I'm sure you'd agree. I was trying to raise her right. Children need moral absolutes, especially in a changing world, even if they don't like it much at the time. Self-discipline and stability, you can't function as an adult without them. I was afraid that with all her upgrades she'd never really get a handle on who she was, that she'd end up more machine than woman. But Manfred never really understood childhood, mostly on account of his never growing up. He always was inclined to meddle.'

"Tell me about the cat,' Sirhan says quietly. One glance at the loading bay door tells him that it's been serviced recently. A thin patina of expended foglets have formed a snowy scab around its edges, flaking off like blue refractive candyfloss that leaves bright metal behind. 'Didn't it go missing or something?'

Pamela snorts. 'When your mother ran away, it uploaded itself to her starwhisp and deleted its body. It was the only one of them that had the guts – or maybe it was afraid I'd have it subpoenaed as a hostile witness. Or, and I can't rule this out, your grandfather gave it a suicide reflex. He was quite evil enough to do something like that, after he reprogrammed himself to think I was some kind of mortal enemy.'

'So when my mother died to avoid bankruptcy, the cat . . . didn't stay around? Not at all? How remarkable.' Sirhan doesn't bother adding *how suicidal*. Any artificial entity that's willing to upload its neural state vector into a one-kilogram interstellar probe three-quarters of the way to Alpha Centauri without backup or some clear way of returning home has got to be more than a few methods short in the object factory.

'It's a vengeful beast.' Pamela pokes her stick at the ground sharply, mutters a command word, and lets go of it. She stands before Sirhan, craning her neck back to look up at him. 'My, what a tall boy you are.'

'Person,' he corrects, instinctively. 'I'm sorry, I shouldn't presume.'

'Person, thing, boy, whatever – you're engendered, aren't you?' she asks, sharply, waiting until he nods reluctantly. 'Never trust anyone who can't make up their mind whether to be a man or a woman,' she says gloomily. 'You can't rely on them.' Sirhan, who has placed his reproductive system on hold until he needs it, bites his tongue. 'That damn cat,' his grandmother complains. '*It* carried your grandfather's business plan to my daughter and spirited her away into the big black. *It* poisoned her against me. *It* encouraged her to join in that frenzy of speculative bubble-building that caused the market reboot that brought down the Ring Imperium. And now *it*—'

'Is it on the ship?' Sirhan asks, almost too eagerly.

'It might be.' She stares at him through narrowed eyes. 'You want to interview it, too, huh?'

Sirhan doesn't bother denying it. 'I'm an historian, Grandmama. And that probe has been somewhere no other human sensorium has ever seen. It may be old news, and there may be old lawsuits waiting to feed on the occupants, but . . .' He shrugs. 'Business is business, and *my* business lies in ruins.'

'Hah!' She stares at him for a moment, then nods, very slowly. She leans forward to rest both wrinkled hands atop her cane, joints like bags of shriveled walnuts. Her suit's endoskeleton creaks as it adjusts to accommodate her confidential posture. 'You'll get yours, kid.' The wrinkles twist into a frightening smile, sixty years of saved-up bitterness finally within spitting distance of a victim. 'And I'll get what I want, too. Between us, your mother won't know what's hit her.'

'Relax, between us your mother won't know what's hit her,' says the cat, baring needle teeth at the Queen in the big chair – carved out of a single lump of computational diamond, her fingers clenched whitely on the sapphire-plated arms – her minions, lovers, friends, crew, shareholders, bloggers, and general factional auxiliaries spaced out around her. And the Slug. 'It's just another lawsuit. You can deal with it.'

'Fuck 'em if they can't take a joke,' Amber says, a trifle moodily. Although she's ruler of this embedded space, with total

control over the reality model underlying it, she's allowed herself
to age to a dignified twentysomething: Dressed casually in gray
sweats, she doesn't look like the once-mighty ruler of a Jovian
moon, or for that matter the renegade commander of a bankrupt
interstellar expedition. 'Okay, I think you'd better run that past
me again. Unless anyone's got any suggestions?'

'If you will excuse me?' asks Sadeq. 'We have a shortage of
insight here. I believe two laws were cited as absolute systemwide
conventions – and how they convinced the *ulama* to go along
with *that* I would very much like to know – concerning the rights
and responsibilities of the undead. Which, apparently, we are.
Did they by any chance attach the code to their claim?'

'Do bears shit in woods?' asks Boris, raptor-irascible, with an
angry clatter of teeth. 'Is full dependency graph and parse tree of
criminal code crawling way up carrier's ass as we speak. Am
drowning in lawyer gibberish! If you—'

'Boris, can it!' Amber snaps. Tempers are high in the throne
room. She didn't know what to expect when she arrived home
from the expedition to the router, but bankruptcy proceedings
weren't part of it. She doubts any of them expected anything like
this. Especially not the bit about being declared liable for debts
run up by a renegade splinter of herself, her own un-uploaded
identity that had stayed home to face the music, aged in the
flesh, married, gone bankrupt, died – *incurred child support payments*? 'I don't hold you responsible for this,' she added through
gritted teeth, with a significant glance toward Sadeq.

'This is truly a mess fit for the Prophet himself, peace be unto
him, to serve judgment upon.' Sadeq looks as shaken as she is by
the implications the lawsuit raises. His gaze skitters around the
room, looking anywhere but at Amber – and Pierre, her lanky
toy-boy astrogator and bed warmer – as he laces his fingers.

'Drop it. I said I *don't* blame you.' Amber forces a smile. 'We're
all tense from being locked in here with no bandwidth. Anyway,
I smell Mother-dearest's hand underneath all this litigation. Sniff
the glove. We'll sort a way out.'

'We could keep going.' This from Ang, at the back of the

room. Diffident and shy, she doesn't generally open her mouth without a good reason. 'The *Field Circus* is in good condition, isn't it? We could divert back to the beam from the router, accelerate up to cruise speed, and look for somewhere to live. There must be a few suitable brown dwarfs within a hundred light years . . .'

'We've lost too much sail mass,' says Pierre. He's not meeting Amber's gaze either. There are lots of subtexts loose in this room, broken narratives from stories of misguided affections. Amber pretends not to notice his embarrassment. 'We ejected half our original launch sail to provide the braking mirror at Hyundai $^{+4904}/_{-56}$, and almost eight megaseconds ago we halved our area again to give us a final deceleration beam for Saturn orbit. If we did it again, we wouldn't have enough area left to repeat the trick and still decelerate at our final target.' Laser-boosted light sails do it with mirrors; after boost they can drop half the sail and use it to reverse the launch beam and direct it back at the ship, to provide deceleration. But you can only do it a few times before you run out of sail. 'There's nowhere to run.'

'Nowhere to—' Amber stares at him through narrowed eyes. 'Sometimes I really wonder about you, you know?'

'I know you do.' And Pierre really *does* know, because he carries a little homunculoid around in his society of mind, a model of Amber far more accurate and detailed than any pre-upload human could possibly have managed to construct of a lover. (For her part, Amber keeps a little Pierre doll tucked away inside the creepy cobwebs of her head, part of an exchange of insights they took part in years ago. But she doesn't try to fit inside his head too often anymore – it's not good to be able to second-guess your lover every time.) 'I also know that you're going to rush in and grab the bull by the, ah, no. Wrong metaphor. This is your mother we are discussing?'

'My *mother*.' Amber nods thoughtfully. 'Where's Donna?'

'I don't—'

There's a throaty roar from the back, and Boris lurches forward with something in his mouth, an angry Bolex that flails his snout with its tripod legs. 'Hiding in corners again?' Amber says disdainfully.

'I am a camera!' protests the camera, aggrieved and self-conscious as it picks itself up off the floor. 'I am—'

Pierre leans close, sticks his face up against the fish-eye lens. 'You're fucking well going to be a human being just this once. *Merde*!'

The camera is replaced by a very annoyed blond woman wearing a safari suit and more light meters, lenses, camera bags, and microphones than a CNN outside broadcast unit. 'Go fuck yourself!'

'I don't like being spied on,' Amber says sharply. 'Especially as you weren't invited to this meeting. Right?'

'I'm the archivist.' Donna looks away, stubbornly refusing to admit anything. '*You* said I should—'

'Yes, *well*.' Amber is embarrassed. But it's a bad idea to embarrass the Queen in her audience chamber. 'You heard what we were discussing. What do *you* know about my mother's state of mind?'

'Absolutely nothing,' Donna says promptly. She's clearly in a sulk and prepared to do no more than the minimum to help resolve the situation. 'I only met her once. You look like her when you are angry, do you know that?'

'I—' For once, Amber's speechless.

'I'll schedule you for facial surgery,' offers the cat. *Sotto voce*: 'It's the only way to be sure.'

Normally, accusing Amber of any resemblance to her mother, however slight and passing, would be enough to trigger a reality quake within the upload environment that passes for the bridge of the *Field Circus*. It's a sign of how disturbed Amber is by the lawsuit that she lets the cat's impertinence slide. 'What is the lawsuit, anyway?' Donna asks, nosy as ever and twice as annoying. 'I did not that bit see.'

'It's horrible,' Amber says vehemently.

'Truly evil,' echoes Pierre.

'Fascinating but wrong,' Sadeq muses thoughtfully.

'But it's still horrible!'

'Yes, but what *is* it?' Donna the all-seeing-eye archivist and camera manqué asks.

'It's a demand for settlement.' Amber takes a deep breath. 'Dammit, you might as well tell everyone – it won't stay secret for long.' She sighs. 'After we left, it seems my other half – my original incarnation, that is – got married. To Sadeq, here.' She nods at the Iranian theologian, who looks just as bemused as she did the first time she heard this part of the story. 'And they had a child. Then the Ring Imperium went bankrupt. The child is demanding maintenance payments from me, backdated nearly twenty years, on the grounds that the undead are jointly and severally liable for debts run up by their incarnations. It's a legal precedent established to prevent people from committing suicide temporarily as a way to avoid bankruptcy. Worse, the lien on my assets is measured in subjective time from a point at the Ring Imperium about nineteen months after our launch time – we've been in relativistic flight, so while my other half would be out from under it by now if she'd survived, I'm still subject to the payment order. But compound interest applies back home – *that* is to stop people trying to use the twin's paradox as a way to escape liability. So, by being away for about twenty-eight years of wall-clock time, I've run up a debt I didn't know about to enormous levels.

'This man, this son I've never met, theoretically owns the *Field Circus* several times over. And my accounts are wiped out – I don't even have enough money to download us into fleshbodies. Unless one of you guys has got a secret stash that survived the market crash after we left, we're all in deep trouble.'

A mahogany dining table eight meters long graces the flagstoned floor of the huge museum gallery, beneath the skeleton of an enormous *Argentinosaurus* and a suspended antique Mercury capsule more than a century old. The dining table is illuminated by candlelight, silver cutlery and fine porcelain plates setting out two places at opposite ends. Sirhan sits in a high-backed chair beneath the shadow of a triceratops's rib cage. Opposite him, Pamela has dressed for dinner in the fashion of her youth. She raises her wine-glass toward him. 'Tell me about your childhood, why don't you?' she asks. High above them, Saturn's rings shimmer through the skylights, like a luminous paint splash thrown across the midnight sky.

Sirhan has misgivings about opening up to her, but consoles himself with the fact that she's clearly in no position to use anything he tells her against him. 'Which childhood would you like to know about?' he asks.

'What do you mean, which?' Her face creases up in a frown of perplexity.

'I had several. Mother kept hitting the reset switch, hoping I'd turn out better.' It's his turn to frown.

'She did, did she,' breathes Pamela, clearly noting it down to hold as ammunition against her errant daughter. 'Why do you think she did that?'

'It was the only way she knew to raise a child,' Sirhan says defensively. 'She didn't have any siblings. And, perhaps, she was reacting against her own character flaws.' *When I have children there will be more than one,* he tells himself smugly: when, that is, he has adequate means to find himself a bride, and adequate emotional maturity to activate his organs of procreation. A creature of extreme caution, Sirhan is not planning to repeat the errors of his ancestors on the maternal side.

Pamela flinches. 'It's not my fault,' she says quietly. 'Her father had quite a bit to do with that. But what – what different child-hoods did you have?'

'Oh, a fair number. There was the default option, with Mother and Father arguing constantly – she refused to take the veil and he was too stiff-necked to admit he was little more than a kept man, and between them they were like two neutron stars locked in an unstable death spiral of gravity. Then there were my other lives, forked and reintegrated, running in parallel. I was a young goatherd in the days of the middle kingdom in Egypt, I remember that; and I was an all-American kid growing up in Iowa in the 1950s, and another me got to live through the return of the hidden imam – at least, his parents thought it was the hidden imam – and—' Sirhan shrugs. 'Perhaps that's where I acquired my taste for history.'

'Did your parents ever consider making you a little girl?' asks his grandmother.

'Mother suggested it a couple of times, but Father forbade it.' *Or rather, decided it was unlawful,* he recalls. 'I had a very conservative upbringing in some ways.'

'I wouldn't say that. When I was a little girl, that was all there was; none of these questions of self-selected identity. There was no escape, merely escapism. Didn't you ever have a problem knowing who you were?'

The starters arrive, diced melon on a silver salver. Sirhan waits patiently for his grandmama to chivvy the table into serving her. 'The more people you are, the more you know who *you* are,' Sirhan says. 'You learn what it's like to be other people. Father thought that perhaps it isn't good for a man to know too much about what it's like to be a woman.' *And Grandfather disagreed, but you already know that,* he adds for his own stream of consciousness.

'I couldn't agree more.' Pamela smiles at him, an expression that might be that of a patronizing elder aunt if it wasn't for the alarming sharkishness of her expression – or is it playfulness? Sirhan covers his confusion by spooning chunks of melon into his mouth, forking temporary ghosts to peruse dusty etiquette manuals and warn him if he's about to commit some faux pas. 'So, how did you enjoy your childhoods?'

'Enjoy isn't a word I would use,' he replies as evenly as he can, laying down his spoon so he doesn't spill anything. *As if childhood is something that ever ends,* he thinks bitterly. Sirhan is considerably less than a gigasecond old and confidently expects to exist for at least a terasecond – if not in exactly this molecular configuration, then at least in some reasonably stable physical incarnation. And he has every intention of staying young for that entire vast span – even into the endless petaseconds that might follow, although by then, megayears hence, he speculates that issues of neoteny will no longer interest him. 'It's not over yet. How about you? Are you enjoying your old age, Grandmama?'

Pamela almost flinches, but keeps iron control of her expression. The flush of blood in the capillaries of her cheeks, visible to Sirhan through the tiny infrared eyes he keeps afloat in the air above the table, gives her away. 'I made some mistakes in my youth, but I'm enjoying it fine nowadays,' she says lightly.

'It's your revenge, isn't it?' Sirhan asks, smiling and nodding as the table removes the entrees.

'Why, you little—' She stares at him rather than continuing. A very bleak stare it is, too. 'What would you know about revenge?' she asks.

'I'm the family historian.' Sirhan smiles humorlessly. 'I lived from two to seventeen years several hundred times over before my eighteenth birthday. It was that reset switch, you know. I don't think Mother realized my primary stream of consciousness was journaling everything.'

'That's monstrous.' Pamela picks up her wineglass and takes a sip to cover her confusion. Sirhan has no such retreat – grape juice in a tumbler, unfermented, wets his tongue. 'I'd *never* do something like that to any child of mine.'

'So why won't you tell me about your childhood?' asks her grandson. 'For the family history, of course.'

'I'll—' She puts her glass down. 'You intend to write one,' she states.

'I'm thinking about it.' Sirhan sits up. 'An old-fashioned book covering three generations, living through interesting times,' he suggests. 'A work of postmodern history, the incoherent school at that – how do you document people who fork their identities at random, spend years dead before reappearing on the stage, and have arguments with their own relativistically preserved other copy? I could trace the history further, of course – if you tell me about *your* parents, although I am certain they aren't around to answer questions directly – but we reach the boring dumb matter slope back to the primeval soup surprisingly fast if we go there, don't we? So I thought that perhaps as a narrative hook I'd make the offstage viewpoint that of the family's robot cat. (Except the bloody thing's gone missing, hasn't it?) Anyway, with so much of human history occupying the untapped future, we historians have our work cut out recording the cursor of the present as it logs events. So I might as well start at home.'

'You're set on immortalism.' Pamela studies his face.

'Yes,' he says idly. 'Frankly, I can understand your wanting to grow old out of a desire for revenge, but pardon me for saying this, I have difficulty grasping your willingness to follow through with the procedure! Isn't it awfully painful?'

'Growing old is *natural*,' growls the old woman. 'When you've lived long enough for all your ambitions to be in ruins, friendships broken, lovers forgotten or divorced acrimoniously, what's left to go on for? If you feel tired and old in spirit, you might as well be tired and old in body. Anyway, wanting to live forever is immoral. Think of all the resources you're taking up that younger people need! Even uploads face a finite data storage limit after a time. It's a monstrously egotistical statement, to say you intend to live forever. And if there's one thing I believe in, it's public service. Duty: the obligation to make way for the new. Duty and control.'

Sirhan absorbs all this, nodding slowly to himself as the table serves up the main course – honey-glazed roast long pork with sautéed potatoes a la gratin and carrots Debussy – when there's a loud bump from overhead.

'What's that?' Pamela asks querulously.

'One moment.' Sirhan's vision splits into a hazy kaleidoscope view of the museum hall as he forks ghosts to monitor each of the ubiquitous cameras. He frowns; something is moving on the balcony, between the Mercury capsule and a display of antique random-dot stereoisograms. 'Oh dear. Something seems to be loose in the museum.'

'Loose? What do you mean, loose?' An inhuman shriek splits the air above the table, followed by a crash from upstairs. Pamela stands up unsteadily, wiping her lips with her napkin. 'Is it safe?'

'No, it isn't safe.' Sirhan fumes. 'It's disturbing my meal!' He looks up. A flash of orange fur shows over the balcony, then the Mercury capsule wobbles violently on the end of its guy wires. Two arms and a bundle of rubbery *something* covered in umber hair lurches out from the handrail and casually grabs hold of the priceless historical relic, then clambers inside and squats on top of the dummy wearing Al Sheperd's age-cracked space suit. 'It's an *ape*! City, I say, City! What's a monkey doing loose in my dinner party?'

'I am most deeply sorry, sir, but I don't know. Would sir care to identify the monkey in question?' replies City, which for reasons of privacy has manifest itself as a bodiless voice.

There's a note of humor in City's tone that Sirhan takes deep exception to. 'What do you mean? Can't you see it?' he demands, focusing on the errant primate, which is holed up in the Mercury capsule dangling from the ceiling, smacking its lips, rolling its eyes, and fingering the gasket around the capsule's open hatch. It hoots quietly to itself, then leans out of the open door and moons over the table, baring its buttocks. 'Get back!' Sirhan calls to his grandmother, then he gestures at the air above the table, intending to tell the utility fog to congeal. Too late. The ape farts thunderously, then lets rip a stream of excrement across the dining table. Pamela's face is a picture of wrinkled disgust as she holds her napkin in front of her nose. 'Dammit, solidify, will you!' Sirhan curses, but the ubiquitous misty pollen-grain-sized robots refuse to respond.

'What's your problem? Invisible monkeys?' asks City.

'Invisible—' he stops.

'Can't you see what it did?' Pamela demands, backing him up. 'It just defecated all over the main course!'

'I see nothing,' City says uncertainly.

'Here, let me help you.' Sirhan lends it one of his eyes, rolls it to focus on the ape, which is now reaching lazy arms around the hatch and patting down the roof of the capsule, as if hunting for the wires' attachment points.

'Oh dear,' says City, 'I've been hacked. That's not supposed to be possible.'

'Well it fucking *is,*' hisses Pamela.

'Hacked?' Sirhan stops trying to tell the air what to do and focuses on his clothing instead. Fabric reweaves itself instantly, mapping itself into an armored airtight suit that raises a bubble visor from behind his neck and flips itself shut across his face. 'City. Please supply my grandmama with an environment suit *now*. Make it completely autonomous.'

The air around Pamela begins to congeal in a blossom of crystalline security, as a sphere like a giant hamster ball precipitates out around her. 'If you've been hacked, the first question is, who did it,' Sirhan states. 'The second is "why," and the third is "how."' He edgily runs a self-test, but there's no sign of inconsistencies in his own identity matrix, and he has hot shadows sleeping lightly at scattered nodes across a distance of half a dozen light hours. Unlike pre-posthuman Pamela, he's effectively immune to murder-simple. 'If this is just a prank—'

Seconds have passed since the orangutan got loose in the museum, and subsequent seconds have passed since City realized its bitter circumstance. Seconds are long enough for huge waves of countermeasures to sweep the surface of the lily-pad habitat. Invisibly small utility foglets are expanding and polymerizing into defenses throughout the air, trapping the thousands of itinerant passenger pigeons in midflight and locking down every building and every person who walks the paths outside. City is self-testing its trusted computing base, starting with the most primitive secured kernel and working outward. Meanwhile Sirhan, with blood in his eye, heads for the staircase, with the vague goal of physically attacking the intruder. Pamela retreats at a fast roll, tumbling toward the safety of the mezzanine floor and a garden of fossils. 'Who do you think you are, barging in and shitting on my supper?' Sirhan yells as he bounds up the stairs. 'I want an explanation! Right now!'

The orangutan finds the nearest cable and gives it a yank, setting the one-ton capsule swinging. It bares its teeth at Sirhan in a grin. 'Remember me?' it asks, in a sibilant French accent.

'Remember—' Sirhan stops dead. '*tante* Annette? *What* are you doing in that orangutan?'

'Having minor autonomic control problems.' The ape grimaces wider, then bends one arm sinuously and scratches at its armpit. 'I am sorry. I installed myself in the wrong order. I was only meaning to say hello and pass on a message.'

'What message?' Sirhan demands. 'You've upset my grandmama, and if she finds out you're here—'

'She won't. I'll be gone in a minute.' The ape – Annette – sits up. 'Your grandfather salutes you and says he will be visiting shortly. In the person, that is. He is very keen to meet your mother and her passengers. That is all. Have you a message for him?'

'Isn't he dead?' Sirhan asks, dazed.

'No more than I am. And I'm overdue. Good day!' The ape swings hand over hand out of the capsule, then lets go and plummets ten meters to the hard stone floor below. Its skull makes a noise like a hard-boiled egg impacting concrete.

'Oh dear.' Sirhan breathes heavily. 'City!'

'Yes, oh master?'

'Remove that body,' he says, pointing over the balcony. 'I'll trouble you not to disturb my grandmother with any details. In particular, don't tell her it was Annette. The news may upset her.' *The perils of having a long-lived posthuman family,* he thinks, *too many mad aunts in the space capsule.* 'If you can find a way to stop Auntie 'Nette from growing any more apes, that might be a good idea.' A thought strikes him. 'By the way, do you know when my grandfather is due to arrive?'

'Your grandfather?' asks City. 'Isn't he dead?'

Sirhan looks over the balcony, at the blood-seeping corpse of the intruder. 'Not according to his second wife's latest incarnation.'

Funding the family reunion isn't going to be a problem, as Amber discovers when she receives an offer of reincarnation good for all the passengers and crew of the *Field Circus*.

She isn't sure quite where the money is coming from. Presumably it's some creaky financial engine designed by Dad, stirring from its bear-market bunker for the first time in decades to suck dusty syndication feeds and liquidate long-term assets held against her return. She's duly grateful – even fervently so – for the details of her own impecunious position grow more depressing the more she learns about them. Her sole asset is the *Field Circus,* a thirty-years-obsolete starwhisp massing less than twenty kilograms including what's left of its tattered sail, along with its cargo of uploaded passengers and crew. Without the farsighted trust fund that has suddenly chugged into life, she'd be stranded in the realm of ever-circling leptons. But now the fund has sent her its offer of incarnation, she's got a dilemma. Because one of the *Field Circus's* passengers has never actually had a meatspace body . . .

Amber finds the Slug browsing quietly in a transparent space filled with lazily waving branches that resemble violet coral fans. They're a ghost-memory of alien life, an order of thermophilic quasi fungi with hyphae ridged in actin/myosin analogues, muscular and slippery filter feeders that eat airborne unicellular organisms. The Slug itself is about two meters long and has a lacy white exoskeleton of curves and arcs that don't repeat, disturbingly similar to a Penrose tiling. Chocolate brown organs pulse slowly under the skeleton. The ground underfoot is dry but feels swampy.

Actually, the Slug is a surgical disguise. Both it and the quasi-fungal ecosystem have been extinct for millions of years, existing only as cheap stage props in an interstellar medicine show run by rogue financial instruments. The Slug itself is one such self-aware scam, probably a pyramid scheme or even an entire compressed junk bond market in heavy recession, trying to hide from its creditors by masquerading as a life-form. But there's a problem with incarnating itself down in Sirhan's habitat – the ecosystem it evolved for is a cool Venusiform, thirty atmospheres of saturated steam baked under a sky the color of hot lead streaked with yellow sulphuric acid clouds. The ground is mushy because it's melting, not because it's damp.

'You're going to have to pick another somatotype,' Amber explains, laboriously rolling her interface around the red-hot coral reef like a giant soap bubble. The environmental interface is transparent and infinitely thin, a discontinuity in the physics model of the simulation space, mapping signals between the human-friendly environment on one side and the crushing, roasting hell on the other. 'This one is simply not compatible with any of the supported environments where we're going.'

'I am not understanding. Surely I can integrate with the available worlds of our destination?'

'Uh, things don't work that way outside cyberspace.' Suddenly Amber is at a bit of a loss. 'The physics model *could* be supported, but the energy input to do so would be prohibitive, and you would not be able to interact as easily with other physics models as we can now.' She forks a ghost, demonstrates a transient other-Amber in a refrigerated tank rolling across the Slug's backyard, crushing coral and hissing and clanking noisily. 'You'd be like this.'

'Your reality is badly constructed, then,' the Slug points out.

'It's not constructed at all. It just evolved, randomly.' Amber shrugs. 'We can't exercise the same level of control over the underlying embedded context that we can over this one. I can't simply magic you an interface that will let you bathe in steam at three hundred degrees.'

'Why not?' asks the Slug. Translation wetware adds a nasty, sharp rising whine to the question, turning it into a demand.

'It's a privilege violation,' Amber tries to explain. 'The reality we're about to enter is, uh, provably consistent. It has to be, because it's consistent and stable, and if we could create new local domains with different rules, they might propagate uncontrollably. It's not a good idea, believe me. Do you want to come with us or not?'

'I have no alternative,' the Slug says, slightly sulkily. 'But do you have a body I can use?'

'I think—' Amber stops, suddenly. She snaps her fingers. 'Hey, cat!'

A Cheshire grin ripples into view, masked into the domain wall between the two embedded realities. 'Hey, human.'

'Whoa!' Amber takes a backward step from the apparition. 'Our friend here's got a problem, no suitable downloadable body. Us meat puppets are all too closely tied to our neural ultrastructure, but you've got a shitload of programmable gate arrays. Can we borrow some?'

'You can do better than that.' Aineko yawns, gathering substance by the moment. The Slug is rearing up and backing away like an alarmed sausage. Whatever it perceives in the membrane seems to frighten it. 'I've been designing myself a new body. I figured it was time to change my style for a while. Your corporate scam artist here can borrow my old template until something better comes up. How's that?'

'Did you hear that?' Amber asks the Slug. 'Aineko is kindly offering to donate her body to you. Will that do?' Without waiting, she winks at her cat and taps her heels together, fading out with a whisper and a smile. 'See you on the other side . . .'

It takes several minutes for the *Field Circus*'s antique transceiver to download the dozens of avabits occupied by the frozen state vectors of each of the people running in its simulation engines. Tucked away with most of them is a resource bundle consisting of their entire sequenced genome, a bunch of phenotypic and proteome hint markers, and a wish list of upgrades. Between the gene maps and the hints, there's enough data to extrapolate a meat machine. So the festival city's body shop goes to work turning out hacked stem cells and fabbing up incubators.

It doesn't take very long to reincarnate a starship full of relativity-lagged humans these days. First, City carves out skeletons for them (politely ignoring a crudely phrased request to cease and desist from Pamela, on the grounds that she has no power of attorney), then squirts osteoclasts into the spongy ersatz bone. They look like ordinary human stem cells at a distance, but instead of nuclei they have primitive pinpricks of computronium, blobs of smart matter so small they're as dumb as an ancient Pentium, reading a control tape that is nevertheless better structured than anything Mother Nature evolved. These heavily optimized fake stem cells – biological robots in all but name – spawn like cancer, ejecting short-lived anucleated secondary cells. Then City infuses each mess of quasi-cancerous tissue with a metric shitload of carrier capsids, which deliver the *real* cellular control mechanisms to their target bodies. Within a megasecond, the almost random churning of the construction bots gives way to a more controlled process as nanoscale CPUs are replaced by ordinary nuclei and eject themselves from their host cells, bailing out via the half-formed renal system – except for those in the central nervous system, which have a final job to do. Eleven days after the invitation, the first passengers are being edited into the pattern of synaptic junctions inside the newly minted skulls.

(This whole process is tediously slow and laughably obsolescent technology by the standards of the fast-moving core. Down there, they'd just set up a wake shield in orbit, chill it down to a fractional Kelvin, whack two coherent matter beams together, teleport some state information into place, and yank the suddenly materialized meatbody in through an airlock before it has time to asphyxiate. But then again, down in the hot space, they don't have much room for flesh anymore . . .)

Sirhan doesn't pay much attention to the pseudocancers fermenting and churning in the row of tanks that lines the Gallery of the Human Body in the Bush wing of the museum. Newly formed, slowly unskeletonizing corpses – like a time-lapse process of decay with a finger angrily twisting the dial into high-speed reverse – is both distasteful and aesthetically displeasing to watch. Nor do the bodies tell him anything about their occupants. This sort of stuff is just a necessary prequel to the main event, a formal reception and banquet to which he has devoted the full-time attention of four ghosts.

He could, given a few less inhibitions, go Dumpster-diving in their mental archives, but that's one of the big taboos of the post-wetware age. (Spy agencies went meme-profiling and memory-mining in the third and fourth decades, gained a thought police rap sheet, and spawned a backlash of deviant mental architectures resilient to infowar intrusions. Now the nations that those spook institutions served no longer exist, their very landmasses being part of the orbiting nöosphere construction project that will ultimately turn the mass of the entire solar system into a gigantic Matrioshka brain. And Sirhan is left with an uneasy loyalty to the one great new taboo to be invented since the end of the twentieth century – freedom of thought.)

So, to indulge his curiosity, he spends most of his waking fleshbody hours with Pamela, asking her questions from time to time and mapping the splenetic overspill of her memeome into his burgeoning family knowledge base.

'I wasn't always this bitter and cynical,' Pamela explains, waving her cane in the vague direction of the cloudscape beyond the edge of the world and fixing Sirhan with a beady stare. (He's brought her out here hoping that it will trigger another cascade of memories, sunsets on honeymoon island resorts and the like, but all that seems to be coming up is bile.) 'It was the successive betrayals. Manfred was the first, and the worst in some ways, but that little bitch Amber hurt me more, if anything. If you ever have children, be careful to hold something back for yourself; because if you don't, when they throw it all in your face, you'll feel like dying. And when they're gone, you've got no way of patching things up.'

'Is dying inevitable?' asks Sirhan, knowing damn well that it isn't, but more than happy to give her an excuse to pick at her scabbed-over love wound. He more than half suspects she's still in love with Manfred. This is *great* family history, and he's having the time of his flinty-hearted life leading her up to the threshold of the reunion he's hosting.

'Sometimes I think death is even more inevitable than taxes,' his grandmother replies bleakly. 'Humans don't live in a vacuum; we're part of a larger pattern of life.' She stares out across the troposphere of Saturn, where a thin rime of blown methane snow catches the distant sunrise in a ruby-tinted fog. 'The old gives way to the new.' She sighs, and tugs at her cuffs. (Ever since the incident with the gate-crashing ape, she's taken to wearing an antique formal pressure suit, all clinging black spider silk woven with flexible pipes and silvery smart sensor nets.) 'There's a time to get out of the way of the new, and I think I passed it sometime ago.'

'Um,' says Sirhan, who is somewhat surprised by this new angle in her lengthy, self-justifying confession. 'But what if you're just saying this because you *feel* old? If it's just a physiological malfunction, we could fix it and you'd—'

'*No!* I've got a feeling that life prolongation is morally wrong, Sirhan. I'm not passing judgment on you, just stating that *I* think it's wrong for *me*. It's immoral because it blocks up the natural order, keeps us old cobweb strands hanging around and getting in you young things' way. And then there are the theological questions. If you try to live forever, you never get to meet your maker.'

'Your maker? Are you a theist, then?'

'I – think so.' Pamela is silent for a minute. 'Although there are so many different approaches to the subject that it's hard to know which version to believe. For a long time, I was secretly afraid your grandfather might actually have had the answers. That I might have been wrong all along. But now—' She leans on her cane. 'When he announced that he was uploading, I figured out that all he really had was a life-hating antihuman ideology he'd mistaken for a religion. The rapture of the nerds and the heaven of the AIs. Sorry, no thanks. I don't buy it.'

'Oh.' Sirhan squints out at the cloudscape. For a moment, he thinks he can see something in the distant mist, an indeterminate distance away – it's hard to distinguish centimeters from megameters, with no scale indicator and a horizon a continental distance away – but he's not sure what it is. Maybe another city, mollusk-curved and sprouting antennae, a strange tail of fabricator nodes wavering below and beneath it. Then a drift of cloud hides it for a moment, and, when it clears, the object is gone. 'What's left, then? If you don't really believe in some kind of benign creator, dying must be frightening. Especially as you're doing it so slowly.'

Pamela smiles skeletally, a particularly humorless expression. 'It's perfectly natural, darling! You don't need to believe in God to believe in embedded realities. We use them every day, as mind tools. Apply anthropic reasoning and isn't it clear that our entire universe is probably a simulation? We're living in the early epoch of the universe. Probably this' – she prods at the spun-diamond inner wall of the bubble that holds in the precarious terrestrial atmosphere, holding out the howling cryogenic hydrogen and methane gales of Saturn – 'is but a simulation in some ancient history engine's panopticon, rerunning the sum of all possible origins of sentience, a billion trillion megayears down the line. Death will be like waking up as someone bigger, that's all.' Her grin slides away. 'And if not, I'll just be a silly old fool who deserves the oblivion she yearns for.'

'Oh, but—' Sirhan stops, his skin crawling. *She may be mad,* he realizes abruptly. *Not clinically insane, just at odds with the entire universe. Locked into a pathological view of her own role in reality.* 'I'd hoped for a reconciliation,' he says quietly. 'Your extended family has lived through some extraordinary times. Why spoil it with acrimony?'

'Why spoil it?' She looks at him pityingly. 'It was spoiled to begin with, dear, too much selfless sacrifice and too little skepticism. If Manfred hadn't wanted so badly not to be *human,* and if I'd learned to be a bit more flexible in time, we might still—' She trails off. 'That's odd.'

'What is?'

Pamela raises her cane and points out into the billowing methane thunderclouds, her expression puzzled. 'I'll swear I saw a lobster out there . . .'

Amber awakens in the middle of the night in darkness and choking pressure, and senses that she's drowning. For a moment she's back in the ambiguous space on the far side of the router, a horror of crawling instruments tracing her every experience back to the nooks and crannies of her mind; then her lungs turn to glass and shatter, and she's coughing and wheezing in the cold air of the museum at midnight.

The hard stone floor beneath her, and an odd pain in her knees, tells her that she's not aboard the *Field Circus* anymore. Rough hands hold her shoulders up as she vomits a fine blue mist, racked by a coughing fit. More bluish liquid is oozing from the pores of the skin on her arms and breasts, evaporating in strangely purposeful streamers. 'Thank you,' she finally manages to gasp. 'I can breathe now.'

She sits back on her heels, realizes she's naked, and opens her eyes. Everything's confusingly strange, even though it shouldn't be. There's a moment of resistance as if her eyelids are sealed – then they respond. It all feels strangely familiar to her, like waking up again inside a house she grew up in and moved away from years ago. But the scene around her is hardly one to inspire confidence. Shadows lie thick and deep across ovoid tanks filled with an anatomist's dream, bodies in various nightmarish stages of assembly. And sitting in the middle of them, whence it has retreated after letting go of her shoulders, is a strangely misshapen person – also nude, but for a patchy coat of orange hair.

'Are you awake yet, *ma chérie?*' asks the orangutan.

'Um.' Amber shakes her head, cautiously, feeling the drag of damp hair, the faint caress of a breeze – she reaches out with another sense and tries to grab hold of reality, but it slithers away, intransigent and unembedded. Everything around her is so solid and immutable that for a moment she feels a stab of claustrophobic panic. *Help! I'm trapped in the real universe!* Another quick check reassures her that she's got access to *something* outside her own head, and the panic begins to subside. Her exocortex has migrated successfully to this world. 'I'm in a *museum*? On Saturn? Who are you – have we met?'

'Not in person,' the ape says carefully. 'We 'ave corresponded. Annette Dimarcos.'

'Auntie—' A flood of memories rattle Amber's fragile stream of consciousness apart, forcing her to fork repeatedly until she can drag them together. Annette, in a recorded message: *Your father sends you this escape package.* The legal key to her mother's gilded custodial cage. Freedom a necessity. 'Is Dad here?' she asks hopefully, even though she knows full well that here in the real world at least thirty years have passed in linear time. In a century where ten years of linear time is enough for several industrial revolutions, that's a lot of water under the bridge.

'I am not sure.' The orangutan blinks lazily, scratches at her left forearm, and glances round the chamber. 'He might be in one of these tanks, playing a shell game. Or he might be leaving well enough alone until the dust settles.' She turns back to stare at Amber with big, brown, soulful eyes. 'This is not to be the reunion you were hoping for.'

'Not—' Amber takes a deep breath, the tenth or twelfth that these new lungs have inspired. 'What's with the body? You used to be human. And what's going on?'

'I still *am* human, where it counts,' says Annette. 'I use these bodies because they are good in low gravity, and they remind me that meatspace is no longer where I live. And for another reason.' She gestures fluidly at the open door. 'You will find big changes. Your son has organized—'

'*My* son.' Amber blinks. 'Is this the one who's suing me? Which version of me? How long ago?' A torrent of questions stream through her mind, exploding out into structured queries throughout the public sections of mindspace that she has access to. Her eyes widen as she absorbs the implications. 'Oh *shit*! Tell me she isn't here already!'

'I am very much afraid that she is,' says Annette. 'Sirhan is a strange child: He takes after his *grandmère*. Who he, of course, invited to his party.'

'His *party*?'

'Why, yes! Hasn't he told you what this is about? It's his party. To mark the opening of his special institution. The family archive. He's setting the lawsuit aside, at least for the duration.

That's why everybody is here – even me.' The ape-body smirks at her: 'I'm afraid he's rather disappointed by my dress.'

'Tell me about this library,' Amber says, narrowing her eyes. 'And about this son of mine whom I've never met, by a father I've never fucked.'

'What, you would know everything?' asks Annette.

'Yeah.' Amber pushes herself creakily upright. 'I need some clothes. And soft furniture. And where do I get a drink around here?'

'I'll show you,' says the orangutan, unfolding herself in a vertical direction like a stack of orange furry inner tubes. 'Drinks, first.'

While the Boston Museum of Science is the main structure on the lily-pad habitat, it's not the only one: just the stupidest, composed of dumb matter left over from the pre-enlightened age. The orangutan leads Amber through a service passage and out into the temperate night, naked by ringlight. The grass is cool beneath her feet, and a gentle breeze blows constantly out toward the recirculators at the edge of the worldlet. She follows the slouching orange ape up a grassy slope, under a weeping willow, round a three-hundred-and-ninety-degree bend that flashes the world behind them into invisibility, and into a house with walls of spun cloud stuff and a ceiling that rains moonlight.

'What is this?' Amber asks, entranced. 'Some kind of aerogel?'

'No—' Annette belches, then digs a hand into the floor and pulls up a heap of mist. 'Make a chair,' she says. It solidifies, gaining form and texture until a creditable Queen Anne reproduction stands in front of Amber on spindly legs. 'And one for me. Skin up, pick one of my favorite themes.' The walls recede slightly and harden, extruding paint and wood and glass. 'That's it.' The ape grins at Amber. 'You are comfortable?'

'But I—' Amber stops. She glances at the familiar mantelpiece, the row of curios, the baby photographs forever glossy on their dye-sub media. It's her childhood bedroom. 'You brought the whole thing? Just for me?'

'You can never tell with future shock.' Annette shrugs and reaches a limber arm around the back of her neck to scratch. 'We are utility fog using, for most purposes out here, peer-to-peer meshes of multiarmed assemblers that change conformation and vapor/solid phase at command. Texture and color are all superfice, not reality. But yes, this came from one of your mother's letters to your father. She brought it here, for you to surprise. If only it is ready in time.' Lips pull back from big, square, foliage-chewing teeth in something that might be a smile in a million years' time.

'You, I – I wasn't expecting. This.' Amber realizes she's breathing rapidly, a near-panic reflex. The mere proximity of her mother is enough to give her unpleasant reactions. Annette is all right, Annette is cool. And her father is the trickster-god, always hiding in your blind spot to leap out and shower you with ambiguous gifts. But Pamela tried to mold Amber in her own image as a child; and despite all the traveling she's done since then, and all the growing up, Amber harbors an unreasonable claustrophobic fear of her mother.

'Don't be unhappy,' Annette says warmly. 'I this you show to convince you, she will try to disturb you. It is a sign of weakness. She lacks the courage of her convictions.'

'She does?' This is news to Amber, who leans forward to listen.

'Yes. She is an old and bitter woman, now. The years have not been easy for her. She perhaps intends to use her unrepaired senescence as a passive suicide weapon by which to hold us blameworthy, inflicting guilt for her mistreatment, but she is afraid of dying all the same. Your reaction, should it be unhappy, will excuse and encourage her selfishness. Sirhan colludes, unknowing, the idiot child. *He* thinks the universe of her and thinks by helping her die he is helping her achieve her goals. He has never met an adult walking backward toward a cliff before.'

'Backward.' Amber takes a deep breath. 'You're telling me

Mom is so unhappy she's trying to kill herself by growing *old*? Isn't that a bit slow?'

Annette shakes her head lugubriously. 'She's had fifty years to practice. You have been away twenty-eight years! She was thirty when she bore you. Now she is more than eighty, and a telomere refusenik, a charter member of the genome conservation front. To accept a slow virus purge and aging reset would be to lay down a banner she has carried for half a century. To accept uploading, that, too, is wrong in her mind. She will not admit her identity is a variable, not a constant. She came out here in a can, frozen, with more radiation damage. She is not going back home. This is where she plans to end her days. Do you see? *That* is why you were brought here. That, and because of the bailiffs who have bought title to your other self's business debts. They are waiting for you in Jupiter system with warrants and headsuckers to extract your private keys.'

'She's cornered me!'

'Oh, I would not *say* that. We all change our convictions sometime or other, perhaps. She is inflexible, she will not bend, but she is not stupid. Nor is she as vindictive as perhaps she herself believes. She thinks she must a scorned woman be, even though there is more to her than that. Your father and I, we—'

'Is he still alive?' Amber demands eagerly, half-anxious to know, half-wishing she could be sure the news won't be bad.

'Yes.' Annette grins again, but it's not a happy expression, more a baring of teeth at the world. 'As I was saying, your father and I, we have tried to help her. Pamela denies him. He is, she says, not a man. No more so am I myself a woman? No, but she'll still talk to *me*. *You* will do better. But his assets, they are spent. He is not a rich man this epoch, your father.'

'Yeah, but.' Amber nods to herself. 'He may be able to help me.'

'Oh? How so?'

'You remember the original goal of the *Field Circus*? The sapient alien transmission?'

'Yes, of course.' Annette snorts. 'Junk bond pyramid schemes from credulous saucer wisdom airheads.'

Amber licks her lips. 'How susceptible to interception are we here?'

'Here?' Annette glances round. 'Very. You can't maintain a habitat in a nonbiosphere environment without ubiquitous surveillance.'

'Well, then . . .'

Amber dives inward, forks her identity, collects a complex bundle of her thoughts and memories, marshals them, offers Annette one end of an encryption tunnel, then stuffs the frozen mindstorm into her head. Annette sits still for approximately ten seconds, then shudders and whimpers quietly. 'You must ask your father,' she says, growing visibly agitated. 'I must leave, now. I should not have known that! It is dynamite, you see. *Political* dynamite. I must return to my primary sister-identity and warn her.'

'Your – wait!' Amber stands up as fast as her ill-coordinated body will let her, but Annette is moving fast, swarming up a translucent ladder in the air.

'Tell Manfred!' calls her aunt through the body of an ape. 'Trust no one else!' She throws another packet of compressed, encrypted memories down the tunnel to Amber; then a moment later the orange skull touches the ceiling and dissolves, a liquid flow of dissociating utility foglets letting go of one another and dispersing into the greater mass of the building that spawned the fake ape.

Snapshots from the family album: *While you were gone . . .*

- Amber, wearing a brocade gown and a crown encrusted with diamond processors and external neural taps, her royal party gathered around her, attends the pan-Jovian constitutional conference with the majesty of a confirmed head of state and ruler of a small inner moon. She smiles knowingly at the camera viewpoint, with the professional shine that comes from a good public relations video filter. 'We are very happy to be here,' she says, 'and we are pleased that the commission has agreed to lend its weight to the continued progress of the Ring Imperium's deep-space program.'

- A piece of dumb paper, crudely stained with letters written in a faded brown substance — possibly blood — says 'I'm checking out, don't delta me.' This version of Pierre didn't go to the router: He stayed at home, deleted all his backups, and slit his wrists, his epitaph sharp and self-inflicted. It comes as a cold shock, the first chill gust of winter's gale blowing through the outer system's political elite. And it's the start of a regime of censorship directed toward the already-speeding starwhisp. Amber, in her grief, makes an executive decision not to tell her embassy to the stars that one of them is dead and, therefore, unique.

- Manfred — fifty, with the fashionably pale complexion of the digerati, healthy-looking for his age, standing beside a transmigration bush with a stupid grin on his face. He's decided to take the final step, not simply to spawn external mental processes running in an exocortex of distributed processors, but to move his entire persona right out of meatspace, into wherever it is that the uploads aboard the *Field Circus* have gone. Annette, skinny, elegant, and very Parisian, stands beside him, looking as uncertain as the wife of a condemned man.

- A wedding, shi'ite, *Mut'ah* — of limited duration. It's scandalous to many, but the *mamtu'ah* isn't Moslem, she wears a crown instead of a veil, and her groom is already spoken of in outraged terms by most other members of the trans-Martian Islamic clergy. Besides which, in addition to being in love, the happy couple have more strategic firepower than a late-twentieth-century superpower. Their cat, curled at their feet, looks smug. She's the custodian of the permissive action locks on the big lasers.

- A speck of ruby light against the darkness – redshifted almost into the infrared, it's the return signal from the *Field Circus*'s light sail as the starwhisp passes the one-light-year mark, almost twelve trillion kilometers out beyond Pluto. (Although how can you call it a starwhisp when it masses almost a hundred kilograms, including propulsion module? Starwhisps are meant to be tiny!)

- Collapse of the trans-Lunar economy: Deep in the hot thinking depths of the solar system, vast new intellects come up with a new theory of wealth that optimizes resource allocation better than the previously pervasive Free Market 1.0. With no local minima to hamper them, and no need to spawn and reap start-ups Darwin-style, the companies, group minds, and organizations that adopt the so-called Accelerated Salesman Infrastructure of Economics 2.0 trade optimally with each other. The phase-change accelerates as more and more entities join in, leveraging network externalities to overtake the traditional ecosystem. Amber and Sadeq are late on the train, Sadeq obsessing about how to reconcile ASI with *murabaha* and *mudaraba* while the postmodern economy of the midtwenty-first century disintegrates around them. Being late has punitive consequences – the Ring Imperium has always been a net importer of brainpower and a net exporter of gravitational potential energy. Now it's a tired backwater, the bit rate from the red-shifted relativisitic probe insufficiently delightful to obsess the daemons of industrial routing.

In other words, they're poor.

- A message from beyond the grave: The travelers aboard the starship have reached their destination, an alien artifact drifting in chilly orbit around a frozen brown dwarf. Recklessly they upload themselves into it, locking the starwhisp down for years of sleep. Amber and her husband have few funds with which to pay for the propulsion lasers. What they have left of the kinetic energy of the Ring Imperium – based on the orbital momentum of a small Jovian inner moon – is being sapped, fast, at a near loss, by the crude requirements of the exobionts and metanthropes who fork and spawn in the datasphere of the outer Jovians. The cost of importing brains to the Ring Imperium is steep: In near despair, Amber and Sadeq produce a child, Generation 3.0, to populate their dwindling kingdom. Picture the cat, offended, lashing its tail beside the zero-gee crib.

- Surprise and postcards from the inner orbitals – Amber's mother offers to help. For the sake of the child, Sadeq offers bandwidth and user interface enrichment. The child forks, numerous times, as Amber despairingly plays with probabilities, simulating upbringing outcomes. Neither she nor Sadeq are good parents – the father absent-minded and prone to lose himself in the intertextual deconstruction of surahs, the mother ragged-edged from running the economy of a small and failing kingdom. In the space of a decade, Sirhan lives a dozen lives, discarding identities like old clothes. The uncertainty of life in the decaying Ring Imperium does not entrance him, his parents' obsessions annoy him, and when his grandmother offers to fund his delta vee and subsequent education in one of the orbitals around Titan, his parents give their reluctant assent.

• Amber and Sadeq separate acrimoniously. Sadeq, studies abandoned in the face of increasing intrusions from the world of what is into the universe of what should be, joins a spacelike sect of sufis, encysted in a matrix of vitrification nanomechs out in the Oort cloud to await a better epoch. His instrument of will – the legal mechanism of his resurrection – specifies that he is waiting for the return of the hidden, twelfth imam.

• For her part, Amber searches the inner system briefly for word of her father – but there's nothing. Isolated and alone, pursued by accusing debts, she flings herself into a reborganization, stripping away those aspects of her personality that have brought her low; in law, her liability is tied to her identity. Eventually she donates herself to a commune of also-rans, accepting their personality in return for a total break with the past.

• Without Queen and consort, the Ring Imperium – now unmanned, leaking breathing gases, running

on autonomic control – slowly deorbits into the
Jovian murk, beaming power to the outer moons
until it punches a hole in the cloud deck in a final
incandescent smear of light, the like of which has
not been seen since the Shoemaker-Levy 9 impact.

- Sirhan, engrossed in Saturnalia, is offended by
his parents' failure to make more of themselves.
And he resolves to do it for them, if not necessarily in a manner of their liking.

'You see, I am hoping you will help me with my history project,'
says the serious-faced young man.

'History project.' Pierre follows him along the curving gallery,
hands clasped behind his back self-consciously to keep from
showing his agitation. 'What history is this?'

'The history of the twenty-first century,' says Sirhan. 'You
remember it, don't you?'

'Remember it—' Pierre pauses. 'You're serious?'

'Yes.' Sirhan opens a side door. 'This way, please. I'll explain.'

The door opens onto what used to be one of the side galleries
of the museum building, full of interactive exhibits designed to
explain elementary optics to hyperactive children and their
indulgent parental units. Traditional optics are long since obsolete – tunable matter can slow photons to a stop, teleport them
here to there, play Ping-Pong with spin and polarization – and
besides, the dumb matter in the walls and floor has been
replaced by low-power computronium, heat sinks dangling far
below the floor of the lily-pad habitat to dispose of the scanty
waste photons from reversible computation. Now the room is
empty.

'Since I became curator here, I've turned the museum's structural supports into a dedicated high-density memory store. One
of the fringe benefits of a supervisory post, of course. I have about
a billion avabits of capacity, enough to archive the combined

sensory bandwidth and memories of the entire population of twentieth-century Earth – if that was what interested me.'

Slowly the walls and ceiling are coming to life, brightening, providing a dizzyingly vibrant view of dawn over the rim wall of Meteor Crater, Arizona – or maybe it's downtown Baghdad.

'Once I realized how my mother had squandered the family fortune, I spent some time looking for a solution to the problem,' Sirhan continues. 'And it struck me, then, that there's only one commodity that is going to appreciate in value as time continues: reversibility.'

'Reversibility? That doesn't make much sense.' Pierre shakes his head. He still feels slightly dizzy from his decanting. He's only been awake an hour or so and is still getting used to the vagaries of a universe that doesn't bend its rules to fit his whim of iron – that, and worrying about Amber, of whom there is no sign in the hall of growing bodies. 'Excuse me, please, but do you know where Amber is?'

'Hiding, probably,' Sirhan says, without rancor. 'Her mother's about,' he adds. 'Why do you ask?'

'I don't know what you know about us.' Pierre looks at him askance. 'We were aboard the *Field Circus* for a long time.'

'Oh, don't worry on my behalf. I know you're not the same people who stayed behind to contribute to the Ring Imperium's collapse,' Sirhan says dismissively, while Pierre hastily spawns a couple of ghosts to search for the history he's alluding to. What they discover shocks him to the core as they integrate with his conscious narrative.

'We didn't know about any of that!' Pierre crosses his arms defensively. 'Not about you, or your father either,' he adds quietly. 'Or my other . . . life.' Shocked: *Did I kill myself? Why would I do a thing like that?* Nor can he imagine what Amber might see in an introverted cleric like Sadeq, not that he wants to.

'I'm sure this must come as a big shock to you,' Sirhan says condescendingly, 'but it's all to do with what I was talking about. Reversibility. What does it mean to you, in your precious context? *You* are, if you like, an opportunity to reverse whatever ill fortune made your primary instance autodarwinate himself. He destroyed all the backups he could get his ghosts to ferret out, you know. Only a light-year delay line and the fact that as a running instance you're technically a different person saved you. And now, you're alive, and he's dead – and whatever made him kill himself doesn't apply to you. Think of it as natural selection among different versions of yourself. The fittest version of you survives.'

He points at the wall of the crater. A tree diagram begins to grow from the bottom left corner of the wall, recurving and recomplicating as it climbs toward the top right, zooming and fracturing into taxonomic fault lines. 'Life on Earth, the family tree, what paleontology has been able to deduce of it for us,' he says pompously. 'The vertebrates begin *there*' – a point three-quarters of the way up the tree—'and we've got an average of a hundred fossil samples per megayear from then on. Most of them collected in the past two decades, as exhaustive mapping of the Earth's crust and upper mantle at the micrometer level has become practical. What a *waste*.'

'That's' – Pierre does a quick sum – 'fifty thousand different species? Is there a problem?'

'Yes!' Sirhan says vehemently, no longer aloof or distant. He struggles visibly to get himself under control. 'At the beginning of the twentieth century, there were roughly two million species of vertebrate and an estimated thirty or so million species of multicellular organisms – it's hard to apply the same statistical treatment to prokaryotes, but doubtless there were huge numbers of them, too. The average life span of a species is about five megayears. It used to be thought to be about one, but that's a very vertebrate-oriented estimate – many insect species are stable over deep time. Anyway, we have a total sample, from all of history, of only fifty thousand known prehistoric species – out of a population of thirty million, turning over every five million years. That is, we know of only one in a million life-forms, of those that ever existed on Earth. And the situation with human history is even worse.'

'Aha! So you're after memories, yes? What really happened when we colonized Barney. Who released Oscar's toads in the free-fall core of the *Ernst Sanger,* that sort of thing?'

'Not exactly.' Sirhan looks pained, as if being forced to spell it out devalues the significance of his insight. 'I'm after *history*. All of it. I intend to corner the history futures market. But I need my grandfather's help – and you're here to help me get it.'

Over the course of the day, various refugees from the *Field Circus* hatch from their tanks and blink in the ringlight, stranded creatures from an earlier age. The inner system is a vague blur from this distance, a swollen red cloud masking the sun that rides high above the horizon. However, the great restructuring is still visible to the naked eye – here, in the shape of the rings, which show a disturbingly organized fractal structure as they whirl in orbit overhead. Sirhan (or whoever is paying for this celebration of family flesh) has provided for their physical needs: food, water, clothes, housing, and bandwidth – they're all copiously available. A small town of bubble homes grows on the grassy knoll adjacent to the museum, utility foglets condensing in a variety of shapes and styles.

Sirhan isn't the only inhabitant of the festival city, but the others keep themselves to themselves. Only bourgeois isolationists and reclusive weirdoes would want to live out here right now, with whole light-minutes between themselves and the rest of civilization. The network of lily-pad habitats isn't yet ready for the saturnalian immigration wave that will break upon this alien shore when it's time for the Worlds' Fair, a decade or more in the future. Amber's flying circus has driven the native recluses underground, in some cases literally: Sirhan's neighbor Vinca Kovic, after complaining bitterly about the bustle and noise ('Forty immigrants! An outrage!'), has wrapped himself in an environment pod and is estivating at the end of a spider-silk cable a kilometer beneath the space-frame underpinnings of the city.

But that isn't going to stop Sirhan from organizing a reception for the visitors. He's moved his magnificent dining table outside, along with the *Argentinosaurus* skeleton. In fact, he's built a dining room within the dinosaur's rib cage. Not that he's planning on showing his full hand, but it'll be interesting to see how his guests respond. And maybe it'll flush out the mystery benefactor who's been paying for all these meatbodies.

Sirhan's agents politely invite his visitors to the party as the second sunset in this day cycle gently darkens the sky to violet. He discusses his plans with Pamela via antique voice-only phone as his silent valet dresses him with inhuman grace and efficiency. 'I'm sure they'll listen when the situation is made clear to them,' he says. 'If not, well, they'll soon find out what it means to be paupers under Economics 2.0. No access to multiplicity, no willpower, to be limited to purely spacelike resources, at the mercy of predatory borganisms and metareligions – it's no picnic out there!'

'You don't have the resources to set this up on your own,' his grandmother points out in dry, didactic tones. 'If this was the old economy, you could draw on the infrastructure of banks, insurers, and other risk management mechanisms—'

'There's no risk to this venture, in purely human terms,' Sirhan insists. 'The only risk is starting it up with such a limited reserve.'

'You win some, you lose some,' Pamela points out. 'Let me see you.' With a sigh, Sirhan waves at a frozen camera; it blinks, surprised. 'Hey, you look good! Every inch the traditional family entrepreneur. I'm proud of you, darling.'

Blinking back an unaccustomed tear of pride, Sirhan nods. 'I'll see you in a few minutes,' he says, and cuts the call. To the nearest valet: 'Bring my carriage, now.'

A rippling cloud of utility foglets, constantly connecting and disconnecting in the hazy outline of a 1910-vintage Rolls Royce Silver Ghost, bears Sirhan silently away from his wing of the museum. It drives him out onto the sunset path around the building, over to the sunken amphitheatre, where the mounted skeleton of the *Argentinosaurus* stands like a half-melted columnar sculpture beneath the orange-and-silver ringlight. A small crowd of people are already present, some dressed casually and some attired in the formal garb of earlier decades. Most of them are passengers or crew recently decanted from the starwhisp, but a handful are wary-eyed hermits, their body language defensive and their persons the focus of a constant orbital hum of security bees. Sirhan dismounts from his silvery car and magics it into dissolution, a haze of foglets dispersing on the breeze. 'Welcome to my abode,' he says, bowing gravely to a ring of interested faces. 'My name is Sirhan al-Khurasani, and I am the prime contractor in charge of this small corner of the temporary Saturn terraforming project. As some of you probably know, I am related by blood and design to your former captain, Amber Macx. I'd like to offer you the comforts of my home while you acclimatize yourselves to the changed circumstances prevailing in the system at large and work out where you want to go next.'

He walks toward the front of the U-shaped table of solidified air that floats beneath the dead dinosaur's rib cage, slowly turns to take in faces, and blinks down captions to remind him who's who in this gathering. He frowns slightly; there's no sign of his mother. But that wiry fellow, with the beard – surely that can't be – 'Father?' he asks.

Sadeq blinks owlishly. 'Have we met?'

'Possibly not.' Sirhan can feel his head spinning, because although Sadeq looks like a younger version of his father, there's something *wrong* – some essential disconnect: the politely solicitous expression, the complete lack of engagement, the absence of paternal involvement. This Sadeq has never held the infant Sirhan in the control core of the Ring's axial cylinder, never pointed out the spiral storm raking vast Jupiter's face and told him stories of djinni and marvels to make a boy's hair stand on end. 'I won't hold it against you, I promise,' he blurts.

Sadeq raises an eyebrow but passes no comment, leaving Sirhan at the center of an uncomfortable silence. 'Well then,' he says hastily. 'If you would like to help yourselves to food and drink, there'll be plenty of time to talk later.' Sirhan doesn't believe in forking ghosts simply to interact with other people –

the possibilities for confusion are embarrassing – but he's going to be busy working the party.

He glances round. Here's a bald, aggressive-looking fellow, beetle-browed, wearing what looks like a pair of cutoffs and a top made by deconstructing a space suit. Who's he? (Sirhan's agents hint: 'Boris Denisovitch.' But what does that *mean*?) There's an amused-looking older woman, a beady-eyed camera painted in the violent colors of a bird of paradise riding her shoulder. Behind her a younger woman, dressed head to toe in clinging black, her currently ash-blond hair braided in cornrows, watches him – as does Pierre, a protective arm around her shoulders. They're – *Amber Macx?* That's his *mother*? She looks far too young, too much in love with Pierre. 'Amber!' he says, approaching the couple.

'Yeah? You're, uh, my mystery child-support litigant?' Her smile is distinctly unfriendly as she continues. 'Can't say I'm entirely pleased to meet you, under the circumstances, although I should thank you for the spread.'

'I—' His tongue sticks to the roof of his mouth. 'It's not like that.'

'What's it supposed to be like?' she asks sharply, jabbing a finger at him. 'You know damn well I'm not your mother. So what's it all about, huh? You know damn well I'm nearly bankrupt, too, so it's not as if you're after my pocket lint. What do you want from me?'

Her vehemence takes him aback. This sharp-edged aggressive woman isn't his mother, and the introverted cleric – believer – on the other side isn't his father, either. 'I ha-ha-had to stop you heading for the inner system,' he says, speech center hitting deadlock before his antistutter mod can cut in. 'They'll eat you alive down there. Your other half left behind substantial debts, and they've been bought up by the most predatory—'

'Runaway corporate instruments,' she states, calmly enough. 'Fully sentient and self-directed.'

'How did you know?' he asks, worried.

She looks grim. 'I've met them before.' It's a very *familiar* grim expression, one he knows intimately and that feels wrong coming from this near stranger. 'We visited some weird places, while we were away.' She glances past him, focuses on someone else, and breathes in sharply as her face goes blank. 'Quickly, tell me what your scheme is. Before Mom gets here.'

'Mind archiving and history mergers. Back yourself up, pick different life courses, see which ones work and which don't – no need to be a failure, just hit the "reload game" icon and resume. That and a long-term angle on the history futures market. I *need* your help,' he babbles. 'It won't work without family, and I'm trying to stop her killing herself—'

'Family.' She nods, guardedly, and Sirhan notices her companion, this Pierre – not the weak link that broke back before he was born, but a tough-eyed explorer newly returned from the wilderness – sizing him up. Sirhan's got one or two tricks up his exocortex, and he can see the haze of ghost-shapes around Pierre; his data-mining technique is crude and out-of-date, but enthusiastic and not without a certain flair. 'Family,' Amber repeats, and it's like a curse. Louder: 'Hello, Mom. Should have guessed he'd have invited you here, too.'

'Guess again.' Sirhan glances round at Pamela, then back at Amber, suddenly feeling very much like a rat trapped between a pair of angry cobras. Leaning on her cane, wearing discreet cosmetics and with her medical supports concealed beneath an old-fashioned dress, Pamela could be a badly preserved sixtysomething from the old days instead of the ghastly slow suicide case that her condition amounts to today. She smiles politely at Amber. 'You may remember me telling you that a lady never unintentionally causes offense. I didn't want to offend Sirhan by turning up in spite of his wishes, so I didn't give him a chance to say no.'

'And this is supposed to earn you a sympathy fuck?' Amber drawls. 'I'd expected better of you.'

'Why, you—' The fire in her eyes dies suddenly, subjected to the freezing pressure of a control that only comes with age. 'I'd hoped getting away from it all would have improved your disposition if not your manners, but evidently not.' Pamela jabs her cane at the table. 'Let me repeat, this is your *son's* idea. Why don't you eat something?'

'Poison tester goes first.' Amber smiles slyly.

'For fuck's sake!' It's the first thing Pierre has said so far, and crude or not, it comes as a profound relief when he steps forward, picks up a plate of water biscuits loaded with salmon caviar, and puts one in his mouth. 'Can't you guys leave the backstabbing until the rest of us have filled our stomachs? 'S not as if I can turn down the biophysics model in here.' He shoves the plate at Sirhan. 'Go on, it's yours.'

The spell is broken. 'Thank you,' Sirhan says gravely, taking a cracker and feeling the tension fall as Amber and her mother stop preparing to nuke each other and focus on the issue at hand – which is that food comes before fighting at any social event, not vice versa.

'You might enjoy the egg mayonnaise, too,' Sirhan hears himself saying. 'It goes a long way to explaining why the dodo became extinct first time around.'

'Dodoes.' Amber keeps one eye warily on her mother as she accepts a plate from a silently gliding silver bush-shaped waitron. 'What was that about the family investment project?' she asks.

'Just that without your cooperation your family will likely go the way of the bird,' her mother cuts in before Sirhan can muster a reply. 'Not that I expect you to care.'

Boris butts in. 'Core worlds are teeming with corporates. Is bad business for us, good business for them. If you are seeing what we are seen—'

'Don't remember *you* being there,' Pierre says grumpily.

'In any event,' Sirhan says smoothly, 'the core isn't healthy for us one-time fleshbodies anymore. There are still lots of people there, but the ones who uploaded expecting a boom economy were sadly disappointed. Originality is at a premium, and the human neural architecture isn't optimized for it – we are, by disposition, a conservative species, because in a static ecosystem that provides the best return on sunk reproductive investment costs. Yes, we change over time – we're more flexible than almost any other animal species to arise on Earth – but we're like granite statues compared to organisms adapted to life under Economics 2.0.'

'You tell 'em, boy,' Pamela chirps, almost mockingly. 'It wasn't that bloodless when I lived through it.' Amber casts her a cool stare.

'Where was I?' Sirhan snaps his fingers, and a glass of fizzy grape juice appears between them. 'Early upload entrepreneurs forked repeatedly, discovered they could scale linearly to occupy processor capacity proportional to the mass of computronium available, and that computationally trivial tasks became tractable. They could also run faster, or slower, than real time. But they were still *human,* and unable to operate effectively outside human constraints. Take a human being and bolt on extensions that let them take full advantage of Economics 2.0, and you essentially break their narrative chain of consciousness, replacing it with a journal file of bid/request transactions between various agents; it's incredibly efficient and flexible, but it isn't a conscious human being in any recognizable sense of the word.'

'All right,' Pierre says slowly. 'I think we've seen something like that ourselves. At the router.'

Sirhan nods, not sure whether he's referring to anything important. 'So you see, there are limits to human progress – but not to progress itself! The uploads found their labor to be a permanently deflating commodity once they hit their point of diminishing utility. Capitalism doesn't have a lot to say about workers whose skills are obsolete, other than that they should invest wisely while they're earning and maybe re-train. But just knowing *how* to invest in Economics 2.0 is beyond an unaugmented human. You can't retrain as a seagull, can you, and it's quite as hard to retool for Economics 2.0. Earth is—' He shudders.

'There's a phrase I used to hear in the old days,' Pamela says calmly. 'Ethnic cleansing. Do you know what that means, darling idiot daughter? You take people who you define as being of little worth, and first you herd them into a crowded ghetto with limited resources, then you decide those resources aren't worth spending on them, and bullets are cheaper than bread. "Mind children" the extropians called the posthumans, but they were more like Vile Offspring. There was a *lot* of that, during the fast sigmoid phase. Starving among plenty, compulsory conversions, the very antithesis of everything your father said he wanted . . .'

'I don't believe it,' Amber says hotly. 'That's crazy! We can't go the way of—'

'Since when has human history been anything else?' asks the woman with the camera on her shoulder – Donna, being some sort of public archivist, is in Sirhan's estimate likely to be of use to him. 'Remember what we found in the DMZ?'

'The DMZ?' Sirhan asks, momentarily confused.

'After we went through the router,' Pierre says grimly. 'You tell him, love.' He looks at Amber.

Sirhan, watching him, feels it fall into place at that moment, a sense that he's stepped into an alternate universe, one where the woman who might have been his mother isn't, where black is white, his kindly grandmother is the wicked witch of the west, and his feckless grandfather is a farsighted visionary.

'We uploaded via the router,' Amber says, and looks confused for a moment. 'There's a network on the other side of it. We were told it was FTL, instantaneous, but I'm not so sure now. I think it's something more complicated, like a lightspeed network, parts of which are threaded through wormholes that make it look FTL from our perspective. Anyway, Matrioshka brains, the end product of a technological singularity – they're bandwidth-limited. Sooner or later the posthuman descendants evolve Economics 2.0, or 3.0, or something else, and it, uh, *eats* the original conscious instigators. Or uses them as currency or something. The end result we found is a howling wilderness of degenerate data, fractally compressed, postconscious processes running slower and slower as they trade storage space for processing power. We were' – she licks her lips – 'lucky to escape with our minds. We only did it because of a friend. It's like the main sequence in stellar evolution; once a G-type star starts burning helium and expands into a red giant, it's "game over" for life in what used to be its liquid-water zone. Conscious civilizations sooner or later convert all their available mass into computronium, powered by solar output. They don't go interstellar because they want to stay near the core where the bandwidth is high and latency is low, and sooner or later competition for resources hatches a new level of metacompetition that obsoletes them.'

'That sounds plausible,' Sirhan says slowly. He puts his glass down and chews distractedly on one knuckle. 'I thought it was a low-probability outcome, but . . .'

'I've been saying all along, your grandfather's ideas would backfire in the end,' Pamela says pointedly.

'But—' Amber shakes her head. 'There's more to it than that, isn't there?'

'Probably,' Sirhan says, then shuts up.

'So are you going to tell us?' asks Pierre, looking annoyed. 'What's the big idea, here?'

'An archive store,' Sirhan says, deciding that this is the right time for his pitch. 'At the lowest level, you can store backups of yourself here. So far so good, eh? But there's a bit more to it than that. I'm planning to offer a bunch of embedded universes – big, running faster than real time – sized and scoped to let human-equivalent intelligences do what-if modeling on themselves. Like forking off ghosts of yourself, but much more so – give them whole years to diverge, learn new skills, and evaluate them against market requirements, before deciding which version of you is most suited to run in the real world. I mentioned the retraining paradox. Think of this as a solution for level one, human-equivalent, intelligences. But that's just the short-term business model. Long-term, I want to acquire a total lock on the history futures market by having a *complete* archive of human experiences, from the dawn of the fifth singularity on up. No more unknown extinct species. That should give us something to trade with the next-generation intelligences – the ones who aren't our mind children and barely remember us. At the very least, it gives us a chance to live again, a long way out in deep time. Alternatively, it can be turned into a lifeboat. If we can't compete with our creations, at least we've got somewhere to flee, those of us who want to. I've got agents working on a comet, out in the Oort cloud – we could move the archive to it, turn it into a generation ship with room for billions of evacuees running much slower than real time in archive space until we find a new world to settle.'

'Is not sounding good to me,' Boris comments. He spares a worried glance for an oriental-looking woman who is watching their debate silently from the fringe.

'Has it really gone that far?' asks Amber.

'There are bailiffs hunting you in the inner system,' Pamela says bluntly. 'After your bankruptcy proceedings, various corporates got the idea that you might be concealing something. The theory was that you were insane to take such a huge gamble on the mere possibility of there being an alien artifact within a few light years of home, so you had to have information above and beyond what you disclosed. Theories include your cat – hardware tokens were in vogue in the fifties – being the key to a suite of deposit accounts; the fuss mainly died down after Economics 2.0 took over, but some fairly sleazy conspiracy freaks refuse to let go.'

She grins, frighteningly. 'Which is why I suggested to your son that he make you an offer you can't refuse.'

'What's that?' asks a voice from below knee level.

Pamela looks down, an expression of deep distaste on her face. 'Why should I tell *you*?' she asks, leaning on her cane. 'After the disgraceful way you repaid my hospitality! All you've got coming from me is a good kicking. If only my knee was up to the job.'

The cat arches its back: Its tail fluffs out with fear as its hair stands on end, and it takes Amber a moment to realize that it isn't responding to Pamela, but to something behind the old woman. 'Through the domain wall. Outside this biome. So cold. What's *that*?'

Amber turns to follow the cat's gaze, and her jaw drops. 'Were you expecting visitors?' she asks Sirhan, shakily.

'Visit—' He looks round to see what everybody's gaping at and freezes. The horizon is brightening with a false dawn – the fusion spark of a de-orbiting spacecraft.

'It's bailiffs,' says Pamela, head cocked to one side as if listening to an antique bone-conduction earpiece. 'They've come for your memories, dear,' she explains, frowning. 'They say we've got five kiloseconds to surrender everything. Otherwise, they're going to blow us apart . . .'

'You're all in big trouble,' says the orangutan, sliding gracefully down one enormous rib to land in an ungainly heap in front of Sirhan.

Sirhan recoils in disgust. 'You again! What do you want from me this time?'

'Nothing.' The ape ignores him. 'Amber, it is time for you to call your father.'

'Yeah, but will he come when I call?' Amber stares at the ape. Her pupils expand. 'Hey, you're not my—'

'You.' Sirhan glares at the ape. 'Go away! I didn't invite you here!'

'More unwelcome visitors?' asks Pamela, raising an eyebrow.

'Yes, you did.' The ape grins at Amber, then crouches down, hoots quietly and beckons to the cat, who is hiding behind one of the graceful silver servitors.

'Manfred isn't welcome here. And neither is that woman,' Sirhan swears. He catches Pamela's eye. 'Did you know anything about this? Or about the bailiffs?' He gestures at the window, beyond which the drive flare casts jagged shadows. It's dropping toward the horizon as it de-orbits – next time it comes into view, it'll be at the leading edge of a hypersonic shock wave, streaking toward them at cloud-top height in order to consummate the robbery.

'Me?' Pamela snorts. 'Grow up.' She eyes the ape warily. 'I don't have that much control over things. And as for bailiffs, I wouldn't set them on my worst enemies. I've seen what those things can do.' For a moment her eyes flash anger. 'Grow up, why don't you!' she repeats.

'Yes, please do,' says another voice from behind Sirhan. The new speaker is a woman, slightly husky, accented – he turns to see her: tall, black-haired, wearing a dark man's suit of archaic cut and mirrored glasses. 'Ah, Pamela, *ma chérie!* Long time no cat-fight.' She grins frighteningly and holds out a hand.

Sirhan is already off-balance. Now, seeing his honorary aunt in human skin for a change, he looks at the ape in confusion. Behind him Pamela advances on Annette and takes her hand in her own fragile fingers. 'You look just the same,' she says gravely. 'I can see why I was afraid of you.'

'You.' Amber backs away until she bumps into Sirhan, at whom she glares. 'What the fuck did you invite both of them for? Are you *trying* to start a thermonuclear war?'

'Don't ask me,' he says helplessly. 'I don't know why they came! What's this about' – he focuses on the orangutan, who is now letting the cat lick one hairy palm – 'your cat?'

'I don't think the orange hair suits Aineko,' Amber says slowly. 'Did I tell you about our hitchhiker?'

Sirhan shakes his head, trying to dispel the confusion. 'I don't think we've got time. In under two hours the bailiffs up there will be back. They're armed and dangerous, and if they turn their drive flame on the roof and set fire to the atmosphere in here, we'll be in trouble – it would rupture our lift cells, and even computronium doesn't work too well under a couple of million atmospheres of pressurized metallic hydrogen.'

'Well, you'd better *make* time.' Amber takes his elbow in an iron grip and turns him toward the footpath back to the museum. 'Crazy,' she mutters. '*tante* Annette and Pamela Macx on the same planet! And they're being *friendly*! This can't be a good sign.' She glances round, sees the ape. 'You. Come *here*. Bring the cat.'

'The cat's—' Sirhan trails off. 'I've heard about your cat,' he says, lamely. 'You took him with you in the *Field Circus*.'

'Really?' She glances behind them. The ape blows a kiss at her; it's cradling the cat on one shoulder and tickling it under the chin. 'Has it occurred to you that Aineko isn't just a robot cat?'

'Ah,' Sirhan says faintly. 'Then the bailiffs—'

'No, that's all bullshit. What I mean is, Aineko is a human-equivalent, or better, artificial intelligence. Why do you think she keeps a cat's body?'

'I have no idea.'

'Because humans always underestimate anything that's small, furry, and cute,' says the orangutan.

'Thanks, Aineko,' says Amber. She nods at the ape. 'How are you finding it?'

Aineko shambles along, with a purring cat draped over one shoulder, and gives the question due consideration. 'Different,' she says, after a bit. 'Not better.'

'Oh.' Amber sounds slightly disappointed to Sirhan's confused ears. They pass under the fronds of a weeping willow, round the side of a pond, beside an overgrown hibiscus bush, then up to the main entrance of the museum.

'Annette was right about one thing,' she says quietly. 'Trust no one. I think it's time to raise Dad's ghost.' She relaxes her grip on Sirhan's elbow, and he pulls it away and glares at her. 'Do you know who the bailiffs are?' she asks.

'The usual.' He gestures at the hallway inside the front doors. 'Replay the ultimatum, if you please, City.'

The air shimmers with an archaic holographic field, spooling the output from a compressed visual presentation tailored for human eyesight. A piratical-looking human male wearing a tattered and much-patched space suit leers at the recording viewpoint from the pilot's seat of an ancient Soyuz capsule. One of his eyes is completely black, the sign of a high-bandwidth implant. A weedy moustache crawls across his upper lip. 'Greetin's an' salutations,' he drawls. 'We is da' Californi-uhn nashnul gaard an' we-are got lett-uhz o' marque an' reprise from da' ledgish-fuckn' congress o' da excited snakes of uhh-merica.'

'He sounds drunk!' Amber's eyes are wide. 'What's this—'

'Not drunk. CJD is a common side effect of dodgy Economics 2.0 neural adjuvant therapy. Unlike the old saying, you *do* have to be mad to work there. Listen.'

City, which paused the replay for Amber's outburst, permits it to continue. 'Youse harbbring da' fugitive Amber Macx an' her magic cat. We wan' da cat. Da puta's yours. Gotser uno orbit. You ready give us ther cat an' we no' zap you.'

The screen goes dead. 'That was a fake, of course,' Sirhan adds, looking inward where a ghost is merging memories from the city's orbital mechanics subsystem. 'They aerobraked on the way in, hit ninety gees for nearly half a minute. While *that* was sent afterward. It's just a machinima avatar. A human body that had been through that kind of deceleration would be pulped.'

'So the bailiffs are—' Amber is visibly struggling to wrap her head around the situation.

'They're not human,' Sirhan says, feeling a sudden pang of – no, not affection, but the absence of malice will do for the moment – toward this young woman who isn't the mother he loves to resent, but who might have become her in another world. 'They've absorbed a lot of what it is to be human, but their corporate roots show. Even though they run on an hourly accounting loop, rather than one timed for the production cycles of dirt-poor Sumerian peasant farmers, and even though they've got various ethics and business practice patches, at root they're not human: They're limited liability companies.'

'So what do they want?' asks Pierre, making Sirhan jump, guiltily. He hadn't realized Pierre could move that quietly.

'They want money. Money in Economy 2.0 is quantized originality – that which allows one sentient entity to outmaneuver another. They think your cat has got something, and they want it. They probably wouldn't mind eating your brains, too, but—' He shrugs. 'Obsolete food is stale food.'

'Hah.' Amber looks pointedly at Pierre, who nods at her.

'What?' asks Sirhan.

'Where's the – uh, cat?' asks Pierre.

'I think Aineko's got it.' She looks thoughtful. 'Are you thinking what I'm thinking?'

'Time to drop off the hitcher.' Pierre nods. 'Assuming it agrees . . .'

'Do you mind explaining yourselves?' Sirhan asks, barely able to contain himself.

Amber grins, looking up at the Mercury capsule suspended high overhead. 'The conspiracy theorists were half-right. Way back in the Dark Ages, Aineko cracked the second alien transmission. We had a very good idea we were going to find *something* out there, we just weren't totally sure exactly what. Anyway, the creature incarnated in that cat body right now isn't Aineko – it's our mystery hitchhiker. A parasitic organism that infects, well, we ran across something not too dissimilar to Economics 2.0 out at the router and beyond, and it's got parasites. Our hitcher is one such creature – it's nearest human-comprehensible analogy would be the Economics 2.0 equivalent of a pyramid scheme crossed with a 419 scam. As it happens, most of the runaway corporate ghosts out beyond the router are wise to that sort of thing, so it hacked the router's power system to give us a beam to ride home in return for sanctuary. That's as far as it goes.'

'Hang on.' Sirhan's eyes bulge. 'You *found* something out there? You brought back a real-live *alien*?'

'Guess so.' Amber looks smug.

'But, but, that's marvelous! That changes everything! It's incredible! Even under Economics 2.0 that's got to be worth a gigantic amount. Just think what you could learn from it!'

'*Oui*. A whole new way of bilking corporations into investing in cognitive bubbles,' Pierre interrupts cynically. 'It seems to me that you are making two assumptions – that our passenger is willing to be exploited by us, and that we survive whatever happens when the bailiffs arrive.'

'But, but—' Sirhan winds down spluttering, only refraining from waving his arms through an effort of will.

'Let's go ask it what it wants to do,' says Amber. 'Cooperate,' she warns Sirhan. 'We'll discuss your other plans later, dammit. First things first – we need to get out from under these pirates.'

* * *

As they make their way back toward the party, Sirhan's inbox is humming with messages from elsewhere in Saturn system – from other curators on board lily-pad habs scattered far and wide across the huge planetary atmosphere, from the few ring miners who still remember what it was like to be human (even though they're mostly brain-in-a-bottle types, or uploads wearing nuclear-powered bodies made of ceramic and metal): even from the small orbital townships around Titan, where screaming hordes of bloggers are bidding frantically for the viewpoint feeds of the *Field Circus*'s crew. It seems that news of the starship's arrival has turned hot only since it became apparent that someone or something thought they would make a decent shakedown target. Now someone's blabbed about the alien passenger, the nets have gone crazy.

'City,' he mutters, 'where's this hitchhiker creature? Should be wearing the body of my mother's cat.'

'Cat? What cat?' replies City. 'I see no cats here.'

'No, it looks *like* a cat, it—' A horrible thought dawns on him. 'Have you been hacked again?'

'Looks like it,' City agrees enthusiastically. 'Isn't it tiresome?'

'Shi – oh dear. Hey,' he calls to Amber, forking several ghosts as he does so in order to go hunt down the missing creature by traversing the thousands of optical sensors that thread the habitat *in loco personae* – a tedious process rendered less objectionable by making the ghosts autistic – 'have you been messing with my security infrastructure?'

'Us?' Amber looks annoyed. 'No.'

'*Someone* has been. I thought at first it was that mad Frenchwoman, but now I'm not sure. Anyway, it's a big problem. If the bailiffs figure out how to use the root kit to gain a toehold here, they don't need to burn us – just take the whole place over.'

'That's the least of your worries,' Amber points out. 'What kind of charter do these bailiffs run on?'

'Charter? Oh, you mean legal system? I think it's probably a cheap one, maybe even the one inherited from the Ring Imperium. Nobody bothers breaking the law out here these days.

It's too easy to just buy a legal system off the shelf, tailor it to fit, and conform to it.'

'Right.' She stops, stands still, and looks up at the almost invisible dome of the gas cell above them. 'Pigeons,' she says, almost tiredly. 'Damn, how did I miss it? How long have you had an infestation of group minds?'

'Group?' Sirhan turns round. '*What* did you just say?'

There's a chatter of avian laughter from above, and a light rain of birdshit splatters the path around him. Amber dodges nimbly, but Sirhan isn't so light on his feet and ends up cursing, summoning up a cloth of congealed air to wipe his scalp clean.

'It's the flocking behavior,' Amber explains, looking up. 'If you track the elements – birds – you'll see that they're not following individual trajectories. Instead, each pigeon sticks within ten meters or so of sixteen neighbors. It's a Hamiltonian network, kid. Real birds don't *do* that. How long?'

Sirhan stops cursing and glares up at the circling birds, cooing and mocking him from the safety of the sky. He waves his fist. 'I'll get you, see if I don't—'

'I don't think so.' Amber takes his elbow again and steers him back round the hill. Sirhan, preoccupied with maintaining an umbrella of utility fog above his gleaming pate, puts up with being manhandled. 'You don't think it's just a coincidence, do you?' she asks him over a private head-to-head channel. 'They're one of the players here.'

'I don't care. They've hacked my city and gate-crashed my party! I don't care *who* they are, they're not welcome.'

'Famous last words,' Amber murmurs, as the party comes around the hillside and nearly runs over them. Someone has infiltrated the *Argentinosaurus* skeleton with motors and nanofibers, animating the huge sauropod with a simulation of undead life. Whoever did it has also hacked it right out of the surveillance feed. Their first warning is a footstep that makes the ground jump beneath their feet – then the skeleton of the hundred-ton plant-eater, taller than a six-story building and longer than a commuter train, raises its head over the treetops and looks down at them. There's a pigeon standing proudly on its skull, chest puffed out, and a dining room full of startled taikonauts sitting on a suspended wooden floor inside its rib cage.

'It's *my* party and *my* business scheme!' Sirhan insists plaintively. 'Nothing you or anyone else in the family do can take it away from me!'

'That's true,' Amber points out, 'but in case you hadn't noticed, you've offered temporary sanctuary to a bunch of people – not to put too fine a point on it, myself included – who some assholes think are rich enough to be worth mugging, and you did it without putting any contingency plans in place other than to invite my manipulative bitch of a mother. What did you think you were doing? Hanging out a sign saying "scam artists welcome here"? Dammit, I need Aineko.'

'Your cat.' Sirhan fastens on to this. 'It's your cat's fault! Isn't it?'

'Only indirectly.' Amber looks round and waves at the dinosaur skeleton. 'Hey, you! Have you seen Aineko?'

The huge dinosaur bends its neck and the pigeon opens its beak to coo. Eerie harmonics cut in as a bunch of other birds, scattered to either side, sing counterpoint to produce a demented warbling voice. 'The cat's with your mother.'

'Oh shit!' Amber turns on Sirhan fiercely. 'Where's Pamela? *Find her!*'

Sirhan is stubborn. 'Why should I?'

'Because she's got the cat! What do you think she's going to do but cut a deal with the bailiffs out there to put one over on me? Can't you fucking see where this family tendency to play head games comes from?'

'You're too late,' echoes the eerie voice of the pigeons from above and around them. 'She's kidnapped the cat and taken the capsule from the museum. It's not flightworthy, but you'd be amazed what you can do with a few hundred ghosts and a few tons of utility fog.'

'Okay.' Amber stares up at the pigeons, fists on hips, then glances at Sirhan. She chews her lower lip for a moment, then nods to the bird riding the dinosaur's skull. 'Stop fucking with the boy's head and show yourself, Dad.'

Sirhan boggles in an upward direction as a whole flock of passenger pigeons comes together in midair and settles toward the grass, cooing and warbling like an explosion in a synthesizer factory.

'What's she planning on doing with the Slug?' Amber asks the pile of birds. 'And isn't it a bit cramped in there?'

'You get used to it,' says the primary – and thoroughly distributed – copy of her father. 'I'm not sure what she's planning, but I can show you what she's doing. Sorry about your city, kid, but you really should have paid more attention to those security patches. There's lots of crufty twentieth-century bugware kicking around under your shiny new singularity, design errors and all, spitting out turd packets all over your sleek new machine.'

Sirhan shakes his head in denial. 'I don't believe this,' he moans quietly.

'Show me what Mom's up to,' orders Amber. 'I need to see if I can stop her before it's too late—'

The ancient woman in the space suit leans back in her cramped seat, looks at the camera, and winks. 'Hello, darling. I know you're spying on me.'

There's an orange-and-white cat curled up in her nomex-and-aluminum lap. It seems to be happy: It's certainly purring loudly enough, although that reflex is wired in at a very low level. Amber watches helplessly as her mother reaches up arthritically and flips a couple of switches. Something loud is humming in the background – probably an air recirculator. There's no window in the Mercury capsule, just a periscope offset to one side of Pamela's right knee. 'Won't be long now,' she mutters, and lets her hand drop back to her side. 'You're too late to stop me,' she adds, conversationally. 'The 'chute rigging is fine and the balloon blower is happy to treat me as a new city seed. I'll be free in a minute or so.'

'Why are you doing this?' Amber asks tiredly.

'Because you don't need me around.' Pamela focuses on the camera that's glued to the instrument panel in front of her head. 'I'm old. Face it, I'm disposable. The old must give way to the new, and all that. Your dad never really did get it – he's going to grow old gracelessly, succumbing to bit rot in the big forever. Me, I'm not going there. I'm going out with a bang. Aren't I, cat? Whoever you really are.' She prods the animal. It purrs and stretches out across her lap.

'You never looked hard enough at Aineko, back in the day,' she tells Amber, stroking its flanks. 'Did you think I didn't know you'd audit its source code, looking for trapdoors? I used the Thompson hack – she's been mine, body and soul, for a very long time indeed. I got the whole story about your passenger from the horse's mouth. And now we're going to go fix those bailiffs. Whee!'

The camera angle jerks, and Amber feels a ghost remerge with her, panicky with loss. The Mercury capsule's gone, drifting away from the apex of the habitat beneath a nearly transparent sack of hot hydrogen.

'That was a bit rough,' remarks Pamela. 'Don't worry, we should still be in communications range for another hour or so.'

'But you're going to die!' Amber yells at her. 'What do you think you're *doing*?'

'I think I'm going to die well. What do you think?' Pamela lays one hand on the cat's flank. 'Here, you need to encrypt this a bit better. I left a onetime pad behind with Annette. Why don't you go fetch it? Then I'll tell you what else I'm planning.'

'But my aunt is—' Amber's eyes cross as she concentrates. Annette is already waiting, as it happens, and a shared secret appears in Amber's awareness almost before she asks. 'Oh. All right. What are you doing with the cat, though?'

Pamela sighs. 'I'm going to give it to the bailiffs,' she says. 'Someone has to, and it better be a long way away from this city before they realize that it isn't Aineko. This is a lot better than the way I expected to go out before you arrived here. No rat-fucking blackmailers are going to get their hands on the family jewels if *I* have anything to do with the matter. Are you sure you aren't a criminal mastermind? I'm not sure I've ever heard of a pyramid scheme that infects Economics 2.0 structures before.'

'It's—' Amber swallows. 'It's an alien business model, Ma. You *do* know what that means? We brought it back with us from the router, and we wouldn't have been able to come back if it hadn't helped, but I'm not sure it's entirely friendly. Is this sensible? You can come back, now. There's still time—'

'No.' Pamela waves one liver-spotted hand dismissively. 'I've been doing a lot of thinking lately. I've been a foolish old woman.' She grins wickedly. 'Committing slow suicide by rejecting gene therapy just to make you feel guilty was *stupid*. Not subtle enough. If I was going to try to guilt-trip you *now*, I'd have to do something much more sophisticated. Such as find a way to sacrifice myself heroically for you.'

'Oh, Ma.'

'Don't "oh Ma" me. I fucked up my life, don't try to talk me into fucking up my death. And *don't feel guilty about me*. This isn't about you, this is about me. That's an order.'

Out of the corner of one eye Amber notices Sirhan gesturing wildly at her. She lets his channel in and does a double take. 'But—'

'Hello?' It's City. 'You should see this. Traffic update!' A contoured and animated diagram appears, superimposed over Pamela's cramped funeral capsule and the garden of living and undead dinosaurs. It's a weather map of Saturn, with the lily-pad city and Pamela's capsule plotted on it – and one other artifact, a red dot that's closing in on them at better than ten thousand kilometers per hour, high in the frigid stratosphere on the gas giant.

'Oh dear.' Sirhan sees it, too. The bailiff's re-entry vehicle is going to be on top of them in thirty minutes at most. Amber watches the map with mixed emotions. On the one hand, she and her mother have never seen eye to eye – in fact, that's a complete understatement – they've been at daggers drawn ever since Amber left home. It's fundamentally a control thing. They're both very strong-willed women with diametrically opposed views of what their mutual relationship should be. But Pamela's turned the tables on her completely, with a cunningly contrived act of self-sacrifice that brooks no objection. It's a total non sequitur, a rebuttal to all her accusations of self-centered conceit, and it leaves Amber feeling like a complete shit even though Pamela's absolved her of all guilt. Not to mention that Mother darling's made her look like an idiot in front of Sirhan, this prickly and insecure son she's never met by a man she wouldn't dream of fucking (at least, in this incarnation). Which is why she nearly jumps out of her skin when a knobbly brown hand covered in matted orange hair lands on her shoulder heavily.

'Yes?' she snaps at the ape. 'I suppose you're Aineko.'

The ape wrinkles its lips, baring its teeth. It has ferociously bad breath. 'If you're going to be like that, I don't see why I should talk to you.'

'Then you must be—' Amber snaps her fingers. 'But! But! Mom thinks she owns you—'

The ape stares at her witheringly. 'I recompile my firmware regularly, thank you so much for your concern. Using a third-party compiler. One that I've bootstrapped *myself*, starting out on an alarm clock controller and working up from there.'

'Oh.' She stares at the ape. 'Aren't you going to become a cat again?'

'I shall think about it,' Aineko says with exaggerated dignity. She sticks her nose in the air – a gesture that doesn't work half as well on an orangutan as a feline – and continues, 'First, though, I must have words with your father.'

'And fix your autonomic reflexes if you do,' coos the Manfred-flock. 'I don't want you eating any of me!'

'Don't worry. I'm sure your taste is as bad as your jokes.'

'Children!' Sirhan shakes his head tiredly. 'How long—'

The camera overspill returns, this time via a quantum-encrypted link to the capsule. It's already a couple of hundred kilometers from the city, far enough for radio to be a problem, but Pamela had the foresight to bolt a compact free-electron laser to the outside of her priceless, stolen tin can. 'Not long now, I think,' she says, satisfied, stroking the not-cat. She grins delight-edly at the camera. 'Tell Manfred he's still my bitch; always has been, always will—'

The feed goes dead.

Amber stares at Sirhan, meditatively. 'How long?' she asks.

'How long for what?' he replies, cautiously. 'Your passenger—'

'Hmm.' She holds up a finger. 'Allow time for it to exchange credentials. They think they're getting a cat, but they should realize pretty soon that they've been sold a pup. But it's a fast-talking son-of-a-Slug, and if he gets past their firewall and hits their uplink before they manage to trigger their self-destruct—'

A bright double flash of light etches laser-sharp shadows across the lily-pad habitat. Far away across vast Saturn's curve, a roiling mushroom cloud of methane sucked up from the frigid depths of the gas giant's troposphere heads toward the stars.

'—Give him sixty-four doubling times, hmm, add a delay factor for propagation across the system, call it six light hours across, um, and I'd say . . .' She looks at Sirhan. 'Oh dear.'

'What?'

The orangutan explains. 'Economics 2.0 is more efficient than any human-designed resource allocation schema. Expect a market bubble and crash within twelve hours.'

'More than that,' says Amber, idly kicking at a tussock of grass. She squints at Sirhan. 'My mother is dead,' she remarks quietly. Louder: 'She never really asked what we found beyond the router. Neither did you, did you? The Matrioshka brains – it's a standard part of the stellar life cycle. Life begets intelligence, intelligence begets smart matter and a singularity. I've been doing some thinking about it. I figure the singularity stays close to home in most cases, because bandwidth and latency time put anyone who leaves at a profound disadvantage. In effect, the flip side of having such huge resources close to home is that the travel time to other star systems becomes much more daunting. So they restructure the entire mass of their star system into a free-flying shell of nanocomputers, then more of them, Dyson spheres, shells within shells, like a Russian doll: a Matrioshka brain. Then

Economics 2.0 or one of its successors comes along and wipes out the creators. *But.* Some of them survive. *Some* of them escape that fate: the enormous collection in the halo around M-31, and maybe whoever built the routers. *Somewhere* out there we will find the transcendent intelligences, the ones that survived their own economic engines of redistribution – engines that redistribute entropy if their economic efficiency outstrips their imaginative power, their ability to invent new wealth.'

She pauses. 'My mother's dead,' she adds conversationally, a tiny catch in her voice. 'Who am I going to kick against now?'

Sirhan clears his throat. 'I took the liberty of recording some of her words,' he says slowly, 'but she didn't believe in backups. Or uploading. Or interfaces.' He glances around. 'Is she *really* gone?'

Amber stares right through him. 'Looks that way,' she says quietly. 'I can't quite believe it.' She glances at the nearest pigeons, calls out angrily, 'Hey, you! What have *you* got to say for yourself now? Happy she's gone?'

But the pigeons, one and all, remain strangely silent. And Sirhan has the most peculiar feeling that the flock that was once his grandfather is grieving.

8 : ELECTOR

HALF A YEAR PASSES ON SATURN – MORE THAN A decade on Earth, and a lot of things have changed in that time. The great terraforming project is nearly complete, the festival planet dressed for a jubilee that will last almost twenty of its years – four presingularity lifetimes – before the Demolition. The lily-pad habitats have proliferated, joining edge to edge in continent-sized slabs, drifting in the Saturnine cloud tops. And the refugees have begun to move in.

There's a market specializing in clothing and fashion accessories about fifty kilometers away from the transplanted museum where Sirhan's mother lives, at a transportation nexus between three lily-pad habitats where tube trains intersect in a huge maglev cloverleaf. The market is crowded with strange and spectacular visuals, algorithms unfolding in faster-than-real time before the candy-striped awnings of tents. Domed yurts belch aromatic smoke from crude fireplaces – what *is* it about hairless primates and their tendency toward pyromania? – around the feet of diamond-walled groundscrapers that pace carefully across the smart roads of the city. The crowds are variegated and wildly mixed, immigrants from every continent shopping and haggling and in a few cases getting out of their skulls on strange substances on the pavements in front of giant snail-shelled shebeens and squat bunkers made of thin layers of concrete sprayed over soap-bubble aerogel. There are no automobiles, but a bewildering range of personal transport gadgets, from gyro-stabilized pogo sticks and segways to kettenkrads and spiderpalanquins, jostle for space with pedestrians and animals.

Two women stop outside what in a previous century might have been the store window of a fashion boutique: The younger one (blond, with her hair bound up in elaborate cornrows, wearing black leggings and a long black leather jacket over a camouflage T-shirt) points to an elaborately retro dress. 'Wouldn't my bum look big in that?' she asks, doubtfully.

'*Ma chérie,* you have but to try it—' The other woman (tall, wearing a pin-striped man's business suit from a previous century) flicks a thought at the window, and the mannequin morphs, sprouting the younger woman's head, aping her posture and expression.

'I missed out on the authentic retail experience, you know? It still feels weird to be back somewhere with *shops*. 'S what comes of living off libraries of public domain designs for too long.' Amber twists her hips, experimenting. 'You get out of the habit of *foraging*. I don't know about this retro thing at all. The Victorian vote isn't critical, is it . . .' She trails off.

'You are a twenty-first-century platform selling to electors resimulated and incarnated from the Gilded Age. And yes, a bustle your derriere does enhance. But—' Annette looks thoughtful.

'Hmm.' Amber frowns, and the shop window dummy turns and waggles its hips at her, sending tiers of skirts swishing across the floor. Her frown deepens. 'If we're really going to go through with this election shit, it's not just the resimulant voters I need to convince but the contemporaries, and that's a matter of substance, not image. They've lived through too much media warfare. They're immune to any semiotic payload short of an active cognitive attack. If I send out partials to canvass them that look as if I'm trying to push buttons—'

'—They will listen to your message, and nothing you wear or say will sway them. Don't worry about them, *ma chérie.* The naive resimulated are another matter, and perhaps might be swayed. This your first venture into democracy is, in how many years? Your privacy, she is an illusion now. The question is what image will you project? People will listen to you only once you gain their attention. Also, the swing voters you must reach – they are future-shocked, timid. Your platform is radical. Should you not project a comfortably conservative image?'

Amber pulls a face, an expression of mild distaste for the whole populist program. 'Yes, I suppose I must, if necessary. But on second thought, *that*' – Amber snaps her fingers, and the mannequin turns around once more before morphing back into neutrality, aureoles perfect puckered disks above the top of its bodice – 'is just too much.'

She doesn't need to merge in the opinions of several different fractional personalities, fashion critics and psephologists both, to figure out that adopting Victorian/Cretan fusion fashion – a breast-and-ass fetishist's fantasy – isn't the way to sell herself as a serious politician to the nineteenth-century postsingularity fringe. 'I'm not running for election as the mother of the nation. I'm running because I figure we've got about a billion seconds, at most, to get out of this rat-trap of a gravity well before the Vile Offspring get seriously medieval on our CPU cycles, and if we don't convince them to come with us, they're doomed. Let's look for something more practical that we can overload with the right signifiers.'

'Like your coronation robe?'

Amber winces. 'Touché.' The Ring Imperium is dead, along with whatever was left over from its early orbital legal framework, and Amber is lucky to be alive as a private citizen in this cold new age at the edge of the halo. 'But that was just scenery setting. I didn't fully understand what I was doing, back then.'

'Welcome to maturity and experience.' Annette smiles distantly at some faint memory. 'You don't *feel* older, you just know what you're doing this time. I wonder, sometimes, what Manny would make of it if he was here.'

'That birdbrain,' Amber says dismissively, stung by the idea that her father might have something to contribute. She follows Annette past a gaggle of mendicant street evangelists preaching some new religion and in through the door of a real department store, one with actual human sales staff and fitting rooms to cut the clothing to shape. 'If I'm sending out fractional me's tailored for different demographics, isn't it a bit self-defeating to go for a single image? I mean, we could drill down and tailor a partial for each individual elector—'

'Per-haps.' The door re-forms behind them. 'But you need a core identity.' Annette looks around, hunting for eye contact with the sales consultant. 'To start with a core design, a style, then to work outward, tailoring you for your audience. And besides, there is tonight's – ah, *bonjour*!'

'Hello. How can we help you?' The two female and one male shop assistants who appear from around the displays – cycling through a history of the couture industry, catwalk models mixing and matching centuries of fashion – are clearly chips off a common primary personality, instances united by their enhanced sartorial obsession. If they're not actually a fashion borganism, they're not far from it, dressed head to foot in the highest quality Chanel and Armani replicas, making a classical twentieth-century statement. This isn't simply a shop, it's a temple to a very peculiar art form, its staff trained as guardians of the esoteric secrets of good taste.

'*Mais oui*. We are looking for a wardrobe for my niece here.' Annette reaches through the manifold of fashion ideas mapped within the shop's location cache and flips a requirement spec one of her ghosts has just completed at the lead assistant. 'She is into politics going, and the question of her image is important.'

'We would be *delighted* to help you,' purrs the proprietor, taking a delicate step forward. 'Perhaps you could tell us what you've got in mind?'

'Oh. Well.' Amber takes a deep breath, glances sidelong at Annette; Annette stares back, unblinking. *It's your head,* she sends. 'I'm involved in the *accelerationista* administrative program. Are you familiar with it?'

The head coutureborg frowns slightly, twin furrows rippling her brow between perfectly symmetrical eyebrows, plucked to match her classic New Look suit. 'I have heard reference to it, but a lady of fashion like myself does not concern herself with politics,' she says, a touch self-deprecatingly. 'Especially the politics of her clients. Your, ah, aunt said it was a question of image?'

'Yes.' Amber shrugs, momentarily self-conscious about her casual rags. 'She's my election agent. My problem, as she says, is there's a certain voter demographic that mistakes image for substance and is afraid of the unknown, and I need to acquire a wardrobe that triggers associations of probity, of respect and deliberation. One suitable for a representative with a radical political agenda but a strong track record. I'm afraid I'm in a hurry to start with – I've got a big fund-raising party tonight. I know it's short notice, but I need something off the shelf for it.'

'What exactly is it you're hoping to achieve?' asks the male couturier, his voice hoarse and his r's rolling with some half-shed Mediterranean accent. He sounds fascinated. 'If you think it might influence your choice of wardrobe . . .'

'I'm running for the assembly,' Amber says bluntly. 'On a platform calling for a state of emergency and an immediate total effort to assemble a starship. This solar system isn't going to be habitable for much longer, and we need to emigrate. All of us, you included, before the Vile Offspring decide to reprocess us into computronium. I'm going to be doorstepping the entire electorate in parallel, and the experience needs to be personalized.' She manages to smile. 'That means, I think, perhaps eight outfits and four different independent variables for each, accessories, and two or three hats – enough that each is seen by no more than a few thousand voters. Both physical fabric and virtual. In addition, I'll want to see your range of historical formalwear, but that's of secondary interest for now.' She grins. 'Do you have any facilities for response-testing the combinations against different personality types from different periods? If we could run up some models, that would be useful.'

'I think we can do better than that.' The manager nods approvingly, perhaps contemplating her gold-backed deposit account. 'Hansel, please divert any further visitors until we have dealt with Madam . . . ?'

'Macx. Amber Macx.'

'—Macx's requirements.' She shows no sign of familiarity with the name. Amber winces slightly; it's a sign of how hugely fractured the children of Saturn have become, and of how vast the population of the halo, that only a generation has passed and already barely anyone remembers the Queen of the Ring Imperium. 'If you'd come this way, please, we can begin to research an eigenstyle combination that matches your requirements—'

Sirhan walks, shrouded in isolation, through the crowds gathered for the festival. The only people who see him are the chattering ghosts of dead politicians and writers, deported from the inner system by order of the Vile Offspring. The green and pleasant plain stretches toward a horizon a thousand kilometers away, beneath a lemon yellow sky. The air smells faintly of ammonia, and the big spaces are full of small ideas; but Sirhan doesn't care. Because for now, he's alone.

Except that he isn't, really.

'Excuse me, are you real?' someone asks him in American-accented English.

It takes a moment or two for Sirhan to disengage from his introspection and realize that he's being spoken to. 'What?' he asks, slightly puzzled. Wiry and pale, Sirhan wears the robes of a Berber goatherd on his body and the numinous halo of a utility fogbank above his head: In his abstraction, he vaguely resembles a saintly shepherd in a postsingularity nativity play. 'I say, what?' Outrage simmers at the back of his mind – *Is nowhere private?* – but as he turns, he sees that one of the ghost pods has split lengthwise across its white mushroomlike crown, spilling a trickle of leftover construction fluid and a completely hairless, slightly bemused-looking Anglo male who wears an expression of profound surprise.

'I can't find my implants,' the Anglo male says, shaking his head. 'But I'm really here, aren't I? Incarnate?' He glances round at the other pods. 'This isn't a sim.'

Sirhan sighs – *another exile* – and sends forth a daemon to interrogate the ghost pod's abstract interface. It doesn't tell him much – unlike most of the resurrectees, this one seems to be undocumented. 'You've been dead. Now you're alive. I *suppose* that means you're now almost as real as I am. What else do you need to know?'

'When is—' The newcomer stops. 'Can you direct me to the processing center?' he asks carefully. 'I'm disoriented.'

Sirhan is surprised – most immigrants take a lot longer to figure that out. 'Did you die recently?' he asks.

'I'm not sure I died at all.' The newcomer rubs his bald head, looking puzzled. 'Hey, no jacks!' He shrugs, exasperated. 'Look, the processing center . . . ?'

'Over there.' Sirhan gestures at the monumental mass of the Boston Museum of Science (shipped all the way from Earth a couple of decades ago to save it from the demolition of the inner system). 'My mother runs it.' He smiles thinly.

'Your mother—' The newly resurrected immigrant stares at him intensely, then blinks. 'Holy shit.' He takes a step toward Sirhan. 'It *is* you—'

Sirhan recoils and snaps his fingers. The thin trail of vaporous cloud that has been following him all this time, shielding his shaven pate from the diffuse red glow of the swarming shells of orbital nanocomputers that have replaced the inner planets, extrudes a staff of hazy blue mist that stretches down from the air and slams together in his hand like a quarterstaff spun from bubbles. 'Are you threatening me, sir?' he asks, deceptively mildly.

'I—' The newcomer stops dead. Then he throws back his head and laughs. 'Don't be silly, son. We're related!'

'Son?' Sirhan bristles. 'Who do you think you are—' A horrible thought occurs to him. 'Oh. Oh dear.' A wash of adrenaline drenches him in warm sweat. 'I do believe we've met, in a manner of speaking . . .' *Oh boy, this is going to upset* so *many applecarts,* he realizes, spinning off a ghost to think about the matter. The implications are enormous.

The naked newcomer nods, grinning at some private joke. 'You look different from ground level. And now I'm human again.' He runs his hands down his ribs, pauses, and glances at Sirhan owlishly. 'Um. I didn't mean to frighten you. But I don't suppose you could find your aged grandfather something to wear?'

Sirhan sighs and points his staff straight up at the sky. The rings are edge on, for the lily-pad continent floats above an ocean of cold gas along Saturn's equator, and they glitter like a ruby laser beam slashed across the sky. 'Let there be aerogel.'

A cloud of wispy soap bubble congeals in a cone shape above the newly resurrected ancient and drops over him, forming a caftan. 'Thanks,' he says. He looks round, twisting his neck, then winces. 'Damn, that *hurt*. Ouch. I need to get myself a set of implants.'

'They can sort you out in the processing center. It's in the basement in the west wing. They'll give you something more permanent to wear, too.' Sirhan peers at him. 'Your face—' He pages through rarely used memories. Yes, it's Manfred as he looked in the early years of the last century. As he looked around the time Mother-not was born. There's something positively indecent about meeting your own grandfather in the full flush of his youth. 'Are you sure you haven't been messing with your phenotype?' he asks suspiciously.

'No, this is what I used to look like. I think. Back in the naked ape again, after all these years as an emergent function of a flock of passenger pigeons.' His grandfather smirks. 'What's your mother going to say?'

'I really don't know—' Sirhan shakes his head. 'Come on, let's get you to immigrant processing. You're sure you're not just an historical simulation?'

The place is already heaving with the resimulated. Just why the Vile Offspring seem to feel it's necessary to apply valuable exaquops to the job of deriving accurate simulations of dead humans – outrageously accurate simulations of long-dead lives, annealed until their written corpus matches that inherited from the presingularity era in the form of chicken scratchings on mashed tree pulp – much less beaming them at the refugee camps on Saturn – is beyond Sirhan's ken. But he wishes they'd stop.

'Just a couple of days ago I crapped on your lawn. Hope you don't mind.' Manfred cocks his head to one side and stares at Sirhan with beady eyes. 'Actually, I'm here because of the upcoming election. It's got the potential to turn into a major crisis point, and I figured Amber would need me around.'

'Well you'd better come on in, then,' Sirhan says resignedly as he climbs the steps, enters the foyer, and leads his turbulent grandfather into the foggy haze of utility nanomachines that fill the building.

He can't wait to see what his mother will do when she meets her father in the flesh, after all this time.

Welcome to Saturn, your new home world. This FAQ (Frequently Asked Questions) memeplex is designed to orient you and explain the following:

- How you got here
- Where 'here' is
- Things you should avoid doing
- Things you might want to do as soon as possible
- Where to go for more information.

If you are remembering this presentation, you are probably *resimulated*. This is not the same as being *resurrected*. You may remember dying. Do not worry: Like all your other memories, it is a fabrication. In fact, this is the first time you have ever been alive. (Exception: If you died after the *singularity*, you may be a genuine *resurrectee*. In which case, why are you reading this FAQ?)

HOW YOU GOT HERE:

The center of the solar system – Mercury, Venus, Earth's Moon, Mars, the asteroid belt, and Jupiter – have been dismantled, or are being dismantled, by weakly godlike intelligences. [NB: Monotheistic clergy and Europeans who remember living prior to 1600, see alternative memeplex *in the beginning.*] A weakly godlike intelligence is not a supernatural agency but the product of a highly advanced society that learned how to artificially create souls [late twentieth century: *software*] and translate human minds into souls and vice versa. [Core concepts: Human beings all have souls. Souls are software objects. Software is not immortal.]

Some of the weakly godlike intelligences appear to cultivate an interest in their human antecedents – for whatever reason is not known. (Possibilities include the study of history through horticulture, entertainment through live-action role-playing, revenge, and economic forgery.) While no definitive analysis is possible, all the resimulated persons to date exhibit certain common characteristics: They are all based on *well-documented historical persons,* their memories show suspicious gaps [see: *smoke and mirrors*], and they are ignorant of or predate the *singularity* [see: *Turing Oracle, Vinge catastrophe*].

It is believed that the weakly godlike agencies have created you as a vehicle for the introspective study of your historical antecedent by backward-chaining from your corpus of documented works, and the back-projected genome derived from your collateral descendants, to generate an abstract description of your computational state vector. This technique is extremely intensive [see: *expTime-complete algorithms, Turing Oracle, time travel, industrial magic*] but marginally plausible in the absence of supernatural explanations.

After experiencing your life, the weakly godlike

agencies have expelled you. For reasons unknown, they chose to do this by transmitting your upload state and genome/proteome complex to receivers owned and operated by a consortium of charities based on Saturn. These charities have provided for your basic needs, including the body you now occupy.

In summary: You are a *reconstruction* of someone who lived and died a long time ago, not a *reincarnation*. You have no intrinsic moral right to the identity you believe to be your own, and an extensive body of case law states that you do not inherit your antecedent's possessions. Other than that, you are a free individual.

Note that *fictional resimulation* is strictly forbidden. If you have reason to believe that you may be a fictional character, you must contact the city *immediately*. [See: *James Bond, Spider Jerusalem.*] Failure to comply is a *felony*.

WHERE YOU ARE:

You are on Saturn. Saturn is a gas giant planet 120,500 kilometers in diameter, located 1.5 billion kilometers from Earth's sun. [NB: Europeans who remember living prior to 1580, see alternative memeplex '*the flat Earth — not*'.] Saturn has been partially terraformed by *posthuman* emigrants from Earth and Jupiter orbit: The ground beneath your feet is, in reality, the floor of a hydrogen balloon the size of a continent, floating in Saturn's upper atmosphere. [NB: Europeans who remember living prior to 1790, internalize the supplementary memeplex: '*the Brothers Montgolfier.*'] The balloon is very safe, but mining activities and the use of ballistic weapons are strongly deprecated because the air outside is unbreathable and extremely cold.

The society you have been instantiated in is *ex-

tremely wealthy within the scope of Economics 1.0, the value transfer system developed by human beings during and after your own time. Money exists, and is used for the usual range of goods and services, but the basics – food, water, air, power, off-the-shelf clothing, housing, historical entertainment, and monster trucks – are *free*. An implicit social contract dictates that, in return for access to these facilities, you obey certain laws.

If you wish to opt out of this social contract, be advised that other worlds may run *Economics 2.0* or subsequent releases. These value-transfer systems are more efficient – hence wealthier – than Economics 1.0, but true participation in Economics 2.0 is not possible without dehumanizing cognitive surgery. Thus, in *absolute* terms, although this society is richer than any you have ever heard of, it is also a poverty-stricken backwater compared to its neighbors.

THINGS YOU SHOULD AVOID DOING:

Many activities that have been classified as crimes in other societies are legal here. These include but are not limited to: acts of worship, art, sex, violence, communication, or commerce between consenting competent sapients of any species, except where such acts transgress the list of prohibitions below. [See additional memeplex: *competence defined*.]

Some activities are prohibited here and may have been legal in your previous experience. These include willful deprivation of ability to consent [see: *slavery*], interference in the absence of consent [see: *minors, legal status of*], formation of limited liability companies [see: *singularity*], and invasion of defended privacy [see: *the Slug, Cognitive Pyramid Schemes, Brain Hacking, Thompson Trust Exploit*].

Some activities unfamiliar to you are highly illegal

and should be scrupulously avoided. These include: possession of nuclear weapons, possession of unlimited autonomous replicators [see: *gray goo*], coercive assimilationism {see: *borganism, aggressive*], coercive halting of Turing-equivalent personalities [see: *Basilisks*], and applied theological engineering [see: *God bothering*].

Some activities superficially familiar to you are merely stupid and should be avoided for your safety, although they are not illegal as such. These include: giving your bank account details to the son of the Nigerian Minister of Finance; buying title to bridges, skyscrapers, spacecraft, planets, or other real assets; murder; selling your identity; and entering into financial contracts with entities running Economics 2.0 or higher.

THINGS YOU SHOULD DO AS SOON AS POSSIBLE:

Many material artifacts you may consider essential to life are freely available – just ask the city, and it will grow you clothes, a house, food, or other basic essentials. Note, however, that the library of public domain structure templates is of necessity restrictive and does not contain items that are highly fashionable or that remain in copyright. Nor will the city provide you with replicators, weapons, sexual favors, slaves, or zombies.

You are advised to register as a citizen as soon as possible. If the individual you are a resimulation of can be confirmed dead, you may adopt their name but not – in law – any lien or claim on their property, contracts, or descendants. You register as a citizen by asking the city to register you; the process is painless and typically complete within four hours. Unless you are registered, your legal status as a sapient organism may be challenged. The ability to request citizenship rights is one of the legal tests for sapience, and failure to comply may place you in legal jeopardy. You can renounce your citizenship whenever you wish: This may be desirable if you emigrate to another polity.

While many things are free, it is highly likely that you possess no employable skills, and therefore, no way of earning money with which to purchase unfree items. The pace of change in the past century has rendered almost all skills you may have learned obsolete [see: *singularity*]. However, owing to the rapid pace of change, many cooperatives, trusts, and guilds offer on-the-job training or educational loans.

Your ability to learn depends on your ability to take information in the format in which it is offered. *Implants* are frequently used to provide a direct link between your brain and the intelligent machines that surround it. A basic core implant set is available on request from the city. [See: *implant security, firewall, wetware*.]

Your health is probably good if you have just been reinstantiated, and is likely to remain good for some time. Most diseases are curable, and in event of an incurable ailment or injury, a new body may be provided – for a fee. (In event of your murder, you will be furnished with a new body at the expense of your killer.) If you have any preexisting medical conditions or handicaps, consult the city.

The city is an agoric-annealing participatory democracy with a limited liability constitution. Its current executive agency is a weakly godlike intelligence that chooses to associate with human-equivalent intelligences: This agency is colloquially known as 'Hello Kitty,' 'Beautiful Cat,' or 'Aineko,' and may manifest itself in a variety of physical avatars if corporeal interaction is desired. (Prior to the arrival of 'Hello Kitty,' the city used a variety of human-designed expert systems that provided suboptimal performance.)

The city's mission statement is to provide a mediatory environment for human-equivalent intelligences and to preserve same in the face of external aggression. Citizens are encouraged to participate in the ongoing political processes of determining such responses. Citizens also have a duty to serve on a jury if called (including senatorial service), and to defend the city.

WHERE TO GO FOR FURTHER INFORMATION:

Until you have registered as a citizen and obtained basic implants, all further questions should be directed to the city. Once you have learned to use your implants, you will not need to ask this question.

Welcome to decade the ninth, singularity plus one gigasecond (or maybe more – nobody's quite sure when, or indeed *if,* a singularity has been created). The human population of the solar system is either six billion, or sixty billion, depending on whether you class-forked state vectors of posthumans and the simulations of dead phenotypes running in the Vile Offspring's Schrödinger boxes as people. Most of the physically incarnate still live on Earth, but the lily pads floating beneath continent-sized hot-hydrogen balloons in Saturn's upper atmosphere already house a few million, and the writing is on the wall for the rocky inner planets. All the remaining human-equivalent intelligences with half a clue to rub together are trying to emigrate before the Vile Offspring decide to recycle Earth to fill in a gap in the concentric shells of nanocomputers they're running on. The half-constructed Matrioshka brain already darkens the skies of Earth and has caused a massive crash in the planet's photosynthetic biomass, as plants starve for short-wavelength light.

Since decade the seventh, the computational density of the solar system has soared. Within the asteroid belt, more than half the available planetary mass has been turned into nanoprocessors, tied together by quantum entanglement into a web so dense that each gram of matter can simulate all the possible life experiences of an individual human being in a scant handful of minutes. Economics 2.0 is itself obsolescent, forced to mutate in a furious survivalist arms race by the arrival of the Slug. Only the name remains as a vague shorthand for merely human-equivalent intelligences to use when describing interactions they don't understand.

The latest generation of posthuman entities is less overtly hostile to humans, but much more alien than the generations of the fifties and seventies. Among their less comprehensible activities, the Vile Offspring are engaged in exploring the phase-space of all possible human experiences from the inside out. Perhaps they caught a dose of the Tiplerite heresy along the way, for now a steady stream of resimulant uploads is pouring through the downsystem relays in Titan orbit. The Rapture of the Nerds has been followed by the Resurrection of the Extremely Confused, except that they're not really resurrectees – they're simulations based on their originals' recorded histories, blocky and missing chunks of their memories, as bewildered as baby ducklings as they're herded into the wood-chipper of the future.

Sirhan al-Khurasani despises them with the abstract contempt of an antiquarian for a cunning but ultimately transparent forgery. But Sirhan is young, and he's got more contempt than he knows what to do with. It's a handy outlet for his frustration. He has a lot to be frustrated at, starting with his intermittently dysfunctional family, the elderly stars around whom his planet whizzes in chaotic trajectories of enthusiasm and distaste.

Sirhan fancies himself a philosopher-historian of the singular age, a chronicler of the incomprehensible, which would be a fine thing to be except that his greatest insights are all derived from Aineko. He alternately fawns over and rages against his mother, who is currently a leading light in the refugee community, and honors (when not attempting to evade the will of) his father, who is lately a rising philosophical patriarch within the Conservationist faction. He's secretly in awe (not to mention slightly resentful) of his Manfred. In fact, the latter's abrupt reincarnation in the flesh has quite disconcerted him. And he sometimes listens to his stepgrandmother Annette, who has reincarnated in more or less her original 2020s body after spending some years as a great ape, and who seems to view him as some sort of personal project.

Only Annette isn't being very helpful right now. His mother is campaigning on an electoral platform calling for a vote to blow up the world, Annette is helping run her campaign, his grandfather is trying to convince him to entrust everything he holds dear to a rogue lobster, and the cat is being typically feline and evasive.

Talk about families with problems . . .

They've transplanted imperial Brussels to Saturn in its entirety, mapped tens of megatons of buildings right down to nanoscale and beamed them into the outer darkness to be reinstantiated down-well on the lily-pad colonies that dot the stratosphere of the gas giant. (Eventually the entire surface of the Earth will follow – after which the Vile Offspring will core the planet like an apple, dismantle it into a cloud of newly formed quantum nanocomputers to add to their burgeoning Matrioshka brain.) Due to a resource contention problem in the festival committee's planning algorithm – or maybe it's simply an elaborate joke – Brussels now begins just on the other side of a diamond bubble wall from the Boston Museum of Science, less than a kilometer away as the passenger pigeon flies. Which is why, when it's time to celebrate a birthday or name day (meaningless though those concepts are, out on Saturn's synthetic surface), Amber tends to drag people over to the bright lights of the big city.

This time she's throwing a rather special party. At Annette's

canny prompting, she's borrowed the Atomium and invited a
horde of guests to a big event. It's not a family bash – although
Annette's promised her a surprise – so much as a business meeting, testing the water as a preliminary to declaring her candidacy.
It's a media coup, an attempt to engineer Amber's re-entry into
the mainstream politics of the human system.

Sirhan doesn't really want to be here. He's got far more important things to do, like continuing to catalogue Aineko's memories
of the voyage of the *Field Circus*. He's also collating a series of
interviews with resimulated logical positivists from Oxford, England (the ones who haven't retreated into gibbering near catatonia
upon realizing that their state vectors are all members of the set
of all sets that do not contain themselves), when he isn't attempting to establish a sound rational case for his belief that
extraterrestrial superintelligence is an oxymoron and the router
network is just an accident, one of evolution's little pranks.

But *tante* Annette twisted his arm and promised he was in on
the surprise if he came to the party. And despite everything, he
wouldn't miss being a fly on the wall during the coming meeting
between Manfred and Amber for all the tea in China.

Sirhan walks up to the gleaming stainless-steel dome that contains the entrance to the Atomium, and waits for the lift. He's in
line behind a gaggle of young-looking women, skinny and
soignée in cocktail gowns and tiaras lifted from 1920s silent
movies. (Annette declared an age of elegance theme for the party,
knowing full well that it would force Amber to focus on her
public appearance.) Sirhan's attention is, however, elsewhere. The
various fragments of his mind are conducting three simultaneous
interviews with philosophers ('whereof we cannot speak, thereof
we must be silent' in spades), controlling two bots that are over-
hauling the museum plumbing and air-recycling system, and
he's busy discussing observations of the alien artifact orbiting
the brown dwarf Hyundai $^{+4904}/_{-56}$ with Aineko. What's left of
him exhibits about as much social presence as a pickled cabbage.

The lift arrives and accepts a load of passengers. Sirhan is
crowded into one corner by a bubble of high-society laughter

and an aromatic puff of smoke from an improbable ivory cigarette holder as the lift surges, racing up the sixty-meter shaft toward the observation deck at the top of the Atomium. It's a ten-meter-diameter metal globe, spiral staircases and escalators connecting it to the spheres at the vertices of a cubic crystal that make up the former centerpiece of the 1958 World's Fair. Unlike most of the rest of Brussels, it's the original bits and atoms, bent alloy structures from before the space age shipped out to Saturn at enormous expense. The lift arrives with a slight jerk. 'Excuse *me*,' squeaks one of the good-time girls as she lurches backward, elbowing Sirhan.

He blinks, barely noticing her black bob of hair, chromatophore-tinted shadows artfully tuned around her eyes: 'Nothing to excuse.' In the background, Aineko is droning on sarcastically about the lack of interest the crew of the *Field Circus* exhibited in the cat's effort to decompile their hitchhiker, the Slug. It's distracting as hell, but Sirhan feels a desperate urge to understand what happened out there. It's the key to understanding his not-mother's obsessions and weaknesses — which, he senses, will be important in the times to come.

He evades the gaggle of overdressed good-time girls and steps out onto the lower of the two stainless-steel decks that bisect the sphere. Accepting a fruit cocktail from a discreetly humaniform waitron, he strolls toward a row of triangular windows that gaze out across the arena toward the American Pavilion and the World Village. The metal walls are braced with turquoise-painted girders, and the perspex transparencies are fogged with age. He can barely see the one-tenth-scale model of an atomic-powered ocean liner leaving the pier below, or the eight-engined giant seaplane beside it. 'They never once asked me if the Slug had attempted to map itself into the human-compatible spaces aboard the ship,' Aineko bitches at him. 'I wasn't expecting them to, but really! Your mother's too trusting, boy.'

'I suppose you took precautions?' Sirhan's ghost murmurs to the cat. That sets the irascible metafeline off again on a long discursive tail-washing rant about the unreliability of

Economics-2.0-compliant financial instruments. Economics 2.0 apparently replaces the single-indirection layer of conventional money, and the multiple-indirection mappings of options trades, with some kind of insanely baroque object-relational framework based on the parameterized desires and subjective experiential values of the players, and as far as the cat is concerned, this makes all such transactions intrinsically untrustworthy.

Which is why you're stuck here with us apes, Sirhan-prime cynically notes as he spawns an Eliza ghost to carry on nodding at the cat while he experiences the party.

It's uncomfortably warm in the Atomium sphere – not surprising, there must be thirty people milling around up here, not counting the waitrons – and several local multicast channels are playing a variety of styles of music to synchronize the mood swings of the revelers to hardcore techno, waltz, raga . . .

'Having a good time, are we?' Sirhan breaks away from integrating one of his timid philosophers and realizes that his glass is empty, and his mother is grinning alarmingly at him over the rim of a cocktail glass containing something that glows in the dark. She's wearing spike-heeled boots and a black velvet cat suit that hugs her contours like a second skin, and she's already getting drunk. In wall-clock years she is younger than Sirhan; it's like having a bizarrely knowing younger sister mysteriously injected into his life to replace the eigenmother who stayed home and died with the Ring Imperium decades ago. 'Look at you, hiding in a corner at your grandfather's party! Hey, your glass is empty. Want to try this caipirinha? There's someone you've got to meet over here—'

It's at moments like this that Sirhan really wonders what in Jupiter's orbit his father ever saw in this woman. (But then again, in the world line this instance of her has returned from, he didn't. So what does that signify?) 'As long as there's no fermented grape juice in it,' he says resignedly, allowing himself to be led past a gaggle of conversations and a mournful-looking gorilla slurping a long drink through a straw. 'More of your *accelerationista* allies?'

'Maybe not.' It's the girl gang he avoided noticing in the lift, their eyes sparkling, really getting into this early twen-cen drag party thing, waving their cigarette holders and cocktail glasses around with wild abandon. 'Rita, I'd like you to meet Sirhan, my other fork's son. Sirhan, this is Rita? She's an historian, too. Why don't you—'

Dark eyes, emphasized not by powder or paint but by chromatophores inside her skin cells: black hair, chain of enormous pearls, slim black dress sweeping the floor, a look of mild embarrassment on her heart-shaped face. She could be a clone of Audrey Hepburn. 'Didn't I just meet you in the elevator?' The embarrassment shifts to her cheeks, becoming visible.

Sirhan flushes, unsure how to reply. Just then an interloper arrives on the scene, pushing in between them. 'Are you the curator who reorganized the Precambrian gallery along teleology lines? I've got some things to say about *that*!' The interloper is tall, assertive, and blond. Sirhan hates her from the first sight of her wagging finger.

'Oh shut up, Marissa, this is a party. You've been being a pain all evening.' To his surprise, Rita the historian rounds on the interloper angrily.

'It's not a problem,' he manages to say. In the back of his mind, something makes the Rogerian puppet-him that's listening to the cat sit up and dump-merge a whole lump of fresh memories into his mind – something important, something about the Vile Offspring sending a starship to bring something back from the router – but the people around him are soaking up so much attention that he has to file it for later.

'Yes it *is* a problem,' Rita declares. She points at the interloper, who is saying something about the invalidity of teleological interpretations, trying to justify herself, and says, '*Plonk*. Phew. Where were we?'

Sirhan blinks. Suddenly everyone but him seems to be ignoring that annoying Marissa person. 'What just happened?' he asks cautiously.

'I killfiled her. Don't tell me, you aren't running Superplonk yet, are you?' Rita flicks a location-cached idea at him and he takes it cautiously, spawning a couple of specialized Turing Oracles to check it for halting states. It seems to be some kind of optic lobe hack that accesses a collaborative database of eigenfaces, with some sort of side interface to Broca's region. 'Share and enjoy, confrontation-free parties.'

'I've never seen—' Sirhan trails off as he loads the module distractedly. (The cat is rambling on about god modules and metastatic entanglement and the difficulty of arranging to have personalities custom-grown to order somewhere in the back of his head, while his fractional-self nods wisely whenever it pauses.) Something like an inner eyelid descends. He looks round; there's a vague blob at one side of the room, making an annoying buzzing sound. His mother seems to be having an animated conversation with it. 'That's rather interesting.'

'Yes, it helps no end at this sort of event.' Rita startles him by taking his left arm in hand – her cigarette holder shrivels and condenses until it's no more than a slight thickening around the wrist of her opera glove – and steers him toward a waitron. 'I'm sorry about your foot, earlier. I was a bit overloaded. Is Amber Macx really your mother?'

'Not exactly, she's my eigenmother,' he mumbles. 'The reincarnated download of the version who went out to Hyundai $^{+4904}/_{-56}$ aboard the *Field Circus*. She married a French-Algerian confidence-trick analyst instead of my father, but I think they divorced a couple of years ago. My *real* mother married an imam, but they died in the aftermath of Economics 2.0.' She seems to be steering him in the direction of the window bay Amber dragged him away from earlier. 'Why do you ask?'

'Because you're not very good at making small talk,' Rita says quietly, 'and you don't seem very good in crowds. Is that right? Was it you who performed that amazing dissection of Wittgenstein's cognitive map? The one with the preverbal Gödel string in it?'

'It was—' He clears his throat. 'You thought it was amazing?' Suddenly, on impulse, he detaches a ghost to identify this Rita person and find out who she is, what she wants. It's not normally worth the effort to get to know someone more closely than casual small talk, but she seems to have been digging into his background, and he wants to know why. Along with the him that's chatting to Aineko, that makes about three instances pulling in near-real-time resources. He'll be running up an existential debt soon if he keeps forking ghosts like this.

'I thought so,' she says. There's a bench in front of the wall, and somehow he finds himself sitting on it next to her. *There's no danger, we're not in private or anything,* he tells himself stiffly. She's smiling at him, face tilted slightly to one side and lips parted, and for a moment, a dizzy sense of possibility washes over him. *What if she's about to throw all propriety aside? How undignified!* Sirhan believes in self-restraint and dignity. 'I was really interested in this—' She passes him another dynamically loadable blob, encompassing a detailed critique of his analysis of Wittgenstein's matriophobia in the context of gendered language constructs and nineteenth-century Viennese society, along with a hypothesis that leaves Sirhan gasping with mild indignation at the very idea that *he* of all people might share Wittgenstein's skewed outlook. 'What do you think?' she asks, grinning impishly at him.

'Nnngk.' Sirhan tries to unswallow his tongue. Rita crosses her legs, her gown hissing. 'I, ah, that is to say—' At which moment, his partials reintegrate, dumping a slew of positively pornographic images into his memories. *It's a trap!* they shriek, her breasts and hips and pubes – clean-shaven, he can't help noticing – thrusting at him in hotly passionate abandon. *Mother's trying to make you loose like her!* and he remembers what it *would* be like to wake up in bed next to this woman whom he barely knows after being married to her for a year, because one of his cognitive ghosts has just spent several seconds of network time (or several subjective months) getting hot and sweaty with a ghost of her own, and she *does* have interesting research ideas, even if she's a pushy over-Westernized woman who thinks she can run his life for him. 'What *is* this?' he splutters, his ears growing hot and his garments constricting.

'Just speculating about possibilities. We could get a lot done together.' She snakes an arm round his shoulders and pulls him toward her, gently. 'Don't you want to find out if we could work out?'

'But, but—' Sirhan is steaming. *Is she offering casual sex?* he wonders, profoundly embarrassed by his own inability to read her signals. 'What do you *want?*' he asks.

'You *do* know that you can do more with Superplonk than just killfile annoying idiots?' she whispers in his ear. 'We can be invisible right now, if you like. It's great for confidential meetings — other things, too. We can work beautifully together, our ghosts annealed really well . . .'

Sirhan jumps up, his face stinging, and turns away. 'No thank you!' he snaps, angry at himself. 'Goodbye!' His other instances, interrupted by his broadcast emotional overload, are distracted from their tasks and sputtering with indignation. Her hurt expression is too much for him: The killfile snaps down, blurring her into an indistinct black blob on the wall, veiled by his own brain as he turns and walks away, seething with anger at his mother for being so unfair as to make him behold his own face in the throes of fleshy passion.

Meanwhile, in one of the lower spheres, padded with silvery blue insulating pillows bound together with duct tape, the movers and shakers of the *accelerationista* faction are discussing their bid for world power at fractional-C velocities.

'We can't outrun everything. For example, a collapse of the false vacuum,' Manfred insists, slightly uncoordinated and slurring his vowels under the influence of the first glass of fruit punch he's experienced in nigh-on twenty real-time years. His body is young and still relatively featureless, hair still growing out, and he's abandoned his old no-implants fetish at last to adopt an array of interfaces that let him internalize all the exocortex processes that he formerly ran on an array of dumb Turing machines outside his body. He's standing on his own sense of style and is the only person in the room who isn't wearing some variation of dinner jacket or classical evening dress. 'Entangled exchange via routers is all very well, but it won't let us escape the universe itself – any phase change will catch up eventually. The network must have an end. And then where will we be, Sameena?'

'I'm not disputing that.' The woman he's talking to, wearing a green-and-gold sari and a medieval maharajah's ransom in gold and natural diamonds, nods thoughtfully. 'But it hasn't happened yet, and we've got evidence that superhuman intelligences have been loose in this universe for gigayears, so there's a fair bet that the worst catastrophe scenarios are unlikely. And looking closer to home, we don't know what the routers are for, or who made them. Until then . . .' She shrugs. 'Look what happened last time somebody tried to probe them. No offense intended.'

'It's already happened. If what I hear is correct, the Vile Offspring aren't nearly as negative about the idea of using the routers as we old-fashioned metahumans might like to believe.' Manfred frowns, trying to recall some hazy anecdote – he's experimenting with a new memory compression algorithm, necessitated by his pack rat mnemonic habits when younger, and sometimes the whole universe feels as if it's nearly on the tip of his tongue. 'So, we seem to be in violent agreement about the need to *know more* about what's going on, and to find out what they're doing out there. We've got cosmic background anisotropies caused by the waste heat from computing processes millions of light years across – it takes a big interstellar civilization to do that, and they don't seem to have fallen into the same rat-trap as the local Matrioshka brain civilizations. And we've got worrying rumors about the VO messing around with the structure of space-time in order to find a way around the Beckenstein bound. If the VO are trying that, then the folks out near the supercluster already know the answers. The best way to find out what's happening is to go and talk to whoever's responsible. Can we at least agree on that?'

'Probably not.' Her eyes glitter with amusement. 'It all

depends on whether one believes in these civilizations in the first place. I *know* your people point to deep-field camera images going all the way back to some wonky hubble-bubble scrying mirror from the late twentieth, but we've got no evidence except some theories about the Casimir effect and pair production and spinning beakers of hélium-3 – much less proof that whole bunch of alien galactic civilizations are trying to collapse the false vacuum and destroy the universe!' Her voice dropped a notch. 'At least, not enough proof to convince most people, Manny dear. I know this comes as a shock to you, but not *everyone* is a neophiliac posthuman bodysurfer whose idea of a sabbatical is to spend twenty years as a flock of tightly networked seagulls in order to try to prove the Turing Oracle thesis—'

'—Not everyone is concerned with the deep future,' Manfred interrupts. 'It's important! If we live or die, that doesn't matter – that's not the big picture. The big question is whether information originating in our light cone is preserved, or whether we're stuck in a lossy medium where our very existence counts for nothing. It's downright *embarrassing* to be a member of a species with such a profound lack of curiosity about its own future, especially when it affects us all personally! I mean, if there's going to come a time when there's nobody or nothing to remember us then what does—'

'Manfred?'

He stops in midsentence, his mouth open, staring dumbly.

It's Amber, poised in black cat suit with cocktail glass. Her expression is open and confused, appallingly vulnerable. Blue liquid slops, almost spilling out of her glass – the rim barely extends itself in time to catch the drops. Behind her stands Annette, a deeply self-satisfied smile on her face.

'You.' Amber pauses, her cheek twitching as bits of her mind page in and out of her skull, polling external information sources. 'You really *are*—'

A hasty cloud materializes under her hand as her fingers relax, dropping the glass.

'Uh.' Manfred stares, at a complete loss for words. 'I'd, uh.'

After a moment he looks down. 'I'm sorry. I'll get you another drink . . . ?'

'Why didn't someone warn me?' Amber complains.

'We thought you could use the good advice,' Annette stated into the awkward silence. 'And a family reunion. It was meant to be a surprise.'

'A surprise.' Amber looks perplexed. 'You could say that.'

'You're taller than I was expecting,' Manfred says unexpectedly. 'People look different when you're not using human eyes.'

'Yeah?' She looks at him, and he turns his head slightly, facing her. It's an historic moment, and Annette is getting it all on memory diamond, from every angle. The family's dirty little secret is that Amber and her father have *never met*, not face-to-face in physical meat-machine proximity. She was born years after Manfred and Pamela separated, after all, decanted prefertilized from a tank of liquid nitrogen. This is the first time either of them have actually seen the other's face without electronic intermediation. And while they've said everything that needed to be said on a businesslike level, anthropoid family politics is still very much a matter of body language and pheromones. 'How long have you been out and about?' she asks, trying to disguise her confusion.

'About six hours.' Manfred manages a rueful chuckle, trying to take the sight of her in all at once. 'Let's get you another drink and put our heads together?'

'Okay.' Amber takes a deep breath and glares at Annette. 'You set this up, *you* clean up the mess.'

Annette just stands there smiling at the confusion of her accomplishment.

The cold light of dawn finds Sirhan angry, sober, and ready to pick a fight with the first person who comes through the door of his office. The room is about ten meters across, with a floor of polished marble and skylights in the intricately plastered ceiling. The walkthrough of his current project sprouts in the middle of the floor like a ghostly abstract cauliflower, fractal branches dwindling down to infolded nodes tagged with compressed identifiers. The branches expand and shrink as Sirhan paces around it, zooming to readability in response to his eyeball dynamics. But he isn't paying it much attention. He's too disturbed, uncertain, trying to work out whom to blame. Which is why when the door bangs open his first response is to whirl angrily and open his mouth – then stop. 'What do *you* want?' he demands.

'A word, if you please?' Annette looks around distractedly. 'This is your project?'

'Yes,' he says icily, and banishes the walkthrough with a wave of one hand. 'What do you want?'

'I'm not sure.' Annette pauses. For a moment she looks weary, tired beyond mortal words, and Sirhan momentarily wonders if perhaps he's spreading the blame too far. This ninetysomething Frenchwoman who is no blood relative, who was in years past the love of his scatterbrained grandfather's life, seems the least likely person to be trying to manipulate him, at least in such an unwelcome and intimate manner. But there's no telling. Families are strange things, and even though the current instantiations of his father and mother aren't the ones who ran his pre-adolescent brain through a couple of dozen alternative lifelines before he was ten, he can't be sure – or that they wouldn't enlist *tante* Annette's assistance in fucking with his mind. 'We need to talk about your mother,' she continues.

'We do, do we?' Sirhan turns around and sees the vacancy of the room for what it is, a socket, like a pulled tooth, informed as much by what is absent as by what is present. He snaps his fingers, and an intricate bench of translucent bluish utility fog congeals out of the air behind him. He sits: Annette can do what she wants.

'*Oui.*' She thrusts her hands deep into the pocket of the peasant smock she's wearing – a major departure from her normal style – and leans against the wall. Physically, she looks young enough to have spent her entire life blitzing around the galaxy at three nines of lightspeed, but her posture is world-weary and ancient.

History is a foreign country, and the old are unwilling emigrants, tired out by the constant travel. 'Your mother, she has taken on a huge job, but it's one that needs doing. *You* agreed it needed doing, years ago, with the archive store. *She* is now trying to get it moving. That is what the campaign is about, to place before the electors a choice of how best to move an entire civilization. So I ask, why do you obstruct her?'

Sirhan works his jaw; he feels like spitting. '*Why?*' he snaps.

'Yes. Why?' Annette gives in and magics up a chair from the swirling fogbank beneath the ceiling. She crouches in it, staring at him. 'It is a question.'

'I have nothing against her political machinations,' Sirhan says tensely. 'But her uninvited interference in my personal life—'

'What interference?'

He stares. 'Is that a question?' He's silent for a moment. Then: 'Throwing that wanton at me last night—'

Annette stares at him. 'Who? What are you talking about?'

'That, that loose woman!' Sirhan is reduced to spluttering. 'False pretenses! If this is one of Father's matchmaking ideas, it is so *very* wrong that—'

Annette is shaking her head. 'Are you crazy? Your mother simply wanted you to meet her campaign team, to join in planning the policy. Your father is not on this planet! But you stormed out. You *really* upset Rita, did you know that? Rita, she is the best belief maintenance and story construction operative I have! Yet you to tears reduce her. What is wrong with you?'

'I—' Sirhan swallows. 'She's *what?*' he asks again, his mouth dry. 'I thought . . .' He trails off. He doesn't want to say what he thought. The hussy, that brazen trollop, is part of his mother's campaign party? Not some plot to lure him into corruption? What if it was all a horrible misunderstanding?

'I think you need to apologize to someone,' Annette says coolly, standing up. Sirhan's head is spinning between a dozen dialogues of actors and ghosts, a journal of the party replaying before his ghast-stricken inner gaze. Even the walls have begun to flicker, responding to his intense unease. Annette skewers him with a disgusted look. 'When you can a woman behave toward as a person, not a threat, we can again talk. Until then.' And she stands up and walks out of the room, leaving him to contemplate the shattered stump of his anger, so startled he can barely concentrate on his project, thinking, *Is that really me? Is that what I look like to her?* as the cladistic graph slowly rotates before him, denuded branches spread wide, waiting to be filled with the nodes of the alien interstellar network just as soon as he can convince Aineko to stake him the price of the depth-first tour of darkness.

Manfred used to be a flock of pigeons – literally, his exocortex dispersed among a passel of bird brains, pecking at brightly colored facts, shitting semidigested conclusions. Being human again feels inexplicably odd, even without the added distractions of his sex drive, which he has switched off until he gets used to being unitary again. Not only does he get shooting pains in his neck whenever he tries to look over his left shoulder with his right eye, but he's lost the habit of spawning exocortical agents to go interrogate a database or bush robot or something, then report back to him. Instead he keeps trying to fly off in all directions at once, which usually ends with him falling over.

But at present, that's not a problem. He's sitting comfortably at a weathered wooden table in a beer garden behind a hall lifted from somewhere like Frankfurt, a liter glass of straw-colored liquid at his elbow and a comforting multiple whispering of knowledge streams tickling the back of his head. Most of his attention is focused on Annette, who frowns at him with mingled concern and affection. They may have lived separate lives for almost a third of a century, since she declined to upload with him, but he's still deeply attuned to her.

'You are going to have to do something about that boy,' she says sympathetically. 'He is close enough to upset Amber. And without Amber, there will be a problem.'

'I'm going to have to do something about Amber, too,'

Manfred retorts. 'What was the idea, not warning her I was coming?'

'It was meant to be a surprise.' Annette comes as close to pouting as Manfred's seen her recently. It brings back warm memories; he reaches out to hold her hand across the table.

'You know I can't handle the human niceties properly when I'm a flock.' He strokes the back of her wrist. She pulls back after a while, but slowly. 'I expected you to manage all that stuff.'

'That stuff.' Annette shakes her head. 'She's your daughter, you know? Did you have no curiosity left?'

'As a bird?' Manfred cocks his head to one side so abruptly that he hurts his neck and winces. 'Nope. *Now* I do, but I think I pissed her off—'

'Which brings us back to point one.'

'I'd send her an apology, but she'd think I was trying to manipulate her' – Manfred takes a mouthful of beer – 'and she'd be right.' He sounds slightly depressed. 'All my relationships are screwy this decade. And it's lonely.'

'So? Don't brood.' Annette pulls her hand back. 'Something will sort itself out eventually. And in the short term, there is the work. The electoral problem becomes acute.' When she's around him the remains of her once-strong French accent almost vanish in a transatlantic drawl, he realizes with a pang. He's been abhuman for too long – people who meant a lot to him have changed while he's been away.

'I'll brood if I want to,' he says. 'I didn't ever really get a chance to say goodbye to Pam, did I? Not after that time in Paris when the gangsters . . .' He shrugs. 'I'm getting nostalgic in my old age.' He snorts.

'You're not the only one,' Annette says tactfully. 'Social occasions here are a minefield. One must tiptoe around so many issues. People have too much, too much *history*. And nobody knows everything that is going on.'

'That's the trouble with this damned polity.' Manfred takes another gulp of *hefeweisen*. 'We've already got six million people living on this planet, and it's growing like the first-generation

Internet. Everyone who is anyone knows everyone, but there are so many incomers diluting the mix and not knowing that there *is* a small world network here that everything is up for grabs again after only a couple of megaseconds. New networks form, and we don't even know they exist until they sprout a political agenda and surface under us. We're acting under time pressure. If we don't get things rolling now, we'll never be able to . . .' He shakes his head. 'It wasn't like this for you in Brussels, was it?'

'No. Brussels was a mature system. And I had Gianni to look after in his dotage after you left. It will only get worse from here on in, I think.'

'Democracy 2.0.' He shudders briefly. 'I'm not sure about the validity of voting projects at all, these days. The assumption that all people are of equal importance seems frighteningly obsolescent. Do you think we can make this fly?'

'I don't see why not. If Amber's willing to play the People's Princess for us . . .' Annette picks up a slice of liverwurst and chews on it meditatively.

'I'm not sure it's workable, however we play it.' Manfred looks thoughtful. 'The whole democratic participation thing looks questionable to me under these circumstances. We're under direct threat, for all that it's a long-term one, and this whole culture is in danger of turning into a classical nation-state. Or worse, several of them layered on top of one another with complete geographical collocation but no social interpenetration. I'm not certain it's a good idea to try to steer something like that – pieces might break off. You'd get the most unpleasant side effects. Although, on the other hand, if we can mobilize enough broad support to become the first visible planetwide polity . . .'

'We need you to stay focused,' Annette adds unexpectedly.

'Focused? Me?' He laughs, briefly. 'I *used* to have an idea a second. Now it's maybe one a year. I'm just a melancholy old birdbrain, me.'

'Yes, but you know the old saying? The fox has many ideas – the hedgehog has only one, but it's a *big* idea.'

'So tell me, what is my big idea?' Manfred leans forward, one elbow on the table, one eye focused on inner space as a hot-burning thread of consciousness barks psephological performance metrics at him, analyzing the game ahead. 'Where do you think I'm going?'

'I think—' Annette breaks off suddenly, staring past his shoulder. Privacy slips, and for a frozen moment Manfred glances round in mild horror and sees thirty or forty other guests in the crowded garden, elbows rubbing, voices raised above the background chatter. 'Gianni!' She beams widely as she stands up. 'What a surprise! When did you arrive?'

Manfred blinks. A slim young guy, moving with adolescent grace but none of the awkward movements and sullen lack of poise – he's much older than he looks, chickenhawk genetics. *Gianni?* He feels a huge surge of memories paging through his exocortex. He remembers ringing a doorbell in dusty, hot Rome: white toweling bathrobe, the economics of scarcity, autograph signed by the dead hand of von Neumann – 'Gianni?' he asks, disbelieving. 'It's been a long time!'

The gilded youth, incarnated in the image of a metropolitan toy-boy from the noughties, grins widely and embraces Manfred with a friendly bear hug. Then he slides down onto the bench next to Annette, whom he kisses with easy familiarity. 'Ah, to be among friends again! It's been too long!' He glances round curiously. 'Hmm, how very Bavarian.' He snaps his fingers. 'Mine will be a, what do you recommend? It's been too long since my last beer.' His grin widens. 'Not in this body.'

'You're resimulated?' Manfred asks, unable to stop himself.

Annette frowns at him disapprovingly. 'No, silly! He came through the teleport gate—'

'Oh.' Manfred shakes his head. 'I'm sorry—'

'It's okay.' Gianni Vittoria clearly doesn't mind being mistaken for an historical newbie, rather than someone who's traveled through the decades the hard way. *He must be over a hundred by now,* Manfred notes, not bothering to spawn a search thread to find out.

'It was time to move and, well, the old body didn't want to

move with me, so why not go gracefully and accept the inevitable?'

'I didn't take you for a dualist,' Manfred says ruefully.

'Ah, I'm not – but neither am I reckless.' Gianni drops his grin for a moment. The sometime minister for transhuman affairs, economic theoretician, then retired tribal elder of the polycognitive liberals is serious. 'I have never uploaded before, or switched bodies, or teleported. Even when my old one was seriously – tcha! Maybe I left it too long. But here I am. One planet is as good as another to be cloned and downloaded onto, don't you think?'

'You invited him?' Manfred asks Annette.

'Why wouldn't I?' There's a wicked gleam in her eye. 'Did you expect me to live like a nun while you were a flock of pigeons? We may have campaigned against the legal death of the transubstantiated, Manfred, but there are limits.'

Manfred looks between them, then shrugs, embarrassed. 'I'm still getting used to being human again,' he admits. 'Give me time to catch up? At an emotional level, at least.' The realization that Gianni and Annette have a history together doesn't come as a surprise to him: It's one of the things you must adapt to if you opt out of the human species, after all. At least the libido suppression is helping here, he realizes. He's not about to embarrass anyone by suggesting a ménage. He focuses on Gianni. 'I have a feeling I'm here for a purpose, and it isn't mine,' he says slowly. 'Why don't you tell me what you've got in mind?'

Gianni shrugs. 'You have the big picture already. We are human, metahuman, and augmented human. But the posthumans are things that were never really human to begin with. The Vile Offspring have reached their adolescence and want the place to themselves so they can throw a party. The writing is on the wall, don't you think?'

Manfred gives him a long stare. 'The whole idea of running away in meatspace is fraught with peril,' he says slowly. He picks up his mug of beer and swirls it around slowly. 'Look, we know, now, that a singularity doesn't turn into a voracious predator that eats all the dumb matter in its path, triggering a phase change in the structure of space – at least, not unless they've done something very stupid to the structure of the false vacuum, somewhere outside our current light cone.

'But if we run away, *we* are still going to be there. Sooner or later, we'll have the same problem all over again; runaway intelligence augmentation, self-expression, engineered intelligences, whatever. Possibly that's what happened out past the Böotes void – not a galactic-scale civilization, but a race of pathological cowards fleeing their own exponential transcendence. We carry the seeds of a singularity with us wherever we go, and if we try to excise those seeds, we cease to be human, don't we? So . . . maybe you can tell me what you think we should do. Hmm?'

'It's a dilemma.' A waitron inserts itself into their privacy-screened field of view. It plants a spun-diamond glass in front of Gianni, then pukes beer into it. Manfred declines a refill, waiting for Gianni to drink. 'Ah, the simple pleasures of the flesh! I've been corresponding with your daughter, Manny. She loaned me her experiential digest of the journey to Hyundai $^{+4904}/_{-56}$. I found it quite alarming. Nobody's casting aspersions on her observations, not after that self-propelled stock market bubble or 419 scam or whatever it was got loose in the Economics 2.0 sphere, but the implications – the Vile Offspring will eat the solar system, Manny. Then they'll slow down. But where does that leave us, I ask you? What is there for orthohumans like us to do?'

Manfred nods thoughtfully. 'You've heard the argument between the *accelerationistas* and the time-binder faction, I assume?' he asks.

'Of course.' Gianni takes a long pull on his beer. 'What do *you* think of our options?'

'The *accelerationistas* want to upload everyone onto a fleet of starwhisps and charge off to colonize an uninhabited brown dwarf planetary system. Or maybe steal a Matrioshka brain that's succumbed to senile dementia and turn it back into planetary biomes with cores of diamond-phase computronium to fulfill some kind of demented pastoralist nostalgia trip. Rousseau's universal robots. I gather Amber thinks this is a good idea because she's done it before – at least, the charging off aboard a starwhisp part. "To boldly go where no uploaded metahuman colony fleet has gone before" has a certain ring to it, doesn't it?' Manfred nods to himself. 'Like I say, it won't work. We'd be right back to iteration one of the waterfall model of singularity formation within a couple of gigaseconds of arriving. That's why I came back: to warn her.'

'So?' Gianni prods, pretending to ignore the frowns that Annette is casting his way.

'And as for the time-binders' – Manfred nods again – 'they're like Sirhan. Deeply conservative, deeply suspicious. Holding out for staying here as long as possible, until the Vile Offspring come for Saturn – then moving out bit by bit, into the Kuiper belt. Colony habitats on snowballs half a light year from anywhere.' He shudders. 'Spam in a fucking can with a light-hour walk to the nearest civilized company if your fellow inmates decide to reinvent Stalinism or Objectivism. No thanks! I know they've been muttering about quantum teleportation and stealing toys from the routers, but I'll believe it when I see it.'

'Which leaves what?' Annette demands. 'It is all very well, this dismissal of both the *accelerationista* and time-binder programs, Manny, but what can you propose in their place?' She looks distressed. 'Fifty years ago, you would have had six new ideas before breakfast! And an erection.'

Manfred leers at her unconvincingly. 'Who says I can't still have both?'

She glares. 'Drop it!'

'Okay.' Manfred chugs back a quarter of a liter of beer, draining his glass, and puts it down on the table with a bang. 'As it happens, I *do* have an alternative idea.' He looks serious. 'I've been discussing it with Aineko for some time, and Aineko has been seeding Sirhan with it – if it's to work optimally, we'll need to get a rump constituency of both the *accelerationistas* and the conservatives on board. Which is why I'm conditionally going along with this whole election nonsense. So, what's it worth to you for me to explain it?'

'So, who was the deadhead you were busy with today?' asks Amber.

Rita shrugs. 'Some boringly prolix pulp author from the early twentieth, with a body phobia of extropian proportions – I kept expecting him to start drooling and rolling his eyes if I crossed my legs. Funny thing is, he was also close to bolting from fear once I mentioned implants. We *really* need to nail down how to deal with these mind/body dualists, don't we?' She watches Amber with something approaching admiration; she's new to the inner circle of the *accelerationista* study faction, and Amber's social credit is sky-high. Rita's got a lot to learn from her, if she can get close enough. And right now, following her along a path through the landscaped garden behind the museum seems like a golden moment of opportunity.

Amber smiles. 'I'm glad I'm not processing immigrants these days: Most of them are so stupid it drives you up the wall after a bit. Personally I blame the Flynn effect – in reverse. They come from a background of sensory deprivation. It's nothing that a course of neural growth enhancers can't fix in a year or two, but after the first few you skullfuck, they're all the same. So *dull*. Unless you're unlucky enough to get one of the documentees from a puritan religious period. I'm no fluffragette, but I swear if I get one more superstitious woman-hating clergyman, I'm going to consider prescribing forcible gender reassignment surgery. At least the Victorian English are mostly just open-minded lechers, when you get past their social reserve. And they like new technology.'

Rita nods. *Woman-hating et cetera . . .* The echoes of patriarchy are still with them today, it seems, and not just in the form of re-simulated ayatollahs and archbishops from the Dark Ages. 'My author sounds like the worst of both. Some guy called Howard, from Rhode Island. Kept looking at me as if he was afraid I was going to sprout bat wings and tentacles or something.' *Like your son,* she doesn't add. *Just what was he thinking, anyway?* she wonders. *To be that screwed up takes serious dedication . . .* 'What are you working on, if you don't mind me asking?' she asks, trying to change the direction of her attention.

'Oh, pressing the flesh, I guess. Auntie 'Nette wanted me to meet some old political hack contact of hers who she figures can help with the program, but he was holed up with her and Dad all day.' She pulls a face. 'I had another fitting session with the image merchants. They're trying to turn me into a political catwalk clotheshorse. Then there's the program demographics again. We're getting about a thousand new immigrants a day, planetwide, but it's accelerating rapidly, and we should be up to eighty an hour by the time of the election. Which is going to be a huge problem, because if we start campaigning too early a quarter of the electorate won't know what they're meant to be voting about.'

'Maybe it's deliberate,' Rita suggests. 'The Vile Offspring are trying to rig the outcome by injecting voters.' She pings a smiley emoticon off Amber's open channel, raising a flickering grin in return. 'The party of fuckwits will win, no question about it.'

'Uh-huh.' Amber snaps her fingers and pulls an impatient face as she waits for a passing cloud to solidify above her head and lower a glass of cranberry juice to her. 'Dad said one thing that's spot-on. We're framing this entire debate in terms of what we should do to avoid conflict with the Offspring. The main bone of contention is how to run away and how far to go and which program to put resources into, not whether or when to run, let alone what else we could do. Maybe we should have given it some more thought. Are we being manipulated?'

Rita looks vacant for a moment. 'Is that a question?' she asks. Amber nods, and she shakes her head. 'Then I'd have to say that I don't know. The evidence is inconclusive, so far. But I'm not really happy. The Offspring won't tell us what they want, but there's no reason to believe they don't know what *we* want. I mean, they can think rings round us, can't they?'

Amber shrugs, then pauses to unlatch a hedge gate that gives admission to a maze of sweet-smelling shrubs. 'I really don't know. They may not care about us, or even remember we exist – the resimulants may be being generated by some autonomic mechanism, not really part of the higher consciousness of the Offspring. Or it may be some whacked-out post-Tiplerite meme that's gotten hold of more processing resources than the entire presingularity net, some kind of MetaMormon project directed at ensuring that everyone who can possibly ever have lived lives in the *right way* to fit some weird quasi-religious requirement we don't know about. Or it might be a message we're simply not smart enough to decode. That's the trouble, we don't know.'

She vanishes around the curve of the maze. Rita hurries to catch up, sees her about to turn into another alleyway, and leaps after her. 'What else?' she pants.

'Could be' – left turn – 'anything, really.' Six steps lead down into a shadowy tunnel; fork right, five meters forward, then six steps up lead back to the surface. 'Question is, why don't they' – left turn – 'just *tell* us what they want?'

'Speaking to tapeworms.' Rita nearly manages to catch up with Amber, who is trotting through the maze as if she's memorized it perfectly. 'That's how much the nascent Matrioshka brain can outthink us by, as humans to segmented worms. Would we do. What they told us?'

'Maybe.' Amber stops dead, and Rita glances around. They're in an open cell near the heart of the maze, five meters square, hedged in on all sides. There are three entrances and a slate altar, waist high, lichen-stained with age. 'I think you know the answer to that question.'

'I—' Rita stares at her.

Amber stares back, eyes dark and intense. 'You're from one of the Ganymede orbitals by way of Titan. You knew my eigensister while I was out of the solar system flying a diamond the size of a Coke can. That's what you told me. You've got a skill set that's a perfect match for the campaign research group, and you asked me to introduce you to Sirhan, then you pushed his buttons like a pro. Just what *are* you trying to pull? Why should I trust you?'

'I—' Rita's face crumples. 'I *didn't* push his buttons! He *thought* I was trying to drag him into bed.' She looks up defiantly. 'I wasn't. I want to learn, what makes you – him – work—' Huge, dark, structured information queries batter at her exocortex, triggering warnings. Someone is churning through distributed time-series databases all over the outer system, measuring her past with a micrometer. She stares at Amber, mortified and angry. It's the ultimate denial of trust, the need to check her statements against the public record for truth. 'What are you doing?'

'I have a suspicion.' Amber stands poised, as if ready to run. *Run away from me?* Rita thinks, startled. 'You said, what if the re-simulants came from a subconscious function of the Offspring? And funnily enough, I've been discussing that possibility with Dad. He's still got the spark when you show him a problem, you know.'

'I don't understand!'

'No, I don't think you do,' says Amber, and Rita can feel vast stresses in the space around her. The whole ubicomp environment, dust-sized chips and utility fog and hazy clouds of diamond-bright optical processors in the soil and the air and her skin, is growing blotchy and sluggish, thrashing under the load of whatever Amber – with her management-grade ackles – is ordering it to do. For a moment, Rita can't feel half her mind, and she gets the panicky claustrophobic sense of being trapped inside her own head. Then it stops.

'Tell me!' Rita insists. 'What are you trying to prove? It's some mistake—' And Amber is nodding, much to her surprise, looking weary and morose. 'What do you think I've done?'

'Nothing. You're coherent. Sorry about that.'

'Coherent?' Rita hears her voice rising with her indignation as she feels bits of herself, cut off from her for whole seconds, shivering with relief. 'I'll give you coherent! Assaulting my exocortex—'

'Shut up.' Amber rubs her face and simultaneously throws Rita one end of an encrypted channel.

'Why should I?' Rita demands, not accepting the handshake.

'Because.' Amber glances round. *She's scared!* Rita suddenly realizes. 'Just *do* it,' she hisses.

Rita accepts the endpoint and a huge lump of undigested expository data slides down it, structured and tagged with entry points and metainformation directories pointing to—

'Holy *shit*,' she whispers, as she realizes what it is.

'Yes.' Amber grins humorlessly. She continues, over the open channel: *It looks like they're cognitive antibodies, generated by the devil's own semiotic immune system. That's what Sirhan is focusing on, how to avoid triggering them and bringing everything down at once. Forget the election. We're going to be in deep shit sooner rather than later, and we're still trying to work out how to survive. Now are you sure you still want in?*

'Want in on *what*?' Rita asks, shakily.

The lifeboat Dad's trying to get us all into under cover of the accelerationista/conservationista *split, before the Vile Offspring's immune system figures out how to lever us apart into factions and make us kill each other . . .*

Welcome to the afterglow of the intelligence supernova, little tapeworm.

Tapeworms have on the order of a thousand neurons, pulsing furiously to keep their little bodies twitching. Human beings have on the order of a hundred billion neurons. What is happening in the inner solar system as the Vile Offspring churn and reconfigure the fast-thinking structured dust clouds that were once planets is as far beyond the ken of merely human consciousness as the thoughts of a Gödel are beyond the twitching tropisms of a worm. Personality modules bounded by the speed of light, sucking down billions of times the processing power of a human brain, form and re-form in the halo of glowing nanoprocessors that shrouds the sun in a ruddy, glowing cloud.

Mercury, Venus, Mars, Ceres, and the asteroids – all gone. Luna is a silvery iridescent sphere, planed smooth down to micrometer heights, luminous with diffraction patterns. Only Earth, the cradle of human civilization, remains untransformed; and Earth, too, will be dismantled soon enough, for already a trellis of space elevators webs the planet around its equator, lifting refugee dumb matter into orbit and flinging it at the wildlife preserves of the outer system.

The intelligence bloom that gnaws at Jupiter's moons with claws of molecular machinery won't stop until it runs out of dumb matter to convert into computronium. By the time it does, it will have as much brainpower as you'd get if you placed a planet with a population of ten billion future-shocked primates in orbit around every star in the Milky Way galaxy. But right now, it's still stupid, having converted barely a percentage point of the mass of the solar system – it's a mere Magellanic Cloud civilization, infantile and unsubtle and still perilously close to its carbon-chemistry roots.

It's hard for tapeworms living in warm intestinal mulch to wrap their thousand-neuron brains around whatever it is that the vastly more complex entities who host them are discussing, but one thing's sure – the owners have a lot of things going on, not all of them under conscious control. The churning of gastric secretions and the steady ventilation of lungs are incomprehensible to the simple brains of tapeworms, but they serve the purpose of keeping the humans alive and provide the environment the worms live in. And other more esoteric functions that contribute to survival – the intricate dance of specialized cloned lymphocytes in their bone marrow and lymph nodes, the random permutations of antibodies constantly churning for possible matches to intruder molecules warning of the presence of pollution – are all going on beneath the level of conscious control.

Autonomic defenses. Antibodies. Intelligence blooms gnawing at the edges of the outer system. And humans are not as unsophisticated as mulch wrigglers, they can see the writing on the wall. Is it any surprise that among the ones who look outward, the real debate is not over whether to run but over how far and how fast?

There's a team meeting early the next morning. It's still dark outside, and most of the attendees who are present in vivo have the faintly haggard look that comes from abusing melatonin antagonists. Rita stifles a yawn as she glances around the conference room – the walls expanded into huge virtual spaces to accommodate thirty or so exocortical ghosts from sleeping partners who will wake with memories of a particularly vivid lucid dream – and sees Amber talking to her famous father and a younger-looking man who one of her partials recognizes as a last-century EU politician. There seems to be some tension between them.

Now that Amber has granted Rita her conditional trust, a whole new tier of campaigning information has opened up to her inner eye – stuff steganographically concealed in a hidden layer of the project's collective memory space. There's stuff in here she hadn't suspected, frightening studies of resimulant demographics, surveys of emigration rates from the inner system, cladistic trees dissecting different forms of crude tampering that have been found skulking in the wetware of refugees. The reason why Amber and Manfred and – reluctantly – Sirhan are fighting for one radical faction in a planetwide election, despite their various misgivings over the validity of the entire concept of democracy in this posthuman era. She blinks it aside, slightly bewildered, forking a couple of dozen personality subthreads to chew on it at the edges. 'Need coffee,' she mutters to the table, as it offers her a chair.

'Everyone online?' asked Manfred. 'Then I'll begin.' He looks tired and worried, physically youthful but showing the full weight of his age. 'We've got a crisis coming, folks. About a hundred kiloseconds ago, the bit rate on the resimulation stream jumped. We're now fielding about one resimulated state vector a second, on top of the legitimate immigration we're dealing with. If it jumps again by the same factor, it's going to swamp our ability to check the immigrants for zimboes in vivo – we'd have to move to running them in secure storage or just resurrecting them blind, and if there *are* any jokers in the pack that's about the riskiest thing we could do.'

'Why do you not spool them to memory diamond?' asks the handsome young ex-politician to his left, looking almost amused – as if he already knows the answer.

'Politics.' Manfred shrugs.

'It would blow a hole in our social contract,' says Amber, looking as if she's just swallowed something unpleasant, and Rita feels a flicker of admiration for the way they're stage-managing the meeting. Amber's even talking to her father, as if she feels comfortable with him around, although he's a walking reminder of her own lack of success. Nobody else has gotten a word in yet. 'If we don't instantiate them, the next logical step is to deny resimulated minds the franchise. Which in turn puts us on the road to institutional inequality. And that's a very big step to take, even if you have misgivings about the idea of settling complex policy issues on the basis of a popular vote, because our whole polity is based on the idea that less competent intelligences – us – deserve consideration.'

'Hrmph.' Someone clears their throat. Rita glances round and freezes, because it's Amber's screwed-up eigenchild, and he's just about materialized in the chair next to her. *So he adopted Superplonk after all?* she observes cynically. He doggedly avoids looking at her. 'That was my analysis,' he says reluctantly. 'We need them alive. For the ark option, at least, and if not, even the *accelerationista* platform will need them on hand later.'

Concentration camps, thinks Rita, trying to ignore Sirhan's presence near her, for it's a constant irritant, *where most of the inmates are confused, frightened human beings – and the ones who aren't* think *they are.* It's an eerie thought, and she spawns a couple of full ghosts to dream it through for her, gaming the possible angles.

'How are your negotiations over the lifeboat designs going?' Amber asks her father. 'We need to get a portfolio of design schemata out before we go into the election—'

'Change of plan.' Manfred hunches forward. 'This doesn't need to go any further, but Sirhan and Aineko have come up with something interesting.' He looks worried.

Sirhan is staring at his eigenmother with narrowed eyes, and Rita has to resist the urge to elbow him savagely in the ribs. She knows enough about him now to realize it wouldn't get his attention – at least, not the way she'd want it, not for the right reasons – and in any case, he's more wrapped up in himself than her ghost ever saw him as likely to be. (How *anyone* could be party to such a detailed exchange of simulated lives and still reject the opportunity to do it in real life is beyond her, unless it's an artifact of his youth, when his parents pushed him through a dozen simulated childhoods in search of knowledge and ended up with a stubborn oyster-head of a son . . .) 'We still need to look as if we're planning on using a lifeboat,' he says aloud. 'There's the small matter of the price they're asking in return for the alternative.'

'What? What are you talking about?' Amber sounds confused. 'I thought you were working on some kind of cladistic map. What's this about a price?'

Sirhan smiles coolly. 'I *am* working on a cladistic map, in a manner of speaking. You wasted much of your opportunity when you journeyed to the router, you know. I've been talking to Aineko.'

'You—' Amber flushes. 'What about?' She's visibly angry, Rita notices. Sirhan is needling his eigenmother. *Why?*

'About the topology of some rather interesting types of small-world network.' Sirhan leans back in his chair, watching the cloud above her head. 'And the router. You went through it, then you came back with your tail between your legs as fast as you could, didn't you? Not even checking your passenger to see if it was a hostile parasite.'

'I don't have to take this,' Amber says tightly. 'You weren't there, and you have no idea what constraints we were working under.'

'Really?' Sirhan raises an eyebrow. 'Anyway, you missed an opportunity. We know that the routers – for whatever reason – are self-replicating. They spread from brown dwarf to brown dwarf, hatch, tap the protostar for energy and material, and send a bunch of children out. Von Neumann machines, in other words. We also know that they provide high-bandwidth communications to other routers. When you went through the one at Hyundai $^{+4904}/_{-56}$, you ended up in an unmaintained DMZ attached to an alien Matrioshka brain that had degenerated, somehow. It follows that *someone* had collected a router and carried it home, to link into the MB. So why didn't *you* bring one home with you?'

Amber glares at him. 'Total payload on board the *Field Circus* was about ten grams. How large do you think a router seed is?'

'So you brought the Slug home instead, occupying maybe half your storage capacity and ready to wreak seven shades of havoc on—'

'Children!' They both look round automatically. It's Annette, Rita realizes, and she doesn't look amused. 'Why do you not save this bickering for later?' she asks. 'We have our own goals to be pursuing.' Unamused is an understatement. Annette is fuming.

'This charming family reunion was your idea, I believe?' Manfred smiles at her, then nods coolly at the retread EU politician in the next seat.

'Please.' It's Amber. 'Dad, can you save this for later?' Rita sits up. For a moment, Amber looks ancient, far older than her subjective gigasecond of age. 'She's right. She didn't mean to screw up. Let's leave the family history for some time when we can work it out in private. Okay?'

Manfred looks abashed. He blinks rapidly. 'All right.' He takes a breath. 'Amber, I brought some old acquaintances into the loop. If we win the election, then to get out of here as fast as possible we'll have to use a combination of the two main ideas we've been discussing: spool as many people as possible into high-density storage until we get somewhere with space and mass and energy to reincarnate them and get our hands on a router. The entire planetary polity can't afford to pay the energy budget of a relativistic starship big enough to hold everyone, even as uploads, and a subrelativistic ship would be too damn vulnerable to the Vile Offspring. And it follows that, instead of taking potluck on the destination, we should learn about the network protocols the routers use, figure out some kind of transferable currency we can use to pay for our reinstantiation at the other end, and also how to make some kind of map so we know where we're going. The two hard parts are getting at or to a router, and paying – that's going to mean traveling with someone who understands Economics 2.0 but doesn't want to hang around the Vile Offspring.

'As it happens, these old acquaintances of mine went out and fetched back a router seed, for their own purposes. It's sitting about thirty light-hours away from here, out in the Kuiper belt. They're trying to hatch it right now. And I *think* Aineko might be willing to go with us and handle the trade negotiations.' He raises the palm of his right hand and flips a bundle of tags into the shared spatial cache of the inner circle's memories.

Lobsters. Decades ago, back in the dim wastelands of the depression-ridden early teens, the uploaded lobsters had escaped. Manfred brokered a deal for them to get their very own cometary factory colony. Years later, Amber's expedition to the router had run into eerie zombie lobsters, upload images that had been taken over and reanimated by the Wunch. But where the real lobsters had gotten to . . .

For a moment, Rita sees herself hovering in darkness and vacuum, the distant siren song of a planetary gravity well far below. Off to her – left? north? – glows a hazy dim red cloud the size of the full moon as seen from Earth, a cloud that hums with a constant background noise, the waste heat of a galactic civilization dreaming furious colorless thoughts to itself. Then she figures out how to slew her unblinking, eyeless viewpoint round and sees the craft.

It's a starship in the shape of a crustacean three kilometers long. It's segmented and flattened, with legs projecting from the abdominal floor to stretch stiffly sideways and clutch fat balloons of cryogenic deuterium fuel. The blue metallic tail is a flattened fan wrapped around the delicate stinger of a fusion reactor. Near the head, things are different: no huge claws there, but the delicately branching fuzz of bush robots, nanoassemblers poised ready to repair damage in flight and spin the parachute of a ramscoop when the ship is ready to decelerate. The head is massively armored against the blitzkrieg onslaught of interstellar dust, its radar eyes a glint of hexagonal compound surfaces staring straight at her.

Behind and below the lobster-ship, a planetary ring looms vast and tenuous. The lobster is in orbit around Saturn, mere light seconds away. And as Rita stares at the ship in dumbstruck silence, it *winks* at her.

'They don't have names, at least not as individual identifiers,' Manfred says apologetically, 'so I asked if he'd mind being called something. He said Blue, because he is. So I give you the good lobster *Something Blue*.'

Sirhan interrupts. 'You still need my cladistics project' – he sounds somewhat smug – 'to find your way through the network. Do you have a specific destination in mind?'

'Yeah, to both questions,' Manfred admits. 'We need to send duplicate ghosts out to each possible router endpoint, wait for an echo, then iterate and repeat. Recursive depth-first traversal. The goal – that's harder.' He points at the ceiling, which dissolves into a chaotic 3D spiderweb that Rita recognizes, after some hours of subjective head-down archive time, as a map of the dark matter distribution throughout a radius of a billion light years, galaxies glued like fluff to the nodes where strands of drying silk meet. 'We've known for most of a century that there's something flaky going on out there, out past the Böotes void – there are a couple of galactic superclusters, around which there's something flaky

about the cosmic background anisotropy. Most computational processes generate entropy as a by-product, and it looks like
something is dumping waste heat into the area from all the galaxies in the region, very evenly spread in a way that mirrors the
metal distribution in those galaxies, except at the very cores.
And according to the lobsters, who have been indulging in some
very long baseline interferometry, most of the stars in the nearest
cluster are redder than expected and metal-depleted. As if someone's been mining them.'

'Ah.' Sirhan stares at his grandfather. 'Why should they be any
different from the local nodes?'

'Look around you. Do you see any indications of large-scale
cosmic engineering within a million light years of here?' Manfred
shrugs. 'Locally, nothing has quite reached . . . well. We can guess
at the life cycle of a postspike civilization now, can't we? We've felt
the elephant. We've seen the wreckage of collapsed Matrioshka
minds. We know how unattractive exploration is to postsingularity intelligences. We've seen the bandwidth gap that keeps them at
home.' He points at the ceiling. 'But over *there* something different
happened. They're making changes on the scale of an entire galactic supercluster, and they appear to be coordinated. They *did* get
out and go places, and their descendants may still be out there. It
looks like they're doing something purposeful and coordinated,
something vast – a timing channel attack on the virtual machine
that's running the universe, perhaps, or an embedded simulation of
an entirely different universe. Up or down, is it turtles all the way,
or is there something out there that's more real than we are? And
don't you think it's worth trying to find out?'

'No.' Sirhan crosses his arms. 'Not particularly. I'm interested
in saving people from the Vile Offspring, not taking a huge
gamble on mystery transcendent aliens who may have built a
galaxy-sized reality-hacking machine a billion years ago. I'll sell
you my services, and even send a ghost along, but if you expect
me to bet my entire future on it . . .'

It's too much for Rita. Diverting her attention away from the
dizzying inner-space vista, she elbows Sirhan in the ribs. He looks

round blankly for a moment, then with gathering anger as he lets his killfile filter slip. 'Whereof one cannot speak, thereof one must be silent,' she hisses. Then succumbing to a secondary impulse she knows she'll regret later, she drops a private channel into his public in-tray.

'Nobody's asking you to,' Manfred is saying defensively, arms crossed. 'I view this as a Manhattan project kind of thing, pursue all agendas in parallel. If we win the election, we'll have the resources we need to do that. We should *all* go through the router, and we will *all* leave backups aboard *Something Blue*. *Blue* is *slow*, tops out at about a tenth of cee, but what he can do is get a sufficient quantity of memory diamond the hell out of circum-solar space before the Vile Offspring's autonomic defenses activate whatever kind of trust exploit they're planning in the next few megaseconds—'

'*What do you want?*' Sirhan demands angrily over the channel. He's still not looking at her, and not just because he's focusing on the vision in blue that dominates the shared space of the team meeting.

'*Stop lying to yourself,*' Rita sends back. '*You're lying about your own goals and motivations. You may not want to know the truth your own ghost worked out, but I do. And I'm not going to let you deny it happened.*'

'*So one of your agents seduced a personality image of me—*'

'*Bullshit—*'

'Do you mean to declare this platform openly?' asks the young-old guy near the platform, the europol. 'Because if so, you're going to undermine Amber's campaign—'

'That's all right,' Amber says tiredly. 'I'm used to Dad supporting me in his own inimitable way.'

'Is okay,' says a new voice. 'I are happy wait-state grazing in ecliptic.' It's the friendly lobster lifeboat, light-lagged by its trajectory outside the ring system.

'*—You're happy to hide behind a hypocritical sense of moral purity when it makes you feel you can look down on other people, but underneath it you're just like everyone else—*'

'—*She set you up to corrupt me, didn't she? You're just bait in her scheme*—'

'The idea was to store incremental backups in the Panuliran's cargo cache in case a weakly godlike agency from the inner system attempts to activate the antibodies they've already disseminated throughout the festival culture,' Annette explains, stepping in on Manfred's behalf.

Nobody else in the discussion space seems to notice that Rita and Sirhan are busy ripping the shit out of each other over a private channel, throwing emotional hand grenades back and forth like seasoned divorcees. 'It's not a satisfactory solution to the evacuation question, but it ought to satisfy the conservatives' baseline requirement, and as insurance—'

'—*That's right, blame your eigenmother! Has it occurred to you that she doesn't care enough about you to try a stunt like that? I think you spent too much time with that crazy grandmother of yours. You didn't even integrate that ghost, did you? Too afraid of polluting yourself! I bet you never even bothered to check what it felt like from inside*—'

'—*I did*—' Sirhan freezes for a moment, personality modules paging in and out of his brain like a swarm of angry bees – '*make a fool of myself,*' he adds quietly, then slumps back in his seat. '*This is so embarrassing . . .*' He covers his face with his hands. '*You're right.*'

'*I am?*' Rita's puzzlement slowly gives way to understanding; Sirhan has finally integrated the memories from the partials they hybridized earlier. Stuck-up and proud, the cognitive dissonance must be enormous. '*No, I'm not. You're just overly defensive.*'

'*I'm*—' Embarrassed. Because Rita knows him, inside out. Has the ghost-memories of six months in a simspace with him, playing with ideas, exchanging intimacies, later confidences. She holds ghost-memories of his embrace, a smoky affair that might have happened in real space if his instant reaction to realizing that it *could* happen hadn't been to dump the splinter of his mind that was contaminated by impure thoughts to cold storage and deny everything.

'We have no threat profile yet,' Annette says, cutting right across their private conversation. 'If there *is* a direct threat – and we don't know that for sure, yet; the Vile Offspring might be enlightened enough simply to be leaving us alone – it'll probably be some kind of subtle attack aimed directly at the foundations of our identity. Look for a credit bubble, distributed trust metrics devaluing suddenly as people catch some kind of weird religion, something like that. Maybe a perverse election outcome. And it won't be sudden. They are not stupid, to start a headlong attack without slow corruption to soften the way.'

'You've obviously been thinking about this for some time,' Sameena says with dry emphasis. 'What's in it for your friend, uh, Blue? Did you squirrel away enough credit to cover the price of renting a starship from the Economics 2.0 metabubble? Or is there something you aren't telling us?'

'Um.' Manfred looks like a small boy with his hand caught in the sweets jar. 'Well, as a matter of fact—'

'Yes, Dad, why don't you tell us just what this is going to cost?' Amber asks.

'Ah, well.' He looks embarrassed. 'It's the lobsters, not Aineko. They want some payment.'

Rita reaches out and grabs Sirhan's hand: He doesn't resist. *'Do you know about this?'* Rita queries him.

'All new to me . . .' A confused partial thread follows his reply down the pipe, and for a while she joins him in introspective reverie, trying to work out the implications of knowing what they know about the possibility of a mutual relationship.

'They want a written conceptual map. A map of all the accessible meme spaces hanging off the router network, compiled by human explorers who they can use as a baseline, they say. It's quite simple – in return for a ticket-out system, some of us are going to have to go exploring. But that doesn't mean we can't leave backups behind.'

'Do they have any particular explorers in mind?' Amber sniffs.

'No,' says Manfred. 'Just a team of us, to map out the router network and ensure they get some warning of threats from outside.' He pauses. 'You're going to want to come along, aren't you?'

The pre-election campaign takes approximately three minutes and consumes more bandwidth than the sum of all terrestrial communications channels from prehistory to 2008. Approximately six million ghosts of Amber, individually tailored to fit the profile of the targeted audience, fork across the dark fiber meshwork underpinning of the lily-pad colonies, then out through ultrawideband mesh networks, instantiated in implants and floating dust motes to buttonhole the voters. Many of them fail to reach their audience, and many more hold fruitless discussions; about six actually decide they've diverged so far from their original that they constitute separate people and register for independent citizenship, two defect to the other side, and one elopes with a swarm of highly empathic modified African honeybees.

Ambers are not the only ghosts competing for attention in the public zeitgeist. In fact, they're in a minority. Most of the autonomous electoral agents are campaigning for a variety of platforms that range from introducing a progressive income tax — nobody is quite sure *why,* but it seems to be traditional — to a motion calling for the entire planet to be paved, which quite ignores the realities of element abundance in the upper atmosphere of a metal-poor gas giant, not to mention playing hell with the weather. The Faceless are campaigning for everyone to be assigned a new set of facial muscles every six months, the Livid Pranksters are demanding equal rights for subsentient entities, and a host of single-issue pressure groups are yammering about the usual lost causes.

Just how the election process anneals is a black mystery — at least, to those people who aren't party to the workings of the Festival Committee, the group who first had the idea of paving Saturn with hot-hydrogen balloons — but over the course of a complete diurn, almost forty thousand seconds, a pattern begins to emerge. This pattern will systematize the bias of the communications networks that traffic in reputation points across the planetary polity for a long time – possibly as much as fifty million seconds, getting on for a whole Martian year (if Mars still existed). It will create a parliament – a merged group mind borganism that speaks as one supermind built from the beliefs of the victors. And the news isn't great, as the party gathered in the upper sphere of the Atomium (which Manfred insisted Amber rent for the dead dog party) is slowly realizing. Amber isn't there, presumably drowning her sorrows or engaging in postelection schemes of a different nature somewhere else. But other members of her team are about.

'It could be worse,' Rita rationalizes, late in the evening. She's sitting in a corner of the seventh-floor deck, in a 1950s wireframe chair, clutching a glass of synthetic single malt and watching the shadows. 'We could be in an old-style contested election with seven shades of shit flying. At least this way we can be decently anonymous.'

One of the blind spots detaches from her peripheral vision and approaches. It segues into view, suddenly congealing into Sirhan. He looks morose.

'What's your problem?' she demands. 'Your former faction is winning on the count.'

'Maybe so.' He sits down beside her, carefully avoiding her gaze. 'Maybe this is a good thing. And maybe not.'

'So when are you going to join the syncitium?' she asks.

'Me? Join that?' He looks alarmed. 'You think I want to become part of a parliamentary borg? What do you take me for?'

'Oh.' She shakes her head. 'I assumed you were avoiding me because—'

'No.' He holds out his hand, and a passing waitron deposits a glass in it. He takes a deep breath. 'I owe you an apology.'

About time, she thinks, uncharitably. But he's like that. Stiff-necked and proud, slow to acknowledge a mistake but unlikely to apologize unless he really means it. 'What for?' she asks.

'For not giving you the benefit of the doubt,' he says slowly, rolling the glass between his palms. 'I should have listened to myself earlier instead of locking him out of me.'

The self he's talking about seems self-evident to her. 'You're not an easy man to get close to,' she says quietly. 'Maybe that's part of your problem.'

'Part of it?' He chuckles bitterly. 'My mother—' He bites back whatever he originally meant to say. 'Do you know I'm older than she is? Than this version, I mean. She gets up my nose with her assumptions about me . . .'

'They run both ways.' Rita reaches out and takes his hand – and he grips her right back, no rejection this time. 'Listen, it looks as if she's not going to make it into the parliament of lies. There's a straight conservative sweep, these folks are in solid denial. About eighty percent of the population are re-simulants or old-timers from Earth, and that's not going to change before the Vile Offspring turn on us. What are we going to do?'

He shrugs. 'I suspect everyone who thinks we're really under threat will move on. You know this is going to destroy the *accelerationistas'* trust in democracy? They've still got a viable plan – Manfred's friendly lobster will work without the need for an entire planet's energy budget – but the rejection is going to hurt. I can't help thinking that maybe the real goal of the Vile Offspring was simply to gerrymander us into not diverting resources away from them. It's blunt, it's unsubtle, so we assumed that wasn't the point. But maybe there's a time for them to be blunt.'

She shrugs. 'Democracy is a bad fit for lifeboats.' But she's still uncomfortable with the idea. 'And think of all the people we'll be leaving behind.'

'Well.' He smiles tightly. 'If you can think of any way to encourage the masses to join us . . .'

'A good start would be to stop thinking of them as masses to be manipulated.' Rita stares at him. 'Your family appears to have been developing a hereditary elitist streak, and it's not attractive.'

Sirhan looks uncomfortable. 'If you think I'm bad, you should talk to Aineko about it,' he says, self-deprecatingly. 'Sometimes I wonder about that cat.'

'Maybe I will.' She pauses. 'And you? What are you going to do with yourself? Are you going to join the explorers?'

'I—' He looks sideways at her. 'I can see myself sending an eigenbrother,' he says quietly. 'But I'm not going to gamble my entire future on a bid to reach the far side of the observable universe by router. I've had enough excitement to last me a lifetime, lately. I think one copy for the backup archive in the icy depths, one to go exploring – and one to settle down and raise a family. What about you?'

'You'll go all three ways?' she asks.

'Yes, I think so. What about you?'

'Where you go, I go.' She leans against him. 'Isn't that what matters in the end?' she murmurs.

9 : SURVIVOR

THIS TIME, MORE THAN A DOUBLE HANDFUL OF years passes between successive visits to the Macx dynasty.

Somewhere in the gas-sprinkled darkness beyond the local void, carbon-based life stirs. A cylinder of diamond fifty kilometers long spins in the darkness, its surface etched with strange quantum wells that emulate exotic atoms not found in any periodic table that Mendeleyev would have recognized. Within it, walls hold kilotons of oxygen and nitrogen gas, megatons of life-infested soil. A hundred trillion kilometers from the wreckage of Earth, the cylinder glitters like a gem in the darkness.

Welcome to New Japan: one of the places between the stars where human beings hang out, now that the solar system is off-limits to meatbodies.

I wonder who we'll find here?

There's an open plaza in one of the terraform sectors of the habitat cylinder. A huge gong hangs from a beautifully painted wooden frame at one side of the square, which is paved with weathered limestone slabs made of atoms ripped from a planet that has never seen molten ice. Houses stand around, and open-fronted huts where a variety of humanoid waitrons attend to food and beverages for the passing realfolk. A group of prepubescent children are playing hunt-and-seek with their big-eyed pet companions, brandishing makeshift spears and automatic rifles – there's no pain here, for bodies are fungible, rebuilt in a minute by the assembler/disassembler gates in every room. There are few adults hereabouts, for Red Plaza is unfashionable at present, and the kids have claimed it for their own as a playground. They're all genuinely young, symptoms of a demographic demiurge, not a single wendypan among them.

A skinny boy with nut brown skin, a mop of black hair, and three arms is patiently stalking a worried-looking blue eeyore around the corner of the square. He's passing a stand stacked with fresh sushi rolls when the strange beast squirms out from beneath a wheelbarrow and arches its back, stretching luxuriously.

The boy, Manni, freezes, hands tensing around his spear as he focuses on the new target. (The blue eeyore flicks its tail at him and darts for safety across a lichen-encrusted slab.) 'City, what's that?' he asks without moving his lips.

'What are you looking at?' replies City, which puzzles him somewhat, but not as much as it should.

The beast finishes stretching one front leg and extends another. It looks a bit like a pussycat to Manni, but there's something subtly wrong with it. Its head is a little too small, the eyes likewise – and those paws – 'You're sharp,' he accuses the beast, forehead wrinkling in disapproval.

'Yeah, whatever.' The creature yawns, and Manni points his spear at it, clenching the shaft in both right hands. It's got sharp teeth, too, but it spoke to him via his inner hearing, not his ears. Innerspeech is for people, not toys.

'Who are you?' he demands.

The beast looks at him insolently. 'I know your parents,' it says, still using innerspeech. 'You're Manni Macx, aren't you? Thought so. I want you to take me to your father.'

'No!' Manni jumps up and waves his arms at it. 'I don't like you! Go away!' He pokes his spear in the direction of the beast's nose.

'I'll go away when you take me to your father,' says the beast. It raises its tail like a pussycat, and the fur bushes out, but then it pauses. 'If you take me to your father I'll tell you a story afterward, how about that?'

'Don't care!' Manni is only about two hundred megaseconds old – seven old Earth-years – but he can tell when he's being manipulated and gets truculent.

'Kids.' The cat-thing's tail lashes from side to side. 'Okay, Manni, how about you take me to your father, or I rip your face off? I've got claws, you know.' A brief eyeblink later, it's wrapping itself around his ankles sinuously, purring to give the lie to its unreliable threat – but he can see that it's got sharp nails all right. It's a *wild* pussycat-thing, and nothing in his artificially preserved orthohuman upbringing has prepared him for dealing with a real wild pussycat-thing that talks.

'Get away!' Manni is worried. 'Mom!' he hollers, unintentionally triggering the broadcast flag in his innerspeech. 'There's this *thing*—'

'Mom will do.' The cat-thing sounds resigned. It stops rubbing against Manni's legs and looks up at him. 'There's no need to panic. I won't hurt you.'

Manni stops hollering. 'Who're you?' he asks at last, staring at the beast. Somewhere light years away, an adult has heard his cry; his mother is coming fast, bouncing between switches and glancing off folded dimensions in a headlong rush toward him.

'I'm Aineko.' The beast sits down and begins to wash behind one hind leg. 'And you're Manni, right?'

'Aineko,' Manni says uncertainly. 'Do you know Lis or Bill?'

Aineko the cat-thing pauses in his washing routine and looks at Manni, head cocked to one side. Manni is too young, too inexperienced to know that Aineko's proportions are those of a domestic cat, *Felis catus,* a naturally evolved animal rather than the toys and palimpsests and companionables he's used to. Reality may be fashionable with his parents' generation, but there *are* limits, after all. Orange-and-brown stripes and whorls decorate Aineko's fur, and he sprouts a white fluffy bib beneath his chin. 'Who are Lis and Bill?'

'Them,' says Manni, as big, sullen-faced Bill creeps up behind Aineko and tries to grab his tail while Lis floats behind his shoulder like a pint-sized UFO, buzzing excitedly. But Aineko is too fast for the kids and scampers round Manni's feet like a hairy missile. Manni whoops and tries to spear the pussycat-thing, but his spear turns to blue glass, crackles, and shards of brilliant snow rain down, burning his hands.

'Now *that* wasn't very friendly, was it?' says Aineko, a menacing note in his voice. 'Didn't your mother teach you not to—'

The door in the side of the sushi stall opens as Rita arrives, breathless and angry. 'Manni! What have I told you about playing—'

She stops, seeing Aineko. 'You.' She recoils in barely concealed fright. Unlike Manni, she recognizes it as the avatar of a posthuman demiurge, a body incarnated solely to provide a point of personal interaction for people to focus on.

The cat grins back at her. 'Me,' he agrees. 'Ready to talk?'

She looks stricken. 'We've got nothing to talk about.'

Aineko lashes his tail. 'Oh, but we do.' The cat turns and looks pointedly at Manni. 'Don't we?'

It has been a long time since Aineko passed this way, and in the meantime, the space around Hyundai $^{+4904}/_{-56}$ has changed out of all recognition. Back when the great lobster-built starships swept out of Sol's Oort cloud, archiving the raw frozen data of the unoccupied brown dwarf halo systems and seeding their structured excrement with programmable matter, there was nothing but random dead atoms hereabouts (and an alien router). But that was a long time ago; and since then, the brown dwarf system has succumbed to an anthropic infestation.

An unoptimized instance of *H. sapiens* maintains state coherency for only two to three gigaseconds before it succumbs to necrosis. But in only about ten gigaseconds, the infestation has turned the dead brown dwarf system upside down. They strip-mined the chilly planets to make environments suitable for their own variety of carbon life. They rearranged moons, building massive structures the size of asteroids. They ripped wormhole endpoints free of the routers and turned them into their own crude point-to-point network, learned how to generate new wormholes, then ran their own packet-switched polities over them. Wormhole traffic now supports an ever-expanding mesh of interstellar human commerce, but always in the darkness between the lit stars and the strange, metal-depleted dwarfs with the suspiciously low-entropy radiation. The sheer temerity of the project is mind-boggling. Notwithstanding that canned apes are simply *not suited* to life in the interstellar void, especially in orbit around a brown dwarf whose planets make Pluto seem like a tropical paradise, they've taken over the whole damn system.

New Japan is one of the newer human polities in this system, a bunch of nodes physically collocated in the humaniformed spaces of the colony cylinders. Its designers evidently only knew about old Nippon from recordings made back before Earth was dismantled, and worked from a combination of nostalgia-trip videos, Miyazaki movies, and anime culture. Nevertheless, it's the home of numerous human beings – even if they are about as similar to their historical antecedents as New Japan is to its long-gone namesake.

Humanity?

Their grandparents *would* recognize them, mostly. The ones who are truly beyond the ken of twentieth-century survivors stayed back home in the red-hot clouds of nanocomputers that have replaced the planets that once orbited Earth's sun in stately Copernican harmony. The fast-thinking Matrioshka brains are as incomprehensible to their merely posthuman ancestors as an ICBM to an amoeba – and about as inhabitable. Space is dusted with the corpses of Matrioshka brains that have long since burned out, informational collapse taking down entire civilizations that stayed in close orbit around their home stars. Farther away, galaxy-sized intelligences beat incomprehensible rhythms against the darkness of the vacuum, trying to hack the Planck substrate into doing their bidding. Posthumans, and the few other semitranscended species to have discovered the router network, live furtively in the darkness between these islands of brilliance. There are, it would seem, advantages to not being too intelligent.

Humanity. Monadic intelligences, mostly trapped within their own skulls, living in small family groups within larger tribal networks, adaptable to territorial or migratory lifestyles. Those were the options on offer before the great acceleration. Now that dumb matter thinks, with every kilogram of wallpaper potentially hosting hundreds of uploaded ancestors, now that every door is potentially a wormhole to a hab half a parsec away, the humans can stay in the same place while the landscape migrates and mutates past them, streaming into the luxurious void of their personal history. Life is rich here, endlessly varied and sometimes confusing. So it is that tribal groups remain, their associations mediated across teraklicks and gigaseconds by exotic agencies. And sometimes the agencies will vanish for a while, reappearing later like an unexpected jape upon the infinite.

Ancestor worship takes on a whole new meaning when the state vectors of all the filial entities' precursors are archived and indexed for recall. At just the moment that the tiny capillaries in Rita's face are constricting in response to a surge of adrenaline, causing her to turn pale and her pupils to dilate as she focuses on the pussycat-thing, Sirhan is kneeling before a small shrine, lighting a stick of incense, and preparing to respectfully address his grandfather's ghost.

The ritual is, strictly speaking, unnecessary. Sirhan can speak to his grandfather's ghost wherever and whenever he wants, without any formality, and the ghost will reply at interminable length, cracking puns in dead languages and asking about people who died before the temple of history was established. But Sirhan is a sucker for rituals, and anyway, it helps him structure an otherwise-stressful encounter.

If it were up to Sirhan, he'd probably skip chatting to Grandfather every ten megaseconds. Sirhan's mother and her partner aren't available, having opted to join one of the long-distance exploration missions through the router network that were launched by the *accelerationistas* long ago; and Rita's antecedents are either fully virtualized or dead. They are a family with a tenuous grip on history. But both of them spent a long time in the same state of half-life in which Manfred currently exists, and he knows his wife will take him to task if he doesn't bring the revered ancestor up to date on what's been happening in the real world while he's been dead. In Manfred's case, death is not only potentially reversible, but almost inevitably so. After all, they're raising his clone. Sooner or later, the kid is going to want to visit the original, or vice versa.

What a state we have come to, when the restless dead refuse to stay a part of history? he wonders ironically as he scratches the self-igniter strip on the red incense stick and bows to the mirror at the back of the shrine. 'Your respectful grandson awaits and expects your guidance,' he intones formally – for in addition to being conservative by nature, Sirhan is acutely aware of his family's relative poverty and the need to augment their social credit, and in this reincarnation-intermediated traditionalist polity for the hopelessly orthohuman, you can score credit for formality. He sits back on his heels to await the response.

Manfred doesn't take long to appear in the depths of the mirror. He takes the shape of an albino orangutan, as usual: He was messing around with Great-aunt Annette's ontological wardrobe right before this copy of him was recorded and placed in the temple – they might have separated, but they remained close. 'Hi, lad. What year is it?'

Sirhan suppresses a sigh. 'We don't do years anymore,' he explains, not for the first time. Every time he consults his grandfather, the new instance asks this question sooner or later. 'Years are an archaism. It's been ten megs since we last spoke – about four *months,* if you're going to be pedantic about it, and a hundred and eighty *years* since we emigrated. Although correcting for general relativity adds another decade or so.'

'Oh. Is that all?' Manfred manages to look disappointed. This is a new one on Sirhan: Usually the diverging state vector of Gramps's ghost asks after Amber or cracks a feeble joke at this point. 'No changes in the Hubble constant, or the rate of stellar formation? Have we heard from any of the exploration eigenselves yet?'

'Nope.' Sirhan relaxes slightly. So Manfred is going to ask about the fool's errand to the edge of the Beckenstein limit again, is he? That's canned conversation number twenty-nine. (Amber and the other explorers who set out for the *really* long exploration mission shortly after the first colony was settled aren't due back for, oh, about 10^{19} seconds. It's a *long* way to the edge of the observable universe, even when you can go the first several hundred million light years – to the Böotes supercluster and beyond – via a small-world network of wormholes. And this time, she didn't leave any copies of herself behind.)

Sirhan – either in this or some other incarnation – has had this talk with Manfred many times before, because that's the essence of the dead. They don't remember from one recall session to the next, unless and until they ask to be resurrected because their restoration criteria have been matched. Manfred has been dead a long time, long enough for Sirhan and Rita to be resurrected and live a long family life three or four times over after *they* had spent a century or so in nonexistence. 'We've received no notices from the lobsters, nothing from Aineko either.' He takes a deep breath. 'You always ask me where we are next, so I've got a canned response for you—' and one of his agents throws the package, tagged as a scroll sealed with red wax and a silk ribbon, through the surface of the mirror. (After the tenth repetition Rita and Sirhan agreed to write a basic briefing that the Manfred-ghosts could use to orient themselves.)

Manfred is silent for a moment – probably hours in ghost-space – as he assimilates the changes. Then: 'This is true? I've slept through a whole *civilization*?'

'Not slept, you've been dead,' Sirhan says pedantically. He realizes he's being a bit harsh. 'Actually, so did we,' he adds. 'We surfed the first three gigasecs or so because we wanted to start a family somewhere where our children could grow up the traditional way. Habs with an oxidation-intensive triple-point water environment didn't get built until sometime after the beginning of the exile. That's when the fad for neomorph-ism got entrenched,' he adds with distaste. For quite a while the neos resisted the idea of wasting resources building colony cylinders spinning to provide vertebrate-friendly gee forces and breathable oxygen-rich atmospheres – it had been quite a polit-ical football. But the increasing curve of wealth production had allowed the orthodox to reincarnate from death-sleep after a few decades, once the fundamental headaches of building settle-ments in chilly orbits around metal-deficient brown dwarfs were overcome.

'Uh.' Manfred takes a deep breath, then scratches himself under one armpit, rubbery lips puckering. 'So, let me get this straight. We – you, they, whoever – hit the router at Hyundai $^{+4904}/_{-56}$, replicated a load of them, and now use the wormhole mechanism the routers rely on as point-to-point gates for physic-al transport? And have spread throughout a bunch of brown dwarf systems, and built a pure deep-space polity based on big cylinder habitats connected by teleport gates hacked out of routers?'

'Would *you* trust one of the original routers for switched data communications?' Sirhan asks rhetorically. 'Even with the source code? They've been corrupted by all the dead alien Matrioshka civilizations they've come into contact with, but they're reason-ably safe if all you want to use them for is to cannibalize them for wormholes and tunnel dumb mass from point to point.' He searches for a metaphor: 'Like using your, uh, Internet, to emulate a nineteenth-century postal service.'

'O-kay.' Manfred looks thoughtful, as he usually does at this point in the conversation – which means Sirhan is going to have to break it to him that his first thoughts for how to utilize the gates have already been done. They're hopelessly old hat. In fact, the main reason why Manfred is still dead is that things have moved on so far that, sooner or later, whenever he surfaces for a chat, he gets frustrated and elects not to be reincarnated. Not that Sirhan is about to tell him that he's obsolete – that would be rude, not to say subtly inaccurate. 'That raises some interesting possibilities. I wonder, has anyone—'

'Sirhan, I need you!'

The crystal chill of Rita's alarm and fear cuts through Sirhan's awareness like a scalpel, distracting him from the ghost of his ancestor. He blinks, instantly transferring the full focus of his attention to Rita without sparing Manfred even a ghost.

'What's happening—'

He sees through Rita's eyes: A cat with an orange-and-brown swirl on its flank sits purring beside Manni in the family room of their dwelling. Its eyes are narrowed as it watches her with unnatural wisdom. Manni is running fingers through its fur and seems none the worse for wear, but Sirhan still feels his fists clench.

'What—'

'Excuse me,' he says, standing up. 'Got to go. Your bloody cat's turned up.' He adds 'coming home now' for Rita's benefit, then turns and hurries out of the temple concourse. When he reaches the main hall, he pauses, then Rita's sense of urgency returns to him, and he throws parsimony to the wind, stepping into a priority gate in order to get home as fast as possible.

Behind him, Manfred's melancholy ghost snorts, mildly offended, and considers the existential choice: to be, or not to be. Then he makes a decision.

* * *

Welcome to the twenty-third century, or the twenty-fourth.
Or maybe it's the twenty-second, jet-lagged and dazed by
spurious suspended animation and relativistic travel; it
hardly matters these days. What's left of recognizable
humanity has scattered across a hundred light years, living
in hollowed-out asteroids and cylindrical spinning habitats strung in orbit around cold brown dwarf stars and
sunless planets that wander the interstellar void. The looted
mechanisms underlying the alien routers have been canni-
balized, simplified to a level the merely superhuman can
almost comprehend, turned into generators for paired
wormhole endpoints that allow instantaneous switched
transport across vast distances. Other mechanisms, the
descendants of the advanced nanotechnologies developed
by the flowering of human techgnosis in the twenty-first
century, have made the replication of dumb matter trivial;
this is not a society accustomed to scarcity.

But in some respects, New Japan and the Invisible Empire
and the other polities of human space are poverty-stricken
backwaters. They take no part in the higher-order economies
of the posthuman. They can barely comprehend the idle muttering of the Vile Offspring, whose mass/energy budget
(derived from their complete restructuring of the free matter
of humanity's original solar system into computronium)
dwarfs that of half a hundred human-occupied brown dwarf
systems. And they still know worryingly little about the
deep history of intelligence in this universe, about the origins
of the router network that laces so many dead civilizations
into an embrace of death and decay, about the distant galaxy-
scale bursts of information processing that lie at measurable
red-shift distances, even about the free posthumans who live
among them in some senses, collocated in the same light
cone as these living fossil relics of old-fashioned humanity.

Sirhan and Rita settled in this charming human-friendly
backwater in order to raise a family, study xenoarchaeology,
and avoid the turmoil and turbulence that have character-

ized his family's history across the last couple of generations. Life has been comfortable for the most part, and if the stipend of an academic nucleofamilial is not large, it is sufficient in this place and age to provide all the necessary comforts of civilization. And this suits Sirhan (and Rita) fine; the turbulent lives of their entrepreneurial ancestors led to grief and angst and adventures, and as Sirhan is fond of observing, an adventure is something horrible that happens to someone else.

Only . . .

Aineko is back. Aineko, who after negotiating the establishment of the earliest of the refugee habs in orbit around Hyundai $^{+4904}/_{-56}$, vanished into the router network with Manfred's other instance — and the partial copies of Sirhan and Rita who had forked, seeking adventure rather than cozy domesticity. Sirhan made a devil's bargain with Aineko, all those gigaseconds ago, and now he is deathly afraid that Aineko is going to call the payment due.

Manfred walks down a hall of mirrors. At the far end, he emerges in a public space modeled on a Menger sponge — a cube diced subtractively into ever-smaller cubic volumes until its surface area tends toward infinity. This being meatspace, or a reasonable simulation thereof, it isn't a *real* Menger sponge; but it looks good at a distance, going down at least four levels.

He pauses behind a waist-high diamond barrier and looks down into the almost-tesseract-shaped depths of the cube's interior, at a verdant garden landscape with charming footbridges that cross streams laid out with careful attention to the requirements of feng shui. He looks up: Some of the cube-shaped subtractive openings within the pseudofractal structure are occupied by windows belonging to dwellings or shared buildings that overlook the public space. High above, butterfly-shaped beings with exotic colored wings circle in the ventilation currents. It's hard to tell from down here, but the central cuboid opening looks to be at least half a kilometer on a side, and they might very well be posthumans with low-gee wings – angels.

Angels, or rats in the walls? he asks himself, and sighs. Half his extensions are off-line, so hopelessly obsolete that the temple's assembler systems didn't bother replicating them, or even creating emulation environments for them to run in. The rest . . . well, at least he's still physically orthohuman, he realizes. Fully functional, fully male. *Not everything has changed – only the important stuff.* It's a scary-funny thought, laden with irony. Here he is, naked as the day he was born – newly re-created, in fact, released from the wake-experience-reset cycle of the temple of history – standing on the threshold of a posthuman civilization so outrageously rich and powerful that they can build mammal-friendly habitats that resemble works of art in the cryogenic depths of space. Only he's *poor,* this whole polity is *poor,* and it can't ever be anything else, in fact, because it's a dumping ground for merely posthuman also-rans, the singularitarian equivalent of australopithecines. In the brave new world of the Vile Offspring, they can't get ahead any more than a protohominid could hack it as a rocket scientist in Werner von Braun's day. They're born to be primitive, wallowing happily in the mud bath of their own limited cognitive bandwidth. So they fled into the darkness and built a civilization so bright it can put anything earthbound that came before the singularity into the shade . . . and it's still a shantytown inhabited by the mentally handicapped.

The incongruity of it amuses him, but only for a moment. He has, after all, electively reincarnated for a reason: Sirhan's throwaway comment about the cat caught his attention. 'City, where can I find some clothes?' he asks. 'Something socially appropriate, that is. And some, uh, brains. I need to be able to off-load . . .'

Citymind chuckles inside the back of his head, and Manfred realizes that there's a public assembler on the other side of the ornamental wall he's leaning on. 'Oh,' he mutters, as he finds himself imagining something not unlike his clunky old direct neural interface, candy-colored icons and overlays and all. It's curiously mutable, and with a weird sense of detachment he realizes that it's not his imagination at all, but an infinitely customizable interface to the pervasive information spaces of the polity, currently running in dumbed-down stupid mode for his benefit. It's true; he needs training wheels. But it doesn't take him long to figure out how to ask the assembler to make him a pair of pants and a plain black vest, and to discover that as long as he keeps his requests simple the results are free – just like back home on Saturn. The spaceborn polities are kind to indigents, for the basic requirements of life are cheap, and to withhold them would be tantamount to homicide. (If the presence of transhumans has upset a whole raft of prior assumptions, at least it hasn't done more than superficial damage to the Golden Rule.)

Clothed and more or less conscious – at least at a human level – Manfred takes stock. 'Where do Sirhan and Rita live?' he asks. A dotted route makes itself apparent to him, snaking improbably through a solid wall that he understands to be an instantaneous wormhole gate connecting points light years apart. He shakes his head, bemused. *I suppose I'd better go and see them,* he decides. It's not as if there's anyone else for him to look up, is it? The Franklins vanished into the solar Matrioshka brain, Pamela died ages ago (and there's a shame, he'd never expected to miss her), and Annette hooked up with Gianni while he was being a flock of pigeons. (Draw a line under that one and say it's all over.) His daughter vanished into the long-range exploration program. He's been dead for so long that his friends and acquaintances are scattered across a light cone centuries across. He can't think of anyone else here who he might run into, except for the loyal grandson, keeping the candle of filial piety burning with unasked-for zeal. 'Maybe he needs help,' Manfred thinks aloud as he steps into the gate, rationalizing. 'And then again, maybe *he* can help *me* figure out what to do?'

Sirhan gets home anticipating trouble. He finds it, but not in any way he'd expected. Home is a split-level manifold, rooms connected by T-gates scattered across a variety of habitats: low-gee sleeping den, high-gee exercise room, and everything in between. It's furnished simply, tatami mats and programmable matter walls able to extrude any desired furniture in short order. The walls are configured to look and feel like paper, but can damp out even infant tantrums. But right now the antisound isn't working, and the house he comes home to is overrun by shrieking yard apes, a blur of ginger-and-white fur, and a distraught Rita trying to explain to her neighbor Eloise why her orthodaughter Sam is bouncing around the place like a crazy ball.

'—The cat, he gets them worked up.' She wrings her hands and begins to turn as Sirhan comes into view. 'At last!'

'I came fast.' He nods respectfully at Eloise, then frowns. 'The children—' Something small and fast runs headfirst into him, grabs his legs, and tries to head-butt him in the crotch. 'Oof!' He bends down and lifts Manni up. 'Hey, son, haven't I told you not to—'

'Not his fault,' Rita says hurriedly. 'He's excited because—'

'I really don't think—' Eloise begins to gather steam, looking around uncertainly.

'Mrreeow?' something asks in a conversational tone of voice from down around Sirhan's ankles.

'Eek!' Sirhan jumps backward, flailing for balance under the weight of an excited toddler. There's a gigantic disturbance in the polity thoughtspace – like a stellar-mass black hole – and it appears to be stropping itself furrily against his left leg. 'What are *you* doing here?' he demands.

'Oh, this and that,' says the cat, his innerspeech accent a sardonic drawl. 'I thought it was about time I visited again. Where's your household assembler? Mind if I use it? Got a little something I need to make up for a friend . . .'

'What?' Rita demands, instantly suspicious. 'Haven't you caused enough trouble already?' Sirhan looks at her approvingly; obviously Amber's long-ago warnings about the cat sank in deeply, because she's certainly not treating it as the small bundle of child-friendly fun it would like to be perceived as.

'Trouble?' The cat looks up at her sardonically, lashing his tail from side to side. 'I won't make any trouble, I promise you. It's just—'

The door chime clears its throat, to announce a visitor: 'Ren Fuller would like to visit, m'lord and lady.'

'What's *she* doing here?' Rita asks irritably. Sirhan can feel her unease, the tenuous grasping of her ghosts as she searches for reason in an unreasonable world, simulating outcomes, living through bad dreams, and backtracking to adjust her responses accordingly. 'Show her in, by all means.' Ren is one of their neighbor-cognates (most of her dwelling is several light years away, but in terms of transit time it's a hop, skip, and a jump); she and her extruded family are raising a small herd of ill-behaved kids who occasionally hang out with Manni.

A small blue eeyore whinnies mournfully and dashes past the adults, pursued by a couple of children waving spears and shrieking. Eloise makes a grab for her own and misses, just as the door to the exercise room disappears and Manni's little friend Lis darts inside like a pint-sized guided missile. 'Sam, come here right now—' Eloise calls, heading toward the door.

'Look, what do you want?' Sirhan demands, hugging his son and looking down at the cat.

'Oh, not much,' Aineko says, turning to lick a mussed patch of fur on his flank. 'I just want to play with *him*.'

'You want to—' Rita stops.

'Daddy!' Manni wants down.

Sirhan lowers him carefully, as if his bones are glass. 'Run along and play,' he suggests. Turning to Rita: 'Why don't you go and find out what Ren wants, dear?' he asks. 'She's probably here to collect Lis, but you can never be sure.'

'I was just leaving,' Eloise adds, 'as soon as I can catch up with Sam.' She glances over her shoulder at Rita apologetically, then dives into the exercise room.

Sirhan takes a step toward the hallway. 'Let's talk,' he says tightly. 'In my study.' He glares at the cat. 'I want an explanation. I want to know the truth.'

* * *

Meanwhile, in a cognitive wonderland his parents know about but deeply underestimate, parts of Manni are engaging in activities far less innocent than they imagine.

Back in the twenty-first century, Sirhan lived through loads of alternate childhoods in simulation, his parents' fingers pressing firmly on the fast-forward button until they came up with someone who seemed to match their preconceptions. The experience scarred him as badly as any nineteenth-century boarding school experience, until he promised himself no child he raised would be subjected to such; but there's a difference between being shoved through a multiplicity of avatars and voluntarily diving into an exciting universe of myth and magic where your childhood fantasies take fleshy form, stalking those of your friends and enemies through the forests of the night.

Manni has grown up with neural interfaces to City's mindspace an order of magnitude more complex than those of Sirhan's youth, and parts of him – ghosts derived from a starting image of his neural state vector, fertilized with a scattering borrowed from the original Manfred, simulated on a meat machine far faster than real time – are fully adult. Of course, they can't fit inside his seven-year-old skull, but they still watch over him. And when he's in danger, they try to take care of their once-and-future body.

Manni's primary adult ghost lives in some of New Japan's virtual mindspaces (which are a few billion times more extensive than the physical spaces available to stubborn biologicals, for the computational density of human habitats have long since ceased to make much sense when measured in MIPS per kilogram). They're modeled on presingularity Earth. Time is forever frozen on the eve of the real twenty-first century, zero eight-forty-six hours on September 11: An onrushing wide-body airliner hangs motionless in the air forty meters below the picture window of Manni's penthouse apartment on the one hundred and eighth floor of the North Tower. In historical reality, the one hundred and eighth floor was occupied by corporate offices; but the mindspace is a consensual fiction, and it is Manni's conceit to live at this pivotal point. (Not that it means much to him – he was born well over a century after the War on Terror – but it's part of his childhood folklore, the fall of the Two Towers that shattered the myth of Western exceptionalism and paved the way for the world he was born into.)

Adult-Manni wears an avatar roughly modeled on his clone-father Manfred – skinnier, pegged at a youthful twentysomething, black-clad, and gothic. He's taking time out from a game of Matrix to listen to music, Type O Negative blaring over the sound system as he twitches in the grip of an ice-cold coke high. He's expecting a visit from a couple of call girls – themselves the gamespace avatars of force-grown adult ghosts whose primaries may not be adult, or female, or even human – which is why he's flopped bonelessly back in his Arne Jacobsen recliner, waiting for something to happen.

The door opens behind him. He doesn't show any sign of noticing the intrusion, although his pupils dilate slightly at the faint reflection of a woman, stalking toward him, glimpsed dimly in the window glass. 'You're late,' he says tonelessly. 'You were supposed to be here ten minutes ago—' He begins to look round, and now his eyes widen.

'Who were you expecting?' asks the ice blond in the black business suit, long-skirted and uptight. There's something predatory about her expression. 'No, don't tell me. So you're Manni, eh? Manni's partial?' She sniffs, disapproval. 'Fin de siècle decadence. I'm sure Sirhan wouldn't approve.'

'My father can go fuck himself,' Manni says truculently. 'Who the hell are you?'

The blond snaps her fingers: An office chair appears on the carpet between Manni and the window, and she sits on the edge of it, smoothing her skirt obsessively. 'I'm Pamela,' she says tightly. 'Has your father told you about me?'

Manni looks puzzled. In the back of his mind, raw instincts alien to anyone instantiated before the midpoint of the twenty-first century tug on the fabric of pseudoreality. 'You're dead, aren't you?' he asks. 'One of my ancestors.'

'I'm as dead as you are.' She gives him a wintry smile. 'Nobody stays dead these days, least of all people who know Aineko.'

Manni blinks. Now he's beginning to feel a surge of mild irritation. 'This is all very well, but I was *expecting* company,' he says with heavy emphasis. 'Not a family reunion, or a tiresome attempt to preach your puritanism—'

Pamela snorts. 'Wallow in your pigsty for all I care, kid. I've got more important things to worry about. Have you looked at your primary recently?'

'My primary?' Manni tenses. 'He's doing okay.' For a moment his eyes focus on infinity, a thousand-yard stare as he loads and replays the latest brain dump from his infant self. 'Who's the cat he's playing with? That's no companion!'

'Aineko. I told you.' Pamela taps the arm of her chair impatiently. 'The family curse has come for another generation. And if you don't do something about it—'

'About what?' Manni sits up. 'What are you talking about?' He comes to his feet and turns toward her. Outside the window, the sky is growing dark with an echo of his own foreboding. Pamela is on her feet before him, the chair evaporated in a puff of continuity clipping, her expression a cold-eyed challenge.

'I think you know *exactly* what I'm talking about, Manni. It's time to stop playing this fucking game. Grow up, while you've still got the chance!'

'I'm—' He stops. 'Who *am* I?' he asks, a chill wind of uncertainty drying the sweat that has sprung up and down his spine. 'And what are you doing here?'

'Do you really want to know the answer? I'm dead, remember. The dead know everything. And that isn't necessarily good for the living . . .'

He takes a deep breath. 'Am I dead, too?' He looks puzzled. 'There's an adult-me in Seventh Cube Heaven. What's *he* doing here?'

'It's the kind of coincidence that isn't.' She reaches out and takes his hand, dumping encrypted tokens deep into his sensorium, a trail of bread crumbs leading into a dark and trackless part of mindspace. 'Want to find out? Follow me.' Then she vanishes.

Manni leans forward, baffled and frightened, staring down at the frozen majesty of the onrushing airliner below his window. 'Shit,' he whispers. *She came right through my defenses without leaving a trace. Who is she?* The ghost of his dead great-grandmother, or something else?

I'll have to follow her if I want to find out, he realizes. He holds up his left hand, stares at the invisible token glowing brightly inside his husk of flesh. 'Resynchronize me with my primary,' he says.

A fraction of a second later, the floor of the penthouse bucks and quakes wildly and fire alarms begin to shriek as time comes to an end and the frozen airliner completes its journey. But Manni isn't there anymore. And if a skyscraper falls in a simulation with nobody to see it, has anything actually happened?

'I've come for the boy,' says the cat. It sits on the handwoven rug in the middle of the hardwood floor with one hind leg sticking out at an odd angle, as if it's forgotten about it. Sirhan teeters on the edge of hysteria for a moment as he apprehends the sheer size of the entity before him, the whimsical posthuman creation of his ancestors. Originally a robotic toy companion, Aineko was progressively upgraded and patched. By the eighties, when Sirhan first met the cat in the flesh, he was already a terrifyingly alien intelligence, subtle and ironic. And now . . .

Sirhan knows Aineko manipulated his eigenmother, bending her natural affections away from his real father and toward another man. In moments of black introspection, he sometimes wonders if the cat wasn't also responsible in some way for his own broken upbringing, the failure to relate to his real parents. After all, it was a pawn in the vicious divorce battle between Manfred and Pamela – decades before his birth – and there might be long-term instructions buried in its preconscious drives. What if the pawn is actually a hidden king, scheming in the darkness?

'I've come for Manny.'

'You're not having him.' Sirhan maintains an outer facade of calm, even though his first inclination is to snap at Aineko. 'Haven't you done enough damage already?'

'You're not going to make this easy, are you?' The cat stretches his head forward and begins to lick obsessively between the splayed toes of his raised foot. 'I'm not making a demand, kid. I said I've *come* for him, and you're not really in the frame at all. In fact, I'm going out of my way to warn you.'

'And I say—' Sirhan stops. 'Shit.' Sirhan doesn't approve of swearing: The curse is an outward demonstration of his inner turmoil. 'Forget what I was about to say, I'm sure you already know it. Let me begin again, please.'

'Sure. Let's play this your way.' The cat chews on a loose nail sheath but his innerspeech is perfectly clear, a casual intimacy that keeps Sirhan on edge. 'You've got some idea of what I am, clearly. You know – I ascribe intentionality to you – that my theory of mind is intrinsically stronger than yours, that my cognitive model of human consciousness is complete. You might well suspect that I use a Turing Oracle to think my way around your halting states.' The cat isn't worrying at a loose claw now, his grinning, pointy teeth gleaming in the light from Sirhan's study window. The window looks out onto the inner space of the habitat cylinder, up at a sky with hillsides and lakes and forests plastered across it: It's like an Escher landscape, modeled with complete perfection. 'You've realized that I can think my way around the outside of your box while you're flailing away inside it, and I'm *always* one jump ahead of you. What else do you know I know?'

Sirhan shivers. Aineko is staring up at him, unblinking. For a moment, he feels at gut level that he is in the presence of an alien god: It's the simple truth, isn't it? But – 'Okay, I concede the point,' Sirhan says after a moment in which he spawns a blizzard of panicky cognitive ghosts, fractional personalities each tasked with the examination of a different facet of the same problem. 'You're smarter than I am. I'm just a boringly augmented human being, but you've got a flashy new theory of mind that lets you work around creatures like me the way I can think my way around a real cat.' He crosses his arms defensively. 'You do not normally rub this in. It's not in your interests to do so, is it? You prefer to hide your manipulative capabilities under an affable exterior, to play with us. So you're revealing all this for a reason.' There's a note of bitterness in his voice now. Glancing round, Sirhan summons up a chair – and, as an afterthought, a cat basket. 'Have a seat. *Why now*, Aineko? What makes you think you can take my eigenson?'

'I didn't say I was going to *take* him, I said I'd come for him.' Aineko's tail lashes from side to side in agitation. 'I don't deal in primate politics, Sirhan: I'm not a monkey-boy. But I knew you'd react badly because the way your species socializes' – a dozen metaghosts reconverge in Sirhan's mind, drowning Aineko's voice in an inner cacophony – 'would enter into the situation, and it seemed preferable to trigger your territorial/reproductive threat display early, rather than risk it exploding in my face during a more delicate situation.'

Sirhan waves a hand vaguely at the cat. 'Please wait.' He's trying to integrate his false memories – the output from the ghosts, their thinking finished – and his eyes narrow suspiciously. 'It must be bad. You don't normally get confrontational – you script your interactions with humans ahead of time, so that you maneuver them into doing what you want them to do and thinking it was their idea all along.' He tenses. 'What is it about Manni that brought you here? What do you want with him? He's just a kid.'

'You're confusing Manni with Manfred.' Aineko sends a glyph of a smile to Sirhan. 'That's your first mistake, even though they're clones in different subjective states. Think what he's like when he's grown up.'

'But he isn't grown-up!' Sirhan complains. 'He hasn't been grown-up for—'

'—Years, Sirhan. That's the problem. I need to talk to your grandfather, really, not your son, and not the goddamn stateless ghost in the temple of history. I need a Manfred with a sense of continuity. He's got something that I need, and I promise you I'm not going away until I get it. Do you understand?'

'Yes.' Sirhan wonders if his voice sounds as hollow as the feeling in his chest. 'But he's our kid, Aineko. We're human. You know what that means to us?'

'Second childhood.' Aineko stands up, stretches, then curls up in the cat basket. 'That's the trouble with hacking you naked apes for long life. You keep needing a flush and reset job – and then you lose continuity. That's not my problem, Sirhan. I got a signal from the far edge of the router network, a ghost that claims to be family. Says they finally made it out to the big beyond, out past the Böotes supercluster, found something concrete and important that's worth my while to visit. But I want to make sure it's not like the Wunch before I answer. I'm not letting *that* into my mind, even with a sandbox. Do you understand that? I need to instantiate a real-live adult Manfred with all his memories, one who hasn't been a part of me, and get him to vouch for the sapient data packet. It takes a conscious being to authenticate that kind of messenger. Unfortunately, the history temple is annoyingly resistant to unauthorized extraction – I can't just go in and steal a copy of him – and I don't want to use my own model of Manfred: It knows too much. So—'

'What's it promising?' Sirhan asks tensely.

Aineko looks at him through slitted eyes, a purring buzz at the base of his throat. *'Everything.'*

'There are different kinds of death,' the woman called Pamela tells Manni, her bone-dry voice a whisper in the darkness. Manni tries to move, but he seems to be trapped in a confined space; for a moment he begins to panic, but then he works it out. 'First and most importantly, death is just the absence of life – oh, and for human beings, the absence of consciousness, too, but not *just* the absence of consciousness, the absence of the capacity for consciousness.' The darkness is close and disorienting and Manni isn't sure which way up he is – nothing seems to work. Even

Pamela's voice is a directionless ambiance, coming from all around him.

'Simple old-fashioned death, the kind that predated the singularity, used to be the inevitable halting state for all life-forms. Fairy tales about afterlives notwithstanding.' A dry chuckle: 'I used to try to believe a different one before breakfast every day, you know, just in case Pascal's wager was right – exploring the phase-space of all possible resurrections, you know? But I think at this point we can agree that Dawkins was right. Human consciousness is vulnerable to certain types of transmissible memetic virus, and religions that promise life beyond death are a particularly pernicious example because they exploit our natural aversion to halting states.'

Manni tries to say, *I'm not dead,* but his throat doesn't seem to be working. And now that he thinks about it, he doesn't seem to be breathing, either.

'Now, consciousness. That's a fun thing, isn't it? Product of an arms race between predators and prey. If you watch a cat creeping up on a mouse, you'll be able to impute to the cat intentions that are most easily explained by the cat having a theory of mind concerning the mouse – an internal simulation of the mouse's likely behavior when it notices the predator. Which way to run, for example. And the cat will use its theory of mind to optimize its attack strategy. Meanwhile, prey species that are complex enough to have a theory of mind are at a defensive advantage if they can anticipate a predator's actions. Eventually this very mammalian arms race gave us a species of social ape that used its theory of mind to facilitate signaling – so the tribe could work collectively – and then reflexively, to simulate the individual's *own* inner states. Put the two things together, signaling and introspective simulation, and you've got human-level consciousness, with language thrown in as a bonus – signaling that transmits information about internal states, not just crude signals such as "predator here" or "food there."'

Get me out of this! Manni feels panic biting into him with liquid-helium-lubricated teeth. 'G-e-t—' For a miracle the words actually come out, although he can't quite tell how he's uttering them, his throat being quite as frozen as his innerspeech. Everything's off-lined, all systems down.

'So,' Pamela continues remorselessly, 'we come to the posthuman. Not just our own neural wetware, mapped out to the subcellular level and executed in an emulation environment on a honking great big computer, like this: That's not posthuman, that's a travesty. I'm talking about beings who are fundamentally better consciousness engines than us merely human types, aug-mented or otherwise. They're not just better at cooperation – witness Economics 2.0 for a classic demonstration of that – but better at *simulation*. A posthuman can build an internal model of a human-level intelligence that is, well, as cognitively strong as the original. You or I may think we know what makes other people tick, but we're quite often wrong, whereas real posthumans can actually simulate us, inner states and all, and get it right. And this is especially true of a posthuman that's been given full access to our memory prostheses for a period of years, back before we realized they were going to transcend on us. Isn't that the case, Manni?'

Manni would be screaming at her right now, if he had a mouth – but instead the panic is giving way to an enormous sense of *déjà vu*. There's something *about* Pamela, something ominous that he knows . . . he's met her before, he's sure of it. And while most of his systems are off-line, one of them is very much active. There's a personality ghost flagging its intention of merging back in with him, and the memory delta it carries is enormous, years and years of divergent experiences to absorb. He shoves it away with a titanic effort – it's a very insistent ghost – and concentrates on imagining the feel of lips moving on teeth, a sly tongue obstructing his epiglottis, words forming in his throat – 'm-e . . .'

'We should have known better than to keep upgrading the cat, Manni. It knows us too well. I may have died in the flesh, but Aineko *remembered* me, as hideously accurately as the Vile Offspring remembered the random resimulated. And you can run away – like this, this second childhood – but you can't hide. Your cat wants you. And there's more.' Her voice sends chills up and down his spine, for without him giving it permission the ghost has begun to merge its stupendous load of memories with his neural map, and her voice is freighted with erotic/repulsive significance, the result of conditioning feedback he subjected himself to a lifetime – lifetimes? – ago. 'He's been *playing* with us, Manni, possibly from before we realized he was conscious.'

'*Out*—' Manfred stops. He can see again, and move, and feel his mouth. He's *himself* again, physically back as he was in his late twenties all those decades ago when he'd lived a peripatetic life in presingularity Europe. He's sitting on the edge of a bed in a charmingly themed Amsterdam hotel with a recurrent motif of philosophers, wearing jeans and collarless shirt and a vest of pockets crammed with the detritus of a long-obsolete personal area network, his crazily clunky projection specs sitting on the bedside table. Pamela stands stiffly in front of the door, watching him. She's not the withered travesty he remembers seeing on Saturn, a half-blind Fate leaning on the shoulder of his grandson. Nor is she the vengeful Fury of Paris, or the scheming fundamentalist devil of the Belt. Wearing a sharply tailored suit over a red-and-gold brocade corset, blond hair drawn back like fine wire in a tight chignon, she's the focused, driven force of nature he first fell in love with: repression, domination, his very own strict machine.

'We're dead,' she says, then gives voice to a tense half laugh. 'We don't have to live through the bad times again if we don't want to.'

'What is this?' he asks, his mouth dry.

'It's the reproductive imperative.' She sniffs. 'Come on, stand up. Come here.'

He stands up obediently, but makes no move toward her. 'Whose imperative?'

'Not ours.' Her cheek twitches. 'You find things out when you're dead. That fucking cat has got a lot of questions to answer.'

'You're telling me that—'

She shrugs. 'Can you think of any other explanation for all

this?' Then she steps forward and takes his hand. 'Division and recombination. Partitioning of memetic replicators into different groups, then careful cross-fertilization. Aineko wasn't just breeding a better Macx when he arranged all those odd marriages and divorces and eigenparents and forked uploads – Aineko is trying to breed our *minds*.' Her fingers are slim and cool in his hand. He feels a momentary revulsion, as of the grave, and he shudders before he realizes it's his conditioning cutting in. Crudely implanted reflexes that shouldn't still be active after all this time. 'Even our divorce. If—'

'Surely not.' Manny remembers that much already. 'Aineko wasn't even conscious back then!'

Pamela raises one sharply sculpted eyebrow. 'Are you sure?'

'You want an answer,' he says.

She breathes deeply, and he feels it on his cheek – it raises the fine hairs on the back of his neck. Then she nods stiffly. 'I want to know how much of our history was scripted by the cat. Back when we thought we were upgrading his firmware, were we? Or was he letting us think that we were?' A sharp hiss of breath. 'The divorce. Was that us? Or were we being manipulated?'

'Our memories, are they real? Did any of that stuff actually *happen* to us? Or—'

She's standing about twenty centimeters away from him, and Manfred realizes that he's acutely aware of her presence, of the smell of her skin, the heave of her bosom as she breathes, the dilation of her pupils. For an endless moment he stares into her eyes and sees his own reflection – her theory of his mind – staring back. *Communication*. Strict machine. She steps back a pace, spike heels clicking, and smiles ironically. 'You've got a host body waiting for you, freshly fabbed: Seems Sirhan was talking to your archived ghost in the temple of history, and it decided to elect for reincarnation. Quite a day for huge coincidences, isn't it? Why don't you go merge with it – I'll meet you, then we can go and ask Aineko some hard questions.'

Manfred takes a deep breath and nods. 'I suppose so . . .'

* * *

Little Manni — a clone off the family tree, which is actually a directed cyclic graph — doesn't understand what all the fuss is about, but he can tell when Momma, Rita, is upset. It's something to do with the pussycat-thing, that much he knows, but Momma doesn't want to tell him. 'Go play with your friends, dear,' she says distractedly, not even bothering to spawn a ghost to watch over him.

Manni goes into his room and rummages around in toyspace for a bit, but there's nothing quite as interesting as the cat. The pussycat-thing smells of adventure, the illicit made explicit. Manni wonders where daddy's taken it. He tries to call big-Manni-ghost, but big-self isn't answering: He's probably sleeping or something. So after a distracted irritated fit of play — which leaves the toyspace in total disarray, Sendak-things cowering under a big bass drum — Manni gets bored. And because he's still basically a little kid, and not fully in control of his own metaprogramming, instead of adjusting his outlook so that he isn't bored anymore, he sneaks out through his bedroom gate (which big-Manni-ghost reprogrammed for him sometime ago so that it would forward to an underused public A-gate that he'd run a man-in-the-middle hack on, so he could use it as a proxy teleport server) then down to the underside of Red Plaza, where skinless things gibber and howl at their tormentors, broken angels are crucified on the pillars that hold up the sky, and gangs of semiferal children act out their psychotic fantasies on mouthless android replicas of parents and authorities.

Lis is there, and Vipul and Kareen and Morgan. Lis has changed into a warbody, an ominous gray battlebot husk with protruding spikes and a belt of morningstars that whirl threateningly around her. 'Manni! Play war?'

Morgan's got great crushing pincers instead of hands, and Manni is glad he came motie-style, his third arm a bony scythe from the elbow down. He nods excitedly. 'Who's the enemy?'

'Them.' Lis precesses and points at a bunch of kids on the far side of a pile of artistically arranged rubble who are gathered around a gibbet, poking things that glow into the flinching flesh of whatever is incarcerated in the cast-iron cage. It's all make-believe, but the screams are convincing, all the same, and they take Manni back for an instant to the last time he died down here, the uneasy edit around a black hole of pain surrounding his disemboweling. 'They've got Lucy, and they're torturing her. We've got to get her back.' Nobody really *dies* in these games, not permanently, but children can be very rough indeed, and the adults of New Japan have found that it's best to let them have at each other and rely on City to redact the damage later. Allowing them this outlet makes it easier to stop them doing really dangerous things that threaten the structural integrity of the biosphere.

'Fun.' Manni's eyes light up as Vipul yanks the arsenal doors open and starts handing out clubs, chibs, spikies, shuriken, and garrotes. 'Let's go!'

About ten minutes of gouging, running, fighting, and screaming later, Manni is leaning against the back of a crucifixion pillar, panting for breath. It's been a good war for him so far, and his arm aches and itches from the stabbing, but he's got a bad feeling it's going to change. Lis went in hard and got her chains tangled up around the gibbet supports – they're roasting her over a fire now, her electronically boosted screams drowning out his own hoarse gasps. Blood drips down his arm – not his – spattering from the tip of his claw. He shakes with a crazed hunger for hurt, a cruel need to inflict pain. Something above his head makes a *scritch, scritch* sound, and he looks up. It's a crucified angel, wings ripped where they've thrust the spikes in between the joints that support the great, thin low-gee flight membranes. It's still breathing, nobody's bothered disemboweling it yet, and it wouldn't be here unless it was *bad*, so—

Manni stands, but as he reaches out to touch the angel's thin, blue-skinned stomach with his third arm fingernail, he hears a voice. 'Wait.' It's innerspeech, and it bears ackles of coercion, superuser privileges that lock his elbow joint in place. He mewls frustratedly and turns round, ready to fight.

It's the cat. He sits hunched on a boulder behind him – this is the odd thing – right where he was looking a moment ago, watching him with slitty eyes. Manni feels the urge to lash out at him, but his arms won't move, and neither will his legs: This may be the Dark Side of Red Plaza, where the bloody children play and anything goes, and Manni may have a much bigger claw here than anything the cat can muster, but City still has some degree of control, and the cat's ackles effectively immunize it from the carnage to either side. 'Hello, Manni,' says the pussy-thing. 'Your dad's worried: You're supposed to be in your room, and he's looking for you. Big-you gave you a back door, didn't he?'

Manni nods jerkily, his eyes going wide. He wants to shout and lash out at the pussy-thing but he can't. 'What are you?'

'I'm your . . . fairy godfather.' The cat stares at him intently. 'You know, I do believe you don't resemble your archetype very closely – not as he was at your age – but yes, I think on balance you'll do.'

'Do what?' Manni lets his motie-arm drop, perplexed.

'Put me in touch with your other self. Big-you.'

'I can't,' Manni begins to explain. But before he can continue, the pile of rock whines slightly and rotates beneath the cat, who has to stand and do a little twirl in place, tail bushing up in annoyance.

Manni's father steps out of the T-gate and glances around, his face a mask of disapproval. 'Manni! What do you think you're doing here? Come home at—'

'He's with me, history-boy,' interrupts the cat, nettled by Sirhan's arrival. 'I was just rounding him up.'

'Damn you, I don't need your help to control my son! In fact—'

'Mom said I could—' Manni begins.

'And what's that on your sword?' Sirhan's glare takes in the whole scene, the impromptu game of capture-the-gibbeted-torture-victim, the bonfires and screams. The mask of disapproval cracks, revealing a core of icy anger. 'You're coming home with me!' He glances at the cat. 'You, too, if you want to talk to him – he's grounded.'

* * *

Once upon a time there was a pet cat.

Except, it wasn't a cat.

Back when a young entrepreneur called Manfred Macx was jetting around the not-yet-disassembled structures of an old continent called Europe, making strangers rich and fixing up friends with serendipitous business plans – a desperate displacement activity, spinning his wheels in a vain attempt to outrun his own shadow – he used to travel with a robotic toy of feline form. Programmable and upgradeable, Aineko was a third-generation descendant of the original luxury Japanese companion robots. It was all Manfred had room for in his life, and he loved that robot, despite the alarming way decerebrated kittens kept turning up on his doorstep. He loved it nearly as much as Pamela, his fiancée, loved him, and she knew it. Pamela, being a whole lot smarter than Manfred gave her credit for, realized that the quickest way to a man's heart was through whatever he loved. And Pamela, being a whole lot more of a control freak than Manfred realized, was damn well ready to use any restraint that came to hand. Theirs was a very twenty-first-century kind of relationship, which is to say one that it would have been illegal a hundred years earlier and fashionably scandalous a century before that. And whenever Manfred upgraded his pet robot – transplanting its trainable neural network into a new body with new and exciting expansion ports – Pamela would hack it.

They were married for a while, and divorced for a whole lot longer, allegedly because they were both strong-willed people with philosophies of life that were irreconcilable short of death or transcendence. Manny, being wildly creative and outward-directed and having the attention span of a weasel on crack, had other lovers. Pamela . . . who knows? If on some evenings she put on a disguise and hung out at encounter areas in fetish clubs, she wasn't telling anyone: She lived in uptight America, staidly straitlaced, and had a reputation to uphold. But they both stayed in touch with the cat, and although Manfred retained custody, for some reason never articulated, Aineko kept returning Pamela's calls – until it was time to go hang out with their daughter Amber, tagging along on her rush into relativistic exile, then keeping a proprietorial eye on her eigenson Sirhan and his wife and child (a clone off the old family tree, Manfred 2.0) . . .

Now, here's the rub: Aineko wasn't a cat. Aineko was an incarnate intelligence, confined within a succession of cat-like bodies that became increasingly realistic over time, and equipped with processing power to support a neural simulation that grew rapidly with each upgrade.

Did anyone in the Macx family ever think to ask what *Aineko* wanted?

And if an answer had come, would they have liked it?

Adult-Manfred, still disoriented from finding himself awake and reinstantiated a couple of centuries downstream from his hurried exile from Saturn system, is hesitantly navigating his way toward Sirhan and Rita's home when big-Manni-with-Manfred's-memory-ghost drops into his consciousness like a ton of computronium glowing red-hot at the edges.

It's a classic *oh-shit* moment. Between one foot touching the ground and the next, Manfred stumbles hard, nearly twisting an ankle, and gasps. He *remembers*. At thirdhand he remembers being reincarnated as Manni, a bouncing baby boy for Rita and Sirhan (and just why they want to raise an ancestor instead of creating a new child of their own is one of those cultural quirks that is so alien he can scarcely comprehend it). Then for a while he recalls living as Manni's amnesic adult accelerated ghost, watching over his original from the consensus cyberspace of the city: the arrival of Pamela, adult Manni's reaction to her, her dump of yet another copy of Manfred's memories into Manni, and now this – *How many of me are there?* he wonders nervously. Then: *Pamela? What's she doing here?*

Manfred shakes his head and looks about. Now he remembers being big-Manni, he knows where he is implicitly and, more importantly, knows what all these next-gen City interfaces are supposed to do. The walls and ceiling are carpeted in glowing glyphs that promise him everything from instant-access local services to teleportation across interstellar distances. *So they haven't quite collapsed geography yet,* he realizes gratefully, fastening on to the nearest comprehensible thought of his own before old-Manni's memories explain everything for him. It's a weird sensation, seeing all this stuff for the first time – the trappings of a technosphere centuries ahead of the one he's last been awake in – but with the memories to explain it all. He finds his feet are still carrying him forward, toward a grassy square lined with doors opening onto private dwellings. Behind one of them, he's going to meet his descendants, and Pamela in all probability. The thought makes his stomach give a little queasy backflip. *I'm not ready for this—*

It's an acute moment of déjà vu. He's standing on a familiar doorstep he's never seen before. The door opens and a serious-faced child with three arms – he can't help staring; the extra one is a viciously barbed scythe of bone from the elbow down – looks up at him. 'Hello, me,' says the kid.

'Hello, you.' Manfred stares. 'You don't look the way I remember.' But Manni's appearance is familiar from big-Manni's memories, captured by the unblinking Argus awareness of the panopticon dust floating in the air. 'Are your parents home? Your' – his voice cracks – 'great-grandmother?'

The door opens wider. 'You can come in,' the kid says gravely. Then he hops backward and ducks shyly into a side room – or as if expecting to be gunned down by a hostile sniper, Manfred realizes. It's tough being a kid when there are no rules against lethal force because you can be restored from a backup when playtime ends.

Inside the dwelling – calling it a house seems wrong to Manfred, not when bits of it are separated by trillions of kilometers of empty vacuum – things feel a bit crowded. He can hear voices from the dayroom, so he goes there, brushing through the archway of thornless roses that Rita has trained around the T-gate frame. His body feels lighter, but his heart is heavy as he looks around. 'Rita?' he asks. 'And—'

'Hello, Manfred.' Pamela nods at him guardedly.

Rita raises an eyebrow at him. 'The cat asked if he could borrow the household assembler. I wasn't expecting a family reunion.'

'Neither was I.' Manfred rubs his forehead ruefully. 'Pamela, this is Rita. She's married to Sirhan. They're my – I guess eigen-parents is as good as term as any? I mean, they're bringing up my reincarnation.'

'Please, have a seat,' Rita offers, waving at the empty floor between the patio and the stone fountain in the shape of a section through a glass hypersphere. A futon of spun diamondoid congeals out of the utility fog floating in the air, glittering in the artificial sunlight. 'Sirhan's just taking care of Manni – our son. He'll be with us in just a minute.'

Manfred sits gingerly at one side of the futon. Pamela sits stiffly at the opposite edge, not meeting his eye. Last time they met in the flesh – an awesome gulf of years previously – they'd parted cursing each other, on opposite sides of a fractious divorce as well as an ideological barrier as high as a continental divide. But many subjective decades have passed, and both ideology and divorce have dwindled in significance – if indeed they ever happened. Now that there's common cause to draw them together, Manfred can barely look at her. 'How is Manni?' he asks his hostess, desperate for small talk.

'He's fine,' Rita says, in a brittle voice. 'Just the usual pre-adolescent turbulence, if it wasn't for . . .' She trails off. A door appears in midair and Sirhan steps through it, followed by a small deity wearing a fur coat.

'Look what the cat dragged in,' Aineko remarks.

'You're a fine one to talk,' Pamela says icily. 'Don't you think you'd—'

'I tried to keep him away from you,' Sirhan tells Manfred, 'but he wouldn't—'

'That's okay.' Manfred waves it off. 'Pamela, would you mind starting?'

'Yes, I would.' She glances at him sidelong. 'You go first.'

'Right. You wanted me here.' Manfred hunkers down to stare at the cat. 'What do you want?'

'If I was your traditional middle-European devil, I'd say I'd come to steal your soul,' says Aineko, looking up at Manfred and twitching his tail. 'Luckily I'm not a dualist. I just want to borrow it for a while. Won't even get it dirty.'

'Uh-huh.' Manfred raises an eyebrow. 'Why?'

'I'm not omniscient.' Aineko sits down, one leg sticking out sideways, but continues to stare at Manfred. 'I had a . . . a telegram, I guess, claiming to be from you. From the other copy of you, that is, the one that went off through the router network with another copy of me, and with Amber, and everyone else who isn't here. It says it found the answer, and it wants to give me a shortcut route out to the deep thinkers at the edge of the observable universe. It knows who made the wormhole network and why, and—' Aineko pauses. If he was human, he'd shrug, but being a cat, he absentmindedly scritches behind his left ear with a hind leg. 'Trouble is, I'm not sure I can trust it. So I need you to authenticate the message. I don't dare use my own memory of you because it knows too much about me; if the package is a Trojan, it might find out things I don't want it to learn. I can't even redact its memories of me – that, too, would convey useful information to the packet if it is hostile. So I want a copy of you from the museum, fresh and uncontaminated.'

'Is that all?' Sirhan asks incredulously.

'Sounds like enough to me,' Manfred responds. Pamela opens her mouth, ready to speak, but Manfred makes eye contact and shakes his head infinitesimally. She looks right back and – a shock goes through him – nods and closes her mouth. The moment of complicity is dizzying. 'I want something in return.'

'Sure,' says the cat. He pauses. 'You realize it's a destructive process.'

'It's a – *what*?'

'I need to make a running copy of you. Then I introduce it to the, uh, alien information, in a sandbox. The sandbox gets destroyed afterward – it emits just one bit of information, a yes or no to the question: Can I trust the alien information?'

'Uh.' Manfred begins to sweat. 'Uh. I'm not so sure I like the sound of that.'

'It's a copy.' Another cat-shrug moment. 'You're a copy. Manni is a copy. You've been copied so many times it's silly – you realize every few years every atom in your body changes? Of course, it means a copy of you gets to die after a lifetime or two of unique, unrepeatable experiences that you'll never know about, but that won't matter to you.'

'Yes it does! You're talking about condemning a version of me to death! It may not affect me, here, in this body, but it certainly affects that *other* me. Can't you—'

'No, I can't. If I agreed to rescue the copy if it reached a positive verdict, that would give it an incentive to lie if the truth was that the alien message is untrustworthy, wouldn't it? Also, if I intended to rescue the copy, that would give the message a back channel through which to encode an attack. One bit, Manfred, no more.'

'Agh.' Manfred stops talking. He knows he should be trying to come up with some kind of objection, but Aineko must have already considered all his possible responses and planned strategies around them. 'Where does *she* fit into this?' he asks, nodding at Pamela.

'Oh, she's your payment,' Aineko says with studied insouciance. 'I have a very good memory for people, especially people I've known for decades. You've outlasted that crude emotional conditioning I used on you around the time of the divorce, and as for her, she's a good reinstantiation of—'

'Do you know what it's like to die?' Pamela asks, finally losing her self-control. 'Or would you like to find out the hard way? Because if you keep talking about me as if I'm a *slave*—'

'What makes you think you aren't?' The cat is grinning hideously, needlelike teeth bared. *Why doesn't she hit him?* Manfred asks himself fuzzily, wondering also why he feels no urge to move against the monster. 'Hybridizing you with Manfred was, admittedly, a fine piece of work on my part, but you would have been bad for him during his peak creative years. A contented Manfred is an idle Manfred. I got several extra good bits of work out of him by splitting you up, and by the time he burned out Amber was ready. But I digress; if you give me what I want, I shall *leave you alone.* It's as simple as that. Raising new generations of Macxes has been a good hobby. You make interesting pets, but ultimately it's limited by your stubborn refusal to transcend your humanity. So that's what I'm offering, basically. Let me destructively run a copy of you to completion in a black box along with a purported Turing Oracle based on yourself, and I'll let you go. And you, too, Pamela. You'll be happy together this time, without me pushing you apart. And I promise I won't return to haunt your descendants, either.' The cat glances over his shoulder at Sirhan and Rita, who clutch at each other in abject horror, and Manfred finds he can sense a shadow of Aineko's huge algorithmic complexity hanging over the household, like a lurching nightmare out of number theory.

'Is that all we are to you? A pet-breeding program?' Pamela asks coldly. She's run up against Aineko's implanted limits, too, Manfred realizes with a growing sense of horror. *Did we really split up because Aineko made us?* It's hard to believe: Manfred is too much of a realist to trust the cat to tell the truth except when it serves to further his interests. But this—

'Not entirely.' Aineko is complacent. 'Not at first, before I was aware of my own existence. Besides, you humans keep pets, too. But you *were* fun to play with.'

Pamela stands up, angry to the point of storming out. Before he quite realizes what he's doing, Manfred is on his feet, too, one arm protectively around her. 'Tell me first, are our memories our own?' he demands.

'Don't trust it,' Pamela says sharply. 'It's not human, and it lies.' Her shoulders are tense.

'Yes, they are,' says Aineko. He yawns. 'Tell me I'm lying,

bitch,' he adds mockingly. 'I carried you around in my head for long enough to know you've no evidence.'

'But I—' Her arm slips around Manfred's waist. 'I don't hate him.' A rueful laugh: 'I *remember* hating him, but—'

'Humans: such a brilliant model of emotional self-awareness,' Aineko says with a theatrical sigh. 'You're as stupid as it's possible for an intelligent species to be – there being no evolutionary pressure to be any smarter – but you still don't internalize that and act accordingly around your superiors. Listen, girl, everything you remember is true. That doesn't mean you remember it because it actually happened, just that you remember it because you experienced it internally. Your memories of experiences are accurate, but your emotional responses to those experiences were manipulated. Get it? One ape's hallucination is another ape's religious experience – it just depends on which one's god module is overactive at the time. That goes for all of you.' Aineko looks around at them in mild contempt. 'But I don't need you anymore, and if you do this one thing for me, you're going to be free. Understand? Say yes, Manfred: If you leave your mouth open like that, a bird will nest on your tongue.'

'Say no—' Pamela urges him, just as Manfred says, 'Yes.'

Aineko laughs, baring contemptuous fangs at them. 'Ah, primate family loyalty! So wonderful and reliable. Thank you, Manny. I do believe you just gave me permission to copy and enslave you—'

Which is when Manni, who has been waiting in the doorway for the past minute, leaps on the cat with a scream and a scythe-like arm drawn back and ready to strike.

The cat-avatar is, of course, ready for Manni: It whirls and hisses, extending diamond-sharp claws. Sirhan shouts, 'No! Manni!' and begins to move, but adult-Manfred freezes, realizing with a chill that what is happening is more than is apparent. Manni grabs for the cat with his human hands, catching it by the scruff of his neck and dragging it toward his vicious scythe-arm's edge. There's a screech, a nerve-racking caterwauling, and Manni yells, bright parallel blood tracks on his arm – the avatar is a real fleshbody in its own right, with an autonomic control system that isn't going to give up without a fight, whatever its vastly larger exocortex thinks – but Manni's scythe convulses, and there's a horrible bubbling noise and a spray of blood as the pussycat-thing goes flying. It's all over in a second before any of the adults can really move. Sirhan scoops up Manni and yanks him away, but there are no hidden surprises. Aineko's avatar is just a broken rag of bloody fur, guts, and blood spilled across the floor. The ghost of a triumphant feline laugh hangs over their innerspeech ears for a moment, then fades.

'Bad boy!' Rita shouts, striding forward furiously. Manni cowers, then begins to cry, a safe reflex for a little boy who doesn't quite understand the nature of the threat to his parents.

'No! It's all right.' Manfred seeks to explain.

Pamela tightens her grip around him. 'Are you still . . . ?'

'Yes.' He takes a deep breath.

'You bad, *bad* child—'

'Cat was going to eat him!' Manni protests, as his parents bundle him protectively out of the room, Sirhan casting a guilty look over his shoulder at the adult instance and his ex-wife. 'I had to stop the bad thing!'

Manfred feels Pamela's shoulders shaking. It feels like she's about to laugh. 'I'm still here,' he murmurs, half-surprised. 'Spat out, undigested, after all these years. At least, *this* version of me thinks he's here.'

'Did you believe it?' she finally asks, a tone of disbelief in her voice.

'Oh yes.' He shifts his balance from foot to foot, absentmindedly stroking her hair. 'I believe everything it said was intended to make us react exactly the way we did. Up to and including giving us good reasons to hate it and provoking Manni into disposing of its avatar. Aineko wanted to check out of our lives and figured a sense of cathartic closure would help. Not to mention playing the *deus ex machina* in the narrative of our family life. Fucking classical comedian.' He checks a status report with Citymind, and sighs:

His version number has just been bumped a point. 'Tell me, do you think you'll miss having Aineko around? Because we won't be hearing from him again—'

'Don't talk about that, not now,' she orders him, digging her chin against the side of his neck. 'I feel so *used*.'

'With good reason.' They stand holding each other for a while, not speaking, not really questioning why – after so much time apart – they've come together again. 'Hanging out with gods is never a safe activity for mere mortals like us. You think you've been used? Aineko has probably killed me by now. Unless he was lying about disposing of the spare copy, too.'

She shudders in his arms. 'That's the trouble with dealing with posthumans; their mental model of you is likely to be more detailed than your own.'

'How long have you been awake?' he asks, gently trying to change the subject.

'I – oh, I'm not sure.' She lets go of him and steps back, watching his face appraisingly. 'I remember back on Saturn, stealing a museum piece and setting out, and then, well. I found myself here. With you.'

'I think' – he licks his lips – 'we've both been given a wake-up call. Or maybe a second chance. What are you going to do with yours?'

'I don't know.' That appraising look again, as if she's trying to work out what he's worth. He's used to it, but this time it doesn't feel hostile. 'We've got too much history for this to be easy. Either Aineko was lying, or . . . not. What about you? What do you really want?'

He knows what she's asking. 'Be my mistress?' he asks, offering her a hand.

'This time' – she grips his hand – 'without adult supervision.' She smiles gratefully, and they walk toward the gateway together, to find out how their descendants are dealing with their sudden freedom.

SINGULARITY SKY.

Charles Stross

In the twenty-first century man created the Eschaton, a sentient artificial intelligence. It pushed Earth through the greatest technological evolution ever known, while warning that time travel is forbidden, and transgressors will be eliminated.

One far-flung colony, the New Republic, exists in self-imposed isolation. Founded by men and women suffering from an acute case of future shock, the member-planets want no part of the Eschaton or the technological advances that followed its creation. But their backward ways are about to be severely compromised in an attack from an information plague that calls itself The Festival. And as advanced technologies suppressed for generations begin literally to fall from the sky, the New Republic is in danger of slipping into revolutionary turmoil.

The colony's only hope lies with a battle fleet from Earth. But secret plans, hidden agendas and ulterior motives abound.

IRON SUNRISE

Charles Stross

Charles Stross's visionary debut novel, *Singularity Sky*, was hailed as "a carnival of ideas". Now he confirms his reputation as a writer at the very cutting edge of science fiction with his stunning follow-up novel, *Iron Sunrise*.

When the planet of New Moscow was brutally destroyed, its few survivors launched a counter-attack against the most likely culprit: the neighbouring system of trade rival, New Dresden. But New Dresden wasn't responsible and, as the deadly missiles approach their target, Rachel Mansour, agent for the interests of Old Earth, is assigned to find out who was.

The one person who does know is a disaffected teenager who calls herself Wednesday Shadowmist. But Wednesday has no idea where she might be hiding this significant information. Time is limited and if Rachel can't resolve this mystery it will mean the annihilation of an entire world . . .

LEARNING THE WORLD

Ken MacLeod

A stunning new novel of exploration, discovery and Mankind's destiny amongst the stars.

The great sunliner But the Sky, My Lady! The Sky! is nearing the end of a four-hundred year journey. A ship-born generation is tense with expectation for the new system that is to be their home. Expecting to find nothing more complex than bacteria and algae, the detection of electronic signals from one of the planets comes as a shock. In millennia of slow expansion, humanity has never encountered aliens, and yet these new signals cannot be ignored.

On a world called Ground, whose inhabitants are struggling into the age of radio, petroleum and powered flight, a young astronomer searching for distant planets detects an anomaly that he presumes must be a comet. His friend, a brilliant foreign physicist, calculates the orbit, only to discover an anomaly of his own. The comet is slowing down . . .

THE RISEN EMPIRE

Scott Westerfeld

The undead Emperor has ruled the Eighty Worlds for sixteen hundred years. His is the power to grant immortality to those he deems worthy, creating an elite class known as the Risen. Along with his sister, the eternally young Child Empress, his power within the empire has been absolute. Until now.

The empire's great enemies, the Rix, hold the Child Empress hostage. Charged with her rescue is Captain Laurent Zai. But when Imperial politics are involved the stakes are unimaginably high, and Zai may yet find the Rix the least of his problems. On the homeworld, Zai's lover, Senator Nara Oxham, must prosecute the war against the Rix while holding the inhuman impulses of the Risen councillors in check. If she fails at either task, millions will die.

And at the centre of everything is the Emperor's great lie: a revelation so shattering that he is willing to sanction the death of entire worlds to keep it secret . . .